OXFORD WORLD'S CLASSICS

A SIMPLE STORY

ELIZABETH INCHBALD was born into a farmer's family in Suffolk in 1753. An early ambition to act led her to London, where at the age of nineteen she married Joseph Inchbald, an actor and fellow-Catholic. The couple acted together in various companies in Scotland, Liverpool, and York. After her husband's death in 1779 Inchbald lived mainly in London, acting at Covent Garden and the Haymarket. Her first play, *The Mogul Tale*, was acted in 1784 and was followed by more farces and comedies, as well as translations and adaptations for the stage. After 1789 she gave up regular acting engagements to concentrate on her writing, which brought her financial success and popular acclaim. In 1791 she published her first novel, *A Simple Story*, on which her reputation now rests. A second novel, *Nature and Art*, followed in 1796. *To Marry or not to Marry* (1805) was Inchbald's last play. Thereafter she wrote prefaces for a 25-volume collection of plays, *The British Theatre*. She died in 1821.

J. M. S. TOMPKINS's books include *The Popular Novel in England, 1770–1800* (1932) and *The Polite Marriage* (1938).

JANE SPENCER is the author of *The Rise of the Woman Novelist: from Aphra Behn to Jane Austen* (1986) and editor of Behn's *The Rover and Other Plays* (1995) in Oxford World's Classics.

T0088455

OXFORD WORLD'S CLASSICS

For over 100 years Oxford World's Classics have brought
readers closer to the world's great literature. Now with over 700
titles—from the 4,000-year-old myths of Mesopotamia to the
twentieth century's greatest novels—the series makes available
lesser-known as well as celebrated writing.

The pocket-sized hardbacks of the early years contained
introductions by Virginia Woolf, T. S. Eliot, Graham Greene,
and other literary figures which enriched the experience of reading.
Today the series is recognized for its fine scholarship and
reliability in texts that span world literature, drama and poetry,
religion, philosophy and politics. Each edition includes perceptive
commentary and essential background information to meet the
changing needs of readers.

OXFORD WORLD'S CLASSICS

ELIZABETH INCHBALD

A Simple Story

Edited with Notes by
J. M. S. TOMPKINS

With an Introduction by
JANE SPENCER

OXFORD
UNIVERSITY PRESS

OXFORD

UNIVERSITY PRESS

Great Clarendon Street, Oxford OX2 6DP

Oxford University Press is a department of the University of Oxford.
It furthers the University's objective of excellence in research, scholarship,
and education by publishing worldwide in

Oxford New York

Athens Auckland Bangkok Bogotá Buenos Aires Calcutta
Cape Town Chennai Dar es Salaam Delhi Florence Hong Kong Istanbul
Karachi Kuala Lumpur Madrid Melbourne Mexico City Mumbai
Nairobi Paris São Paulo Singapore Taipei Tokyo Toronto Warsaw

with associated companies in Berlin Ibadan

Oxford is a registered trade mark of Oxford University Press
in the UK and in certain other countries

Published in the United States
by Oxford University Press Inc., New York

Note on the Text, Chronology,
Explanatory Notes © Oxford University Press 1967
Introduction and Bibliography © Jane Spencer 1988

First published 1967 by Oxford University Press
First issued as a World's Classics paperback 1988
Reissued as an Oxford World's Classics paperback 1998
Reissued 2009

British Library Cataloguing in Publication Data

Data available

Library of Congress Cataloging in Publication Data
Inchbald, Mrs., 1753–1821.
A simple story/Elizabeth Inchbald; edited by J. M. S. Tompkins,
with a new introduction by Jane Spencer.
p. cm.—(Oxford world's classics)
Bibliography: p.
I. Tompkins, J. M. S. (Joyce Marjorie Sanxter), 1897–
II. Title.
823'.6—dc19 PR3518.A73 1988 88–4022

ISBN 978-0-19-955472-0

15

Printed and bound in Great Britain by Clays Ltd, Elcograf S.p.A.

CONTENTS

ACKNOWLEDGEMENTS

I AM indebted to the General Editor of *Oxford English Novels*, Professor Herbert Davis, for his friendly help in all my difficulties. Miss G. Guiney of Oxford kindly entrusted her copy of the rare second edition of *A Simple Story* to me, and Associate Professor Devendra P. Varma of Dalhousie University, Nova Scotia, Canada, procured for me through the University Librarian Xerox copies of parts of the third edition from Princeton University Library.

I am deeply grateful to the Revd. Gervase Mathew, O.P., for answering my questions about Catholic practices in England in the eighteenth century, and for directing me to Archbishop Mathew's *Catholicism in England*.

J.M.S.T.

INTRODUCTION

DARING in theme, elegant in style, *A Simple Story* is one of the most remarkable novels of the late eighteenth century. Its heroine, Miss Milner, known to us only by her formal title, breaks through the formalities surrounding women with a beautifully modulated expression of her scandalous feelings for the priest who is her guardian: 'Oh, Miss Woodley! I love him with all the passion of a mistress, and with all the tenderness of a wife.' Her emotions are doubly forbidden, by the code of feminine delicacy and by Dorriforth's religious vows. The Catholic interest in the novel is important mainly because it adds the shocking hint of sacrilege to the heroine's desire: that desire and its prohibition are Inchbald's main concerns. The bold theme is skilfully handled. Drawing on her long experience as a dramatist, Inchbald uses lively dialogue and telling gesture to convey her meaning with a lightness of touch rare in the fiction of her time. Equally, she finds new opportunities in her move from theatrical to narrative writing. It suits her to introduce sharp commentary, to cut down on external action, to narrow her focus, and to concentrate on the minute signals of her protagonists' inner drama. Her few characters move in a world of tea-tables and evenings at the fireside. Reactions to the insurgent heroine define her companions, and there is deft comedy of manners in Mrs Horton's fascination with family quarrels, Miss Woodley's gentle benevolence and lack of insight, and Mr Sandford's austere reception of Miss Milner's cheeky challenges. The warm heroine's dislike of cool Miss Fenton has a suggestion of Emma's reaction to Jane Fairfax: 'not to admire Miss Fenton was impossible—to find a fault in her person or sentiments equally impossible—and yet to love her, was very unlikely'. Inchbald's concise, ironic narrative style anticipates Austen, while the passionate heroine she creates to disrupt the world of social comedy looks further forward, to the work of the Brontës.

The careful handling of potentially shocking situations which characterizes Inchbald's novel might well be applied to her life. As a woman and as a writer, the author of *A Simple Story* was used to treading with utmost care the narrow line between permissible and forbidden female behaviour. Daughter of a Suffolk farming family with friends in the provincial theatre, she had an early ambition to be an actress, and eventually achieved limited success, despite her stammer, through stubborn determination. In her late teens, an attempt to live independently and find acting work in London was made difficult by sexual harassment. Eventually she agreed to marry the much older Joseph Inchbald, an actor and fellow-Catholic known to her family, evidently because this was the only way to enter her chosen profession with respectable protection. (Interestingly, they first acted together as father and daughter—Lear and Cordelia.) Their marriage was stormy, with frequent quarrels over her flirtations; but it seems her most serious attraction was to a man who never flirted at all, the actor John Philip Kemble, who has been identified as the prototype for Dorriforth. Like Dorriforth, Kemble was educated at Douai, but he entered the theatre instead of the priesthood. After her husband's sudden death Inchbald may have hoped for Kemble to propose, but he never did. He remained her friend, and she, like her own Miss Milner, enjoyed encouraging an entourage of admirers while committing herself to none. The beautiful young widow's situation was a morally dangerous one in contemporary eyes, and Catholic friends spent some energy dissuading her from flirtation and encouraging more frequent confession and attendance at mass. Some of Miss Milner's exploits seem to have been based on her creator's: in particular, the masquerade which the heroine attends, dressed in an ambiguous costume suggestive of male attire, recalls the author's visit to a masquerade in the 1780s, dressed as Bellario in *Philaster*—a female character in male disguise, which she had acted on stage.[1]

---

[1] *Philaster* was adapted from Beaumont and Fletcher by Colman the Elder in 1763.

Inchbald, however, unlike her heroine, seems to have known exactly how far she could go. Mud never stuck to her. There was gossip that she spent a night with Harris, manager of the Covent Garden theatre, in exchange for an acting job; but the story was not generally believed, and her detractors apologized. Harris himself complained, 'that woman, Inchbald, has solemnly devoted herself to *virtue* and a *garret*'.[2] Maybe she devoted herself to virtue for the sake of the garret; no woman writer seems to have been more committed to a room of one's own. Late in life she joined a Catholic boarding-house community, but up till then she lived alone in a succession of lodgings, keeping herself fiercely independent. As she made more money from writing she gave generously to friends and family, but lived frugally herself. A lively picture of her is given by George Hardinge, who wrote after first meeting her,

She is perfectly modest; but arch, clever, and so interesting, that if she had no genius you would long to be acquainted with her. What [her friends] seem to enjoy in her most is her *naiveté*, and she gave us two or three capital traits of it. She lives alone—her character has no *tache* upon it—and Mrs Siddons said she was as cold as ice: but I cannot believe it, for at least I see a little of the coquette in her, but well disciplined, and well bred.[3]

All the rambling anecdotes of interrupted courtships related by her biographer, Boaden, and all his meticulous accounts of the money she earned and invested, suggest the picture of a lively woman whose feelings were strictly controlled in the interests of her strongest desire, for independence.

It was this that led her to write. From her early twenties, as well as acting, she studied hard and experimented with writing, partly for her own satisfaction and partly in the hope of building alternative sources of income. She was well aware that she would never be a brilliant success as an actress, and writing for

[2] James Boaden, *Memoirs of Mrs. Inchbald* (London, 1833), I, pp. 191–2. The account of Inchbald's life given here is based on Boaden.
[3] John Nichols, *Illustrations of the Literary History of the Eighteenth Century*, vol. III (London, 1818), p. 38n.

INTRODUCTION

the stage was in any case much more likely to be lucrative. Her
French studies did eventually lead to her making money from
dramatic translations and adaptations. She also wrote original
farces and comedies. For some years she could not get her work
accepted, but in 1784 her farce *The Mogul Tale* was accepted by
Colman at the Haymarket. It was very successful and earned
her a hundred guineas. From then on her works were frequently
performed and published, with varying success. The comedy
Such Things Are (1787) was especially popular, and she had the
pleasure of seeing Bow Street crowded with people trying to get
in to see her work. She estimated that she made £900 altogether
from this play. By 1789 she had sufficient income from her
writing to give up her regular acting engagements.

With the increasing refinement of the theatre, writing comedies was no longer considered incompatible with a woman's
modesty, but Inchbald's position was still tricky. Some of her
early farces were attacked for 'indecencies' such as *double
entendre*, found most objectionable in a woman writer. Her
comedy *All On A Summer's Day* (1787) was criticized because
of the character of the heroine, Lady Carrol, a married woman
who flirts. Though Inchbald intended Lady Carrol as an
amiable coquette, with every virtue except prudence, some
critics found her behaviour too close to vice for their taste.[4] The
author probably kept this experience in mind when creating
Miss Milner, in whom she managed to portray more dangerous
behaviour without offending her readers.

She had begun writing a novel in 1777, soon after her first
meeting with Kemble, who read the work in progress. She
completed it in 1779 soon after her husband's death, but it was
rejected for publication, and she turned back to dramatic
writing. Boaden indicates that this novel was *A Simple Story*,
but as no manuscript or sufficiently detailed comments on it
survive, a recent scholar has cast some doubt on this claim,
arguing that the characterization of Miss Milner could not have
been achieved before Inchbald's experience with comedy had

Patricia Sigl, *The Literary Achievement of Elizabeth Inchbald [1753–1821]*, Ph.D.
University of Wales (Swansea), 1980, pp. 75–6 and 102–10.

taught her to develop the witty heroine, and that Sandford depends on a prototype in her comedy.[5] This does not rule out the possibility that Inchbald was working on an early version of the story of Dorriforth and Miss Milner in the 1770s. The new friendship with Kemble at the time of composition seems to support the idea, though we may wonder whether he recognized himself in the hero, and if so, what his reaction was. It seems most probable, however, that if the early novel was a version of *A Simple Story*, the work was given extensive revision, if not a complete recasting, in 1789–90. It was then that Inchbald turned back to fiction, and according to Boaden worked on two separate narratives for some time before deciding to combine them into one, the two-part novel as we have it. The manuscript was purchased for £200 by Robinson, who had already published several of her plays.

The publication of her novel in 1791 brought Inchbald a degree of critical esteem which she had never enjoyed before. Her plays, for all their popularity, had their detractors, including her friend Francis Twiss who told her that though she could write a passable light comedy she was not in the same class as Sheridan. In the novel, on the other hand, she was hailed as an original. A reviewer in the *Gentleman's Magazine* announced that he did not admire her plays, but her novel proved her worth as a writer, while the *Critical Review*, which did praise her plays, agreed that in turning to fiction 'Mrs Inchbald has discovered the true path which she ought to pursue'.[6] She followed such advice only to the extent of writing one more novel, *Nature and Art* (1796), a somewhat over-schematic contrast between different upbringings which, like Robert Bage's *Hermsprong* in the same year, praises the natural democrat and criticizes the tyrant produced by the false art of British civilization with its inequalities of rank and wealth. *Nature and Art* contains some very effective scenes but as a whole it lacks the power of her earlier novel.

---

[5] Sigl, ibid., pp. 229–31.

[6] *Gentleman's Magazine*, vol. 61, pt. 1 (1791), p. 255; *Critical Review*, 2nd ser. 1 (1791), p. 207.

The pre-eminence of Inchbald's first novel among all her works is partly explained by the personal significance of the story of Miss Milner and Dorriforth, which meant that she drew on a theme long thought about, and probably written upon at an earlier date. (It may be significant that a few years before the novel appeared Inchbald had completed an autobiography which she subsequently destroyed.) Another source of its strength is the relevance of her story to some of the central concerns of her culture. In creating Miss Milner, the author was not only using aspects of her own personality but drawing on the literary tradition of the coquette, a key figure for contemporary notions of womanhood. At a time when the rights of woman were about to become the subject of fierce discussion, Inchbald offered new insight into a character type which had always been associated with a form of feminine rebellion.

In an era that demanded a suitable moral lesson from its fiction, Inchbald was careful to provide one. That women should have 'A PROPER EDUCATION' is her emphatic conclusion, placing *A Simple Story* within a main current of eighteenth-century thought. From Rousseau who argued that women should be trained to please men, to Wollstonecraft who maintained that they should be taught to govern themselves, the proper education of women was a central subject of debate. It was a particular concern of women novelists, much of whose authority derived from their claim to contribute to proper female education through their didactic fictions. But what was a proper education? Apart from some 'bluestocking' support for women's access to the male preserves of learning—classical languages, science, mathematics—there was little real interest in the intellectual content of the curriculum. Most writers were concerned with education as moral development, and worked with a basic distinction between 'frivolous' accomplishments—dancing, singing, drawing, and so on—and 'serious' reading in languages, religion, philosophy, or just books of moral homily. The point about 'serious' study was the self-control and rational behaviour it was supposed to encourage, while accomplishments, a means of young women's self-display on the marriage-market, were associated with feminine irrationality. Rousseau, who considered women naturally inclined not to thought but to display, complained in *Emile* about religious moralizers who objected to singing and dancing. 'By making good women the slaves of dismal duties, we have deprived marriage of its charm for men. ... I would have an English maiden cultivate the talents which will delight her husband as zealously as the Circassian cultivates the accomplishments of an Eastern harem.'[7] Understandably, women writers, claiming for their sex a place outside the harem, took a different view. Novelists like Sarah Fielding and Frances Sheridan criticized feminine display and defended heroines of sense and learning.[8]

Advocates for women supported serious education leading to rational thinking and distrusted accomplishments. Towards the end of the century, the link between education and feminism was strengthened by the new faith in education's politically progressive powers expressed by radical writers like Thomas Holcroft and William Godwin; and, most importantly, by Mary Wollstonecraft. In her *Vindication of the Rights of Woman* (1792), she attacked educationalists for considering women only as sexual beings: 'the important years of youth, the usefulness of age, and the rational hopes of futurity, are all to be sacrificed to render women an object of desire for a *short* time. ... how could Rousseau expect them to be virtuous and constant when reason is neither allowed to be the foundation of their virtue, nor truth the object of their inquiries?'[9]

Because Elizabeth Inchbald had Revolutionary sympathies and numbered both Holcroft and Godwin among her friends, it is tempting to see *A Simple Story*—written with the aid of Holcroft's comments, and perhaps revised with Godwin's help—as a kind of 'Jacobin' novel, concerned with the progressive possibilities of education.[10] Her mother and daughter pair of

[7] Jean-Jacques Rousseau, *Emile*, tr. Barbara Foxley (London, 1974), p. 337.
[8] Sarah Fielding, *The Adventures of David Simple* (London, 1744); Frances Sheridan, *Memoirs of Miss Sidney Bidulph* (London, 1761).
[9] Mary Wollstonecraft, *Vindication of the Rights of Woman*, ed. Miriam Kramnick (London, 1974), p. 189.
[10] See Gary Kelly, *The English Jacobin Novel 1780–1805* (Oxford, 1976), pp. 64–93.

heroines illustrate the effects of bad and good education: Miss Milner, frivolously accomplished and without a serious thought in her head, has no control over herself and ends unhappily, while her daughter, Lady Matilda, given a serious education, avoids her mother's errors and achieves a happy ending. Seen in this way, the novel fails to satisfy. Wollstonecraft herself, reading it in these terms less than a year before producing *Rights of Woman*, was disappointed. There was not enough contrast between mother and daughter; 'the vain, giddy Miss Milner' was presented in too favourable a light, allowed too many virtues; and her daughter was no advertisement for the better education she received.

[Lady Matilda] should have possessed greater dignity of mind. Educated in adversity she should have learned (to prove that a cultivated mind is a real advantage) how to bear, nay, rise above her misfortunes, instead of suffering her health to be undermined by the trials of her patience, which ought to have strengthened her under-standing.[11]

Wollstonecraft evidently wanted a feminist moral which Inchbald failed to provide. There is much more to *A Simple Story*, however, than its insistent but unintegrated moral tag. The novel has a feminist interest, not because it shares the contemporary advocacy of a rational education for women, but because it reveals what was repressed in order to make that case. Miss Milner embodies the female sexuality that women writers of Inchbald's time were busy denying in the interests of their own respectability, and women's claims for better treatment.

Neither Miss Milner's education nor her daughter's is much elaborated on. If Lady Matilda spends much of her time reading instead of going to balls and assemblies like her mother, this is the sign rather than the source of her better mind. Suffering and deprivation have been her true mentors. The significant difference between Miss Milner's education and her

---

[11] *Analytical Review*, vol. 10 (1791), pp. 101–2. I attribute this review to Wollstonecraft on internal evidence and because one of the initials she used, 'M', is the next signature to appear in the issue (after the following article). See R. M. Wardle, 'Mary Wollstonecraft, *Analytical Reviewer*', *PMLA*, 62 (1947), 1000–9.

daughter's is that Miss Milner's failed to subdue the sexual
desire and the will to power which make her such a disruptive
figure. Because she has not been educated a Catholic, Miss
Milner is able to desire a priest; and because she has not been
seriously educated at all she cannot suppress her desire. The
proper education 'would have given such a prohibition to her
love, that she had been precluded from it, as by that barrier
which divides a sister from a brother'. However Inchbald
laments her heroine's unfortunate lack, it is clear that education
in this novel functions negatively, not adding wisdom but
imposing taboos. The female desire which it is meant to stifle is
the novel's more fundamental concern. Miss Milner, as a
coquette, wants to prolong the courtship period because it is the
one time in a woman's life when she is allowed power over a
man. Wollstonecraft was to reject the coquette's power in *Rights
of Woman*, but in doing so she also devalues female sexuality.
Inchbald links her heroine's shocking desire for Dorriforth to
her struggle against his control over her, and thus reveals, what
the early feminist position could not acknowledge, the disruptive potential of female desire.[12]

Only Inchbald's extreme delicacy of handling could have
made her theme acceptable to her readership. The novel as a
form had only recently gained its respectability by suppressing
the passionate fallen heroines of pre-Richardsonian days, and
the convention of the pure sex-free heroine was setting in. Apart
from the explicit moment of Miss Milner's passionate declaration of her love for Dorriforth, Inchbald renders desire spar-
ingly and obliquely. Though this strategy was enjoined on her
by social constraints it does not weaken her work, for hers is an
art of excision and compression. As Maria Edgeworth re-
marked, she gains from her omissions. 'I am of the opinion',
she wrote to Inchbald in 1810, after rereading her novel, 'that it
is by leaving more than most other writers to the imagination,
that you succeed so eminently in affecting it. By the force that is
necessary to repress feeling, we judge of the intensity of the

<hr/>

[12] Wollstonecraft herself was to revise her attitude to desire in her later novel, *Maria;
or the Wrongs of Woman* (London, 1798).

feeling; and you always contrive to give us by intelligible but simple signs the measure of this force.'[13]

Miss Milner's emotions are conveyed by minute signs like the movement of her knife and fork in her hand, or a mistake at cards. If Inchbald is skilled at revealing unspoken communication, she also manages to convey its ambiguities. Under the influence of her unmentionable passion for Dorriforth, the verbally aggressive Miss Milner is forced into communicating, like a sentimental heroine, through blushes and other body-language. The irony is that the bodily signs which usually, in the literature of sensibility, speak more truly than words, are radically ambiguous in Inchbald's world. Her characters misread each other. She exploits the cultural ambivalence over women's blushes—are they, because they suggest lack of self-confidence, a sign of innocence and modesty, or rather, because they indicate sexual consciousness, a sign of guilt? Miss Milner's guardian reads her innocently, and seeing in her red face a proof of modesty, promises her, 'while you thus continue to blush, I shall reverence your internal sensations': the heroine and the reader, conscious of the erotic nature of those sensations, watch the hero caught in a lovers' dialogue without his knowledge.

Inchbald can compress a world of significance into a moment's uneasiness. One such moment occurs early in the novel, when Lord Frederick sneers at Miss Milner and her guardian by quoting Pope's *Eloisa to Abelard*:

> 'From Abelard it came,
> And Heloisa still must love the name.'

Whether from an inattention to the quotation, or from a consciousness it was wholly inapplicable, Dorriforth heard it without one emotion of shame or of anger—while Miss Milner seemed shocked at the implication; her pleasantry was immediately depressed, and she threw open the sash and held her head out at the window to conceal the embarrassment these lines had occasioned.

Eloisa and Abelard, twelfth-century lovers made famous for

[13] Boaden, op. cit., II, pp. 152–3.

Inchbald's era by Pope's poem, are relevant to Dorriforth and Miss Milner both as teacher and pupil, and (potentially) as breakers of religious vows. Miss Milner's sexual consciousness, revealed by embarrassment here, distinguishes her story from contemporary English novels where hero and heroine are teacher and pupil. Eliza Haywood's Mr Trueworth tries to reform the frivolous Betsy Thoughtless, Burney's Evelina asks Lord Orville for guidance, but these are relationships of strict propriety.[14] The reference to Eloisa and Abelard recalls the French literary tradition which includes these lovers and their eighteenth-century descendants, the teacher-pupil pair of illicit lovers in *La Nouvelle Héloise*. Inchbald is reintroducing danger-ous French eroticism into the English novel.

There are various ways of interpreting this eroticism. Undoubtedly Inchbald's subject was daring for her time, and Terry Castle, in a recent critique of her novel, presents her as an anti-authoritarian writer who makes female desire triumph over masculine authority.[15] On the other hand, there is much that is relevant to *A Simple Story* in Rosalind Coward's psychoanalyti-cal study of today's popular romantic fiction, which points to the regressive aspect of their dominant fantasies.

[Popular romantic stories] are directly reminiscent of infantile fanta-sies. In the adoration of the powerful male, we have the adoration of the father by the small child. . . . The qualities which make [romantic heroes] so desirable are, actually, the qualities which feminists have chosen to ridicule: power (the desire to dominate others); privilege (the exploitation of others); emotional distance (the inability to communi-cate); and singular love for the heroine (the inability to relate to anyone other than the sexual partner).[16]

Dorriforth/Lord Elmwood, for all the greater skill shown in his portrait, has some resemblance to such heroes; and he is a father-figure to the first heroine, and the father of the second.

---

[14] Eliza Haywood, *The History of Miss Betsy Thoughtless* (London, 1751); Fanny Burney, *Evelina* (London, 1778).

[15] Terry Castle, *Masquerade and Civilization: The Carnivalesque in Eighteenth-Century English Culture and Fiction* (London, 1986), pp. 290–330.

[16] Rosalind Coward, *Female Desire: Women's Sexuality Today* (London, 1984), pp. 191–2.

The novel's denouement suggests the infantile fantasy of union with a powerful father described by Coward. Where Inchbald does depart from the regressive romantic pattern, however, is in the first two volumes. In Miss Milner we have the expression, however carefully coded, of active sexuality, whereas female desire in the novels Coward discusses is always passive. While Mills and Boon or Harlequin writers endorse a passive feminine role, Inchbald's earlier romance offers a more challenging view of femininity.

Inchbald's hero attracted particular notice from the critics. To take a Roman Catholic priest as a central figure was new and exciting, and Dorriforth/Lord Elmwood provided the necessary link between the first and second halves of the story. In some respects he is the centrepiece: the story begins with him and traces the effect on him of his relationship to the two successive heroines. At the beginning, we get to know Dorriforth and his fears about taking on the guardianship of Miss Milner, while our picture of her, built upon hearsay, is puzzling. She is said to be wild and frivolous, but the one definite testimony to her behaviour is the praise of a woman who has benefited from her generosity. It seems that Dorriforth's quest to understand the enigmatic personality of this warm-hearted coquette is to be a central concern. Yet when Miss Milner appears she, rather than Dorriforth, is given to the reader from the inside. She is incomprehensible to her companions, but the reader is helped to understand her. Her growing love for her guardian means that she has to start acting the character that once came naturally to her, and to appear incessantly changeable because the truth of her constant love would be so shocking. It is a subtle rendering of a favourite eighteenth-century theme, the deceitfulness forced on women by social restrictions. Our understanding of the hero is less complete. Repeatedly, the narrative informs us of his religious principles, goodness, generosity, and feeling heart, but—apart from his gentleness towards Miss Milner whenever she is miserable or submissive—they seem very little in evidence. Another enigmatic male character is Sandford, whose pretence of hating and despising the heroine in order to shock her into repentance makes him at least as much of a deceiver as she is. The pretence takes on so much reality that the reader is hardly prepared for the volte-face at the end of the second volume. It is male behaviour, not female, which appears fascinating, wayward, and contradictory in this novel.

Miss Milner and Dorriforth are opposites in conflict, like Richardson's Lovelace and Clarissa with the sexual roles reversed. It is Miss Milner who, Lovelace-like, is attracted by the very quality which debars the fulfilment of desire, the beloved's purity. Unlike Clarissa, though, Dorriforth has social power on his side. In fact the best key to understanding him is his insistence on controlling any wilfulness in his subordinates, especially in women. We see this from his treatment of Harry Rushbrook, son of his disobedient sister, as well as in his efforts to curb his ward's activities. Miss Milner's coquetry, and the warm-heartedness that supposedly makes up for it, are both expressions of her deep opposition to such control. Her generosity always appears in opposition to masculine tyranny, from the secret financial aid to her father's debtors (which, ironically, first arouses Dorriforth's admiration for her), to the befriending of Harry Rushbrook. The first half of *A Simple Story* presents the enigma of the powerful male from the point of view of a woman resentful of, yet fascinated by him.

The third and fourth volumes of the novel offer a very different heroine, in a very different position. Although, in its surface detail, this second half is as convincing a domestic narrative as the first, its dramatic situation is reminiscent of the Gothic novels so popular in Inchbald's time. It presents us with an extreme of patriarchal tyranny—an obsession not only of Gothic narrative but of many of the tragedies Inchbald had seen and acted in during her stage career. Lord Elmwood has not so much altered as become a heightened version of the tyrant he always was. External restraints to his power have disappeared and he is an isolated and terrible figure. The other characters, even Sandford the Jesuit, talk about him almost as if he were God. The denouement may, as has recently been argued, repeat

the earlier overturning of patriarchal commands,[17] but only in
the interests of restoring a socialized version of the father's
power. Lady Matilda, unlike her mother, is a passive maiden
waiting to be rescued; she does not challenge authority or assert
her desires; and unlike her mother, she ends happily.

The second half of the novel, then, can be read as a kind of
atonement on Inchbald's part for the boldness of the first. Miss
Milner's wit, her sexuality, her will to dominate, threaten the
masculine rule represented by her guardian. Recognizing that
her unruly heroine could not be incorporated into the tradition-
al happy ending of the courtship novel, Inchbald created a
meeker daughter, who could. Rather than see the novel's double
structure, and the gap in time which swallows Miss Milner and
her shocking actions, as flaws spoiling narrative unity, we can
read them as symptoms of the disruptive power of Inchbald's
theme of female self-assertion. The double narrative is a
necessary form for containing that disruption and restoring
both feminine propriety and narrative closure. All the troubling
questions raised by Miss Milner are laid to rest by Lady
Matilda, a submissive and properly feminine father's daughter.

[17] Castle, op. cit., p. 324.

NOTE ON THE TEXT

THE text is that of the first edition of February 1791. This has never been reprinted since it was superseded by the second edition of March 1791. It is now preferred chiefly because its combination of provincialisms, colloquial ellipses, and irregular grammar with pointed and eloquent expression brings us close to the 'piquant mixture of a milkmaid and a fine lady', as Godwin, on Mary Shelley's testimony, described Mrs. Inchbald; also, by analogy, to the charmer whose sparkling talk had to break through the impediment of a stumbling tongue. In the second edition the milkmaid has been suppressed. In preparing this, Mrs. Inchbald had, on internal evidence, the help of classically educated friends, most probably of William Godwin. There are hundreds of small corrections of order, syntax, and vocabulary, in the interest of logic, precision, and accepted literary usage. Nearly all of these were taken into the fourth and the 'new' (1810) editions, though very occasionally she went back to the simpler word and the shorter statement. More emendations of the same kind were added in the fourth edition and a few in 1810. There is a constant gain in lucidity and formal literacy, but some loss of spontaneity and flexibility of tone. These changes are the fruits of her attentive self-culture; but it is possible to prefer the flavour of the wild berry.

The care Mrs. Inchbald took to surmount the drawbacks of an imperfect education and to deserve her success by an improved presentation of her novel is illustrated below by a classification of the more frequent types of emendation. Nearly all the changes are stylistic, but there is a small handful

of afterthoughts and alterations of detail. There is also in
the frequent slight rearrangements of words in the dialogue
a consciousness of the speaker's voice, and of what emphasis will bring out the full meaning, explicit and implicit,
of the dialogue, which confirms the dramatic quality of her
imagination. It would take too much space to illustrate
this.

A few misprints and misspellings have been corrected (e.g.
assylum, *buiscuit*), and eighteenth-century spellings, where
these are inconsistent (e.g. *chearful* and *cheerful*; *suspence* and
suspense), have been normalized. A few omitted words have
been supplied and some half-dozen grammatical tangles have
been straightened out by the second edition; these may be in
part due to the difficulties of Mrs. Inchbald's manuscript.
(In one place the printers read *maintaining* as *mentioning*.)
The treatment of titles varies between lower-case in all
positions in vols. I and II (*lady Evans*; *lord Frederick*) and
capitals in all positions in vols. III and IV (*your Lordship*;
'*No, Madam*'); it has therefore been reduced to modern
usage.

The errata at the end of each volume have been taken into
the text, but have not been generalized. Thus, she makes a few
token corrections of her verbal forms (e.g. *shaked* to *shook*;
run to *ran*; *forbid* to *forbad*) and these have been respected,
but not carried through the rest of the book. Such variants
were not, in her time, a positive mark of imperfect education.
Parson Woodforde, her contemporary, an Oxford man and
former Fellow of his College, writing his diary in the next
county to hers, uses 'had went' for the past conditional form
and confuses the parts of the verbs 'lie' and 'lay' as she does.
The cases of the pronouns doubtless conform to her speech
habits. Verbs and pronouns are regularized in the second
edition.

No correction later than the second edition has been introduced into the text.

Punctuation. The first edition exhibits a type of punctuation often found in the minor novel at the end of the eighteenth century. It is a guide to dramatic emphasis, and only accidentally combines this with a syntactical function. Except in one respect (see below) it has been retained. It should give no trouble to the reader who remembers

(*a*) that a comma (or semicolon or colon) frequently marks an emphasis on the preceding word (e.g. 'Lord Elmwood gazed on him with wonder! . . . She, sighed with a trembling kind of ecstasy');

(*b*) but can sometimes indicate a break or short pause before the important word (e.g. 'He felt upon this occasion, a reluctance');

(*c*) and that the comma or semicolon marks off the group of words that would naturally be uttered in one impulse, rather than a syntactical portion of a sentence, though the two may coincide, as they often do in noun clauses.

The full stop performs its natural function, but, within a paragraph, is often replaced by the dash.

A usage, unparalleled in my experience, occurs in dialogue. After a remark, complete in itself and conclusive in tone, there is a full stop, even though it is followed by, for example, 'replied Miss Milner'. This punctuation seems to be Mrs. Inchbald's idiosyncrasy—probably a dramatic notation—and the compositors were puzzled. In vols. I and II such a full stop is followed by a capital letter (e.g. '"I hope they won't quarrel." Said Mrs. Horton'); in vol. III and the first half of vol. IV by a lower-case letter (e.g. '"I did not know it was proper". she replied timidly'), and in the last half of vol. IV the compositors fall back on normal usage, which also appears in many passages of similar dialogue throughout. This oddity, then, is inconsistent, largely disappears in the second edition, and has not been retained in this.

In the later editions the punctuation as a whole is progressively modernized. Some dramatic punctuation survives in the fourth edition (1799), but none from the 'new' edition of 1810 onward.

TYPES OF EMENDATION IN THE SECOND EDITION

(a) Elimination of provincialisms, colloquialisms, incorrect grammar, and misused words:

e.g. *shaked, had shook, had rose*; *neither—or*; *laid* for *lay*; *dare* for *dares*; *durst* for *dared*; *provided* for *even if*; *moreover* for *on the contrary*.

Relative pronouns and connectives inserted.

Prepositions at the end of sentences avoided.

Mortally > *dangerously*; *innate feeling* > *genuine feeling*; *stationary* pulses > *the placid ones that moved in a more equal course*.

We should probably include among provincialisms the extensive use of titles—his lordship, her ladyship—which are replaced by proper names and descriptions such as 'her guardian', 'his patron'; a proverbial image 'red as scarlet' which is replaced by 'flushed with resentment'; and such small points of fashion as Miss Milner's 'woman', who becomes her 'maid'.

(b) Clarification of form and meaning:

Avoidance of change of construction in sentences.

Clarification of antecedents of pronouns.

Avoidance of ambiguity in the conditional mood:

e.g. 'and *had been cured* of all his pride' > 'and *would have been cured* of all his pride'.

Avoidance of tautology:

e.g. the italicized words are deleted in: something *more* essential; *all* omnipotent; *unexpectedly* surprised; *future* fate; *sprightly* vivacity; *necessary* duty; rising briskly *from his seat*; the postmark *on the outside*.

Precision of vocabulary and order:

e.g. 'the *monastic precepts* of hypocrisy' > 'the *injunctions* of monkish hypocrisy'. In connexion with Dorriforth's duel: 'the law of justice and *equity*' > 'the law of *honour* and justice'.

Complete, logical statement:

e.g. 'these airy charms . . . had yielded their transcendent power, *to less potent sadness*' > 'to *the weaker influence of filial sorrow*'; 'with that vast store of prudence he possesses I will force him still *to yield to his love*' > 'to *make a sacrifice of just resentment to partial affection*'.

Recension of exaggerated, playful, or paradoxical expressions, and those possibly liable to misunderstanding on any grounds:

e.g. 'with all the *pomp and dignity of a clergyman*' > 'with all the *dignity of his official character*'; 'and *almost* petrified' > '*as it were*, petrified'; 'to fly the roof of two such *un-seductive* innocent females' > 'two such innocent females'; 'where all the passions tumultuous strove by turns, one among them soon found the means to occupy all vacancies —*that one was love*' > '*a passion, commencing innocently, but terminating in guilt*'; 'Lord Margrave's *reserve of virtue*' > 'a *reserve of specious virtue*'.

Under this head might be included the excision of Sandford's argument on judging by construction in vol. II, chapter vii.

(c) Elegance:

Replacement of the simple, effective word by the dignified and sometimes conventional one:

e.g. *says* > *intimates*; *to tell him so* > *to apprize him of this arrangement*; *gnawing* sorrows > *corroding* sorrows; a foreboding of disaster ... *darted* over all his face > *spread a gloom*; Sandford looked *as if he could have struck her* > looked *enraged*.

The minute consideration which Mrs. Inchbald gave her text over twenty years may be illustrated from the various versions of one phrase in the first chapter of the book:

First edition: ... 'although the house which they themselves may have built'.

Second and third[1] editions: ... 'although the very house which they may have built themselves'.

Fourth edition: ... 'although the very house which they may have themselves built'.

'New' edition: ... 'although the very fabric which they may have themselves erected'.

(d) There are a few modifications of detail which cannot be classified. Miss Woodley's age is raised to thirty-five. Two references to the West Indies are introduced into vol. II to prepare for Lord Elmwood's absence. The homely details of a smoky house and of gentlemen taking their candles from the sideboard on going to bed are excised. 'Chariot' is replaced by 'chaise'. Tears no longer fall in 'floods', though they continue to fall. Slight touches affect Dorriforth's demeanour to his ward while he is still in orders. He is no longer allowed to 'shed tears' over the letter he writes her before his duel; rather, 'he could with difficulty preserve the usual firmness of his

---

[1] But see p. xxviii *n*.

mind'. A few heightening touches are added. Miss Milner, relinquishing the ball, 'sat down at the table by the side of *her delighted friend*' (first edition: *Miss Woodley*). Emotive repetitions raise the pitch of her speech ('can never—*oh! never* be erased'; 'my heart, *my heart* by nature sincere'); and, by a fine touch, her last letter to her husband in its '*Farewell Dorriforth*—farewell Lord Elmwood' is made to echo the petulant anguish of her stormy courtship—'No, call him Dorriforth ... for by that name alone, is he dear to me' (vol. II, chapter vii).

Mrs. Inchbald's imagination could always reinhabit her book. In the fourth edition she strengthens the pathos of Sandford's position by changing 'the old *man*' to 'the old *priest*' (vol. IV, chapter ix) and in the 'new' edition of 1810 he speaks to the miserable girl '*rather kindly*' instead of '*good-naturedly*' (vol. II, chapter xi).

SELECT BIBLIOGRAPHY

[NEITHER the *Bibliography* of G. L. Joughin nor the lists of publications in the studies of S. R. Littlewood and W. McKee (see below) give any information about the state of the text in the different editions. The following is a tentative statement. The first, second, and fourth editions and that of 1908 have been fully checked, the others by samples only. Editions listed by Joughin or Littlewood, which I have not seen, are marked (J.) or (L.). The place of publication is London, unless otherwise stated.]

Feb.	1791	1st edition: 4 vols.		(Robinson)
(J.)	1791	„	„ 2 „	(Dublin: Wilson, Wogan, Byrne, etc.)
March	1791	2nd	„ 4 „	(Robinson) (extensively revised)
	1793	3rd	„ 4 „	(Robinson)[1]
	1799	4th	„ 4 „	(Robinson) (revised)
(J.)	1804	„	„ (?) 2 „	(Dublin: Wogan, Porter, Browne, etc.)
	1808	„	„ 2 „	(Paris: Theophilus Barrois, Junior)[2]
	1810	'A new edition with the last corrections of the author'		In Mrs. Barbauld's *British Novelists*, vol. xxviii. With an introduction by Mrs. Barbauld. (Rivington) (revised).
	1820	'A new edition'[3]		(Longman, Hurst, Rees, etc.)

The 1810 revision, which is slight, appears to be the last. After Mrs. Inchbald's death (1821) *A Simple Story* appeared in several

---

[1] Judging by Xerox samples of four chapters from the copy in Princeton University Library, this was a reprint of the second edition. Vol. i of the Princeton set, however, appears to be from a copy of the first edition.

[2] Though described as 'A New Edition with Plates', this appears to be a reprint of the fourth edition.

[3] i.e. Mrs. Barbauld's text.

collections through the nineteenth century: e.g. Limbird's *The British Novelist*, no. 5 (1823), Bentley's Standard Novels and Romances, vol. xxvi (1833), *The Parlour Library*, vol. 85 (Simms, etc., 1852), and (L.) Cassell's *National Library*, vol. 24 (1886). Mrs. Barbauld's and Bentley's *Collections* were reissued several times. In most cases *A Simple Story* is coupled with *Nature and Art*. In 1880 de la Rue published both novels with a good introductory memoir by William Bell Scott. The text used in all these editions appears to be that of the 1810 revision. In 1908 *A Simple Story* appeared in the *Oxford Miscellany* (Frowde) with an introduction by G. L. Strachey. The text is an exact reprint of the 1799 edition.

There was a translation into French, by J. M. Deschamps (Paris, 1792), reprinted several times, and one into German by Margarethe Liebeskind (1792). Details are to be found in Joughin.

BIBLIOGRAPHY

1934 G. L. Joughin, *An Inchbald Bibliography* (reprinted from the University of Texas *Studies in English*, 1934. Austin; Texas).

(This is chiefly based on the holdings of Harvard College Library, with a few locations in European National Libraries. There is a useful list of periodical references.)

BIOGRAPHICAL AND LITERARY

The chief source of biographical information is *Memoirs of Mrs. Inchbald* by James Boaden, Esq., 2 vols. (1833), together with his *Memoirs of the Life of John Philip Kemble*, 2 vols. (1825). References and anecdotes are to be found in the theatrical memoirs of the late eighteenth and the nineteenth century, from Tate Wilkinson, *A Wandering Patentee* (York, 1795), to Frances Ann Kemble, *Record of a Girlhood*, 3 vols. (1879), and also in biographical studies of her friends, such as C. Kegan Paul, *William Godwin, his Friends and Contemporaries*, 2 vols. (1876). Many of these are utilized in S. R. Littlewood's *Mrs. Inchbald and her Circle* (1921).

Useful critical accounts of *A Simple Story* are to be found in
the introductions to various editions, especially G. L. Strachey's introduction to the 1908 *Oxford Miscellany* edition, and
J. M. S. Tompkins's introduction to the 1967 Oxford English
Novels edition. William McKee's Ph.D. dissertation, 'Elizabeth
Inchbald, Novelist' (Washington, 1935) is helpful on the Catho-
lic background to the novel. Discussion of its literary and
theatrical background is to be found in Patricia Sigl, 'The
Literary Achievement of Elizabeth Inchbald [1753–1821]',
Ph.D. University of Wales (Swansea), 1980, which includes
transcripts of a large number of contemporary reviews of
Inchbald's work. Some of Sigl's findings are summarized in
'The Elizabeth Inchbald Papers', *Notes and Queries* (June,
1982), pp. 220–4.

The most important recent criticism of *A Simple Story* is to
be found in Gary Kelly, *The English Jacobin Novel 1780–1805*
(1976), and Terry Castle, *Masquerade and Civilization: The
Carnivalesque in Eighteenth-Century English Culture and Fiction*
(1986). Shorter treatments of the novel are in Marilyn Butler,
Jane Austen and the War of Ideas (1975), Jane Spencer, *The Rise
of the Woman Novelist: from Aphra Behn to Jane Austen* (1986),
and Dale Spender, *Mothers of the Novel* (1986). Katharine M.
Rogers discusses it in her article 'Inhibitions on Eighteenth-
Century Women Novelists: Elizabeth Inchbald and Charlotte
Smith', *Eighteenth-Century Studies*, 11 (1977–8), 63–78, mater-
ial from which is included in her *Feminism in Eighteenth-
Century England* (1982).

J.S.

CHRONOLOGY OF
ELIZABETH INCHBALD

Age

1753 (15 October) Born at Standingfield, near Bury St. Edmunds, youngest but one of the nine children of John Simpson, farmer, and Mary (née Rushbrook). A Catholic family

1761 John Simpson dies. His widow struggles on with the farm. The elder girls marry   8

1770 George Simpson becomes an actor in the Norwich company. Elizabeth, beautiful but hampered by an impediment in her speech, applies to Richard Griffith, the manager, without result   17

1771 First London visit. Meets Joseph Inchbald, 36, actor, painter, and Catholic   18

1772 (11 April) Leaves secretly for London, to get a place in a theatrical company. Experiences convince her that she needs a protector

(9 June) Marries Joseph Inchbald

(4 September) Makes her theatrical début at Bristol as Cordelia to Inchbald's Lear

(October) The Inchbalds join West Digges's company in Scotland   19

1774 (9 January) Mrs. Inchbald begins to study French   20

1776 (12 June) Inchbald has a 'great dispute' with an Edinburgh audience. Engagement with Digges terminated

(23 July) The Inchbalds go to Paris, he to study painting and she French

(end of August) Return penniless to England. Mrs. Inchbald begins her first farce on 31 August

(October) Join Younger's company at Liverpool. Mrs. Inchbald begins 45 years' friendship with Mrs. Siddons   23

1777 (18 January) Meets John Philip Kemble, Mrs. Siddons's brother, aged 20, when he joins the company

(February) Begins an outline of *A Simple Story* (the first half)

(July) The Inchbalds at Canterbury. Meet Holcroft

(October) Join Tate Wilkinson's York Company at Hull   24

Age

1778 First Catholic Relief Act

(October) J. P. Kemble joins the York circuit   25

1779 (6 June) Inchbald dies suddenly; Kemble writes a Latin epitaph for him

(September) Mrs. Inchbald finishes her novel. It is offered to Stockdale and declined. Works at farces   25

1780 (September) London. Engaged by Harris at Covent Garden   26

1782 Summer engagement with Colman at the Haymarket. Also in later years   28

1782-3 (November to May) Engaged for tragedy in Dublin, where she supports Kemble in Jephson's *Count of Narbonne*   29

1784 (6 July) Her farce *The Mogul Tale* (publ. 1786), based on the ballooning excitement of 1783-4, brilliantly successful at the Haymarket   30

1785 *I'll Tell you What* (comedy) (publ. 1786)
Appearance is against them (publ. 1785)   32

1786 *The Widow's Vow* (publ. 1786)   33

1787 *All on a Summer's Day* (not published)
Such Things Are (publ. 1788)
The Midnight Hour (publ. 1788)   34

1788 *The Child of Nature* (publ. 1788)
Animal Magnetism (publ. 1789)   35

1789 *The Married Man* (publ. 1789). Mrs. Inchbald retires from the stage. Her investments yield £58 p.a.   36

1790 Second Catholic Relief Act   37

1791 (10 February) *A Simple Story*. Robinson pays £200 for it
Hue and Cry (not published)
Next Door Neighbours (publ. 1791)   38

1792 *Young Men and Old Women* (not published)
She writes *The Massacre* and *A Case of Conscience*, dealing with the French Revolution. Not produced nor published, until added by James Boaden to his *Memoirs of Mrs. Inchbald* (1833)   39

1793 *Everyone has his Fault* (publ. 1793)   40

1794 *The Wedding Day* (publ. 1794)
Finishes her second novel, *Nature and Art*   41

A SIMPLE STORY

PREFACE[1]

I T is said, *a book should be read with the same spirit with which it has been written.*[2] In that case, fatal must be the reception of this—for the writer frankly avows, that during the time she has been writing it, she has suffered every quality and degree of weariness and lassitude, into which no other employment could have betrayed her.

It has been the destiny of the writer of this Story, to be occupied throughout her life, in what has the least suited either her inclination or capacity—with an invincible impediment in her speech, it was her lot for thirteen years to gain a subsistence by public speaking—and, with the utmost detestation to the fatigue of inventing, a constitution suffering under a sedentary life, and an education confined to the narrow boundaries prescribed her sex, it has been her fate to devote a tedious seven years[3] to the unremitting labour of literary productions—whilst a taste for authors of the first rank has been an additional punishment, forbidding her one moment of those self-approving reflections which are assuredly due to the industrious.—But, alas! in the exercise of the arts, industry scarce bears the name of merit.—What then is to be substituted in the place of genius? GOOD FORTUNE. —And if these volumes should be attended by the good fortune that has accompanied her other writings, to that divinity, and that alone, she shall attribute their success.

Yet, there is a *first cause* still, to whom I cannot here forbear to mention my obligations.

The Muses, I trust, will pardon me, that to them I do not

feel myself obliged—for, in justice to their heavenly inspira-
tions, I believe they have never yet favoured me with one
visitation; but sent in their disguise NECESSITY, who, being
the mother of Invention, gave me all mine—while FORTUNE
kindly smiled, and was accessary to the cheat.

But this important secret I long wished, and endeavoured
to conceal; yet one unlucky moment candidly, though un-
wittingly, divulged it—I frankly owned, 'That Fortune having
chased away Necessity, there remained no other incitement
to stimulate me to a labour I abhorred.'—It happened to be
in the power of the person[1] to whom I confided this secret, to
send NECESSITY once more.—Once more, then, bowing to its
empire, I submit to the task it enjoins.

This case has something similar to a theatrical anecdote
told (I think) by Colly Cibber:[2]

'A performer of a very mean salary, played the Apothecary in
Romeo and Juliet so exactly to the satisfaction of the audience, that
this little part, independent of the other characters, drew immense
houses whenever the play was performed—The manager in consequence, thought it but justice to advance the actor's salary; on
which the poor man (who, like the character he represented, had
been half starved before) began to live so comfortably, he became
too plump for the part; and being of no importance in any thing
else, the manager of course now wholly discharged him—and thus,
actually reducing him to the want of a piece of bread, in a short
time he became a proper figure for the part again.'

Welcome, then, thou all-powerful principle, NECESSITY!—
THOU, who art the instigator of so many bad authors and actors
—but, to their shame, not of all:—THOU, who from my infancy
seldom hast forsaken me, still abide with me.—I will not complain of any hardship thy commands require, so thou doest not
urge my pen to prostitution.——In all thy rigour, oh! do not
force my toil to libels—or, what is equally pernicious—pane-
gyric on the unworthy!

VOLUME I

CHAPTER I

DORRIFORTH, bred at St. Omer's[1] in all the scholastic rigour of that college, was by education, and the solemn vows of his order, a Roman Catholic priest—but nicely discriminating between the philosophical and the superstitious part of that character,[2] and adopting the former only, he possessed qualities not unworthy the first professors of Christianity— every virtue which it was his vocation to preach, it was his care to practise; nor was he in the class of those of the religious, who, by secluding themselves from the world, fly the merit they might have in reforming mankind. He refused to shelter himself from the temptations of the layman by the walls of a cloister, but sought for, and found that shelter in the centre of London, where he dwelt, in his own prudence, justice, fortitude, and temperance.[3]

He was about thirty, and had lived in the metropolis near five years, when a gentleman, above his own age, but with whom he had from his youth contracted a most sincere friendship, died, and left him the sole guardian of his daughter, a young lady of eighteen.

The deceased Mr. Milner, on his approaching dissolution, perfectly sensible of his state, thus reasoned to himself before he made the nomination: 'I have formed no intimate friendship during my whole life, except one—I can be said to know the heart of no man except the heart of Dorriforth—After knowing his, I never sought acquaintance with another—I did not wish to lessen the exalted estimation of human nature he had inspired. In this moment of trembling apprehension

from every thought that darts across my mind, much more for
every action which soon I must be called to answer for; all
worldly views here thrown aside, I act as if that tribunal before
which I every moment expect to appear, were now sitting in
judgment upon my purpose.—The care of an only child is
the great charge that in this tremendous crisis I have to
execute—these earthly affections that bind me to her by
custom, sympathy, or what I fondly call parental love, would
direct me to study her present happiness, and leave her to the
care of some of those she styles her dearest friends; but they
are friends only in the sunshine of fortune; in the cold nipping
frost of disappointment, sickness, or connubial strife, they
will forsake the house of care, although the house which they
themselves may have built.'

Here the excruciating anguish of the father, overcame that
of the dying man.

'In the moment of desertion,' continued he, 'which I now
picture to myself, where will my child find comfort?—That
heavenly aid religion gives, which now amidst these agonizing
tortures, cheers with the bright ray of consolation my frightened
soul; that, she will be denied.'

It is in this place proper to remark, that Mr. Milner was a
member of the church of Rome, but on his marriage with a lady
of Protestant tenets, they mutually agreed their sons should be
educated in the religious opinion of their father, and their
daughters in that of their mother.[1] One child only was the
result of their union, the child whose future welfare now occupied the thoughts of her expiring father—from him the care
of her education had been withheld, as he kept inviolate the
promise made to her departed mother on the article of religion,
and therefore consigned his daughter to a Protestant boarding-
school, from whence she was sent with merely such sentiments
of religion, as young ladies of fashion mostly imbibe. Her little

heart employed in all the endless pursuits of personal accomplishments, had left her mind without one ornament, except those which nature gave, and even they were not wholly preserved from the ravages made by its rival, *Art*.

While her father was in health he beheld with the extreme of delight, his accomplished daughter without one fault with which taste or elegance could have reproached her, nor ever enquired what might be her other failings—Cast on a bed of sickness, and upon the point of leaving her to her future fate, those failings at once rushed on his memory—and all the pride, the fond enjoyment he had taken in beholding her open the ball, or delight her hearers with her sprightly wit, escaped his remembrance; or not escaping, were thought of with a sigh of contrition, or at best a contemptuous frown, at the frivolous qualification.

'Something more essential,' said he to himself, 'must be considered—something to prepare her for an hour like this I now experience—can I then leave her to the charge of those who themselves never remember such an hour will come?—Dorriforth is the only person I know, who, uniting every moral virtue to those of religion, and native honour to pious faith; will protect without controlling, instruct without tyrannizing, comfort without flattering, and perhaps in time make good by choice rather than by constraint, the dear object of his dying friend's sole care.'

Dorriforth, who came post from London to visit Mr. Milner in his illness, received a few moments before his death all his injunctions, and promised to fulfil them—but in this last token of Mr. Milner's perfect esteem of his friend, he still restrained him from all authority to direct his ward in one religious opinion contrary to those her mother had professed, and in which she herself had been educated.

'Never perplex her mind with an idea that may disturb, but

cannot reform'—were his latest words, and Dorriforth's reply gave him entire satisfaction.

Miss Milner[1] was not with her father at this affecting period—some delicately nervous friend, with whom she was on a visit at Bath, thought proper to conceal from her not only the danger of his death, but even his indisposition, lest it might alarm a mind she thought too susceptible. This refined tenderness gave poor Miss Milner the almost insupportable agony, of hearing her father was no more, even before she was told he was not in health. In the bitterest anguish she flew to pay her last duty to his remains, and performed it with the truest filial love, while Dorriforth, upon important business, was obliged to return to town.

CHAPTER II

DORRIFORTH returned to London heavily afflicted for the loss of his friend, and yet perhaps with his thoughts more engaged upon the trust that friend had reposed in him. He knew the life Miss Milner had been accustomed to lead; he dreaded the repulses his admonitions might possibly meet from her; and feared he had undertaken a task he was too weak to execute—the protection of a young woman of fashion.

Mr.[2] Dorriforth was nearly related to one of our first catholic peers; his income was by no means confined, but approaching to affluence, yet his attention to those in poverty, and the moderation of his own desires were such, that he lived in all the careful plainness of œconomy—his habitation was in the house of a Mrs. Horton, an elderly lady, who had a maiden niece residing with her not many years younger than herself— But although Miss Woodley was thirty,[3] and in person exceedingly plain, yet she possessed such an extreme cheerfulness of temper, and such an inexhaustible fund of good nature, that she escaped not only the ridicule, but even the appellation of an old maid.

In this house Dorriforth had lived before the death of Mr. Horton, nor upon that event did he think it necessary, notwithstanding his religious vow of celibacy, to fly the roof of two such unseductive innocent females as Mrs. Horton and her niece—on their part, they regarded him with all that respect and reverence which the most religious flock shews to its pastor; and his friendly society they not only esteemed a spiritual, but a temporal advantage, as the liberal stipend he allowed for his apartments and board enabled them to continue in the large and commodious house, where they had resided during the life of Mr. Horton.

Here, upon Mr. Dorriforth's return from his journey, preparations were made for the reception of his ward, her father having made it one of his requests that she might, for a time at least, dwell in the same house with her guardian, receive the same visits, and cultivate the acquaintance of his acquaintances and friends.

When the will of her father was made known to Miss Milner, she submitted without the smallest reluctance to all he had required—her mind, at that time impressed with the most poignant sorrow for his loss, made no distinction of happiness that was to come; and the day was appointed, with her silent acquiescence, when she was to arrive in London, and take up her abode at Mrs. Horton's, with all the retinue of a rich heiress.

Mrs. Horton was delighted with the addition this acquisition to her family was likely to make to her annual income, and to the style of her living.—The good natured Miss Woodley was overjoyed at the expectation of their new guest, yet she herself could not tell why—but the reason was, her kind heart wanted more ample field for its benevolence; and now her thoughts were all pleasingly employed how she should render, not only the lady herself, but even all her attendants, happy in their new situation.

The thoughts of Dorriforth were less agreeably engaged—Cares, doubts, fears, possessed his mind—so forcibly possessed it, that upon every occasion which offered, he would inquisitively try to gain intelligence of his ward's disposition before he saw her; for he was, as yet, a stranger not only to the real propensities of her mind, but even to her person; a constant round of visits having prevented his meeting her at her father's, the very few times he had been at his house, since her return from boarding-school. The first person whose opinion he, with all proper reserve, asked concerning Miss Milner was Lady Evans, the widow of a baronet who frequently visited at Mrs. Horton's.

But that the reader may be interested in what Dorriforth says and does, it is necessary to give some description of his person and manners. His figure was tall and elegant, but his face, except a pair of dark bright eyes, a set of white teeth, and a graceful fall in his clerical curls of dark brown hair, had not one feature to excite admiration—he possessed notwithstanding such a gleam of sensibility diffused over each, that many people mistook his face for handsome, and all were more or less attracted by it—in a word, the charm that is here meant to be described is a countenance—on his countenance you beheld the feelings of his heart—saw all its inmost workings—the quick pulses that beat with hope and fear, or the placid ones that were stationary with patient resignation. On this countenance his thoughts were pictured, and as his mind was enriched with every virtue that could make it valuable, so was his honest face adorned with every emblem of those virtues—and they not only gave a lustre to his aspect, but added a harmonious sound to all he uttered; it was persuasive, it was perfect eloquence, whilst in his looks you beheld his thoughts moving with his lips, and ever coinciding with what he said.

With one of those interesting looks which revealed the anxiety of his heart, and with that graceful restraint of all gesticulation, for which he was remarkable even in his most anxious concerns, he addressed Lady Evans who had called on Mrs. Horton to hear and to tell the news of the day: 'Your ladyship was at Bath last spring—you know the young lady to whom I have the honour of being appointed guardian.— Pray'—

He was earnestly intent upon asking a question, but was prevented by her ladyship.

'Dear Mr. Dorriforth, do not ask me any thing about the lady—when I saw her she was very young; though indeed that is but three months ago, and she can't be much older now.'

'She is eighteen,' answered Dorriforth, colouring with regret at the doubts her ladyship had increased, but not inspired.

'And she is very beautiful, that I can assure you,' replied her ladyship.

'Which I call no qualification,' said Dorriforth, rising from his seat in evident uneasiness.

'But where there is nothing else,' returned Lady Evans, 'let me tell you, beauty is something.'

'Much worse than nothing, in my opinion,' returned Dorriforth.

'But now, Mr. Dorriforth, do not from what I have said, frighten yourself, and imagine the young lady worse than she really is—all I know of her, is merely, that she's a young, idle, indiscreet, giddy girl, with half a dozen lovers in her suite;

some coxcombs, some men of gallantry, some single, and some married.'

Dorriforth started.—'For the first time of my life,' cried he with a manly sorrow, 'I wish I had never known her father.'

'Nay,' said Mrs. Horton, who expected every thing to happen just as she wished, (for neither an excellent education, the best company, or long experience had been able to cultivate or brighten this good lady's understanding,) 'Nay,' said she, 'I am sure, Mr. Dorriforth, you will soon convert her from all her evil ways.'

'Dear me,' returned Lady Evans, 'I am sure I never meant to hint at any thing evil—and for what I have said, I will give you up my authors if you please; for they were not observations of my own; all I do is to mention them again.'

The good natured Miss Woodley, who sat working at the window, an humble listener to this discourse, ventured on this to say exactly six words: 'Then don't mention them any more.'

'Let us change the subject,' said Dorriforth.

'With all my heart,' cried her ladyship, 'and I am sure it will be to the young lady's advantage.'

'Is she tall, or short?' asked Mrs. Horton, still wishing for farther information.

'Oh, tall enough of all conscience,' returned Lady Evans; 'I tell you again there is no fault can be found with her person.'

'But if her mind is defective'—exclaimed Dorriforth with a sigh—

'—That may be improved as well as the person,' cried Miss Woodley.

'No my dear,' returned her ladyship, 'I never heard of a pad to make strait an ill-shapen disposition.'

'O yes, Lady Evans,' answered Miss Woodley, 'good

company, good books, experience, and the misfortunes of others, may have more power to form the mind to virtue, than'——

Her ladyship would not suffer her to go on, but rising hastily from her seat, cried, 'I must be gone—I have fifty people waiting for me at home—besides, were I inclined to hear a sermon, I should desire Mr. Dorriforth to preach, and not you.'

Just then Mrs. Hillgrave was announced.—'And here is Mrs. Hillgrave,'—continued Lady Evans—'I believe Mrs. Hillgrave you know Miss Milner, don't you? The young lady who has lately lost her father.'

Mrs. Hillgrave was the wife of a merchant who had met with some severe losses, and as soon as the name of Miss Milner was uttered, she lifted up her hands, and the tears started in her eyes.

'There!' cried Lady Evans, 'I desire you will give your opinion of her, and I am sorry I cannot stay to hear it.' Saying this, she courtesied and took her leave.

When Mrs. Hillgrave had been seated a few minutes, Mrs. Horton, who loved information equal to the most inquisitive of her sex, begged that lady,—'if she might be permitted to know, why, at the mention of Miss Milner, she had seemed so much affected?'

This question interesting the fears of Dorriforth, he turned anxiously round attentive to the reply.

'Miss Milner,' answered she, 'has been my benefactress, and the best I ever had.' As she spoke, she took out her handkerchief and wiped away the tears that ran down her face.

'How so?' cried Dorriforth eagerly, with his eyes moistened with joy, nearly as much as her's were with gratitude.

'My husband, at the commencement of his distresses,'

replied Mrs. Hillgrave, 'owed a sum of money to her father, and from repeated provocations, Mr. Milner was determined to seize upon all our effects—his daughter, however, procured us time in order to discharge the debt; and when she found that time was insufficient, and her father no longer to be dissuaded from his intention, she secretly sold some of her most valuable ornaments to satisfy his demand and screen us from its consequences.'

Dorriforth, pleased at this recital, took Mrs. Hillgrave by the hand, and told her 'she should never want a friend.'

'Is Miss Milner tall, or short?' again asked Mrs. Horton, fearing from the sudden pause which had ensued the subject should be dropped.

'I don't know,' answered Mrs. Hillgrave.

'Is she handsome, or ugly?'

'I really can't tell.'

'It is very strange you should not take notice!'

'I did take notice, but I cannot depend upon my own judgment—to me she appeared beautiful as an angel, but perhaps I was deceived by the beauties of her disposition.'

CHAPTER III

This gentlewoman's visit inspired Mr. Dorriforth with some confidence in the principles and character of his ward.—The day arrived on which she was to leave her late father's seat, to take up her abode at Mrs. Horton's; and he, accompanied by Miss Woodley, went in his carriage to meet her, and waited at an inn on the road for her reception.

After many a sigh paid to the memory of her father, Miss Milner, upon the tenth of November, arrived at the place, half way on her journey to town, where Dorriforth and Miss Woodley were expecting her.—Besides attendants, she had with her a gentleman and a lady, distant relations of her mother's, who thought it but a proper testimony of their civility to attend her part of the way, but who so much envied her guardian the trust Mr. Milner had reposed in him, that as soon as they had delivered her safe into his care they returned.

When the carriage which brought Miss Milner stopped at the inn gate, and her name was announced to Dorriforth, he turned pale—something like a foreboding of disaster trembled at his heart, and consequently darted over all his face.—Miss Woodley was even obliged to rouze him from the dejection into which he was cast, or he would have sunk beneath it—she was obliged also to be the first to welcome his lovely charge.— Lovely beyond description.

But the sprightly vivacity, the natural gaiety, which report had given to Miss Milner, were softened by her recent sorrow to a meek sadness—and that haughty display of charms, imputed to her manners, was changed to a pensive demeanour. —The instant Dorriforth was introduced to her by Miss Woodley as her 'Guardian, and her deceased father's most beloved friend,' she burst into a flood of tears, knelt down to him for a moment, and promised ever to obey him as her father.—He had his handkerchief to his face at the time, or she would have beheld the agitation of his heart—the remotest sensations of his soul.

This affecting introduction being over, and some minutes passed in general conversation, the carriages were again ordered, and, bidding farewell to the friends who had accompanied her, Miss Milner, her guardian, and Miss Woodley departed for town; the two ladies in Miss Milner's carriage, and Dorriforth in that in which he came.

Miss Woodley, as they rode along, made no attempts to

ingratiate herself with Miss Milner; though, perhaps, it might constitute one of her first wishes—she behaved to her but as she constantly behaved to every other creature—that was sufficient to gain the esteem of one, possessed of an understanding equal to this young lady's—she had penetration to discover Miss Woodley's unaffected worth, and was soon induced to reward it with the warmest friendship.

CHAPTER IV

AFTER a night's rest in London, less strongly impressed with the loss of her father, reconciled, if not already attached to her new acquaintance, her thoughts pleasingly occupied with the reflection she was in that gay metropolis—a wild rapturous picture of which her active fancy had often formed—Miss Milner arose from a peaceful and refreshing sleep, with much of that vivacity, and all those airy charms, which for a while had yielded their transcendent power, to less potent sadness.

Beautiful as she had appeared to Miss Woodley and to Dorriforth the preceding day, when she joined them the next morning at breakfast, repossessed of her lively elegance and dignified simplicity, they gazed at her, and at each other alternately, with wonder!—and Mrs. Horton, as she sat at the head of her tea-table, felt herself but as a menial servant, such command has beauty if united with sense and with virtue.—In Miss Milner it was so united.—Yet let not our over-scrupulous readers be misled, and extend their idea of her virtue so as to magnify it beyond that which frail mortals commonly possess; nor must they cavil, if, on a nearer view, they find it less—but let them consider, that if Miss Milner had more faults than generally belong to others, she had likewise more temptations.

From her infancy she had been indulged in all her wishes to the extreme of folly, and habitually started at the unpleasant voice of control—she was beautiful, she had been too frequently told the high value of that beauty, and thought those moments passed in wasteful idleness during which she was not gaining some new conquest—she had besides a quick sensibility, which too frequently discovered itself in the immediate resentment of injury or neglect—she had acquired also the dangerous character of a wit; but to which she had no real pretensions, although the most discerning critic, hearing her converse, might fall into this mistake.—Her replies had all the effect of repartee, not because she possessed those qualities which can properly be called wit, but that what she said was spoken with an energy, an instantaneous and powerful perception of what she said, joined with a real or well-counterfeited simplicity, a quick turn of the eye, and an arch smile of the countenance.—Her words were but the words of others, and, like those of others, put into common sentences; but the delivery made them pass for wit, as grace in an ill proportioned figure, will often make it pass for symmetry.

And now—leaving description—the reader must form a judgment of her by her actions; by all the round of great or trivial circumstances that shall be related.

At breakfast, which was just begun at the beginning of this chapter, the conversation was lively on the part of Miss Milner, wise on the part of Dorriforth, good on the part of Miss Woodley, and an endeavour at all three on the part of Mrs. Horton. —The discourse at length drew from Mr. Dorriforth this observation.

'You have a greater resemblance of your father, Miss Milner, than I imagined you had from report: I did not expect to find you so like him.'

'Nor did I, Mr. Dorriforth, expect to find you any thing like what you are.'[1]

'No?—pray, madam, what did you expect to find me?'

'I expected to find you an elderly man, and a plain man.'

This was spoken in an artless manner, but in a tone which obviously declared she thought her guardian both young and handsome.—He replied, but not without some little embarrassment, 'A plain man you shall find me in all my actions.'

She returned, 'Then your actions are to contradict your looks.'

For in what she said, Miss Milner had the quality peculiar to wits, to speak the thought that first occurs, which thought has generally truth on its side.—On this he ventured to pay her a compliment in return.

'You, Miss Milner, I should suppose, must be a very bad judge of what is plain, and what is not.'

'How so, sir?'

'Because I am sure you will readily own you do not think yourself handsome; and allowing that, you instantly want judgment.'

'And I would rather want judgment than beauty,' she replied, 'and so I give up the one for the other.'

With a serious face, as if proposing a most serious question, Dorriforth continued, 'And you really believe you are not handsome?'

'I should from my own opinion believe so, but in some respects I am like you Roman Catholics; I don't believe from my own understanding, but from what other people tell me.'

'And let this be the criterion,' replied Dorriforth, 'that what we teach is truth; for you find you would be deceived did you not trust to persons who know better than yourself.— But, my dear Miss Milner, we will talk upon some other topic, and never resume this again—we differ in opinion, I dare say, on one subject only, and this difference I hope will never extend itself to any other.—Therefore, let not religion be named between us; for as I have resolved never to persecute you, in pity be grateful, and do not persecute me.'

Miss Milner looked with surprise that any thing so lightly said, should be so seriously received.—The kind Miss Woodley ejaculated a short prayer to herself, that heaven would forgive her young friend the involuntary sin of ignorance—while Mrs. Horton, unperceived as she imagined, made the sign of the cross upon her forehead to prevent the infectious taint of heretical opinions. This, pious ceremony, Miss Milner, by chance, observed, and now shewed such an evident propensity to burst into a fit of laughter, that the good lady of the house could no longer contain her resentment, but exclaimed, 'God forgive you,' with a severity so far different from the idea the words conveyed, that the object of her anger was, on this, obliged freely to indulge that risibility which she had been struggling to smother; and without longer suffering under the agony of restraint, she gave way to her humour, and laughed with a liberty so uncontrolled, that in a short time left her in the room with none but the tender-hearted Miss Woodley a witness of her folly.

'My dear Miss Woodley,' (then cried Miss Milner, after recovering herself,) 'I am afraid you will not forgive me.'

'No, indeed I will not,' returned Miss Woodley.

But how unimportant, how weak, how ineffectual are *words* in conversation—looks and manners alone express—for Miss Woodley, with her charitable face and mild accents, saying she would not forgive, implied only forgiveness—while Mrs. Horton, with her enraged voice and aspect, begging heaven to pardon the offender, palpably said, she thought her unworthy of all pardon.

CHAPTER V

SIX weeks have now elapsed since Miss Milner has been in London, partaking with delight in all its pleasures, whilst Dorriforth has been sighing with apprehension, attending with precaution, and praying with the most zealous fervour for her safety.—Her own and her guardian's acquaintance, and the new friendships (to speak in the unmeaning language of the world) which she was continually forming, crowded so perpetually to the house, that seldom had Dorriforth even a moment left from her visits or visitors, to warn her of her danger—yet when a moment offered, he snatched it eagerly—pressed the necessity of 'time not always passed in society; of reflection; of reading; of thoughts for a future state; and of virtues acquired to make old age supportable.'—That forcible power of innate feeling, which directs the tongue to eloquence, had its effect while she listened to him, and she sometimes put on the looks and gesture of assent, and sometimes even spoke the language of conviction; but this, the first call of dissipation would change to ill-timed raillery, or peevish remonstrance at being limited in delights her birth and fortune entitled her to enjoy.

Among the many visitors who attended at her levees, and followed wherever she went, was one that seemed, even when absent, to share her thoughts.—This was Lord Frederick Lawnly, the son of a duke, and the avowed favourite of all the most discerning women of taste.

Lord Frederick was not more than twenty-three; sprightly, elegant, extremely handsome, and possessed of every accomplishment to captivate a heart less susceptible of love than Miss Milner's was supposed to be.—With these allurements, no wonder if she took a pleasure in his company—no wonder

if she took a pride to have it known he was among the number
of her most devoted admirers.—Dorriforth beheld the growing intimacy with alternate pain and pleasure—he wished to
see Miss Milner married, to see his charge in the protection
of another, rather than of himself; yet under the care of a
young nobleman, immersed in all the vices of the town, without one moral excellence, but such as might result eventually
from the influence of the moment—under such care he
trembled for her happiness—yet trembled more lest her heart
should be purloined, without even the authority of matrimonial views.

With these sentiments Dorriforth could never disguise his
uneasiness at the sight of Lord Frederick, nor could his lordship but discern the suspicion of the guardian, and consequently each was embarrassed in the presence of the other.
—Miss Milner observed, but observed with indifference, the
sensations of both—there was but one passion which at present
held a place in her heart, and that was vanity; vanity defined
into all the species of pride, vain-glory, self-approbation—an
inordinate desire of admiration, and an immoderate enjoyment of the art of pleasing, for her own individual happiness,
and not for the happiness of others.—Still had she a heart
inclined, and oftentimes affected by tendencies less unworthy;
but those approaches to what was estimable, were generally
arrested in their first impulse by some darling folly.

Miss Woodley (who could discover virtue, although of
the most diminutive kind, and scarcely through the magnify-
ing glass of calumny could ever perceive a fault) was Miss
Milner's constant companion, and her advocate with Dorriforth, whenever, during her absence, she became the subject of discourse—he listened with hope to the praises of
her friend, but saw with despair how little they were merited.
—Sometimes he struggled to contain his anger, but

oftener strove to suppress tears of pity for her hapless state.

By this time all her acquaintance had given Lord Frederick to her as a lover, the servants whispered it, and some of the public prints[1] had even fixed the day of marriage;—but as no explanation had taken place on the part of his lordship, Dorriforth's uneasiness was encreased, and he seriously told his ward he thought it prudent to entreat Lord Frederick to desist visiting her.—She smiled with ridicule at the caution, but finding it a second time repeated, and in a manner that savoured of authority, she promised to make, and to enforce the request.—The next time his lordship came she did so, assuring him it was by her guardian's desire; 'who from motives of delicacy had permitted her rather to solicit as a favour, what he himself would make as a demand.'—Lord Frederick reddened with anger—he loved Miss Milner, but he doubted whether (from the frequent proofs he had experienced of his own inconstancy) he should continue to love— and this interference of her guardian threatened an explanation or a dismission, before he became thoroughly acquainted with his own heart.—Alarmed, confounded, and provoked, he replied,

'By heaven I believe Mr. Dorriforth loves you himself, and it is jealousy makes him treat me thus.'

'For shame, my lord!' cried Miss Woodley, who was present, and trembling with horror at the sacrilegious idea.

'Nay, shame for him if he be not in love'—answered his lordship, 'for what but a savage could behold beauty like her's, and not own its power?'

'Habit,' replied Miss Milner, 'is every thing—and Mr. Dorriforth sees and converses with beauty, and from habit does not fall in love, as you, my lord, merely from habit do.'

'Then you believe,' cried he, 'love is not in my nature?'

'No more of it, my lord, than habit could very soon extinguish.'

'But I would not have it extinguished—I would rather it should mount to a flame, for I think it a crime to be insensible of the blessings love can bestow.'

'Then your lordship indulges the passion to avoid a sin?—the very motive which deters Mr. Dorriforth.'

'Which ought to deter him, madam, for the sake of his oaths —but monastic[1] vows, like those of marriage, were made to be broken—and surely when your guardian looks on you, his wishes'——

'Are never less pure,' returned Miss Milner eagerly, 'than those which dwell in the bosom of my celestial guardian.'

At that instant Dorriforth entered the room. The colour had mounted into Miss Milner's face from the warmth with which she had delivered her opinion, and his entering at the very moment this compliment had been paid in his absence, heightened the blush to a deep glow on every feature, and a confusion that trembled on her lips and shook through all her frame.

'What's the matter?' cried Dorriforth, looking with concern on her discomposure.

'A compliment paid by herself to you, sir,' replied his lordship, 'has thus affected the lady.'

'As if she blushed at the untruth,' said Dorriforth.

'Nay, that is unkind,' cried Miss Woodley, 'for if you had been here'——

'—I would not have said what I did,' replied Miss Milner, 'but left him to vindicate himself.'

'Is it possible I can want vindication?' returned Dorriforth, 'Who would think it worth their while to slander so unimportant a person as I am?'

'The man who has the charge of Miss Milner,' replied Lord Frederick, 'derives a consequence from her.'

'No ill consequence, I hope, my lord?' replied Dorriforth with a firmness in his voice, and an eye fixed so steadfastly, that his lordship hesitated for a moment in want of a reply—and Miss Milner softly whispering to him, as her guardian turned his head, to avoid an argument, he bowed acquiescence.—And then, as in compliment to her, he wished to change the subject, with a smile of ridicule he cried,

'I wish, Mr. Dorriforth, you would give me absolution of all my sins, for I confess they are many, and manifold.'

'Hold, my lord,' exclaimed Dorriforth, 'do not confess before the ladies, lest in order to excite their compassion, you should be tempted to accuse yourself of sins, you have never yet committed.'

At this Miss Milner laughed, seemingly so well pleased, that Lord Frederick with a sarcastic sneer, repeated,

'From Abelard it came,
And Heloisa still must love the name.'[1]

Whether from an inattention to the quotation, or from a consciousness it was wholly inapplicable, Dorriforth heard it without one emotion of shame or of anger—while Miss Milner seemed shocked at the implication; her pleasantry was immediately depressed, and she threw open the sash and held her head out at the window to conceal the embarrassment these lines had occasioned.

The Earl of Elmwood was at this juncture announced—a Catholic nobleman, just come of age, and on the eve of marriage—his lordship's visit was to his cousin, Mr. Dorriforth, but as all ceremonious visits were alike received by Dorriforth, Miss Milner, and Mrs. Horton's family in one common apartment, Lord Elmwood was ushered into this, and for the present directed the conversation to a different subject.

CHAPTER VI

IN anxious desire that the affection, or acquaintance, between Lord Frederick Lawnly and Miss Milner might be finally broken, her guardian received with the highest satisfaction, overtures from Sir Edward Ashton, in behalf of his passion for that young lady.—Sir Edward was not young or handsome; old or ugly; but immensely rich, and possessed of qualities that made him, in every sense, worthy the happiness to which he aspired.—He was the man Dorriforth would have chosen before any other for the husband of his ward, and his wishes made him sometimes hope, against his reason, that Sir Edward would not be rejected—and he resolved to try the force of his own power in the strongest recommendation of him.

Notwithstanding that dissimilarity of opinion, which in almost every respect, subsisted between Miss Milner and her guardian, there was generally the most punctilious observance of good manners from each towards the other—on the part of Dorriforth more especially; for his politeness would sometimes appear even like the result of a system he had marked out for himself, as the only means to keep his ward restrained within the same limitations.—Whenever he addressed her there was an unusual reserve upon his countenance, and more than usual gentleness in his tone of voice; which seemed the effect of sentiments her birth and situation inspired, joined to a studied mode of respect best suited to enforce the same from her.—The wished-for consequence was produced—for though there was an instinctive rectitude in the understanding of Miss Milner that would have taught her, without other instruction, what manners to observe towards her deputed father; yet, from some volatile thought, or some quick sense of feeling, she had not been accustomed to subdue, she was perpetually on the verge of treating him with levity; but he would immediately recall her recollection by a reserve too awful, and a gentleness too sacred for her to violate. The distinction which both required, was thus, by his skilful management alone, preserved.

One morning he took an opportunity, before her and Miss Woodley, to introduce and press the subject of Sir Edward Ashton's hopes. He first spoke warmly in his praise, then plainly told Miss Milner he believed she possessed the power to make so deserving a man happy to the summit of his wishes. A laugh of ridicule was the only answer,—but a sudden and expressive frown from Dorriforth having quickly put an end to it, he resumed his wonted politeness and said,

'I wish, Miss Milner, you would shew more good taste than thus pointedly to disapprove of Sir Edward.'

'How, Mr. Dorriforth,' replied she, 'can you expect me to give proofs of a good taste, when Sir Edward, whom you consider with such high esteem, has given so bad an example of his, in approving of me?'

Dorriforth wished not to flatter her frailty by a compliment she seemed to have fought for, and for a moment hesitated what to say.

'Answer, sir, that question,' she cried.

'Why then, madam,' replied he, 'it is my opinion, that supposing what your humility has advanced to be just, yet Sir Edward will not suffer by the suggestion; for in cases where the heart is so immediately concerned, as I believe Sir Edward's to be, good taste, or rather reason, has not proper power to act.'

'You are right, Mr. Dorriforth; this is a thorough justification of Sir Edward—and when I fall in love, I must beg you will make the same excuse for me.'

'Then,' returned he earnestly, 'before your heart is in that state I have described, exert your reason.'

'I shall,' answered she, 'and not consent to marry a man whom I could never love.'

'Unless your heart is already given away, Miss Milner, what can make you speak with such a degree of certainty?'

He thought on Lord Frederick while he said this, and he fixed his eyes upon her as if he wished to penetrate her sentiments, and yet trembled for what he might find there.—She blushed, and her looks would have confirmed her guilty, had not a free and unembarrassed tone of voice, more than her words, preserved her from that sentence.

'No,' she replied, 'my heart is not given away, and yet I can venture to declare Sir Edward will never possess an atom of it.'

'I am sorry, for both your sakes, these are your sentiments,' —he replied. 'But as your heart is still your own,' (and he seemed rejoiced to find it was) 'permit me to warn you how you part with a thing so precious—the dangers, the sorrows you hazard in bestowing it, are greater than you may be aware of. The heart once gone, our thoughts, our actions, are no more our own, than that is.'——He seemed *forcing* himself to utter all this, and yet to break off as if he could have said much more, had not the extreme delicacy of the subject prevented him.

When he left the room, and Miss Milner heard the door shut after him, she said with a thoughtful and inquisitive earnestness, 'What can make good people so skilled in all the weaknesses of the bad? Mr. Dorriforth, with all those prudent admonitions, appears rather like a man who has passed his life in the gay world, experienced all its dangerous allurements, all its repentant sorrows, than like one who has lived his whole time secluded in a monastery or his own study.— Then he speaks with such exquisite sensibility on the subject of love, he commends the very thing he would decry.—I do not think my lord Frederick could make the passion appear in more pleasing colours by painting its delights, than Mr. Dorriforth can in describing its sorrows—and if he talks to me frequently in this manner, I shall certainly take pity on his lordship, for the sake of his enemy's eloquence.'

Miss Woodley, who heard the conclusion of this speech with the tenderest concern, cried, 'Alas! you then think seriously of Lord Frederick!'

'Suppose I do, wherefore that *alas!* Miss Woodley?'

'Because I fear you will never be happy with him.'

'That is plainly telling me he will not be happy with me.'

'I cannot speak of marriage from experience,' answered Miss Woodley, 'but I think I can guess what it is.'

'Nor can I speak of love from experience,' replied Miss Milner, 'but I think I can guess what it is.'

'But do not fall in love, my dear Miss Milner,' (cried Miss Woodley, with an earnestness as if she had been asking a favour that depended upon the will of the person entreated,) 'do not fall in love without the approbation of your guardian.'

Her young friend laughed at the inefficacious prayer, but promised to do 'all she could to oblige her.'

CHAPTER VII

SIR EDWARD, not wholly discouraged by the denial with which Dorriforth had, with delicacy, acquainted him, still hoped for a kinder reception, and was so frequently in the house of Mrs. Horton, that Lord Frederick's jealousy was excited, and the tortures he suffered in consequence, convinced him beyond a doubt of the sincerity of his affection.

He now, every time he beheld the object of his passion, (for he still continued his visits, tho' less frequently than before) pleaded his cause so ardently, that Miss Woodley, who was occasionally present, and ever compassionate, could scarce resist wishing him success. He now unequivocally offered marriage, and entreated to be suffered to lay his proposals before Mr. Dorriforth, but this Miss Milner positively forbad.

Her reluctance he imputed, however, more to the known partiality of her guardian to the addresses of Sir Edward, than to any motive which depended upon herself; and to Mr. Dorriforth his lordship conceived a greater dislike than ever; believing that through his interposition, in spite of his ward's attachment, he might yet be deprived of her—but Miss Milner declared both to him and to her friend, Love had, at present, gained no one influence over her mind.—Yet did the watchful Miss Woodley oftentimes hear a sigh burst forth, unknown to herself, till she was reminded of it, and then a sudden blush of shame would instantly spread over her face.—This seeming struggle with her passion, endeared her more than ever to Miss Woodley, and she would even risk the displeasure of Dorriforth by her ready compliance in every new pursuit that might amuse the time, she else saw passed by her friend in heaviness of heart.

Balls, plays, incessant company, at length rouzed her guardian from that mildness with which he had been accustomed to treat her—night after night, his sleep had been disturbed by fears for her safety while abroad; morning after morning, it had been broken by the clamour of her return.— He therefore said to her one forenoon as he met her accidentally upon the stair case,

'I hope, Miss Milner, you pass this evening at home?'

Unprepared for the sudden question, she blushed and replied, 'Yes.' While she knew she was engaged to a brilliant assembly, for which she had been a whole week consulting her milliner in preparation.

She, however, flattered herself what she had said to Mr. Dorriforth might be excused as a slight mistake, the lapse of memory, or some other trifling fault, when he should know the truth—the truth was earlier divulged than she expected—for just as dinner was removed, her footman delivered a message to her from her milliner concerning a new dress for the evening—the *present evening* particularly marked.—Dorriforth looked astonished.

'I thought, Miss Milner, you gave me your word you would pass this evening at home?'

'I mistook then—for I had before given my word I should pass it abroad.'

'Indeed?' cried he.

'Yes, indeed;' returned she, 'and I believe it is right I should keep my first promise; is it not?'

'The promise you gave me then, you do not think of any consequence.'

'Yes, certainly; if you do.'

'I do.'

'And mean, perhaps, to make it of much more consequence than it deserves, by being offended.'

'Whether or not, I am offended—you shall find I am.' And he looked so.

She caught his piercing, steadfast eye—her's were immediately cast down; and she trembled—either with shame or with resentment.

Mrs. Horton rose from her seat—moved the decanters and the fruit round the table—stirred the fire—and came back to her seat again, before another word was uttered. —Nor had this good woman's officious labours taken the least from the aukwardness of the silence, which as soon as the bustle she had made was over, returned in its full force.

At last, Miss Milner rising with alacrity, was preparing to go out of the room, when Dorriforth raised his voice, and in a tone of authority said,

'Miss Milner, you shall not leave the house this evening.'

'Sir?'—she exclaimed with a kind of doubt of what she had heard—a surprise, which fixed her hand on the door she had half opened, but which now she shewed herself irresolute whether to open wide in defiance, or to shut submissive.— Before she could resolve, Dorriforth arose from his seat, and said with a degree of force and warmth she had never heard him speak with before,

'I command you to stay at home this evening.'

And he walked immediately out of the apartment by the opposite door.—Her hand fell motionless from that she held— she appeared motionless herself for some time;—till Mrs. Horton, 'beseeching her not to be uneasy at the treatment she had received,' caused a flood of tears to flow, and her bosom to heave as if her heart was breaking.

Miss Woodley would have said something to comfort her, but she had caught the infection and could not utter a word— not from any real cause of grief did this lady weep; but there was a magnetic quality in tears, which always drew forth her's.

Mrs. Horton secretly enjoyed this scene, although the real well meaning of her heart, and ease of her conscience, did not tell her so—she, however, declared she had 'long prognosticated it would come to this;' and she 'now only thanked heaven it was no worse.'

'What would you have worse, madam?' cried Miss Milner, 'am not I disappointed of the ball?'

'You don't mean to go then?' said Mrs. Horton; 'I commend

your prudence; and I dare say it is more than your guardian gives you credit for.'

'Do you think I would go,' answered Miss Milner, with an earnestness that for a time suppressed her tears, 'in contradiction to his will?'

'It is not the first time, I believe, you have acted contrary to that, Miss Milner,' returned Mrs. Horton, and affected a tenderness of voice, to soften the harshness of her words.

'If that is the case, madam,' replied Miss Milner, 'I see nothing that should prevent me now.' And she flung out of the room as if she had resolved to disobey him.—This alarmed poor Miss Woodley.

'Dear Aunt,' she cried to Mrs. Horton, 'follow and prevail upon Miss Milner to give up her design; she means to go to the ball in opposition to her guardian's will.'

'Then,' cried Mrs. Horton, 'I'll not be an instrument in deterring her—if she does, it may be for the best; it may give Mr. Dorriforth a clearer knowledge what means are proper to use, to convert her from evil.'

'But, dear madam, she must be prevented the evil of disobedience; and as you tempted, you will be the most likely to dissuade her—but if you will not, I must endeavour.'

Miss Woodley was leaving the room to perform this good design, when Mrs. Horton, in humble imitation of the example given her by Dorriforth, cried,

'Niece, I command you not to stir out of this room, this evening.'

Miss Woodley obediently sat down—and though her thoughts and heart were in the chamber with her friend, she never shewed by one impertinent word, or by one line of her face, the restraint she suffered.

At the usual hour, Mr. Dorriforth and his ward were summoned to tea:—Dorriforth entered with a countenance which

evinced the remains of anger; his eye gave testimony of his
absent thoughts; and although he took up a pamphlet and
affected to read, it was plain to discern he scarcely knew he
held it in his hand.

Mrs. Horton began to make tea with a mind as wholly
intent upon something else, as Dorriforth's—she was longing for the event of this misunderstanding, (for to age trivial
matters are important,) and though she wished no ill to Miss
Milner, yet with an inclination bent upon seeing something
new—without the fatigue of going out of her own house—she
was not over scrupulous what that novelty might be.—But
for fear she should have the imprudence to speak a word upon
the subject which employed her thoughts, or even look as if
she thought of it at all; she pinched her lips close together, and
cast her eyes on vacancy, lest their significant regards might
detect her.—And for fear any noise should intercept even the
sound of what might happen, she walked across the room more
softly than usual, and more softly touched every thing she was
obliged to lay her hand on.

Miss Woodley thought it her duty to be mute, and now the
gentle gingle of a tea-spoon, was like a deep-toned bell, all was
so quiet.

Mrs. Horton too, in the self-approving reflection that she
herself was not in any quarrel, or altercation of any kind, felt
at this moment remarkably peaceful, and charitable.—Miss
Woodley did not recollect *herself* so, but was so in reality—in
her peace and charity were instinctive virtues, accident could
not encrease them.

The first cups of tea were scarcely poured out, when a servant came with Miss Milner's compliments and she should
drink none.—The book shook in Dorriforth's hand while this
message was delivered—he believed her to be dressing for
her evening's entertainment, and now studied in what manner

to prevent, or to resent it.—He coughed—drank his tea—endeavoured to talk, but found it difficult—sometimes read—and in this manner near two hours were passed away, when Miss Milner came into the room.——Not drest for a ball, but as she rose from dinner.—Dorriforth read on, and seemed afraid to look up, lest he should behold what he could not have pardoned.—She drew a chair and sat down at the table by the side of Miss Woodley.

After a few minutes pause, and some small embarrassment on the part of Mrs. Horton, at the disappointment she had to contend with from Miss Milner's unexpected obedience, she asked that young lady 'if she would now take tea?'—to which Miss Milner replied, 'No, I thank you, ma'am,' in a voice so languid, compared to her usual one, that Dorriforth lifted his eyes from the book; and seeing her in the same negligent dress she had worn all the day, cast them away again—not with a look of triumph, but of confusion.

And whatever he might have suffered had he beheld her decorated, and on the point of bidding defiance to his commands, yet even upon that trial, he had not endured half the painful sensations he now for a moment felt—he felt himself to blame.

He feared he had treated her with too much severity—he admired her condescension, accused himself for exacting it—he longed to ask her pardon, he did not know how.

A cheerful reply from her, to a question of Miss Woodley's, embarrassed him still more—he wished she had been sullen, he then would have had a temptation, or a pretence, to have been so too.

With all these thoughts crowding fast on his mind he still read, or seemed to read, and to take no notice of what was passing; till a servant entered and asked Miss Milner what time she should want the chariot? to which she replied,

'I don't go out to night.'—He then laid the book out of his hand, and by the time the servant had left the room, thus began.

'Miss Milner, I give you, I fear, some unkind proofs of my regard—it is often the ungrateful task of a friend to be troublesome—sometimes unmannerly.—Forgive the duty of my office, and believe no one is half so much concerned if it robs you of any amusements, as I myself am.'

What he said, he looked with so much sincerity, that had she been burning with rage at his behaviour, she must have forgiven him, for the regret he so forcibly exprest.—She was going to reply, but found she could not without accompanying her words with tears, therefore as soon as she attempted she desisted.

On this he rose from his seat, and going to her, said, 'Once more shew your submission by obeying me a second time to day.—Keep your appointment, and be assured I shall issue my commands with greater circumspection for the future, as I find how strictly they are complied with.'

Miss Milner, the gay, the proud, the haughty Miss Milner, sunk underneath this kindness, and wept with a gentleness and patience, which did not give more surprise than it gave satisfaction to Dorriforth.—He was charmed to find her disposition so little untractable—foreboded the future prosperity of his guardianship, and her eternal, as well as temporal happiness from this specimen.

CHAPTER VIII

ALTHOUGH Dorriforth was that good man that has been described, there was in his nature shades of evil—there was an obstinacy; such as he himself, and his friends termed firmness of mind; but had not religion and some opposite virtues[1] weighed heavy in the balance, it would frequently have degenerated into implacable stubbornness.

The child of a once beloved sister, who married a young officer[2] against her brother's consent, was at the age of three years left an orphan, destitute of every support but from his uncle's generosity: but though Dorriforth maintained, he would never see him. Miss Milner, whose heart was a receptacle for the unfortunate, no sooner was told the melancholy history of Mr. and Mrs. Rushbrook, the parents of the child, than she longed to behold the innocent inheritor of her guardian's resentment, and took Miss Woodley with her to see the boy—he was at a farm house a few miles from town; and his extreme beauty and engaging manners, needed not the sorrows to which he had been born, to give him farther recommendation to the kindness of her, who had come to visit him. She beheld him with admiration and pity, and having endeared herself to him by the most affectionate words and caresses, on her bidding him farewell, he cried most sorrowfully to go along with her. Unused to resist temptations, whether to reprehensible, or to laudable actions, she yielded to his supplications, and having overcome a few scruples of Miss Woodley's, determined to take young Rushbrook[3] to town and present him to his uncle. This idea was no sooner formed than executed.—By making a present to the nurse, she readily gained her consent to part with him for a day or two, and the signs of joy the child denoted on being put into the carriage, seemed to repay her before-hand, for every reproof she might receive from her guardian, for the liberty she had taken.

'Besides,' said she to Miss Woodley, who had still her apprehensions, 'do you not wish his uncle should have some warmer interest in his care than duty?—it is that alone, which induces Mr. Dorriforth to provide for him, but it is proper, affection, should have some share in his benevolence—and how, hereafter, will he be so fit an object for that love, which compassion must excite, as he is at present?'

Miss Woodley acquiesced.—But before they arrived at their own door it came into Miss Milner's remembrance, there was a grave sternness in the manners of her guardian when provoked; the recollection of which, made her something apprehensive for what she had done—Miss Woodley was more so.—They both became silent as they approached the street where they lived—for Miss Woodley having once represented her fears, and having suppressed them in resignation to Miss Milner's better judgment, would not repeat them—and Miss Milner would not confess they were now troubling her.

Just, however, as the coach stopt, she had the forecast and the humility to say, 'We will not tell Mr. Dorriforth the child is his nephew, Miss Woodley, unless he should appear fond, and pleased with him, and then we may venture without any danger.'

This was agreed, and when Dorriforth entered the room just before dinner, poor Harry Rushbrook was introduced to him as the son of a lady who frequently visited there. The deception passed—Dorriforth shook hands with him, and at length highly pleased with his engaging wiles, and applicable replies, took him on his knee, and kissed him with affection. Miss Milner could scarcely restrain the joy this gave her; but unluckily, Dorriforth said soon after to the child, 'And now tell me your name.'

'Harry Rushbrook,' replied he with great force and clearness in his voice.

Dorriforth was holding him fondly round the waist as he stood with his feet upon his knees; and at this reply he did not throw him from him—but he removed his hands, which supported him, so suddenly, that the child to prevent falling on the floor, threw himself about his uncle's neck.—Miss Milner and Miss Woodley turned aside to conceal their tears. 'I had like to have been down,' cried Harry, fearing no other danger.—But his uncle took hold of each hand that had twined around him, and placed him immediately on the ground; and dinner being that instant served, he gave no greater marks of his resentment than calling for his hat, and walking instantly out of the house.

Miss Milner cried for anger; yet she did not treat with less kindness the object of this vexatious circumstance: she held him in her arms all the while she sat at table, and repeatedly said to him, (though he had not the sense to thank her) 'she would always be his friend.'

The first emotions of resentment against Dorriforth being over, she was easily prevailed upon to return with poor Rushbrook to the farm house, before it was likely his uncle should come back; another instance of obedience which Miss Woodley was impatient her guardian should know; she therefore enquired where he was, and sent him a note to acquaint him with it, offering at the same time an apology for what had happened. He returned in the evening seemingly reconciled, nor was a word mentioned of the incident which had occurred during the day; yet there remained in the austere looks of Dorriforth a perfect remembrance of it, and not one trait of compassion for his helpless nephew.

CHAPTER IX

THERE are few things so mortifying to a proud spirit as to suffer by immediate comparison—men, can scarcely bear this humiliation, but to women the punishment is intolerable; and Miss Milner now laboured under the disadvantage to a degree, which gave her no small inquietude.

Miss Fenton, a young lady of the most delicate beauty, elegant manners, gentle disposition, and discreet conduct, was introduced to Miss Milner's acquaintance by her guardian; and frequently, sometimes inadvertently, held up by him as a pattern for her to follow—for, when he did not say this in direct terms, it was insinuated by the warmth of his pane-gyrics on those virtues in which Miss Fenton excelled, and his ward was obviously deficient. Conscious of her inferiority in these subjects of her guardian's praise, Miss Milner, instead of being inspired to emulation, was provoked to envy.

Not to admire Miss Fenton was impossible—to find a fault in her person or sentiments was equally impossible—and yet to love her, was very unlikely.

That serenity of mind which kept her features in a continual placid form, though enchanting at the first glance, upon a second, or third, fatigued the sight for a want of variety; and to have seen her distorted with rage, convulsed with mirth, or in deep dejection had been to her advantage.—But her superior soul appeared above those natural commotions of the mind, and there was more inducement to worship her as a saint, than to love her as a woman.—Yet Dorriforth, whose heart was not formed (at least not educated) for love; regarding her in the light of friendship, beheld her as the most perfect model for her sex, Lord Frederick on first seeing her was struck with her beauty, and Miss Milner apprehended she had introduced a rival; but he had not seen her three times, before he called her 'the most insufferable of Heaven's creatures,' and vowed there was more charming variation in the features of Miss Woodley.

Miss Milner had a heart affectionate to her sex, even where she saw them in the possession of charms superior to her own; but whether from the spirit of contradiction, whether from feeling herself more than ordinarily offended by her guardian's praise of this lady, or whether there was something in the reserve of Miss Fenton that did not accord with her own frank and ingenuous disposition so as to engage her esteem, it is certain she took infinite satisfaction in hearing her beauty and her virtues depreciated, or turned to ridicule, particularly if Mr. Dorriforth was present. This was very painful to him upon many accounts; perhaps regard to Miss Milner's conduct was not among the least; and whenever the circumstance occurred, he could with difficulty restrain his anger. Miss Fenton was not only a young lady whose amiable qualities Dorriforth admired, but she was soon to be allied to him by her marriage with his nearest relation, Lord Elmwood, a young nobleman whom he sincerely loved.

Lord Elmwood had discovered all that beauty in Miss Fenton which every common observer could not but see— the charms of her mind and her fortune had been pointed out to him by his Tutor; and the utility of their marriage in perfect submission to his precepts, his lordship never permitted himself to question.

This Preceptor, held with a magisterial power the government of his pupil's passions; nay, governed them so entirely, no one could perceive (nor did the young lord himself know) that he had any.

This rigid monitor and friend, was a Mr. Sandford, bred a jesuit in the same college where Dorriforth was educated, but before his time the order was compelled to take another name.[1]—Sandford had been the tutor of Dorriforth as well as of his cousin Lord Elmwood, and by this double tie seemed now entailed upon the family.—As a jesuit, he was consequently a man of learning; possessed of steadiness to accomplish the end of any design once meditated, and of wisdom to direct the conduct of men more powerful, but less ingenious than himself. The young earl accustomed in his infancy to fear him as his master, in his youth and manhood received every new indulgence with which his preceptor favoured him with gratitude, and became at length to love him as his father— nor had Dorriforth as yet shook off similar sensations.

Mr. Sandford perfectly knew how to work upon the passions of all human nature, but yet had the conscience not to 'draw all hearts towards him.'—There were of mankind, those, whose hate he thought not unworthy his holy labour; and in that, he was more rapid in his success than even in procuring esteem. In this enterprize he succeeded with Miss Milner, even beyond his most sanguine wish.

She had been educated at an English boarding school, and had no idea of the superior, and subordinate state of characters in a foreign seminary—besides, as a woman, she was privileged to say any thing she pleased; and as a beautiful woman, she had a right to expect whatever she pleased to say, should be admired.

Sandford knew the hearts of women, as well as those of men, notwithstanding he had passed but little of his time in their society—he saw Miss Milner's heart at the first view of her person; and beholding in that little circumference a weight of folly he wished to see eradicated, he began to toil in the vineyard, eager to draw upon him her detestation, in the hope he could also make her abominate herself. The mortifications of slight he was expert in, and being a man of talents, such as all companies, especially those Miss Milner often frequented, looked on with respect, he did not begin by wasting that reverence so highly valued upon ineffectual remonstrances, of which he could foresee the reception, but awakened the attention of the lady solely by his neglect of her. He spoke of her in her presence as of an indifferent person; sometimes forgot to name her when the subject required it; and then would ask her pardon and say he 'did not recollect her,' with such seeming sorrow for his fault, she could not think the offence intended, and of course felt the affront much more severely.

While, with every other person she was the principle, the first cause upon which a whole company depended for conversation, music, cards, or dancing, with Mr. Sandford she found she was of no importance.—Sometimes she tried to consider this disregard of her as merely the effect of ill-breeding, but he was not an ill-bred man; he was a gentleman by birth, and one who had kept the best company; a man of sense and learning.—'And does such a man slight me without knowing it?' she cried—for she had not dived so deep into the powers of simulation, as to suspect such careless manners were the result of art.

This behaviour of Mr. Sandford's had its desired effect; it humbled Miss Milner in her own opinion, more than a thousand sermons would have done preached on the vanity of youth and beauty. She felt an inward nothingness she never knew before, and had been cured of all her pride, had she not possessed a degree of spirit beyond the generality of her sex, and such as even Mr. Sandford with all his penetration did not expect.—She determined to resent his treatment, and entering the lists as his declared enemy, give reasons to the beholders[1] why he did not, with them, acknowledge her sovereignty.

She now commenced hostilities on all his arguments, his

learning, and his favourite axioms; and by a happy turn for ridicule, in want of other weapons, threw in the way of the holy Father as great trials for his patience, as any his order could have substituted in penance. Some things he bore like a martyr—at others, his fortitude would forsake him, and he would call on her guardian, his late pupil, to interpose with his authority; on which she would declare she only acted 'to try the good man's temper,' and had he combated with his fretfulness but a few minutes longer, she would have acknowledged his right to canonization; but having yielded to the sallies of his anger, he must now go through numerous other probations.

If Miss Fenton was admired by Dorriforth, by Sandford she was adored—and instead of giving her as an example to Miss Milner, he spoke of her as of one, endowed beyond Miss Milner's power of imitation.—Often with a shake of his head and a sigh would he say,

'No, I am not so hard upon you as your guardian; I only desire you to love Miss Fenton; to resemble her, I believe, is above your ability.'

This was something too much—and poor Miss Woodley, who was generally a witness of these controversies, suffered a degree of sorrow at every sentence that distrest Miss Milner. —Yet as she suffered for Mr. Sandford too, the joy of her friend's reply was abated by the uneasiness it gave to him. But Mrs. Horton felt for none but the right reverend priest; and often did she feel so violently interested in his cause, she could not refrain giving an answer herself in his behalf—thus, doing the duty of an adversary.

CHAPTER X

MR. SANDFORD finding his friend Dorriforth frequently perplexed in the management of his ward, and he himself thinking her incorrigible, gave his advice, that a proper match should be immediately sought out for her, and the care of so dangerous a person given into other hands. Dorriforth acknowledged the propriety of this counsel, but lamented the difficulty there was in pleasing his ward as to the quality of her lover, for she had refused, besides Sir Edward Ashton, many others of equal pretensions. 'Depend upon it then,' cried Mr. Sandford, 'her affections are already engaged, and it is proper you should know to whom.'—Dorriforth thought he did know, and mentioned Lord Frederick Lawnly; but said he had no farther authority for the supposition, than what his observation had given him, for that every explanation both on his lordship's side, and on that of the lady's, were evaded.—'Take her then,' cried Sandford, 'into the country, and if his lordship does not follow, there is an end to your suspicions.'—'I shall not easily prevail upon Miss Milner to leave the town,' replied Dorriforth, 'while it is in its highest fashion; while all the gay world are resorted hither.'—'You can but try,' returned Sandford, 'and if you should not succeed now; at least fix the time you mean to go during the Autumn, and keep to your determination.'—'But in the Autumn,' replied Dorriforth, 'Lord Frederick will of course be in the country, and as his uncle's estate is near to our residence, he will not then so evidently follow Miss Milner, as he would, could I induce her to go now.'

It was agreed the attempt should be made—and instead of receiving the proposal with uneasiness, Miss Milner, to the surprise of every one present, immediately consented; and

gave her guardian an opportunity of saying several of the
kindest and politest things upon her ready compliance.

'A token of approbation from you, Mr. Dorriforth,'
returned she, 'I always considered with the highest estimation—but your commendations are now become infinitely
superior in value, by their scarcity; for I do not believe that
since Miss Fenton and Mr. Sandford came to town, I have
received one testimony of your friendship.'

Had these words been uttered with pleasantry, they might
have passed without observation; but at the conclusion of the
period, resentment flew to Miss Milner's face, and she darted
a piercing look at Mr. Sandford, which more pointedly
expressed she was angry with him, than had she spoken
volumes in her usual strain of raillery.—Dorriforth looked
confused—but the concern which she had so plainly evinced
for his good opinion throughout what she had said, silenced
any rebuke he might else have been tempted to give her, for
this unwarrantable charge against his friend.—Mrs. Horton
was shocked at the irreverent manner in which Mr. Sandford
was treated—while Miss Woodley turned to him with a smile
upon her face, hoping to set him an example of the manner in
which he should receive this reproach.—Her good wishes did
not succeed—yet he was perfectly unruffled, and replied with
coolness, .

'The air of the country has affected the young lady already
—but it is a comfortable thing,' continued he, 'that in the
variety of humours some women are exposed to, they cannot
be steadfast even in deceit.'

'Deceit,' cried Miss Milner, 'in what am I deceitful? did I
ever pretend sir, I had an esteem for you?'

'That had not been deceit, madam, but merely good
manners.'

'I never, Mr. Sandford, sacrificed truth to politeness.'

'Except when the country has been proposed, and you thought it politeness to appear satisfied.'

'And I was satisfied, till I recollected you might probably be of the party—then every grove was changed to a wilderness, every rivulet into a stagnated pool, and every singing bird into a croaking raven.'

'A very poetical description,' returned he calmly.—'But, Miss Milner, you need not have had any apprehensions of my company in the country, for I understand the seat to which your guardian means to go, belongs to you; and depend upon it, madam, I shall never enter a house where you are the mistress.'

'Nor any house I am certain, Mr. Sandford, but where you yourself are the master.'

'What do you mean, madam? (and for the first time he elevated his voice,) am I the master here?'

'Your servants,' replied she looking at the company, 'will not tell you so, but I do.'

'You condescend, Mr. Sandford,' cried Mrs. Horton, 'in talking so much to a young woman; but I know you do it for her good.'

'Well, Miss Milner,' cried Dorriforth, (and the most cutting thing he could say,) 'since I find my proposal of the country has put you out of humour, I shall mention it no more.'

With all that vast quantity of resentment, anger, or rage which sometimes boiled in the veins of Miss Milner, she was yet never wanting in that respect towards her guardian, which withheld her from uttering one angry sentence, immediately directed to him; and a severe word on his side, instead of exasperating, was sure to soften her. Such was the case at present—his words seemed to cut her to the heart, but she had not the asperity to reply to them as she thought they

merited, and she burst into tears.—Dorriforth, instead of
being concerned, as he usually was at seeing her uneasy,
appeared on the present occasion provoked.—He thought her
weeping was a new reproach to his friend Mr. Sandford, and
to suffer himself to be moved by it, he considered would be a
tacit condemnation of his friend's conduct.—She understood
his thoughts, and getting the better of her tears, apologized
for the weakness of which she had been guilty; adding,

'She could never bear with indifference an unjust accusation.'

'To prove mine was such, madam,' replied Dorriforth, 'be
prepared to quit London, without any marks of regret, within
a few days.'

She bowed assent; the necessary preparations were agreed
upon; and while Miss Milner with apparent satisfaction
adjusted the plan of her journey, (like those persons who
behave well, not so much to please themselves as to vex their
enemies,) she secretly triumphed in the mortification she supposed Mr. Sandford would receive, from her obedient
behaviour.

The news of this intended journey was soon made public.
There is a secret charm in being pitied, when the misfortune
is but ideal, and Miss Milner found immense gratification in
being told, 'her's was a cruel case,' and that it was 'unjust and
barbarous to force so much beauty to be concealed in the
country, while London was filled with admirers; who, like
her, would languish in consequence of the separation.' These
things, and a thousand such, a thousand times repeated, she
still listened to with pleasure; yet preserved the constancy not
to shrink from her resolution of submitting.

Those sighs, which Miss Woodley had long ago observed,
became, however, more frequent still; and a tear half starting
to her eye was an additional matter of her friend's observation.

Yet though Miss Milner at those times was softened to melancholy, she by no means appeared unhappy. Miss Woodley was acquainted with the name of love only, yet she concluded from these encreased symptoms, what she before only suspected, that love *must* be their basis. 'Her senses have been captivated by the person and accomplishments of Lord Frederick,' said Miss Woodley to herself, 'while her understanding beholds his faults, and reproaches her passion—and, oh!' cried she, 'could her guardian and Mr. Sandford know of this conflict, how much more would they have to admire than to condemn!'

With these friendly thoughts, joined to the most perfect good intent, Miss Woodley did not fail to give both gentlemen cause to believe, a contention of this nature was the present state of Miss Milner's mind.—Dorriforth was affected at the description, and Sandford urged more than ever the necessity of the country expedition.——In a few days' time they undertook it; Mrs. Horton, Miss Woodley, Miss Milner, and Mr. Dorriforth, accompanied by Miss Fenton, whom Miss Milner, as she knew it to be the wish of her guardian, invited to pass the three months previous to her marriage, at her country seat. Elmwood House, or rather Castle,[1] the seat of Lord Elmwood, was only a few miles from this residence, and his lordship was expected to pass great part of the summer there with his tutor, Mr. Sandford.

In the neighbourhood was also an estate belonging to an uncle of Lord Frederick's, and many of the company suspected they should soon see his lordship on a visit there, and to that expectation did they in great measure attribute Miss Milner's visible content.

CHAPTER XI

WITH this party Miss Milner arrived at her country house, and for near six weeks all around was the perfect picture of tranquillity;—her satisfaction was as evident as every other person's; and every severe reflection being at this time unnecessary, either to tease her to her duty, or to warn her against her follies, she was even in perfect good humour with Miss Fenton, and added to the hospitality of a host, the kindness of a friend.

Mr. Sandford, who came with Lord Elmwood to the neighbouring seat about a week after the arrival of Miss Milner at her's, was so scrupulously exact in the observance of his word, '*never to enter a house of Miss Milner's*,' that he would not even call upon his friend Dorriforth there—but in their walks, and at Lord Elmwood's, the two parties would occasionally join, and of course Sandford and she at those times met—yet so distant was the reserve on either side, that not a single word was upon any occasion, ever exchanged between them.

Miss Milner did not like Mr. Sandford; yet, as there was no real cause for inveterate rancour, admiring him too as a man who meant well, and being besides of a most forgiving temper, she frequently felt concerned that he did not speak to her, although it had been to find fault as usual—and one morning as they were all, after a long ramble, drawing towards her house, where Lord Elmwood was invited to dine, she even burst into tears at seeing Sandford turn back and wish them a 'good day.'

But though she had generosity to forgive an affront, she had not the humility to make a concession; and she foresaw that nothing less than some very humble atonement on her part, would prevail upon the haughty priest to be reconciled.

Dorriforth saw her concern upon this trifling occasion with a secret pleasure, and an admiration she had never before excited. She insinuated to him to be a mediator between them; but before any accommodation could take place, the peace and composure of their abode was disturbed by the arrival of Sir Edward Ashton at Lord Elmwood's, where it appeared as if he had been invited in order to pursue his matrimonial plan.

At a dinner at Lord Elmwood's Sir Edward was announced as an unexpected visitor; Miss Milner did not suppose him such, and turned pale when his name was uttered—Dorriforth fixed his eyes upon her with some tokens of compassion, while Sandford seemed to exult, and by his repeated 'Welcomes' to the baronet, gave evident proofs how much he was rejoiced to see him. All the declining enmity of Miss Milner was renewed at this behaviour, and suspecting Sandford to be the instigator of his visit, she could not overcome her displeasure, but gave way to it in a manner she thought the most mortifying.—Sir Edward in the course of conversation, enquired 'what neighbours were in the country;' and she with the highest appearance of satisfaction, named Lord Frederick Lawnly, as one who was hourly expected at his uncle's. The colour spread over Sir Edward's face—Dorriforth looked confounded—and Mr. Sandford as if he could have struck her.

'Did Lord Frederick tell *you* he should be down?' Sandford asked of Dorriforth.

To which he replied, 'No.'

'But I hope, Mr. Sandford, you will permit me to know?' cried Miss Milner.—For as she now meant to torment him by what she said, she no longer constrained herself to silence—and as he harboured the same kind intent towards her, he had no longer any objection to make a reply, and therefore answered,

'No, madam, if it depended upon my permission, you should *not* know.'

'Not *any thing*, sir, I dare say;—you would keep me in utter ignorance.'

'I would.'

'From a self-interested motive, Mr. Sandford—that I might have a greater respect for you.'

Some of the persons present laughed—Mrs. Horton coughed—Miss Woodley blushed—Lord Elmwood sneered —Dorriforth frowned—and Miss Fenton, looked just as she did before.

The conversation was changed as soon as possible, and early in the evening the company returned home.

Miss Milner had scarce left her dressing room, where she had been taking off some part of her dress, when Dorriforth's servant came to acquaint her his master was alone in his study, and begged to speak with her.—She felt herself tremble—she immediately experienced a consciousness she had not acted properly at Lord Elmwood's; for she had a prescience her guardian was going to upbraid her, and her heart told her, he had never yet reproached her without a cause.

Miss Woodley just then entered the apartment, and she even found herself so much a coward, as to propose her going to Dorriforth along with her, and aiding her with a word or two occasionally in her excuse.

'What you, my dear,' returned Miss Woodley, 'who not two hours ago, had the courage to vindicate your own cause before a whole company, of whom many were your adversaries; do you want an advocate before your guardian only? and he, who has ever treated you with tenderness.'

'It is that tenderness which frightens me, Miss Woodley; that intimidates, and strikes me dumb—is it possible I can return impertinence to the language and manners Mr. Dorriforth uses? and as I am debarred from that, what can I do but stand before him like a guilty creature, acknowledging my faults.'

She again entreated Miss Woodley to go with her, but on a positive refusal, from the impropriety of such an intrusion, she was at length obliged to go by herself.

How much do different circumstances influence not only the manners, but even the persons of some people!—Miss Milner in the drawing room at Lord Elmwood's surrounded by listeners, by admirers, (for even her enemies beheld her with admiration,) and warm with their approbation and applause—and Miss Milner, with no giddy observer to give a false éclat to her actions, left destitute of all but her own understanding, (which secretly condemns her,) and upon the point of receiving the censure of her guardian and friend, are two different beings.—Though still beautiful beyond description, she does not look even in person the same.—In the last mentioned situation, she was shorter in stature than in the former—she was paler—she was thinner—and a very different contour presided over her whole air, and all her features.

When she arrived at the study door, she opened it with a trepidation she could hardly account for, and entered to Dorriforth the altered woman she has been represented. His heart had taken the most decided part against her, and his face assumed the most severe aspect of reproach; when her appearance gave an instantaneous change to *his* whole mind, and countenance.

She halted, as if she feared to approach—he hesitated, as if he knew not how to speak.—Instead of the warmth with which he was prepared to begin, his voice involuntarily softened, and without knowing what he said, he began,

'My dear Miss Milner'—

She expected he was angry, and in her confusion his gentleness was lost upon her—she imagined what he said might be severe, and she continued to tremble, although he repeatedly assured her, he meant only to advise, not to up-braid her.

'For in respect to all those little disputes between Mr. Sand-ford and you,' said he, 'I should be partial if I blamed you more than him—indeed, when you take the liberty to censure him, his character makes the freedom appear in a more serious light than when he complains of you yet, if he provokes your retorts, he alone must answer for them; nor will I undertake to decide betwixt you.——But I have a question to ask you, and to which I require a serious and unequivocal answer.—Do you expect Lord Frederick in the country?'

Without hesitation she replied, 'she did.'

'I have one more question to ask, madam, and to which I expect a reply equally unreserved.—Is Lord Frederick the man you approve for a husband?'

Upon this close interrogation she discovered an embarrass-ment, and a confusion beyond any she had ever before given proofs of; and in this situation she faintly replied,

'No, he is not.'

'Your words tell me one thing,' answered Dorriforth, 'while your looks declare another—which am I to trust?'

'Which you please,' she returned with an insulted dignity, that astonished, awed, yet did not convince him.

'But then why encourage him to follow you hither, Miss Milner?'

'Why commit a thousand follies (she replied in tears) every hour of my life?'

'You then promote the hopes of Lord Frederick without one serious intention of completing them? This is a conduct which it is my duty to guard you against, and you shall no longer deceive either him or yourself. The moment he arrives it is my fixed resolution you refuse to see him, or agree to become his wife.'

In answer to this, she appeared averse both to the one pro-
position and the other, yet came to no explanation why; but
left her guardian at the conclusion of the conversation as much
at a loss to decide upon her real sentiments, as he was before
he had thus seriously requested to be informed of them; but
having steadfastly taken the resolution which he had declared
to her, he found that determination a certain relief to his
mind.

CHAPTER XII

SIR EDWARD ASHTON, though not invited by Miss Milner,
yet frequently did himself the favour to come to her house;
sometimes he accompanied Lord Elmwood on a visit to her,
at other times he came to see Dorriforth only, who generally
introduced him to the ladies. But Sir Edward was either so
unwilling to give pain to the object of his love, or so much
intimidated by her frowns, that he seldom addressed a single
word to her, except the common compliments at entering,
and retiring.—This apprehension of offending, without one
hope of pleasing, had the most aukward effect upon the manners of the worthy baronet, and his endeavours to insinuate
himself into the affections of the woman he loved, merely by
the means of not giving her offence either by speaking or looking at her, was a circumstance so whimsical, that it frequently
forced a smile from Miss Milner, though the very name of Sir
Edward was of power to throw a gloom over her face; for she
looked upon him as the cause why she should be hurried to
make an election of a lover, before her own mind could well
direct her where to fix.—Besides, his pursuit was a trouble,
while it was not the smallest triumph to her vanity, which

by the addresses of Lord Frederick, was in the highest manner gratified.

His lordship now arrives in the country, and calls at Miss Milner's; her guardian sees his chariot coming along the lawn and gives orders to the servants, to say their lady is not at home, but that Mr. Dorriforth is; Lord Frederick leaves his compliments and goes away.

The ladies all saw his carriage and servants at the door; Miss Milner flew to the glass to adjust her dress, and in her looks expressed signs of palpitation—but in vain she keeps her eyes fixed upon the door of the apartment; he does not enter.

After some minutes' expectation, the door opens and her guardian comes in; she was disappointed, he perceived she was, and he looked at her with a very serious face; she immediately called to mind the assurance he had given her, 'that her acquaintance with Lord Frederick in its present state should not continue,' and between chagrin and confusion, she was at a loss how to behave.

Notwithstanding the ladies were all present, Dorriforth said to her, without the smallest reserve, 'Perhaps, Miss Milner, you may think I have taken an unwarrantable liberty in giving orders to your servants to deny you to Lord Frederick but until his lordship and I have had a private conference, or you condescend to declare your sentiments more fully in regard to his visits, I think it my duty to put an end to them.'

'You will always perform your duty, Mr. Dorriforth, I have no doubt, whether I concur or not.'

'Yet believe me, madam, I should do it much more cheerfully, could I hope it was sanctioned by your inclinations.'

'I am not mistress of my inclinations, sir, or they should conform to yours.'

'Place them under my direction, madam, and I'll answer they will.'

A servant entered.—'Lord Frederick is returned, sir, and says he should be glad to see you.'—'Shew him into the study,' cried Dorriforth hastily, and rising from his seat, left the room.

'I hope they won't quarrel,' said Mrs. Horton, meaning, she thought they would.

'I am sorry to see you so uneasy, Miss Milner,' said Miss Fenton, with the most perfect unconcern.

As the badness of the weather had prevented their usual morning's exercise, the ladies sat employed at their needles till the dinner bell called them away.—'Do you think Lord Frederick is gone?' then, whispered Miss Milner to Miss Woodley.—'I think not,' returned Miss Woodley.—'Go ask of the servants, dear creature.' And Miss Woodley went out of the room.—She soon returned and said, apart, 'He is now getting into his chariot, I saw him pass hastily through the hall; he seemed to fly.'

'Ladies, the dinner is waiting,' cried Mrs. Horton, and they repaired to the dining room; where Dorriforth soon after came, and engrossed their whole attention by his disturbed looks, and unusual silence. Before dinner was over he was, however, more himself, but still he appeared thoughtful and dissatisfied. At the time of their evening walk he excused himself, and was seen in a distant field with Mr. Sandford in earnest conversation; for they frequently stopt on one spot for a quarter of an hour, as if the interest of the subject had so totally engaged them, they stood still without knowing it. Lord Elmwood, who had joined the ladies, walked home with them; Dorriforth entered soon after, in a much less gloomy humour than when he went out, and told his lordship he and the ladies would dine with him to-morrow if he was disengaged, and it was fixed they should.

Still Dorriforth was in some perturbation, but the immediate cause was concealed till the next day, when, about an hour before the company's departure from the Castle, Miss Milner and Miss Woodley were desired, by a servant, to walk into a separate apartment, where they found Dorriforth with Mr. Sandford waiting their coming. Her guardian made an apology to Miss Milner for the form, the ceremony, of which he was going to make use, but he trusted, the extreme weight with which his mind was oppressed, lest he should mistake the real sentiments of a lady whose happiness depended upon his being correct in the knowledge of them, would plead his excuse.

'I know, Miss Milner,' continued he, 'the world in general, allows to unmarried women great latitude in disguising their mind with respect to the man they love.—I too, am willing to pardon any little dissimulation that is but consistent with that modesty, becoming every woman on the subject of marriage. But to what point I may limit, or you may think proper to extend this kind of venial deceit, may so widely differ, that it is not impossible I remain wholly unacquainted with your sentiments, even after you have revealed them to me.—Under this consideration, I wish once more to hear your thoughts in regard to matrimony, and to hear them before one of your own sex, that I may be enabled to form my opinion by her constructions.'

To all this serious oration, Miss Milner made no other reply than by turning to Mr. Sandford, and asking, 'If he was the person of her own sex, to whose judgment her guardian meant to submit his own?'

'Madam,' cried Sandford very angrily, 'you are come hither upon serious business.'

'Any business must be serious to me, Mr. Sandford, in which you are concerned; and if you had called it *sorrowful*, the epithet would have suited as well.'

'Miss Milner,' said her guardian, 'I did not bring you here to contend with Mr. Sandford.'

'Then why, sir, bring him hither? for where he and I are, there must be contention.'

'I brought him hither, madam, or rather brought you to this house, merely that he might be present on this occasion, and with his discernment relieve me from a suspicion, that my own judgment can neither suppress or confirm.'

'Is there any more company you may wish to call in, sir, to clear up your doubts of my veracity? if so, pray send for them before you begin your interrogations.'

He shook his head—she continued. 'The whole world is welcome to hear what I say, and every different judge welcome, if they please, to judge me differently.'

'Dear Miss Milner—,' cried Miss Woodley, with a tone of reproach for the vehemence with which she spoke.

'Perhaps, Miss Milner,' said Dorriforth, 'you will not now, reply to those questions I was going to put to you?'

'Did I ever refuse, sir,' returned she with a self-approving air, 'to comply with any request you have seriously made me? Have I ever refused to obey your commands whenever you thought proper to lay them upon me? if not, you have no right to suppose I will now.'

He was going to reply, when Mr. Sandford sullenly interrupted him, and making towards the door, cried, 'When you come to the point for which you brought me here, send for me again.'

'Stay now,' cried Dorriforth. 'And Miss Milner,' continued he, 'I not only entreat, but command you to tell me.—Have you given your promises, your word, or your affections to Lord Frederick Lawnley?'

The colour spread over her face, and she replied—'I thought confessions were only permitted in secrecy; however,

as I am not a member of your church, I submit to the persecution of a heretic, and answer—Lord Frederick has
neither my word, my promise, nor any share in my affections.'

Sandford, Dorriforth, and Miss Woodley all looked at each
other with a surprise that was for some time dumb.—At length
Dorriforth said, 'And it is your firm intention never to become
his wife?'

To which she answered—'At present it is.'

'At present! do you suspect you shall change your sentiments?'

'Women, sometimes do.'

'But before that change can take place, madam, your acquaintance will be broken off: for it is that, I shall next insist
upon; and to which you can have no objection.'

She replied, 'I had rather it would continue.'

'On what account?' cried Dorriforth.

'Because it entertains me.'

'For shame, for shame!' returned he, 'it endangers both
your character and your happiness.—Yet again, do not suffer
me to break with his lordship if you should like to become his
wife; if in that respect it militates against your felicity?'

'By no means,' she answered; 'Lord Frederick makes part
of my amusement, but could never constitute my felicity.'

'Miss Woodley,' said Dorriforth, 'do you comprehend your
friend in the same literal and unequivocal sense I do?'

'Certainly I do, sir,' answered Miss Woodley.

'And pray, Miss Woodley,' said he, 'were those the sentiments which you have always entertained?'

Miss Woodley hesitated—he continued, 'Or has the present conversation altered them?'

She hesitated again, then answered—'The present conversation has altered them.'

'And yet you confide in it!' cried Sandford, looking at her with contempt.

'Certainly I do,' replied Miss Woodley.

'Do not you then, Mr. Sandford?' asked Dorriforth.

'I would advise you to act the same as if I did,' replied Sandford.

'Then, Miss Milner,' said Dorriforth, 'you see Lord Frederick no more—and I hope I have your permission to tell him so?'

'You have, sir,' she replied with a completely unembarrassed countenance and voice.

Miss Woodley looked hard at her, to discover some lurking wish adverse to all these protestations, but she could not discern one.—Sandford too fixed his penetrating eyes as if he would look through her soul, but finding it perfectly composed, he cried out,

'Why then not write his lordship's dismission herself, and save you, Mr. Dorriforth, the trouble of any farther contest with him?'

'Indeed, Miss Milner,' said Dorriforth, 'that would oblige me; for it is with the greatest reluctance I meet his lordship upon this subject—he was extremely impatient and importunate the last time he was with me—he took advantage of my ecclesiastic situation to treat me with a levity, and ill-breeding, I could ill have suffered upon any other consideration, than the complying with my duty to you.'

'Dictate what you please, Mr. Dorriforth, and I will write it,' said she with a warmth like the most unaffected inclination.—'And while you, sir,' she continued, 'are so indulgent as not to distress me with the importunities of any gentleman to whom I am averse, I think myself equally bound to rid you of the impertinence of every one, to whom you may have objection.'

'But,' answered he, 'be assured I have no material objection to my lord Frederick, except from that dilemma, into which your acquaintance with him has involved us all; and the same I should conceive against any other man, where the same circumstance occurred.—As you have now, however, freely and politely consented to the manner in which it has been proposed, you shall break with him, I will not trouble you a moment longer upon a subject on which I have so frequently explained my wishes, but conclude it by assuring you, your ready acquiescence has given me the sincerest satisfaction.'

'I hope, Mr. Sandford,' said she, turning to him with a smile, 'I have given you satisfaction likewise.'

Sandford could not say yes, and was ashamed to say no; he, therefore, made no answer except by his looks, which were full of suspicion. She, notwithstanding, made him a very low courtesy.—Her guardian then handed her out of the apartment into her coach, which was waiting to take her, Miss Woodley, and himself home.

CHAPTER XIII

NOTWITHSTANDING the seeming readiness with which Miss Milner had resigned all farther acquaintance with Lord Frederick, during the short ride home she appeared to have lost great part of her wonted spirits; she was thoughtful, and once sighed most heavily. Dorriforth began to fear she had not only made a sacrifice of her affections, but of her veracity; yet, why she had done so, he could not comprehend.

As the carriage moved slowly thro' a lane between Elmwood Castle and her house, on casting her eyes out of the window, Miss Milner's countenance was brightened in an instant, and that instant Lord Frederick on horse-back was at the coach door, and the coachman stopt.

'Oh, Miss Milner,' cried he, (with a voice and manner that could give little suspicion of the truth of what he said) 'I am over-joyed at the happiness of seeing you, even though it is but an accidental meeting.'

She was evidently glad to see him, but the earnestness with which he spoke, put her upon her guard not to express the like, and she said in a cool constrained manner, she 'was glad to see his lordship.'

The reserve with which she spoke, gave Lord Frederick immediate suspicion who was in the coach with her, and turning his head quickly, he met the stern eye of Dorriforth; upon which, without the smallest salutation, he turned from him again abruptly and rudely. Miss Milner was confused, and Miss Woodley in torture at the palpable affront; to which Dorriforth alone appeared indifferent.

'Go on,' said Miss Milner to the footman, 'desire the coachman to drive on.'

'No,' cried Lord Frederick, 'not till you have told me when I shall see you again.'

'I will write you word, my lord,' replied she, something alarmed; 'You shall have a letter immediately after I get home.'

As if he guessed what its contents were to be, he cried out with warmth, 'Take care then, madam, how you treat me in that letter—and you, Mr. Dorriforth,' turning to him, 'do you take care what it contains, for if it is dictated by you, to you I shall send the answer.'

Dorriforth, without making his lordship a reply, or casting a look at him, put his head out of the window on the opposite side, and called, in a very angry tone to the coachman, 'How dare you not drive on, when your lady orders you?'

The sound of Dorriforth's voice in anger was to the servants so unusual, it acted like a stroke of electricity on the man, and he drove on at the instant so swiftly, that Lord Frederick was in a moment left many yards behind. As soon, however, as he recovered from the surprise into which this sudden command had thrown him, he rode with speed after the carriage, and followed it till they all arrived at the door of Miss Milner's house; there his lordship, giving himself up to the rage of love, or to rage against Dorriforth for the contempt with which he had treated him, leapt from his horse as Miss Milner stept from her carriage, and seizing her hand, entreated her 'Not to desert him, in compliance to the monastic precepts of hypocrisy.'

Dorriforth heard this, standing silently by, with a manly scorn painted on his countenance.

Miss Milner struggled to loose her hand, saying, 'Excuse me from replying to you now, my lord.'

In return to which his lordship brought her hand to his lips, and began to devour it with kisses, when Dorriforth with an instantaneous impulse, rushed forward, and struck him a blow in the face.—Under the force with which this assault was given, and the astonishment it excited, his lordship staggered, and letting fall the hand of Miss Milner, her guardian immediately laid hold of it, and led her into the house.

She was terrified beyond description; and it was with difficulty Mr. Dorriforth could get her to her own chamber, without taking her in his arms.—When, with the assistance of her woman, he had placed her upon a sopha—all shame and confusion for what he had done, he dropped upon his knees before her, and earnestly 'entreated her forgiveness for the indelicacy he had been guilty of in her presence.'—And that he had alarmed her, and lost sight of the respect which he thought sacredly her due, seemed to be the only circumstance that dwelt upon his thoughts.

She felt the indecorum of the posture he had condescended to take, and was shocked—to see her guardian at her feet, struck her with the same impropriety as if she had beheld a parent there; and all agitation and emotion, she implored him to rise, and with a thousand protestations declared, 'she thought the rashness of the act, was the highest proof of his regard for her.'

Miss Woodley now entered; for her care being ever employed upon the unfortunate, Lord Frederick on this occasion, had been the object of it; and she had waited by his side, and with every good purpose, preached patience to him, while he was smarting under the pain and shame of his chastisement.—At first, his fury threatened to retort upon the servants around him, and who refused his entrance into the house, the punishment he had received—But in the certainty of an honourable amends which must hereafter be made, he overcame the many temptations which the moment offered, and remounting his horse, rode from the place.

No sooner had Miss Woodley entered the room, and Dorriforth had resigned to her the care of his ward, than he flew to the spot where he had left his lordship, negligent what might have been the event had he still remained there.—After enquiring, and being told he was gone, Dorriforth returned to his own apartment; and with a bosom torn by more excruciating sensations far, than those he had given to his adversary.

The remorse that first struck him as he shut the door upon himself was—I have departed from my character—from the sacred character, and dignity of my profession and sentiments—I have departed from myself.——I am no longer the philosopher, but the ruffian—I have treated with an unpardonable insult a young nobleman, whose only crime was love, and a fond desire to insinuate himself into the favour of his mistress.

—I must atone for this outrage in whatever manner he may choose, and the law of justice and equity (though in this one instance, contrary to the law of religion) enjoins, that if he demands my life, in satisfaction for his wounded honour, it is his due. 'Alas,' cried he, 'that I could have laid it down this morning, unsullied with the cause, for which it will make but poor atonement.'

He next reflected—I have offended, and filled with horror a beautiful young lady, whom it was my duty to have protected from the brutal manners, to which I myself have exposed her.

Again—I have drawn upon me the just reproaches of my faithful preceptor and friend; the man in whose judgment it was my delight to be approved—above all, I have drawn upon myself, the stings of my own conscience.

'Where shall I pass this sleepless night?' cried he, walking repeatedly across his chamber; 'Can I go to the ladies? I am a brute, unworthy such society.—Shall I go and repose my disturbed mind on Sandford? I am ashamed to tell him the cause of my uneasiness.—Shall I go to Lord Frederick, and humbling myself before him, beg his forgiveness? He would spurn me for a coward.—No'——(and he lifted up his eyes to Heaven) 'Thou all great, all wise, and all omnipotent being, whom I have above any other offended, to thee alone I apply in this hour of tribulation, and from thee alone I expect comfort.—And the confidence with which I now address myself to thee, encouraged by that long intercourse religion has effected, in this one moment pays me amply, for the many years of my past life wholly devoted to thy service.'

CHAPTER XIV

ALTHOUGH Miss Milner had foreseen no fatal event from
the indignity offered Lord Frederick, yet she passed a night
very different from those to which she had been accustomed.
No sooner was she falling into a sleep, than a thousand vague,
but distressing ideas darted across her imagination.—Her
heart would at times whisper to her as she was half asleep,
'Lord Frederick is banished from you for ever.'—She shakes
off the uneasiness this idea brings along with it—she then
starts, and beholds the blow still aimed at him by Dorriforth.
—And no sooner has she driven away this painful image, than
she is again awakened by seeing her guardian at her feet suing
for pardon.—She sighs, she trembles, she is chilled with
terror.

Relieved by a flood of tears; towards the morning she sinks
into a refreshing slumber, but waking, finds the self-same
images crowding all together upon her mind—she is doubtful
to which to give the preference—one, however, rushes the
foremost, and will continue so—she knows not the consequence of ruminating, nor why she dwells upon that, more
than upon all the rest, and yet it will give place to none.

She rises in a languid and disordered state, and at breakfast adds fresh pain to Dorriforth by her altered appearance.

He had scarce left the breakfast room when an officer
waited upon him charged with a challenge from Lord
Frederick. To the message delivered to him by this gentleman, Dorriforth replied,

'As a clergyman, more especially in the church of Rome,
I know not whether I am not exempt from answering a claim
of this kind; but not having had forbearance to avoid an

offence, I have no right to a privilege that would only indemnify me from making reparation.'

'You will then meet his lordship, sir, at the appointed time?' said the officer.

'I will,' answered Dorriforth, 'and my immediate care shall be to procure a gentleman to accompany me.'

The officer withdrew, and as soon as Dorriforth was once more alone, he was going once more to reflect, but he durst not—since yesterday, reflection, for the first time of his life, was become painful to him; and even as he rode the short way to Lord Elmwood's immediately after, he found his own thoughts so insufferable, he was obliged to enter into conversation with his servant. Solitude, that he was formerly so charmed withal, at those moments had been worse than death.

At Lord Elmwood's, he met Sandford in the hall, and the sight of him was no longer welcome, but displeasing—he knew how different the principles he had just adopted were to those of that reverend friend's, and without his complaining, or even suspecting what had happened, his presence was a sufficient reproach.—Dorriforth passed him as hastily as he could, and enquiring for Lord Elmwood, disclosed to him his errand, which was to ask him to be his second; his lordship started, and wished to consult his tutor, but that his kinsman strictly forbad; and having urged his reasons with arguments, such as his lordship could not refute; he at length prevailed upon him to promise he would accompany him to the field, which was at a few miles distance only, and the parties were to be there at seven on the same evening.

As soon as his business with Lord Elmwood was settled, Dorriforth returned home, to make some necessary preparations for the event which might ensue from this meeting—he wrote letters to several of his friends; and one to his ward, over which he shed tears.

Sandford going into Lord Elmwood's library soon after Dorriforth had left it, expressed his surprise at finding him gone; upon which that young nobleman, after answering a few questions, and giving a few significant tokens, that he was entrusted with a secret, frankly confessed, what he had promised to conceal.

Sandford, as much as a holy man could be, was enraged at Dorriforth for the cause of this challenge, but was still more enraged at him for his wickedness in accepting it—he applauded his pupil's virtue in making the discovery, and congratulated himself that he should be the instrument, of saving not only the blood of his friend, but of preventing the scandal of his being engaged in a duel.

In the ardour of his designs he went immediately to Miss Milner's—entered the house he had so long refused to enter, and at a time when he was on aggravated bad terms with its owner.

He asked for Dorriforth, went hastily into his apartment, and poured upon him a torrent of rebukes.—Dorriforth bore all he said with the patience of a devotee, but with the firmness of a man.—He owned his fault, but no eloquence could make him recall the promise he had given to repair the injury. —Unshaken by the arguments, persuasions, and menaces of Sandford, he gave a fresh proof of that inflexibility for which he has been described—and after two hours dispute they parted, neither of them the better for what either had advanced, but Dorriforth something the worse; his conscience gave testimony to Sandford's opinion, 'that he was bound by ties more sacred than worldly honour,' but while he owned, he would not yield to the duty.

Sandford left him, determined, however, that Lord Elmwood should not be accessary in his guilt, and this he declared, on which Dorriforth took the resolution of seeking another second.

In passing through the house on his return home, Sandford met, by accident, Mrs. Horton, Miss Milner, and the other two ladies returning from a saunter in the garden.—Surprised at the sight of Mr. Sandford in her house, Miss Milner would not express that surprise, but going up to him with all the friendly benevolence which generally played about her heart, she took hold of one of his hands, and pressed it with a kindness which told him he was welcome more forcibly, than if she had made the most elaborate speech to convince him of it.— He, however, seemed little touched with her behaviour, and as an excuse for breaking his word, cried,

'I beg your pardon, madam, but I was brought hither in my anxiety to prevent murder.'

'Murder!' exclaimed all the ladies.

'Yes,' answered he, addressing himself to Miss Fenton, 'your betrothed husband is a party concerned; he is going to be second to Mr. Dorriforth, who means this very evening to be killed by my lord Frederick, or to kill him, in addition to the blow he gave him last night.'

Mrs. Horton exclaimed, 'If Mr. Dorriforth dies, he dies a martyr.'

Miss Woodley cried with fervour, 'Heaven forbid!'

Miss Fenton cried, 'Dear me!'

While Miss Milner, without uttering one word, sunk speechless on the floor.

They lifted her up and brought her to the door which entered the garden. She soon recovered; for the tumult of her mind would not suffer her to remain inactive, and she was rouzed, in spite of her weakness, to endeavour to ward off the present disaster.—In vain, however, she tried to walk to Dorriforth's apartment—in the trial she sunk as before, and was taken to a settee, while Miss Woodley was dispatched to bring her guardian to her.

Informed of the cause of her swoonings, he followed Miss Woodley with a tender anxiety for her health, and with grief and confusion that he had so carelessly endangered it.—On his entering the room Sandford beheld the inquietude of his mind, and cried, 'Here is your *guardian*,' with a cruel emphasis on the word.

He was too much engaged by the indisposition of his ward to reply to Sandford.—He placed himself on the settee by her, and with the utmost tenderness, reverence, and pity, entreated her not to be concerned at an accident in which he, and he only, had been to blame; but which he had still no doubt would be accommodated in the most amicable manner.

'I have one favour to require of you, Mr. Dorriforth,' said she, 'and that is your promise, your solemn promise, which I know is sacred, that you will not fight with my lord Frederick.'

He hesitated.

'Oh, madam,' cried Sandford, 'he is grown a libertine now, and I would not believe his word were he to give it you.'·

'Then, sir,' returned Dorriforth angrily, 'you *may* believe my word, for I will keep that, I have passed to you.—I will give Lord Frederick all the restitution in my power.—But my dear Miss Milner, let not this alarm you; we may not find it convenient to meet this many a day; and most probably some fortunate explanation may yet take place and prevent our meeting at all. If not, reckon but among the many duels that are fought, how few are fatal; and even in that case, how small would be the loss to society'—He was proceeding.

'I should ever deplore the loss,' cried Miss Milner, 'I could not survive the death of either, in such a case.'

'For my part,' returned Dorriforth, 'I look upon my life as much forfeited to his lordship, to whom I have given a high offence, as it might in other instances have been forfeited to the offended laws of the land. Honour, is the law of the polite part of the land; we know it; and when we transgress against it knowingly, we justly incur our punishment.—However, Miss Milner, this business is not to be settled immediately, and I have no doubt but all will be as you could wish.—Do you think I should appear thus easy,' added he with a smile, 'if I were going to be shot at by my lord Frederick?'

'Very well!' cried Sandford, with a look that demonstrated he knew better.

'You will stay within then, all this day?' said Miss Milner.

'I am engaged out to dinner,' he replied, 'it is unlucky—I am sorry for it—but I'll be at home early in the evening.'

'Stained with human blood,' cried Sandford, 'or yourself a corpse.'

The ladies all lifted up their hands, and Miss Milner rose from her seat and threw herself at her guardian's feet.

'You knelt to me last night, I now kneel to you,' (she cried) 'kneel, never desiring to rise more, if you persist in your intention.—I am weak, I am volatile, I am indiscreet, but I have a heart from whence some impressions can never be erased.'

He endeavoured to raise her, she persisted to kneel—and here the trouble, the affright, the terror she endured, discovered to her for the first time her own sentiments—which, till that moment, she had doubted—and she continued,

'I no longer pretend to conceal my passion—I love Lord Frederick Lawnly.'

Her guardian started.

'Yes, to my shame I love him:' (cried she, all emotion) 'I meant to have struggled with the weakness, because I supposed it would be displeasing to you—but apprehension for his safety takes away every power of restraint, and I beseech you to spare his life.'

'This is exactly what I thought,' cried Sandford, triumphantly.

'Good heaven!' cried Miss Woodley.

'But it is very natural,' said Mrs. Horton.

'I own,' said Dorriforth, (struck with amaze, and now taking her from his feet with a force she could not resist) 'I own, Miss Milner, I am greatly affected at this contradiction in your character'——

'But did not I say so?' cried Sandford, interrupting him.

'However,' continued he, 'you may take my word, though you have deceived me in your's, that Lord Frederick's life is secure.—For your sake, I would not endanger it for the universe.—But let this be a warning to you'——

He was proceeding with the most poignant language, and austere looks, when observing the shame, the terror, and the self-reproach which agitated her mind, he divested himself in great measure of his austerity, and said, mildly,

'Let this be a warning to you, how you deal in future with the friends who wish you well—you have hurried me into a mistake that might have cost me my life, or the life of the man you love; and thus exposed *you* to misery, more bitter than death.'

'I am not worthy your friendship, Mr. Dorriforth,' said she, sobbing with grief, 'and from this moment forsake me.'

'No, madam, not in the moment you first discover to me, how I can make you happy.'

The conversation appearing now to become of that nature in which the rest of the company could have no share whatever; they all, except Mr. Sandford, were retiring; when Miss Milner called Miss Woodley back, saying, 'Stay you with me; I was never so unfit to be left without your friendship.'

'Perhaps for the present you can much easier dispense with mine?' said Dorriforth. She made no answer: he therefore having once more assured her Lord Frederick's life was safe, was quitting the room; when he recollected in what a state of humiliation he had left her, and turning towards her as he opened the door, added,

'And be assured, madam, my esteem for you, shall be the same as ever.'

Sandford, as he followed Dorriforth, bowed to Miss Milner too, and repeated the self-same words.—'And, madam, be assured my esteem for you, shall be *the same as ever*.'

CHAPTER XV

THIS taunting reproof from Sandford made little impression upon Miss Milner, whose thoughts were all fixed on a subject of much more importance than the opinion he entertained of her.—She threw her arms about Miss Woodley as soon as they were left alone, and asked, with anxiety, 'What she thought of her behaviour?' Miss Woodley, who could not approve of the duplicity her friend had betrayed, still wished to reconcile her as much as possible to her own conduct, and replied, she 'highly commended the frankness with which she had, at last, acknowledged her sentiments.'

'Frankness!' cried Miss Milner, starting. 'Frankness, my dear Miss Woodley!—what you have just now heard me say, is all a falsehood.'

'How, Miss Milner!'

'Oh, my dear Miss Woodley,' returned she, sobbing upon her bosom, 'pity the agonies of my heart, by nature sincere, when such are the fatal propensities it cherishes, I must submit to the grossest falsehoods rather than reveal the truth.'

'What do you mean?' cried Miss Woodley, with the strongest amazement painted on her face.

'Do you suppose I love Lord Frederick?' returned the

other. 'Do you suppose I *can* love him?—Oh fly, Miss Woodley, and prevent my guardian from telling him such an untruth.'

'What do you mean?' repeated Miss Woodley; 'I protest you frighten me:'—and this inconsistency in the behaviour of Miss Milner, really appeared as if her senses had been deranged.

'Only fly,' resumed she, 'and prevent the inevitable ill consequence which must ensue from Lord Frederick's being told this falsehood.—It will involve us all in greater disquietude than we suffer at present.'

'Then what has influenced you, my dear Miss Milner?'——

'That which impels my every action,' returned she; 'an unsurmountable instinct—a fatality, that will ever render me the most miserable of human beings; and yet you, even you, my dear Miss Woodley, will not pity me.'

Miss Woodley pressed her close in her arms, and vowed, 'That while she was unhappy, from whatever cause, she still would pity her.'

'Go to Mr. Dorriforth then, and prevent him from imposing upon Lord Frederick.'

'But that imposition is the only means to prevent the duel,' replied Miss Woodley. 'The moment I have told him you have no regard for his lordship, he will no longer refuse to fight with him.'

'Then at all events I am undone,' exclaimed Miss Milner, 'for the duel is horrible, even beyond every thing else.'

'How so?' returned Miss Woodley, 'since you have declared you do not care for Lord Frederick.'

'But are you so blind,' returned Miss Milner with a degree of madness in her looks, 'to believe I do not care for Mr. Dorriforth? Oh, Miss Woodley! I love him with all the passion of a mistress, and with all the tenderness of a wife.'

Miss Woodley at this sentence sat down—it was on a chair that was close to her—her feet could not have taken her to any other.—She trembled—she was white as ashes, and deprived of speech. Miss Milner, taking her by the hand, said,

'I know what you feel—I know what you think of me—and how much you hate and despise me.—But Heaven is witness to all my struggles—nor would I, even to myself, acknowledge the shameless prepossession, till forced by a sense of his danger'——

'Silence,' cried Miss Woodley, struck with horror.

'And even now,' resumed Miss Milner, 'have I not concealed it from all but you, by plunging myself into a new difficulty, from whence I know not how I shall be extricated? —And do I entertain a hope? No, Miss Woodley, nor ever will.—But suffer me to own my folly to you—to entreat your soothing friendship to free me from my weakness.—And, oh! give me your friendly advice to deliver me from the difficulties which surround me.'

Miss Woodley was still pale, and still silent.

Education, is called second nature; in the strict (but not enlarged) education of Miss Woodley, it was more powerful than the first—and the violation of oaths, persons, or things consecrated to Heaven, was, in her opinion, if not the most enormous, the most horrid among the catalogue of crimes.

Miss Milner had lived too long in a family who had imbibed those opinions not to be convinced of their existence; nay, her own reason told her that solemn vows of whatever kind, ought to be binding; and the more she respected her guardian's understanding, the less she called in question his religious tenets—in esteeming him, she esteemed all his notions; and among the rest, even venerated those of his religion.—Yet that passion, which had unhappily taken possession of her whole soul, would not have been inspired, had there not

subsisted an early difference, in their systems of divine faith—
had she been early taught what were the sacred functions of
a Roman ecclesiastic, though all her esteem, all her admiration, had been attracted by the qualities and accomplishments
of her guardian; yet education would have given such a prohibition to her love, that she had been precluded from it, as
by that barrier which divides a sister from a brother.

This, unfortunately, was not the case; and Miss Milner
loved Dorriforth without one conscious check to tell her she
was wrong, except that which convinced her, her love would
be avoided by him, with detestation, with horror.

Miss Woodley, something recovered from her first surprise, and suffering—for never did her susceptible mind suffer
so exquisitely—amidst all her grief and abhorrence felt that
pity was still predominant—and reconciled to the faults of
Miss Milner by her misery, she once more looked at her with
friendship, and asked, 'what she could do, to render her less
unhappy?'

'Make me forget,' replied Miss Milner, 'every moment of
my past life since I first saw you—that moment was teeming
with a weight of cares I must labour under till my death.'

'And even in death,' replied Miss Woodley, 'do not be so
presumptuous as to hope to shake them off—if unrepented in
this world'——

She was proceeding—but the anxiety her friend endured,
would not suffer her to be wholly free from the apprehension,
that notwithstanding the positive assurance of her guardian,
(should he and Lord Frederick meet) the duel might still take
place; she therefore rung the bell and enquired if Mr. Dorriforth was still at home?—the answer was—'He is rode out.'—
'You remember,' said Miss Woodley, 'he told you he should
dine out.'—This did not, however, dismiss her fears, and she
dispatched two servants different ways in pursuit of him,

acquainting them with her suspicions, and charging them to prevent his and Lord Frederick's meeting. Sandford had also taken his precautions; but though he knew the time, he did not know the exact place of their appointment, for that, Lord Elmwood had forgot to enquire.

The excessive alarm which Miss Milner discovered upon this occasion, was imputed by the servants, and others who were witness of it, to her affection for Lord Frederick, while none but Miss Woodley knew, or had the most distant suspicion of the real cause.

Mrs. Horton and Miss Fenton, who were sitting together expatiating on the duplicity of their own sex in the instance just before them, had, notwithstanding the interest of the discourse, a longing desire to break it off; for they were impatient to see this poor frail being whom they were loading with their innocent—as it was among friends—calumny. They longed to see if she would have the confidence to look them in the face: them, to whom she had so often protested, she had not the smallest attachment to Lord Frederick but from motives of vanity.

These ladies heard with much satisfaction dinner was served, but met Miss Milner at table with a less degree of pleasure than they expected; for her mind was so totally abstracted from them, they could not discern a single blush, or confused glance, which their presence occasioned. No, Miss Milner had before them divulged nothing of which she was ashamed, she only was ashamed what she had said was not truth. In the bosom of Miss Woodley alone, was that secret entrusted which could call a blush into her face, and before her she *did* feel confusion—before the gentle friend, to whom she had till this time communicated all her faults without embarrassment, she now cast down her eyes in shame, and scarce durst lift them up to meet her's.

At table there was little talking, and less eating; Miss
Milner did not attempt to eat; Miss Woodley endeavoured,
but could not.

Soon after the dinner was removed, Lord Elmwood entered;
and that gallant nobleman declared—'Mr. Sandford had used
him ill in not permitting him to accompany his relation; for he
feared Dorriforth would now throw himself upon the sword
of Lord Frederick without a friend by to defend him.'—A
rebuke from the eye of Miss Woodley, which from this day
forward had a command over Miss Milner, restrained her
from expressing the affright she suffered from this supposition of his lordship's. Miss Fenton replied, 'As to that, my
lord, I see no reason why Mr. Dorriforth and Lord Frederick
should not now be friends.'—'Certainly,' said Mrs. Horton,
'for as soon as my lord Frederick is made acquainted with
Miss Milner's confession, all differences must be reconciled.'
—'What confession?' asked his lordship.

Miss Milner, to avoid hearing a repetition of that which
gave her pain but to think of, arose in order to retire into her
own apartment, but was obliged to sit down again—and
received the assistance of her friend and Lord Elmwood to
lead her into her dressing-room. Reclined upon a sopha there,
a silence ensured between her and Miss Woodley for near half
an hour; and when the conversation began, the name of Dorriforth was never uttered—they were both grown cool and
considerate since the discovery, and both were equally
ashamed and fearful of naming him.

The vanity of the world, the folly of riches, the pleasures of
retirement, and such topics engaged their discourse, but not
their thoughts, for near two hours; and the first time the word
Dorriforth was spoken, a servant with alacrity opened the
dressing room door, without previously rapping, and cried,
'Mr. Dorriforth, madam.'

Dorriforth immediately came in, and went eagerly to Miss Milner.—Miss Woodley beheld the glow of joy, and guilt upon her face, and did not rise to give him her seat, as was her custom if he came with intelligence to his ward, and she was sitting next her—he therefore stood while he repeated all that had happened in his interview with Lord Frederick.

But with her gladness to see her guardian safe, Miss Milner had forgot to enquire for the safety of his lordship; the man whom she had pretended to love so passionately—even a smile of rapture was upon her face, though Dorriforth might be returned from putting him to death. This incongruity of behaviour Miss Woodley saw, and was confounded—but Dorriforth, in whose thoughts a suspicion either of her love to him, or want of love for Lord Frederick, had not the smallest place, easily reconciled this inconsistency, and said,

'You see by my countenance all is well, and therefore you smile on me before I tell you what has passed.'

This brought her to the recollection of her conduct, and now with a countenance constrained to some show of gravity, she tried to express alarm she did not feel.

'Nay, I have the pleasure to assure you Lord Frederick is safe,' resumed Dorriforth, 'and the disgrace of his blow washed entirely away, by a few drops of blood from this arm,' and he laid his hand upon his left arm, which rested in his waistcoat as a sling.

She cast her eyes there, and seeing where the ball had entered the coat sleeve, she gave an involuntary scream, and sunk on the side of the sopha. Instead of that tender sympathy with which Miss Woodley used to attend her upon the slightest illness or affliction, she now addressed her in a sharp tone, and cried, 'Miss Milner, you have heard Lord Frederick is safe, you have then nothing to alarm you.'—Nor did she run to offer a smelling bottle, or to raise her head. Her guardian seeing her near fainting, and without this assistance from her friend, was going himself to give it; but on this, Miss Woodley interfered, and having taken her head upon her arm, assured him, 'It was a trifling weakness to which Miss Milner was accustomed, and that she would ring for her woman, who knew how to relieve her instantly with a few drops.'—Satisfied with this, Dorriforth left the room; and a surgeon being arrived to dress his wound, he retired into his own chamber.

CHAPTER XVI

THE power delegated to the keeper of our secrets, Miss Woodley was the last person on earth to abuse—but she was also the last, who, by her complacency would participate in the guilt of her friend—and there was no guilt, except that of murder, which she thought equal to the crime in question, provided it was ever perpetrated.—Adultery, her reason would perhaps have informed her, was a more pernicious evil to society; but to a religious mind, what sounds so horrible as sacrilege? Of vows made to God or to man, the former must weigh the heavier.—Moreover, the dreadful sin of infidelity in the marriage state, is much softened to a common understanding, by the frequency of the crime; whereas, of vows broken by a devotee she had scarce heard of any; or if any, they were generally followed by such examples of divine vengeance, such miraculous punishments in this world, (as well as eternal punishment in the other) that served to exaggerate their wickedness.

She, who could, and did pardon Miss Milner, was the person who saw her passion in the severest light, and resolved to take every method, however harsh, to root it from her heart

—nor did she fear success, resting on the certain assurance, that however deep her love was fixed, it would never be returned. Yet this confidence did not prevent her taking every precaution, lest Dorriforth should come to the knowledge of it—she would not have his composed mind disturbed with such a thought—his steadfast principles so much as shook by the imagination—nor overwhelm him with those self-reproaches which his fatal attraction, unpremeditated as it was, would still have drawn upon him.

With this plan of concealment, in which the natural modesty of Miss Milner acquiesced, there was but one effort to make which that young lady was not prepared for; and that was an entire separation from her guardian.—She had, from the first, cherished her passion without the most distant prospect of a return—she was prepared to see Dorriforth without ever seeing him nearer to her than her guardian and friend, but not to see him at all—for that, she was not prepared.

But Miss Woodley reflected upon the inevitable necessity of this step before she made the proposal, and then made it with a firmness, that might have done honour to the inflexibility of Dorriforth himself.

During the few days that intervened between her open confession of love for Lord Frederick, and this proposal, the most intricate incoherence appeared to the whole family, in the character of Miss Milner—and in order to evade a marriage with his lordship, and to conceal, at the same time, the shameful propensity which lurked in her breast, she was once, even on the point of declaring a passion for Sir Edward Ashton.

In the duel which had taken place between Lord Frederick and Dorriforth, the latter had received his antagonist's fire, but positively refused to return it; by which he had kept his promise not to endanger his lordship's life, and had reconciled Sandford, in great measure, to his behaviour—and Sandford now (his resolution once broken) no longer refused entering Miss Milner's house, but came every time it was convenient, though he yet avoided its mistress as much as possible; or shewed by every word and look, when she was present, that she was still less in his favour than she had ever been.

He visited Dorriforth on the evening after his engagement with Lord Frederick, and again the next morning breakfasted with him in his own chamber; nor did Miss Milner see her guardian since his first return from that engagement till the following noon. She enquired, however, of the servant how his master did, and was rejoiced to hear his wound was but very slight—yet this enquiry she durst not make before Miss Woodley, but waited till she was absent.

When Dorriforth made his appearance the next day, it was evident he had thrown from his heart a load of cares; and though they had left a languor upon his face, there was content in his voice, his manners, in his every word and action.— Far from seeming to retain any resentment towards his ward, for the trouble and danger into which her imprudence had led him, he appeared rather to pity her weakness, and to wish to sooth the perturbation which the recollection of her own conduct had obviously raised in her mind—His endeavours were most successful—she was soothed every time he spoke to her; and had not the watchful eye of Miss Woodley stood guard over her inclinations, she had plainly evinced, she was enraptured with the joy of seeing him again himself, after the danger to which he had been exposed.

These emotions, which she laboured to subdue, passed, however, the bounds of her ineffectual resistance; when at the time of retiring after dinner, he said to her in a low voice, but such as it was meant the company should hear, 'Do me the favour, Miss Milner, to call at my study sometime in the evening; I have to speak to you upon business.'

She answered, 'I will, sir.' And her eyes swam with delight in expectation of the interview.

Let not the reader, nevertheless imagine, there was in that ardent expectation, one idea which the most spotless mind, in love, might not have indulged without reproach.—Sincere love, (at least among the delicate of the female sex) is often gratified by that degree of enjoyment, or rather forbearance, which would be torture in the pursuit of any other passion—real, delicate, and restrained love, like that of Miss Milner's, was indulged in the sight of the object only; and having bounded her wishes by her hopes, the height of her happiness was limited to a conversation in which no other but themselves partook a part.

Miss Woodley was one who heard the appointment, but the only one who conceived with what sensation it was received.

While the ladies remained in the same room with Dorriforth, Miss Milner thought of little, except of him—as soon as they withdrew into another apartment, she remembered Miss Woodley, and turning her head suddenly, saw Miss Woodley's face imprinted with suspicion and displeasure—this at first was painful to her—but recollecting that in a couple of hours time she was to meet her guardian alone—speak to him, and hear him speak to herself only—every other thought was absorbed in that one, and she considered with indifference, the uneasiness, or the anger of her friend.

Miss Milner, to do justice to her heart, did not wish to beguile Dorriforth into the snares of love.—Could any supernatural power have endowed her with the means, and at the same time shewn to her the ills that must arise from such an effect of her charms, she had assuredly enough of virtue to have declined the conquest; but without enquiring of herself what she proposed? she never saw him without previously endeavouring to look more attractive than she would have desired, in any other company.—And now, without listening to the thousand exhortations that were speaking in every feature of Miss Woodley's face, she flew to a looking-glass, to adjust her dress in a manner that she thought most enchanting.

Time stole away, and the time to go to her guardian arrived. In his presence, unsupported by the presence of a third person, every grace she had practised, every look she had borrowed to set off her charms were annihilated, and she became a native beauty, with the artless arguments of reason, only for her aid.—Awed thus, by his power, from every thing but what she really was, she never was perhaps half so bewitching as in those timid, respectful, and embarrassed moments she passed alone with him.—He caught at those times her respect, her diffidence, nay, even her embarrassment; and never would one word of anger pass on either side.

On the present occasion, he first, expressed the highest satisfaction that she had at length, revealed to him the state of her mind.

'And taking every thing into consideration, Miss Milner,' added he, 'I rejoice that your sentiments happen to be such as you have owned—for although my lord Frederick is not the very man I could have wished for your perfect happiness, yet in the state of human perfection and human happiness, you might have fixed your affections with much less propriety; and yet, where my unwillingness to thwart your inclinations, might not have permitted me to contend with them.'

Not a word of reply did this demand, or if it had, not a word could she have given.

'And now, madam, the reason of my desire to speak with you—is to know from yourself, the means you think most proper to pursue, in order to acquaint his lordship, that notwithstanding this late repulse, there are hopes of your partiality in his favour.'

'Defer the explanation,' returned she, eagerly.

'I beg your pardon, Miss Milner, that cannot be—besides, how can you indulge a disposition thus unpitying?—even so ardently did I desire to render his lordship happy, though he came armed against my life, that had I not reflected, previous to our engagement it would appear like fear, and the means of bartering for his forgiveness; I should have revealed your sentiments the moment I had seen him. When the engagement was over, I was too impatient to acquaint you of his safety, to think then on gratifying him.—And indeed, the delicacy of the declaration, after the many denials you have no doubt given him, should be considered—I therefore entreat your approbation of the manner in which it shall be made.'

'Mr. Dorriforth, can you allow nothing to the moments of surprise? and that pity, which the fate impending inspired; and which might urge me to express myself of Lord Frederick, in a manner my cooler thoughts will not warrant?'

'There was nothing in your expressions, my dear Miss Milner, the least equivocal—if you were off your guard, when you pleaded for Lord Frederick, as I believe you were, you said more sincerely what you thought; and no discreet, or rather indiscreet retractions, can make me change my opinion.'

'I am very sorry,' she replied, confused, and trembling.

'Why sorry? Come, give me commission to reveal these sentiments.—I'll not be too hard upon you—a hint from me to his lordship will do—hope, is ever apt to interpret the slightest words to its own use, and a lover's hope, is beyond all others, sanguine.'

'I never gave Lord Frederick hope.'

'But did you ever plunge him into despair?'

'His pursuit says I never have, but he has no other proof.'

'However light and frivolous you have been upon frivolous subjects, yet I must own, Miss Milner, I expected, that when a case of this importance came seriously before you, you would have discovered a proper stability in your behaviour.'

'I do, sir; and it was only while I was affected with a weakness, which arose from accident, that I have ever shewn an inconsistence.'

'You then still assert you have no affection for my lord Frederick?'

'Not sufficient to become his wife.'

'You are alarmed at marriage, and I do not wonder you should be so; it shews a prudent foresight that does you honour—but, my dear, are there no dangers in a single state? —if I may judge, Miss Milner, there are many more to a young lady of your accomplishments, than were you under the protection of a husband.'

'My father, Mr. Dorriforth, thought your protection sufficient.'

'But that protection was rather to direct your choice, than to be the cause of your not choosing at all.—Give me leave to point out an observation which, perhaps, I have too frequently done before, but upon this occasion I must intrude it once again.—Miss Fenton is its object—her fortune is inferior to your's, her personal attractions less.'——

Here the strong glow of joy, and of gratitude, for an opinion so negligently, and yet so sincerely expressed, flew to Miss Milner's face, neck, and even to her hands and fingers; the blood mounted to every part of her skin that was visible, for not a fibre but felt the secret transport, that Dorriforth thought her more beautiful than the beautiful Miss Fenton.

If he observed her blushes, he was unsuspicious of the cause, and went on.

'There is, besides, in the temper of Miss Fenton, a

sedateness that might with less hazard secure her safety in an unmarried life; and yet she very properly thinks it her duty, as she does not mean to seclude herself by any vows to the contrary, to become a wife—and in obedience to the counsel of her friends, will be married within a very few weeks.'

'Miss Fenton may marry from obedience, I never will.'

'You mean to say, Love shall alone induce you?'

'I do.'

'If, madam, you would point out a subject upon which I am the least able to speak, and on which my sentiments, such as they are, are formed alone from theory (and even there instructed but with caution) it is the subject of love.—And yet, Miss Milner, even that little I know, tells me, without a doubt, that what you said to me yesterday, pleading for Lord Frederick's life, was the result of the most violent and tender love.'

'The *little you know* then, Mr. Dorriforth, has deceived you; had you *known more*, you would have judged otherwise.'

'I submit to the merit of your reply; but without allowing me a judge at all, I will appeal to those who were present with me.'

'Are Mrs. Horton and Mr. Sandford to be the connoisseurs?'

'No; I'll appeal to Miss Fenton and Miss Woodley.'

'And yet, I believe,' replied she with a smile, 'I believe, theory, must only be the judge even there.'

'Then from all you have said, madam, on this occasion, I am to conclude you still refuse to marry Lord Frederick?'

'You are.'

'And you submit never to see him again?'

'I do.'

'All you then said to me, yesterday, was false?'

'I was not mistress of myself at the time.'

'Therefore it was truth—for shame, for shame!'

At that moment the door opened, and Mr. Sandford walked

in—he started back on seeing Miss Milner, and was going away again; but Dorriforth called to him to stay, and said with warmth,

'Tell me, Mr. Sandford, by what power, by what persuasion, I can prevail upon this lady to confide in me as her friend; to lay her heart open, and credit mine when I declare to her, I have no view in all the advice I give, but her immediate welfare?'

'Mr. Dorriforth, you know my opinion of the lady,' replied Sandford, 'it has been formed ever since my first acquaintance with her, and it still remains the same.'

'But instruct me how I am to inspire her with confidence;' returned Dorriforth, 'how I am to impress her with that which is for her advantage?'

'You can work no miracles,' replied Sandford, 'you are not holy enough.'

'And yet Miss Milner,' answered Dorriforth, 'appears to be acquainted with that mystery; for what but the force of a miracle, can induce her to contradict to-day, what before you, and several other witnesses, she positively acknowledged yesterday?'

'Do you call that miraculous?' cried Sandford, 'the miracle had been if she had not done so—for did she not yesterday, contradict what she acknowledged the day before?—and will she not to-morrow, disavow what she says to-day?'

'I wish she may,' replied Dorriforth mildly, for he beheld the tears flowing down her face at the rough and severe manner in which Sandford had spoken, and began to feel for her uneasiness.

'I beg pardon,' cried Sandford, 'for speaking so rudely to the mistress of the house—I have no business here, I know; but where you are, Mr. Dorriforth, unless I am turned out, I shall ever think it my duty to come.'

Miss Milner courtesied, as much as to say he was welcome to come.—He continued,

'I was to blame, that on a nice punctilio, I left you so long without my visits, and without my counsel; in the time, you have run the hazard of being murdered, and what is worse, of being excommunicated;[1] for had you been so rash as to have returned your opponent's fire, not all my interest at Rome would have obtained remission of the punishment.'

Miss Milner, through all her tears, could not now restrain her laughter—on which he resumed;

'And here do I venture like a missionary among savages—but if I can only save you from the scalping knives of some of them; from the miseries which that lady is preparing for you, I am rewarded.'

Sandford spoke this with great fervour, and the crime of her love never appeared to Miss Milner in so tremendous a point of view as thus, unknowingly alluded to by him.

'*The miseries that lady is preparing for you,*' hung upon her ears like the notes of a raven, and equally ominous.—The words '*murder*' and '*excommunication*' he had likewise uttered; all the fatal effects of sacrilegious love.—Frightful superstitions[2] struck to her heart, and she could scarcely prevent falling down under their oppression.

Dorriforth beheld the difficulty she had in sustaining herself, and went with the utmost tenderness and supported her; saying, 'I beg your pardon—I invited you hither with a far different view than your uneasiness.'—

Sandford was beginning to speak. 'Hold, Mr. Sandford,' resumed he, 'the lady is under my protection, and I know not whether it is not necessary you should apologize to her, and to me, for what you have already said.'

'You asked my opinion, or I had not given it you—would you have me, like her, speak what I do not think?'

'Say no more, Mr. Sandford,' cried Dorriforth—and leading her kindly to the door, as if to defend her from his malice, told her 'He would take another opportunity to renew the subject.'

CHAPTER XVII

WHEN Dorriforth was alone with Sandford, he explained to him what before, he had only hinted; and this learned jesuit frankly confessed, 'That the mind of a woman was far above, or rather beneath, his comprehension.'—It was so, indeed—for with all his penetration, and he had a great deal, he had not yet penetrated into the recesses of Miss Milner's heart.

Miss Woodley, to whom she repeated all that had passed between herself, her guardian, and Sandford, took this moment, during the alarm and agitation of her spirits, to alarm them still more by her prophetic insinuations; and at length represented to her here, for the first time, the necessity, 'That Mr. Dorriforth and she should remain no longer under the same roof.' This was like the stroke of sudden death to Miss Milner, and clinging to life, she endeavoured to avert the blow by prayers, and by promises—her friend loved her too sincerely, however, to be prevailed upon.

'But in what manner can I bring about the separation?' cried she, 'for till I marry we are obliged, by my father's request, to live in the same house.'

'Miss Milner,' answered Miss Woodley, 'much as I respect the will of a dying man, I regard your and Mr. Dorriforth's present, and eternal happiness much more; and it is my resolution you *shall part*—if you will not contrive the means, that duty falls on me, and without any invention, I see the measure at once.'

'What is it?' cried Miss Milner eagerly.

'To go and reveal to Mr. Dorriforth, without hesitation, the real state of your heart; which your present inconsistent conduct will but too readily confirm.'

'You would not plunge me into so much shame, into so much anguish!' cried she, distractedly.

'No,' replied Miss Woodley, 'not for the world, provided you will separate from him, by any method of your own—but that you *shall* separate is my determination; and in spite of all your sufferings, this shall be the means, unless you instantly agree to some other.'

'Good Heaven, Miss Woodley! is this your friendship?'

'Yes—and the truest friendship I have to bestow.—Think what a task I undertake for your sake and his, when I condemn myself to explain to him your weakness—what astonishment! what confusion! what remorse, do I foresee painted upon his face!—I hear him call you by the harshest names, and behold him fly from your sight for ever, as an object of his detestation.'

'Oh spare the dreadful picture.—Fly from my sight for ever—detest my name. Oh! my dear Miss Woodley, let his friendship for me but still remain, and I will consent to any thing.—You may command me—I will go away from him directly—but let us part in friendship—Oh! without the friendship of Mr. Dorriforth, life would be a heavy burthen indeed.'

Miss Woodley immediately began to plan schemes for their separation; and with all her invention alive on the subject, this was the only probable one she could form.

Miss Milner was to write to her distant relation at Bath, complaining of the melancholy of a country life, which she was to say her guardian imposed upon her, and entreat the lady to send a pressing invitation for her to pass a month or two with her; this invitation was to be shewn to Dorriforth for his approbation, and both Miss Woodley and Miss Milner were to enforce it, by expressing their earnest wishes for his consent. This plan properly regulated, the necessary letter was sent by Miss Milner to Bath, and Miss Woodley waited with patience, but with a watchful guard upon the conduct of her friend till the answer arrived.

During this interim a most tender and complaining epistle from Lord Frederick was delivered Miss Milner; to which as he received no answer, his lordship prevailed upon his uncle, with whom he resided, to wait upon her, and obtain her verbal reply; for he still flattered himself, fear of her guardian's anger, or perhaps his interception of the letter he had sent, was the cause of her seeming contempt.

The old gentleman was introduced to Miss Milner, and after to Mr. Dorriforth, but received from each an answer so explicit, that left his nephew no longer in doubt but all farther pursuit was vain.

Sir Edward Ashton about this time also, submitted to a formal dismission, and had the mortification to reflect, he was bestowing upon the object of his affections the tenderest proof of his regard, by absenting himself wholly from her society.

Upon this serious and certain conclusion to the hopes of Lord Frederick, Dorriforth was more astonished than he had ever yet been at the conduct of his ward—he had once thought her behaviour, in respect to his lordship, was ambiguous, but since her confession of a passion for him, he had no doubt but that in the end, she would become his wife.— He lamented to find himself mistaken, and now thought it proper to give some important marks of his condemnation of her pernicious caprice; and not merely in words, but by the general tenour of his behaviour. He consequently became much more reserved, and more austere than he had been, since his first acquaintance with her; for his manners, not from design, but unknowingly, were softened since his guardianship, by that tender respect he had never ceased to pay to the object of his protection.

Notwithstanding this severity he assumed, his ward in the prospect of parting from him grew melancholy; Miss Woodley's love to her friend rendered her little otherwise; and Dorriforth's peculiar gravity, oftentimes rigour, could not but make the whole party much less cheerful than they had been. Lord Elmwood too was lying dangerously ill of a fever; Miss Fenton of course was as much in sorrow as her nature would suffer her to be, and both Sandford and Dorriforth in extreme concern on his lordship's account.

In this state of affairs, the letter of invitation arrives from Lady Luneham at Bath: it was shewn to Dorriforth; and to prove to his ward he is so much offended, as no longer to feel that excessive interest in her concerns he once did, he gives his opinion on the subject with indifference—he desires 'Miss Milner will do as she herself thinks proper.'—Miss Woodley instantly accepts this permission, writes back, and appoints the day, her friend means to set off for the visit.

She is wounded to the heart by the cold and unkind manners of her guardian, but dares not take one method to retrieve his opinion.—Alone, and to Miss Woodley she sighs and weeps; he discovers her sorrow, and is doubtful whether the departure of Lord Frederick from that part of the country, is not the cause.

When the day on which she was to set off for Bath, was within two days distance only; the behaviour of Dorriforth took, by degrees, its usual form; if not a greater share of polite and tender attention than ever.—It was the first time he had parted from Miss Milner since he became her guardian, and he felt upon the occasion, a reluctance.—He had been angry with her, he had shewn her he was so, and he now began to wish he had not.—She is not happy, (he considered within himself) every word and action declares she is not, and I may have been too severe, and added to her uneasiness.—'At least we will part on good terms,'—said he—'Indeed my regard for her is such, I cannot part otherwise.'

She soon discerned his returning kindness, and it was a gentle tie that would have fastened her to the spot where she was, but for the firm resistance of Miss Woodley.

'What will a few months absence effect?' cried she, pleading her cause; 'At the end of a few months at farthest, he will expect me back, and where will be the merit in this short separation?'

'In that time,' replied Miss Woodley, 'we may find some method to make it still longer.'—To this she listened with a kind of despair, but uttered she 'was resigned;' and accordingly prepared for her departure.

Dorriforth was all anxiety that every circumstance of her journey should be commodious; he was eager she should be happy, and he was eager she should see he entirely forgave her.—He would have gone part of the way with her, but for the extreme illness of Lord Elmwood, in whose chamber he passed chief of the day, and slept in Elmwood House every night.

On the morning of her journey, when Dorriforth gave his hand and conducted Miss Milner to the carriage, all the way he led her she could not restrain a flood of tears; which encreased, as he parted from her, to convulsive sobs.—He was affected; and notwithstanding he had previously bid her farewell, he drew her gently on one side and said, with his eyes moistened from regard of the most laudable nature,

'My dear Miss Milner, we part friends?—I hope we do?—on my side, depend upon it, I regret nothing so much at this short separation, as having ever given you a moment's pain.'

'I believe so,' was all she could say, for she hastened to break from him, lest his discerning eye should discover the cause of the weakness which thus overcame her.—But her apprehensions were groundless; the rectitude of his own heart was a bar to the suspicion of her's.—He once more kindly bade her adieu, and the carriage drove away.

Miss Fenton and Miss Woodley accompanied Miss Milner part of the journey, about thirty miles, where they were met by Sir Harry and Lady Luneham.—Here was a parting nearly as affecting as that between her and her guardian: Miss Woodley, who for several weeks had treated her friend with a rigidness she herself hardly supposed was in her nature, now bewailed her own severity, begged her forgiveness, promised to correspond with her punctually, and to omit no opportunity of giving her every consolation short of cherishing her fatal passion; but in that, and that only, was the heart of Miss Milner to be consoled.

VOLUME II

CHAPTER I

WHEN Miss Milner arrived at Bath, she thought it the most altered place she had ever seen—she was mistaken—it was she herself, who was changed.

The walks were melancholy, the company insipid, the ball-room fatiguing—in fine, she had left behind, all that could charm or please her.

Though she found herself far less happy than when she was at Bath before, yet she felt, she would not, to enjoy all that past happiness, be again reduced to the being she was at that time. Thus, does the lover consider the extinction of his passion, with the same horror as the libertine[1] looks upon annihilation; the one would rather live hereafter (though in all the tortures with which his future state is described) than cease to exist; so there are no tortures a lover would not suffer, rather than cease to love.

In the wide prospect of melancholy before her, Miss Milner's fancy caught hold of the only comfort which presented itself; and this, slender as it was, in the total absence of every other, her imagination pictured as excessive. The comfort was a letter from Miss Woodley—a letter wherein the subject of her love would most assuredly be mentioned, and in whatever terms, must still be the means of delight.

A letter arrived—she devoured it with her eyes.—The post mark on the outside denoting from whence it came, the name of 'Milner Lodge' written on the top, were all sources of pleasure—and she read slowly every line it contained to procrastinate the pleasing expectation she enjoyed, till she should arrive at the name of Dorriforth. At last her impatient eye, caught the word three lines beyond the place she was reading —irresistibly, she skipped over those lines, and fixed on the point to which she was attracted.

Miss Woodley was cautious in her indulgence; she made the slightest mention of Dorriforth, saying only, 'He was extremely concerned, and even dejected, at the little hope there was of his cousin, Lord Elmwood's, recovery.'—Short and trivial as this passage was, it was still more important to Miss Milner than any other in the letter—she read it again and again, considered, and reflected upon it.—Dejected, thought she, what does that word exactly mean?—did I ever see Mr. Dorriforth dejected?—how I wonder does he look in that state?—Thus did she muse, while the cause of his dejection, though a most serious one, and pathetically described by Miss Woodley, scarce arrested her attention once.—She run over with haste the account of Lord Elmwood's state of health; she certainly pitied him while she thought of him, but she did not think of him long. To die was a hard fate for a young nobleman just in possession of his immense fortune, and on the eve of marriage with a beautiful young woman; but Miss Milner thought Heaven might be still better than all this, and she had no doubt but his lordship would go there. The forlorn state of Miss Fenton ought to have been a subject for compassion, but she knew that lady had resignation to bear any lot with patience, and that a trial of her fortitude, might be more flattering to her vanity than to be Countess of Elmwood: in a word, she saw nobody's misfortunes equal to her own, because she saw no one so little able to bear misfortune.

She replied to Miss Woodley's letter, and dwelt very long on that subject which Miss Woodley had taken care to pass over lightly; this was another indulgence; and to hear from, and to write to her friend, were now the only enjoyments she possessed. From Bath Miss Milner paid several festive visits with Lady Luneham—all were alike tedious and melancholy.

But her guardian wrote to her, and though the subject was sorrowful, the letter gave her joy—the sentiments it expressed were but trite and common-place, yet she valued them as the dearest effusions of friendship and affection; and her hand trembled, and her heart beat with rapture while she wrote the answer, though she knew it would not be received with one emotion, such as those which she experienced. In her second letter to Miss Woodley she prayed like a person insane to be taken home from confinement, and like a lunatic protested, in sensible language, she 'had no disorder.' But her friend replied, 'that very declaration proves its violence.' And assured her that nothing less than placing her affections else-where, should induce her to believe, but that she was incurable.

Miss Woodley's third letter acquainted Miss Milner with the death of Lord Elmwood—Miss Woodley was exceedingly affected by this event, and said little else on any other subject. —Miss Milner was shocked when she read the words 'he is dead,' and instantly thought, 'How transient are all sublunary things!—within a few years I shall be dead—and how felicitous will it then be, if I have resisted every temptation to the delusive pleasures of this life!'—The happiness of a peaceful death occupied her contemplation for near an hour; but at length every virtuous and pious sentiment this meditation inspired, served but to remind her of the many sentences she had heard fall from her guardian's lips upon the same subject —her thoughts were again fixed on him, and she could think of nothing beside.

In a very short time after, her health became impaired from the indisposition of her mind; she languished, and was once in imminent danger. During a slight delirium of her fever, Miss Woodley's name and her guardian's were repeated incessantly; Lady Luneham sent them immediate word of this, and they both hastened to Bath, and arrived there, just as her disorder had taken a most favourable turn. As soon as she became perfectly recollected, her first care was, knowing the frailty of her heart, to enquire what she had uttered while delirious.—Miss Woodley, who was by her bed-side, begged her not to be alarmed on that account, and assured her she knew, from all her attendants, that she had only spoken with a friendly remembrance (as was really the case) of those persons who were dear to her.

She wished to know whether her guardian was come to see her, but she had not the courage to ask before Miss Woodley; and her friend was afraid by the too sudden mention of his name to discompose her. Her woman, however, after some little time, entered the chamber and whispered Miss Woodley. Miss Milner asked inquisitively 'What she said?' and the woman going to her, replied softly, 'Lord Elmwood, madam, would wish to come and see you for a few moments, if you will allow him?' Miss Milner turned her head, and stared wildly.

'I thought,' said she, 'I thought Lord Elmwood had been dead—are my senses disordered still?'

'No, my dear,' answered Miss Woodley, 'it is the present Lord Elmwood who wishes to see you; he whom you left ill when you came hither, is dead.'

'And who is the present Lord Elmwood?' she asked.

Miss Woodley after a short hesitation replied—'Your guardian.'

'And so he is,' cried Miss Milner, 'he is the next heir—I had forgot.—But is it possible he is here?'

'Yes—' returned Miss Woodley with a grave voice and manner, to moderate that glow of satisfaction which for a moment sparkled even in her languid eye, and blushed over her pallid countenance—'Yes—as he heard you were ill, he thought it right to come and see you.'

'He is very good,' answered she, and the tears started in her eyes.

'Would you please to admit his lordship?' asked her woman.

'Not yet, not yet,' she replied, 'let me recollect myself first.' And she looked with a timid doubt upon her friend, to ask if it was proper.

Miss Woodley could scarce support this humble reference to her judgment from the wan face of the poor invalid, and taking her by the hand, whispered in tears, 'You shall do what you please.'—In a few minutes Lord Elmwood was introduced.

To those who sincerely love, every change of situation or circumstances in the object beloved, appears an advantage.—So, the acquisition of a title and estate, was in Miss Milner's eye an immeasurable advantage to her guardian, not on the score of their real value, but any change instead of diminishing her passion would have served but to encrease it—even a change to the utmost poverty.

When he entered—the sight of him seemed to be too much for her, and after the first glance she turned her head away—the sound of his voice encouraged her, however, to look once more—and now she riveted her eyes upon him.

'It is impossible, my dear Miss Milner,' he gently whispered, 'to say, the joy I feel that your disorder has subsided.'

But though it was impossible to say, it was possible to *look* what he felt, and his looks expressed his feelings.—In the zeal of those sensations, he laid hold of her hand, and held it between his—this he himself did not know——but she did.

'You have prayed for me, my lord, I dare say?' said she, with a smile of thanks for those prayers.

'Fervently, ardently!'—returned he, and the fervency with which he prayed, spoke in every feature.

'But I am a protestant, my lord, and if I had died such, do you believe I should have gone to Heaven?'

'Most assuredly, that would not have prevented you.'

'But Mr. Sandford does not think so.'

'He must; for he means to go there himself.'

To keep her guardian with her, Miss Milner seemed inclined to converse; but Miss Woodley perceived the temporal as well as the spiritual evil of this, and advised his lordship to retire.

They had only one more interview before he left the place; at which Miss Milner was capable of sitting up—he was with her, however, but a very short time, some necessary concerns relative to the late Lord Elmwood's affairs, calling him in haste to London. Miss Woodley continued with her friend till she saw her entirely reinstated in her health: during which time his lordship was frequently the subject of their private conversation; and upon those occasions Miss Milner has sometimes brought Miss Woodley to acknowledge, 'That could Mr. Dorriforth have foreseen the early death of the late Lord Elmwood, it had been for the greater honour of his religion (considering that ancient title would now after him become extinct), had he preferred marriage vows, to those of celibacy.'

CHAPTER II

WHEN the time for Miss Woodley to depart arrived, Miss Milner entreated earnestly to accompany her home, and made the most solemn promises that she would guard not only her behaviour, but her very thoughts within the limitation her friend should prescribe. Miss Woodley at length yielded thus much, 'That as soon as Lord Elmwood was set out on his journey to Italy, where she had heard him say he should shortly be obliged to go, she would no longer deny her the pleasure of returning; and if (after the long absence which must consequently take place between him and her) she should then, positively affirm the suppression of her passion was the happy result, she would at that time take her word, and risk the danger of their once more residing together.'

With this concession on the side of Miss Woodley they parted; and as winter was now far advanced, that lady returned to her aunt's house in town, from whence Mrs. Horton was, however, preparing to remove, in order to superintend Lord Elmwood's house, (which had been occupied by the late earl,) in Grosvenor-square; and Miss Woodley was to accompany her.

If Lord Elmwood was not desirous Miss Milner should conclude her visit and return to his protection, it was partly from the multiplicity of affairs in which he was at this time engaged, and partly from having Mr. Sandford now entirely placed with him as his chaplain; for he dreaded that living in the same house their natural antipathy might be encreased to aversion—upon this account he once thought of advising Mr. Sandford to take up his abode elsewhere; but the great pleasure his lordship took in his society, joined to the great mortification he knew such a proposal would be to his friend, would not suffer him to make it.

Miss Milner all this time was not thinking upon those she hated, but on those she loved.—Sandford never came into her thoughts, while the image of Lord Elmwood never left them. One morning, as she sat talking to Lady Luneham on various subjects, but thinking alone on him; Sir Harry,[1] with another gentleman, a Mr. Fleetmond, came in, and the conversation turned upon the great improbability there was, during the present Lord Elmwood's youth, that he should ever inherit the title and estate that had now fallen to him—and said Mr. Fleetmond, 'Independent of the fortune, it must be matter of infinite joy to Dorriforth.'—'No,' answered Sir Harry, 'independent of the fortune, it must be a motive of concern to him; for he must now regret, beyond measure, his folly in taking priest's orders—thus depriving himself of the hopes of an heir, by which the title, at his death, will be lost.'

'By no means,' replied Mr. Fleetmond, 'he may yet have an heir, for he will certainly marry.'

'Marry!' cried Sir Harry.

'Yes,' answered the other, 'it was that I meant by the joy it might probably give him, beyond the possession of his estate and title.'

'How be married?' said Lady Luneham, 'Has he not taken a vow never to marry?'

'Yes,' answered Mr. Fleetmond, 'but there are no religious vows, from which the great Pontiff of Rome cannot grant a dispensation—those commandments made by the church, the church has always the power to dispense withal; and when it is for the general good of religion, his holiness thinks it incumbent on him, to publish his bull to remit all pains and penalties for their non-observance; and certainly it is for the honour of the catholics, that this earldom should continue in a catholic family[1]—In short, I'll lay a wager my Lord Elmwood is married within the twelvemonth.'

Miss Milner, who listened with attention, feared she was in a dream, or deceived by the pretended knowledge of Mr. Fleetmond, who might know nothing—but on consideration, all that he had said was very probable; and to confirm its truth, he was himself a Roman Catholic, and must be well

informed on the subject upon which he spoke.———If she
had heard the direst news that ever sounded in the ears of the
most susceptible of mortals, the agitation of her mind and
person could not have been stronger—she felt, while every
word was speaking, a chill through all her veins—it was a
pleasure too exquisite, not to bear along with it the sensation
of exquisite pain; of which she was so sensible, that for a few
moments it caused her to wish she had not heard the intelligence; though, very soon after, she would not but have
heard it for the world.

As soon as she had recovered from her first astonishment
and joy, she wrote to Miss Woodley an exact account of what
she had heard, and received this answer.

'I am sorry any body should have given you this piece of
information, because it was a task, in the executing of which,
I had promised myself the most extreme satisfaction—but
from the fear your health was not sufficiently returned to support, without danger, the burthen of hopes which I knew would,
upon this occasion, press upon you, I deferred my pleasing
communication, and have had it anticipated. Yet, as you seem
in the utmost doubt as to the truth of what you have been told,
perhaps this confirmation of it, may fall little short of the first
news; especially when it is strengthened by my entreating you
to come to us, as soon as you can with propriety leave Lady
Luneham.

'Come, my dear Miss Milner, and find in your once rigid
monitor, a faithful confidant—I will no longer threaten to disclose a secret you have trusted me with, but leave it to the
wisdom and sensibility of his heart, (who is now to penetrate
into the hearts of our sex, in search of one consonant to his
own) to find it out.—I no longer condemn, but congratulate
you on your passion; and will assist you with all my advice
and earnest wishes, that you may obtain a return.'

This letter was another of those excruciating pleasures, that nearly reduced Miss Milner to the grave—it took away from her all appetite to food, and from her eyes the power of being closed for several nights—she thought so much upon the prospect of accomplishing her wishes, that she could think of nothing beside; not even invent a probable excuse for leaving Lady Luneham before the appointed time, which was yet two months to come. She wrote to Miss Woodley to beg her contrivance, to reproach her for keeping the secret so long from her, and to thank her for having revealed it to her in so kind a manner at last.—She begged also to be acquainted how Mr. Dorriforth (for still she called him by that name) spoke and thought of this sudden change in his destiny.

Miss Woodley's reply was a summons for her to town upon some pretended business, which she avoided explaining, but which entirely silenced her ladyship's entreaties for her stay.

To her question concerning Lord Elmwood she answered, 'It is a subject on which he seldom speaks—he appears just the same he ever did, nor could you by any part of his conduct, conceive that any such change had taken place.' Miss Milner exclaimed to herself, 'I am glad he is not altered—if his words, looks, or manners were any thing different from what they formerly were, I should not like him so well.' And just the reverse would have been the case, had Miss Woodley sent her word he was changed. The day for her leaving Bath was fixed; she expected it with rapture, but before its arrival sunk under the care of expectation; and when it came, was so much indisposed as to be forced to defer her journey for a week.

At length she found herself in London—in the house of her guardian—and that guardian no longer bound to a single life, but *enjoined* to marry. He appeared in her eyes, as in Miss Woodley's, the same as ever; or perhaps more endearing than ever, as it was the first time she had beheld him with hope.—

Mr. Sandford did *not* appear the same; yet he was in reality as surly and as disrespectful in his behaviour to her as usual; but she did not observe, or she did not feel his morose temper as heretofore—he seemed amiable, mild, and gentle; at least such was the happy medium through which she saw him now; for good humour, like the jaundice, makes every one of its own complexion.

CHAPTER III

LORD ELMWOOD was preparing to go abroad to receive in form, the dispensation from his vows; it was, however, a subject he seemed carefully to avoid speaking upon; and when by any accident he was obliged to mention it, it was without any marks either of satisfaction or concern.

Miss Milner's pride, for the first time, began to take the alarm—while he was Mr. Dorriforth, and confined to a single life, his indifference to her charms was rather an honourable, than a reproachful trait in his character, and in reality she admired him for the insensibility—but on the eve of being at liberty, and on the eve of making his choice, she was offended that choice was not immediately fixed upon her[1]—She had been accustomed to receive the devotion of every man who saw her, and not to obtain it of the man from whom, of all others, she most wished it, was cruelly humiliating.—She complained to Miss Woodley, who advised her to have patience, but that was one of the virtues in which she was the least practised.

Encouraged, nevertheless, by her friend in the commendable desire of gaining the affections of him, who possessed all her's, she, however, left no means unattempted to make the conquest—but she began with too great certainty of success,

not to be sensible of the deepest mortification in the disappointment—nay, she anticipated a disappointment as she
had before anticipated her success, and by turns felt the
keenest emotions from hope and from despair.

As these passions alternately governed her, she was alternately in spirits or dejected; in good or in ill humour; and the
frequent vicissitudes of her prospects, at length gave to her
behaviour an air of capriciousness, which not all her follies
had till now produced.—This was not the way to obtain the
affections of Lord Elmwood; she knew it was not; and before
him she was under some restriction.—Sandford observed this,
and added to her many other failings, hypocrisy. It was plain
to see Mr. Sandford esteemed her less and less every day; and
as he was the person who most of all influenced the opinion
of her guardian, he became to her, very soon, an object not
merely of dislike, but of abhorrence.

These sentiments for each other, were discoverable in
every word and action while they were in each other's company; but still in his absence, Miss Milner's good nature, and
little malice, never suffered her to utter a sentence injurious
to his interest.—Sandford's charity did not extend thus far;
and speaking of her with severity one evening while she was
at the opera, 'His meaning,' as he said, 'but to caution her
guardian against her faults,' Lord Elmwood replied,

'There is one fault, however, Mr. Sandford, I cannot lay
to her charge.'

'And what is that, my lord?' (cried Sandford, eagerly)
'What is that one fault, which Miss Milner has not?'

'I never,' replied his lordship, 'heard Miss Milner, in your
absence, utter a syllable to your disadvantage.'

'She durst not, my lord, because she is in fear of you; and
she knows you would not suffer it.'

'She then,' answered his lordship, 'pays me a much higher

compliment than you do; for you freely censure her, and yet imagine I will suffer it.'

'My lord,' replied Sandford, 'I am undeceived now, and shall never take that liberty again.'

As his lordship always treated Sandford with the utmost respect, he began to fear he had been deficient upon this occasion; and the disposition which had induced him to take his ward's part, was likely, in the end, to prove unfavourable to her; for perceiving Sandford was offended at what had passed, as the only means of retribution, his lordship began himself to lament her volatile and captious propensities; in which lamentation Sandford, now forgetting his affront, joined with the heartiest concurrence, adding,

'That you, sir, having now other cares to employ your thoughts, ought to insist upon her marrying, or her retiring wholly into the country.'

She returned home just as this conversation was finished, and Sandford the moment she entered rung for his candle to retire. Miss Woodley, who had been at the opera with Miss Milner, cried,

'Bless me, Mr. Sandford, are you not well; you are going to leave us so early?'

He replied, 'No, I have a pain in my head.'

Miss Milner, who never heard complaints without sympathy, rose immediately from her seat, saying,

'I think I never heard you, Mr. Sandford, complain of indisposition before—will you accept of my specific for the head-ache? indeed it is a certain relief—I'll fetch it instantly.'

She went hastily out of the room, and returned with a bottle, which, she assured him, 'was a present from Lady Luneham, and would certainly cure him.'—And she pressed it upon him with such an anxious earnestness, that with all his churlishness he could not refuse taking it.

This was but a common-place civility, such as is paid by one enemy to another every day; but the *manner* was the material part—the unaffected concern, the attention, the good will, she demonstrated in this little incident, was that which was remarkable; and which immediately took from Lord Elmwood the displeasure to which he had been just before excited, or rather transformed it into a degree of admiration. Even Sandford was not insensible to her behaviour, and in return, when he left the room, 'wished her a good night.'

To her and to Miss Woodley, who had not been witnesses of the preceding conversation, what she had done appeared of no merit, but to the mind of Lord Elmwood it had much; and upon the departure of Sandford he began to be unusually cheerful. He first, reproached the ladies for not offering him a place in their box at the opera.

'Would you have gone, my lord?' asked Miss Milner, highly delighted.

'Certainly,' returned he, 'had you invited me.'

'Then from this day, my lord, I give you a general invitation: nor shall any other company be admitted, but what you approve.'

'I am very much obliged to you,' answered his lordship.

'And you,' continued she, 'who have been only accustomed to church-music, you will be more than any one, enchanted on hearing the soft, harmonious sounds of love.'

'What ravishing pleasures are you preparing for me!' returned he, 'I know not whether my weak senses will be able to support them.'

She had her eyes upon him as he spoke this, and discovered in his, which were fixed upon her, a sensibility unexpected— a kind of fascination which enticed her to look on, while her eye-lids fell involuntarily before its mighty force; and a thousand blushes crowded over her face:——He was struck with these sudden signals; hastily recalled his former countenance, and stopt the conversation.

Miss Woodley, who had been a silent observer for some time, now thought a word or two from her, would be acceptable rather than troublesome.

'And pray, my lord,' said she, 'when do you go to France?'

'To Italy you mean,'—said he, 'not at all—my superiors are very indulgent, for they dispense with all my duties.—I ought, and meant, to have gone abroad; but as variety of concerns require my presence in England, every necessary ceremony has taken place here.'

'Then your lordship is no longer in orders?' said Miss Woodley.

'No, they have been resigned these five days.'

'My lord, I give you joy,' said Miss Milner.

He thanked her, but added with a sigh, 'If I have given up content in search of joy, I shall probably be a loser by the venture.'—Soon after this, he wished the ladies good night, and retired.

Happy as Miss Milner found herself in his company, she saw him leave the room with infinite satisfaction, because her heart was impatient to give a loose to its hopes on the bosom of Miss Woodley.—She bad Mrs. Horton immediately good night, and in her friend's apartment gave way to all the language of the tenderest passion, warm with the confidence of meeting its return.—She described the sentiments she had read in Lord Elmwood's looks, and though Miss Woodley had beheld them too, Miss Milner's fancy heightened every glance; and her construction became, by degrees, so extremely favourable to her own wishes, that had not her friend been present, and known in what measure to estimate those symptoms; she must infallibly have thought, by the joy to which they gave birth, his lordship had openly avowed a passion for her.

Miss Woodley, therefore, thought it her duty to allay those ecstasies, and represented to her, she might be deceived in her hopes—or even supposing his lordship's inclinations tended towards her, there were yet great obstacles between them.—'Would Sandford, who governed, or at least directed his almost every thought and purpose, not be consulted upon this? and if he was; on what, but the most romantic affection on the part of Lord Elmwood, had Miss Milner to depend? and his lordship was not a man to be suspected of submitting to the excess of any passion.'—Thus did Miss Woodley argue, for fear her friend should be misled by her wishes, yet in her own mind she scarce harboured a doubt that any thing would thwart them.—The succeeding circumstance proved she was mistaken.

Another gentleman of family and fortune made overtures to Miss Milner, and her guardian, so far from having his thoughts inclined towards her on his own account, pleaded this lover's cause even with more zeal, than he had formerly pleaded for Sir Edward and Lord Frederick; and thus at once destroyed all those plans of happiness poor Miss Milner had meditated.

In consequence, her melancholy humour was now predominant; and for several days she staid entirely at home, and yet was denied to all her visitants.—Whether this arose from pure melancholy, or the still lingering hope of making her conquest, by that sedateness of manners she knew her guardian admired, perhaps she herself did not know.—Be that as it may, Lord Elmwood could not but observe this change, and one morning thought fit to mention, and applaud it.

Miss Woodley and she were working together when he came into the room; and after sitting several minutes, and talking upon indifferent subjects; to which his ward replied with a dejection in her voice and manner—he said,

'Perhaps I am wrong, Miss Milner, but I have observed you are lately grown more thoughtful than usual.'

She blushed, as she always did when the subject was herself.—He continued, 'Your health appears perfectly restored, and yet you do not take delight in your former recreations.'

'Are you sorry for that, my lord?'

'No, madam, I am extremely glad; and I was going to congratulate you upon the change—but give me leave to enquire, to what lucky accident we are to attribute this alteration?'

'Your lordship then thinks all my commendable deeds, arise from accident; and that I have no virtues of my own.'

'Pardon me, Miss Milner, I think you have many.' This he spoke emphatically; and the blood flowed to her face more than at first.

He resumed—'How can I doubt of a lady's virtues, when her countenance gives such evident proofs of them?—believe me, Miss Milner, that in the midst of your gayest follies; while you thus continue to blush, I shall reverence your internal sensations.'

'Oh! my lord, did you know some of them, I am afraid you would think them unpardonable.'

This was so much to the purpose, Miss Woodley found herself uneasy—but she needed not—Miss Milner loved too sincerely, to reveal it to the object.——His lordship answered,

'And did you, Miss Milner, know some of mine, you might think them equally unpardonable.'

She turned pale, and could no longer guide her needle—in the fond transports of her heart she imagined, the sensations to which he alluded, was his love for her.—She was too much embarrassed to reply, and he continued,

'We have all a great deal to pardon in one another; and I

know not whether the officious person who forces, even his good advice, is not as blameable as the obstinate one, who will not listen to it.—And now, having made a preface to excuse you, should you once more refuse mine, I will venture to give it.'

'My lord,' returned she, 'I have never yet refused to follow your advice, but where my own peace of mind was so nearly concerned, as to have made me culpable, had I complied.'

'Well, madam, I submit to your determinations; and shall never again oppose your inclination to remain single.'

This sentence, as it excluded his ever soliciting for himself, gave her the utmost pain; and she cast a glance of her eye at him full of reproach.—He did not observe it, but went on.

'Continuing unmarried, it seems to have been your father's intention, you should continue under my immediate care; but as I mean for the future to reside chiefly in the country—answer me candidly, do you think you could be happy there, for at least three parts of the year?'

After a short hesitation, she replied,—'I have no objection.'

'I am glad to hear it,' he returned eagerly, 'for it is my earnest desire to have you with me—your welfare is dear to me as my own; and were we apart, continual apprehensions would prey upon my mind.'

The tear started in her eye, at the earnestness with which this was spoken;—he saw it, and to soften her still more with the sense of his esteem for her, he encreased his earnestness while he said,

'If you will take the resolution to quit London for the time I mention, there shall be no means unemployed to make the country all you can wish—I shall insist upon Miss Woodley's accompanying you; and it will not only be *my* study to form such a society as you may approve, but I am certain it will be likewise the study of Lady Elmwood——'

He was going on, but as if a poniard had thrust her heart, she writhed under this unexpected stroke.

He saw her countenance change—he looked at her steadfastly.

It was not a common change from joy to sorrow, from content to uneasiness, which Miss Milner discovered—she felt, and she expressed anguish.—Lord Elmwood was alarmed and shocked.—She did not weep, but she called Miss Woodley to come to her, with a voice that indicated a degree of agony.

'My lord,' (cried Miss Woodley, seeing his consternation, and trembling lest he should guess the secret), 'My lord, Miss Milner has again deceived you—you must not take her from London—it is that, which is the cause of her uneasiness.'

He seemed more amazed still, and still more shocked at her duplicity than at her torture.—'Good Heaven,' exclaimed he, 'how am I to accomplish her wishes? what am I to do? how can I judge, while she will not confide in me, but thus grossly deceives me?'

She leaned, pale as death, on the shoulder of Miss Woodley, her eyes fixed, with a seeming insensibility to all that was said, while he continued,

'Heaven is my witness, if I knew—if I could conceive the means how to make her happy, I would sacrifice my own happiness to her's.'

'My lord,' cried Miss Woodley with a smile, 'perhaps I may call upon you hereafter, to fulfil your word.'

He was totally ignorant what she meant, nor had he leisure from the confusion of his thoughts to reflect upon her meaning; he nevertheless replied, with warmth, 'Do—you will find I'll perform it.——Do—I will faithfully perform it.'

Though Miss Milner was conscious this declaration could

not, in delicacy, ever be brought against him; yet the fervent and solemn manner in which he made it, cheered her spirits; and as persons enjoy the reflection of having in their possession some valuable gem, although they are determined never to use it, so she upon this, was comforted and grew better.—She now lifted up her head from Miss Woodley, and leaned it on her hand as she sat by the side of a table—still she did not speak, but seemed overcome with sorrow.—As her situation became, however, less alarming; her guardian's pity and affright began to take the colour of resentment; and though he did not say so, he was, and looked highly offended.

At this juncture Mr. Sandford entered.—On beholding the present party, it needed not his sagacity to see, at the first view, they were all uneasy; but instead of the sympathy this might have excited in some dispositions, Mr. Sandford, after casting a look at each of them, appeared in high spirits.

'You seem unhappy, my lord,' said he, with a smile.

'You do *not*—Mr. Sandford,' replied his lordship.

'No, my lord, nor would I, were I in your situation,'—returned he, 'What should make a man of sense out of temper but a worthy object?'—And he looked at Miss Milner.

'There are no objects unworthy our care,' replied Lord Elmwood.

'But there are objects on whom all care is fruitless, your lordship will allow.'

'I never yet despaired of any one, Mr. Sandford.'

'And yet there are persons, of whom it is presumption, to entertain hopes.'—And he looked again at Miss Milner.

'Does your head ache, Miss Milner?' asked Miss Woodley, seeing her hold it with her hand.

'Very much,' returned she.

'Mr. Sandford,' said Miss Woodley, 'Did you use all those drops Miss Milner gave you for a pain in the head?'

'Yes,' answered he, 'I did.'—But the question at that moment somewhat embarrassed him.

'And I hope you found benefit from them,' said Miss Milner, with great kindness, as she rose from her seat, and walked slowly and despondently out of the room.

Though Miss Woodley followed her, so that Mr. Sandford was left alone with Lord Elmwood, and might have continued his unkind insinuations without one restraint; yet his lips were closed for the present.—He looked down on the carpet—twitched himself upon his chair—and began to talk of the weather.

CHAPTER IV

As soon as the first transports of despair were over, Miss Milner suffered herself to be once more in hope—she found there were no other means to support her life; and to her no small joy, her friend, Miss Woodley, was much less severe on the present occasion than she expected.—No engagement between mortals, was, in Miss Woodley's opinion, binding like that entered into with heaven; and whatever vows Lord Elmwood had made to another, she justly supposed, no woman's love for him, equalled Miss Milner's—it was prior to all others too, and that established a claim, at least to contend for success; and in a contention, what rival would not fall before her?

It was not difficult to guess who this rival was; or if they were a little time in suspense, Miss Woodley soon arrived at the certainty, by inquiring of Mr. Sandford; who, unsuspicious why she asked, readily informed her the intended Lady Elmwood, was no other than Miss Fenton; and that her marriage with his lordship would be solemnized as soon as the mourning for the late Lord Elmwood was expired.—This last intelligence made Miss Woodley shudder—however, she repeated it to Miss Milner, word for word.

'Happy! happy, woman!' exclaimed Miss Milner of Miss Fenton; 'she has received the first fond impulses of his heart, and has had the transcendent happiness of teaching him to love!'

'By no means,' returned Miss Woodley, finding there was no other method to comfort her; 'do not suppose Lord Elmwood's marriage is the result of love—it is no more than a duty, a necessary piece of business, and this you may plainly see by the wife on whom he has fixed.—Miss Fenton was thought a proper match for his cousin, and this same propriety, you must perceive still exists.'

It was easy to convince Miss Milner all her friend said was truth, for she wished it to be so. 'And oh!' she exclaimed, 'could I but stimulate passion, in the place of propriety——— do you think my dear Miss Woodley,' (and she looked with such begging eyes, it was impossible not to answer as she wished,) 'do you think it would be unjust to Miss Fenton, were I to inspire her destined husband with a passion which she may not have inspired, and which I believe she herself cannot feel?'

Miss Woodley paused a minute, and then answered, 'No;' —but there was a hesitation in her manner of delivery—she did say, 'No,' but she looked as if she was afraid she ought to have said 'Yes.'—Miss Milner, however, did not wait to give her time to recall the word, or to alter its meaning by adding others to it, but run on eagerly, and declared, 'As that was her opinion, she would abide by it, and do all she could to supplant her rival.'—In order, nevertheless, to justify this determination, and satisfy the conscience of Miss Woodley, they both concluded, Miss Fenton's heart was not engaged in the intended marriage, and consequently she was indifferent whether it took place or not.

Since the death of the late earl, that young lady had not been in town; nor had the present lord been near the spot where she resided since the week her lover died; of course, nothing like love could be declared at so early a period; and if it had been made known since, it must only have been by letter, or by the deputation of Mr. Sandford, who they knew had been once in the country to visit her; but how little he was qualified to enforce a tender passion, was a comfortable reflection.

Revived with these conjectures, of which some were true, and others false; the very next day a dark gloom overspread their bright prospects, on Mr. Sandford's saying, as he entered the breakfast-room,

'Miss Fenton, ladies, desired me to present her compliments to you.'

'Is she in town?' asked Mrs. Horton.

'She came to town yesterday morning,' returned Sandford, 'and is at her brother's, in Ormond street; my lord and I supped there last night, and that made us so late home.'

His lordship entered soon after, and confirmed what had been said, by bowing to his ward, and telling her, 'Miss Fenton had charged him with her kindest respects.'

'How does poor Miss Fenton look?' Mrs. Horton asked Lord Elmwood.

To which question Sandford replied, 'Beautiful—she looks beautifully.'

'She has got over her uneasiness, I suppose then?' said Mrs. Horton—not knowing she was asking the question before her new lover.

'Uneasy!' replied Sandford, 'uneasy at any trial this world can send? that had been highly unworthy of her.'

'But sometimes women do fret at such things,' replied Mrs. Horton innocently.

Lord Elmwood asked Miss Milner—'If she meant to ride, this charming day?'

While she was hesitating—

'There are very different kinds of women,' (answered Sandford, directing his discourse to Mrs. Horton,) 'there is as much difference between some women, as between good and evil spirits.'

Lord Elmwood asked Miss Milner again—if she took an airing?

She replied, 'No.'

'And beauty,' continued Sandford, 'when endowed upon spirits that are evil, is a mark of their greater, their more extreme wickedness.—Lucifer was the most beautiful of all the angels in paradise——'

'How do you know?' said Miss Milner.

'But the beauty of Lucifer' (continued Sandford, in perfect neglect and contempt of her question,) 'was an aggravation of his guilt; because it shewed a double share of ingratitude to the Divine Creator of that beauty.'

'Now you talk of angels,' said Miss Milner, 'I wish I had wings; and I should like to fly through the park this morning.'

'You would be taken for an angel in good earnest,' said Lord Elmwood.

Sandford was angry at this little compliment, and cried, 'Then instead of the wings, I would advise the serpent's skin.'[1]

'My lord,' cried she, 'does not Mr. Sandford use me ill?'—Vext with other things, she felt herself extremely hurt at this, and made the appeal almost in tears.

'Indeed, I think he does,' answered his lordship, and he looked at Sandford as if he was displeased.

This was a triumph so agreeable to her, she immediately pardoned the offence; but the offender did not so easily pardon her.

'Good morning, ladies,' said his lordship, rising to go away.

'My lord,' said Miss Woodley, 'you promised Miss Milner to accompany her one evening to the opera; this is opera night.'

'Will you go, my lord?' asked Miss Milner, in a voice so soft, he seemed as if he wished, but could not resist it.

'I am to dine at Mr. Fenton's to-day,' he replied, 'and if he and his sister will go; and you will allow them part of your box, I will promise to come.'

This was a condition that did not please her, but as she felt a strong desire to see him in the company of his intended bride, (for she fancied she could perceive his most secret sentiments, could she once see them together) she answered not ungraciously, 'Yes, my compliments to Mr. and Miss Fenton, and I hope they will favour me with their company.'

'Then, madam, if they come, you may expect me—else not.' And he bowed and left the room.

All the day was passed in anxious expectation by Miss Milner, what would be the event of the evening; for upon the skill of her penetration that evening, all her future prospects she thought depended.—If she saw by his looks, his words, or assiduity, he loved Miss Fenton, she flattered herself she would never think of him again with hope; but if she observed him treat her with inattention or indifference, she meant to cherish from that moment the fondest expectations.—Against that short evening her toilet was consulted the whole day; and the alternate hope and fear which fluttered at her heart, gave a more than usual brilliancy to her eyes, and more than usual bloom to her complexion.—But in vain was her beauty; vain all the pains she had taken to decorate that beauty; vain the many looks she cast towards her box-door to see it open; Lord Elmwood did not come.

The music was discord—every thing she saw, was disgusting—in a word, she was miserable.

She longed impatiently for the curtain to drop, because she was uneasy where she was—yet she asked herself, 'Shall I be less unhappy at home? yes, at home I shall see Lord Elmwood, and that will be happiness—but he will behold me with neglect, and that will be misery.—Ungrateful man! I will no longer think of him,' she said to herself.—Or could she have thought of him without joining in the same idea Miss Fenton, her anguish had been supportable; but while she pictured them as lovers, the tortures of the rack give but a few degrees more pain than she endured.

There are but few persons who ever felt the real passion of jealousy, because few have felt the real passion of love; but to those who have experienced them both, jealousy not only affects the mind, but every fibre of the frame is a victim to it; and Miss Milner's every limb ached, with agonizing torment, while Miss Fenton, courted and beloved by Lord Elmwood, was present to her imagination.

The moment the opera was finished, she flew hastily down stairs, as if to fly from the sufferings she experienced.—She did not go into the coffee-room, though repeatedly persuaded by Miss Woodley, but waited at the door till her carriage drew up.

Piqued—heart-broken—full of resentment to the object of her uneasiness; as she stood inattentive to all that passed, a hand gently laid hold of her's, and the most humble and insinuating voice said, 'Will you permit me to hand you to your carriage?' She was awaked from her reverie, and found Lord Frederick Lawnly by her side.—Her heart, just then melting with tenderness to another, was perhaps more accessible than heretofore, or bursting with resentment, thought this the moment to retaliate. Whatever passion reigned that instant, it was favourable to the desires of Lord Frederick, and she looked as if she was glad to see him; he beheld this with the rapture and the humility of a lover; and though she did not feel the slightest love in return, she felt a gratitude proportionate to the insensibility with which she had been treated by her guardian, and Lord Frederick was not very erroneous if he mistook this gratitude for a latent spark of affection. The mistake, however, did not force from him his respect: he handed her to her carriage, bowed lowly, and disappeared. Miss Woodley wished to divert her thoughts from the object which could only make her wretched, and as they rode home, by many encomiums upon Lord Frederick, endeavoured to incite her to a regard for him; Miss Milner was displeased at the attempt, and exclaimed,

'What, love a rake, a man of professed gallantry? impossible. —To me, a common rake is as odious, as a common prostitute is to a man of the nicest feelings.—Where can be the pride of inspiring a passion, fifty others can equally inspire? or the transport of bestowing favours, where the appetite is already cloyed by fruition of the self-same enjoyments?'

'Strange,' cried Miss Woodley, 'that you, who possess so many follies incident to your sex, should, in the disposal of your heart, have sentiments so contrary to women in general.'

'My dear Miss Woodley,' returned she, 'put in competition the languid love of a debauchee, with the vivid affection of a sober man, and judge which has the dominion? Oh! in my calendar of love, a solemn lord chief justice, or a devout archbishop ranks before a licentious king.'

Miss Woodley smiled at an opinion which she knew half her sex would laugh at; but by the air of sincerity with which it was delivered, she was convinced, her late

behaviour to Lord Frederick was but the mere effect of
chance.

Lord Elmwood's carriage drove to his door just at the time
her's did; Mr. Sandford was with him, and they were both
come from passing the evening at Mr. Fenton's.

'So, my lord,' said Miss Woodley, as soon as they met in
the apartment, 'you did not come to us.'

'No,' answered his lordship, 'I was sorry; but I hope you
did not expect me.'

'Not expect you, my lord?' cried Miss Milner, 'did not
you say you would come?'

'If I had, I certainly should have come,' returned he, 'but
I only said so conditionally.'

'That I am witness to,' cried Sandford, 'for I was present
at the time, and his lordship said it should depend upon Miss
Fenton.'

'And she, with her gloomy disposition,' said Miss Milner,
'chose to sit at home.'

'Gloomy disposition?' repeated Sandford, 'She is a young
lady with a great share of sprightliness—and I think I never
saw her in better spirits than she was this evening, my lord?'

Lord Elmwood did not speak.

'Bless me, Mr. Sandford,' cried Miss Milner, 'I meant no
reflection upon Miss Fenton's disposition; I only meant to
censure her taste for staying at home.'

'I think,' replied Sandford, 'a much greater censure should
be passed upon those, who prefer rambling abroad.'

'But I hope, ladies, my not coming,' said his lordship, 'was
no cause of inconvenience to you; you had still a gentleman
with you, or I should certainly have come.'

'Oh! yes, two gentlemen,' answered the young son of Lady
Evans, a lad from school, whom Miss Milner had taken along
with her, and to whom his lordship had alluded.

'What two?' asked Lord Elmwood.

Neither Miss Milner or Miss Woodley answered.

'You know, madam,' said young Evans, 'that handsome gentleman who handed you into your carriage, and you called my lord.'

'Oh! he means Lord Frederick Lawnly,' said Miss Milner carelessly, but a blush of shame spread over her face.

'And did he hand you into your coach?' asked his lordship, earnestly.

'By mere accident, my lord,' Miss Woodley replied, 'for the crowd was so great——'

'I think, my lord,' said Sandford, 'it was very lucky you were *not* there.'

'Had Lord Elmwood been with us, we should not have had occasion for the assistance of any other,' said Miss Milner.

'Lord Elmwood has been with you, madam,' returned Sandford, 'very frequently, and yet——'

'Mr. Sandford,' said his lordship, interrupting him, 'it is near bed-time, your conversation keeps the ladies from retiring.'

'Your lordship's does not,' said Miss Milner, 'for you say nothing.'

'Because, madam, I am afraid to offend.'

'But does not your lordship also hope to please? and without risking the one, it is impossible to arrive at the other.'

'I think, at present, the risk of one would be too hazardous, and so I wish you a good night.' And he went out of the room somewhat abruptly.

'Lord Elmwood,' said Miss Milner, 'is very grave—he does not look like a man who has been passing his evening with the woman he loves.'

'Perhaps he is melancholy at parting from her,' said Miss Woodley.

'More likely offended,' said Sandford, 'at the manner in which that lady has spoken of her.'

'Who, I?' cried Miss Milner, 'I protest I said nothing but——'

'Nothing, madam? did not you say she was gloomy?'

'But, what I thought—I was going to add, Mr. Sandford.'

'When you think unjustly, you should not express your thoughts.'

'Then, perhaps, I should never speak.'

'And it were better you did not, if what you say, is to give pain.—Do you know, madam, that my lord is going to be married to Miss Fenton?'

'Yes,' answered Miss Milner.

'Do you know that he loves her?'

'No,' answered Miss Milner.

'How, madam! do you suppose he does not?'

'I suppose he does, yet I don't know it.'

'Then supposing he does, how can you have the imprudence to find fault with her before him?'

'I did not—to call her gloomy, was, I knew, to praise her both to him and to you, who admire such tempers.'

'Whatever her temper is, *every one* admires it; and so far from its being what you have described, she has a great deal of vivacity; vivacity which proceeds from the heart.'

'No, if it proceeded, I should admire it too; but it rests there, and no one is the better for it.'

'Come, Miss Milner,' said Miss Woodley, 'it is time to retire; you and Mr. Sandford must finish your dispute in the morning.'

'Dispute, madam!' said Sandford, 'I never disputed with any one beneath a doctor of divinity in my life.—I was only cautioning your friend not to make light of virtues, which it would do her honour to possess.—Miss Fenton is a most

amiable young woman, and worthy just such a husband as my
Lord Elmwood will make her.'

'I am sure,' said Miss Woodley, 'Miss Milner thinks so—
she has a high opinion of Miss Fenton—she was at present
only jesting.'

'But, madam, jests are very pernicious things, when
delivered with a malignant sneer.—I have known a jest destroy
a lady's reputation—I have known a jest give one person a
distaste for another—I have known a jest break off a marriage.'

'But I suppose there is no apprehension of that, in the
present case?' said Miss Woodley—wishing he might answer
in the affirmative.

'Not that I can foresee,' replied he.—'No, Heaven forbid;
for I look upon them to be formed for each other—their dispositions, their pursuits, their inclinations the same.—Their
passions for each other just the same—pure—white as snow.'

'And I dare say, not warmer,' replied Miss Milner.

He looked provoked beyond measure.

'Dear Miss Milner,' cried Miss Woodley, 'how can you
talk thus? I believe in my heart you are only envious my lord
did not offer himself to you.'

'To her!' said Sandford, affecting an air of the utmost surprise, 'to her? Do you think his lordship received a dispensation from his vows to become the husband of a coquette—
a——' he was going on.

'Nay, Mr. Sandford,' cried Miss Milner, 'I believe my
greatest crime in your eyes, is being a heretic.'

'By no means, madam—it is the only circumstance that can
apologize for your faults; and had you not that excuse, there
would be none for you.'

'Then, at present, there is an excuse—I thank you, Mr.
Sandford; this is the kindest thing you ever said to me. But
I am vext to see you are sorry, you have said it.'

'Angry at your being a heretic?' he resumed, 'Indeed I should be much more concerned to see you a disgrace to our religion.'

Miss Milner had not been in a good humour during the whole evening—she had been provoked to the full extent of her patience several times; but this harsh sentence hurried her beyond all bounds, and she arose from her seat in the most violent agitation, and exclaimed, 'What have I done to be treated thus?'

Though Mr. Sandford was not a man easily intimidated, he was on this occasion evidently alarmed; and stared about him with so strong an expression of surprise, that it partook in some degree of fear.—Miss Woodley clasped her friend in her arms, and cried with the tenderest affection and pity, 'My dear Miss Milner, be composed.'

Miss Milner sat down, and was so for a minute; but her dead silence was nearly as alarming to Sandford as her rage had been; and he did not perfectly recover himself till he saw a flood of tears pouring down her face; he then heaved a sigh of content that it had so ended, but in his heart resolved never to forget the ridiculous affright into which he had been put.— He stole out of the room without uttering a syllable—But as he never retired to rest before he had repeated a long form of evening prayers, so when he came to that part which supplicates 'Grace for the wicked,' he named Miss Milner's name, with the most fervent devotion.

CHAPTER V

Of the many restless nights Miss Milner passed, this was not one; it is true she had a weight of care upon her heart, even heavier than usual, but its burthen had overcome her strength;

and wearied out with hopes, with fears, and at the end with disappointment and rage, she sunk into a profound slumber as soon as she was laid down—but the more forgetfulness had prevailed, the greater was the force of remembrance when she awoke—At first, so sound had her sleep been, she had a difficulty in calling to mind why she was unhappy; but that she was unhappy, she well recollected—and when the cause came to her memory, she would have slept again, but that was impossible.

Though her rest had been sound, it had not been refreshing; she was far from well, and sent word so as an apology for not being present at breakfast. Lord Elmwood looked concerned when the message was delivered; Mr. Sandford shook his head.

'Miss Milner's health is not good,' said Mrs. Horton a few minutes after.

Lord Elmwood laid down the newspaper to attend to her.

'To me there is something very extraordinary about her,' continued Mrs. Horton, finding she had caught his lordship's attention.

'So there is to me,' added Sandford, with a sarcastic sneer.

'And so there is to me,' said Miss Woodley, with a most serious face, and heartfelt sigh.

Lord Elmwood gazed by turns at each, as each delivered their sentiments—and when they were all silent, he looked bewildered, not knowing what judgment to form from any of these sentences.

Soon after breakfast, Mr. Sandford withdrew to his own apartment; Mrs. Horton in a little time went to her's, and Lord Elmwood and Miss Woodley were left alone.—His lordship immediately rose from his seat, and said,

'I think, Miss Woodley, Miss Milner was extremely to blame, though I did not choose to tell her so before Mr.

Sandford, in giving my lord Frederick an opportunity of speaking to her; unless she means he shall renew his addresses.'

'That, I am sure, my lord,' replied Miss Woodley, 'she does not mean—and I assure you, my lord, seriously, it was by mere accident she saw him yesterday evening; or permitted him to attend her to her carriage.'

'I am glad to hear it;' he returned quickly; 'for although I am not of a suspicious nature, yet in regard to her affection for him, I cannot but have my doubts.'

'You need have none, my lord,' replied Miss Woodley, with a smile of confidence.

'And yet you must own her behaviour has warranted them—has it not been in this particular incoherent, undefinable, unaccountable!'

'The behaviour of a person in love, no doubt,' said Miss Woodley.

'Don't I say so?' replied he warmly, 'And is not that a just reason for my suspicions?'

'But is there only one man in the world on whom these suspicions should fix?' said Miss Woodley with the colour mounting into her face.

'Not that I know of—not one more that I know of,' returned he, with astonishment at what she had insinuated, and yet with a perfect assurance she was in the wrong.

'Perhaps I am mistaken,' replied she.

'Nay, that is impossible too—' returned he with anxiety, 'You share her confidence; you are perpetually with her; and provided she did not confide in you, you must know, must be acquainted with her inclinations.'

'I believe I am *perfectly* acquainted with them,' replied Miss Woodley, with a significance in her voice and manner which convinced him there was some secret to learn.

After a hesitation;

'It is far from me,' replied he, 'to wish to be entrusted with the private sentiments of those who desire to withhold them from me, much less would I take any unfair means of being informed of them—to ask any more from you, I believe, would be unfair—yet I cannot but lament, that I am not as well informed as you are.—I wish to prove my friendship to Miss Milner, but she will not suffer me—and every step I take for her happiness, I take in the most perplexing uncertainty.'

Miss Woodley sighed, but did not speak.—He seemed to wait for her reply, but as she made none, he proceeded.

'If ever a breach of confidence could be tolerated, I certainly know no occasion that would so justly authorise such a measure as the present.—I am not only proper from my character, but from my circumstances to be relied upon—my interest is so nearly connected with the interest, and my happiness with the happiness of my ward, that those principles as well as my honour, would protect her from every peril arising from my being trusted.'

'Oh! my lord,' cried Miss Woodley, with a most forcible accent, '*you* are the last person on earth, she would pardon me for intrusting.'

'Why so?' (said he warmly,) 'But that is the way—the person who is our friend we misdoubt—where a common interest is concerned, we are ashamed of drawing on a common danger—Afraid of advice, though that advice is to save us.——Miss Woodley,' said he, (changing his voice with excess of earnestness) 'do you believe that I would do any thing to make Miss Milner happy?'

'Any thing in honour, my lord.'

'She can desire nothing farther.'—He replied in agitation—'Are her desires so unwarrantable I cannot grant them?'

Miss Woodley again did not speak—and he continued.

'Great as my friendship is, there are certainly bounds to it;

bounds, that shall save her in spite of herself.'—And he raised his voice.

'In the disposal of themselves,' resumed he, with a less vehement tone, 'that great, that terrific disposal in marriage, (at which I have ever looked with affright and dismay) there is no accounting for the rashness of a woman's choice, or sometimes for the depravity of her taste.—But in such a case, Miss Milner's election of a husband shall not direct mine—if she does not know her own value, I do.—Independent of her fortune, she has beauty to captivate the heart of any man; and with all her follies, she has a frankness in her manner, an unaffected wisdom in her thoughts, a vivacity in her conversation, and withal, a softness in her demeanour, that might alone engage the affections of a man of the nicest sentiments, and the strongest understanding.—I will not see all these qualities and accomplishments debased.—It is my office to protect her from the consequences of a degraded choice, and I will.'

'My lord, Miss Milner's taste is not a depraved one; it is but too much refined.'

'What do you mean by that, Miss Woodley? you talk mysteriously.—Is she not afraid I will thwart her inclinations?'

'She is sure you will, my lord.'

'Then must not the person be unworthy of her?'

Miss Woodley rose from her seat, the tears trinkled[1] down her cheeks, she clasped her hands, and every look, every gesture proved her alternate resolution, and irresolution of proceeding farther.—Lord Elmwood's attention was arrested before, but now it was fixed to a degree, which her manner could only occasion.

'My lord,' said she, with a tremulous voice, 'promise me, declare to me, swear to me, it shall ever remain a secret in your own breast, and I will reveal to you, on whom she has placed her affections.'

This solemn preparation made Lord Elmwood tremble; and he ran over instantly in his mind all the persons he could recollect, in order to arrive at the knowledge by thought, quicker than by words.—It was in vain he tried, and he once more turned his enquiring eyes upon Miss Woodley.—He saw her silent and covered with confusion.—Again he searched his own thoughts, nor ineffectually as before.—At the first glance the object was presented, and he beheld *himself*.

The rapid emotion of varying passions, which immediately darted over his features, informed Miss Woodley her secret was discovered—she hid her face, while the tears that fell down to her bosom, confirmed him in the truth of his suggestion beyond what oaths could have done.—A short interval of silence followed, during which she suffered tortures for the manner in which he would next speak to her—two seconds gave her this reply.

'For God's sake take care what you are doing—you are destroying my prospects of futurity—you are making this world too dear to me.'

Her drooping head was then lifted up, and as she caught the eye of Dorriforth, she saw it beam expectation, amaze, joy, ardour, love.——Nay, there was a fire, a vehemence in the quick fascinating rays it sent forth, she never before had seen —it filled her with alarm—she wished him to love Miss Milner but to love her with moderation.—Miss Woodley was too little versed in the subject to know, that, had been, not to love at all;[1] at least not to the extent of breaking through engagements, and all the various obstacles, that still militated against their union.

Lord Elmwood was sensible of the embarrassment his presence gave Miss Woodley, and understood the reproaches

which she seemed to vent upon herself in silence.—To relieve
her from both, he laid his hand with force upon his heart, and
said, 'Do you believe me?'

'I do, my lord,' she answered, trembling.

'I will make no unjust use of what I know,' returned he,
with firmness.

'I believe you, my lord.'

'But for what my passions now dictate,' continued he, 'I
will not answer.—They are confused—they are triumphant
at present.—I have never yet, however, been vanquished by
them; and even upon this occasion, my reason shall combat
to the last—that, shall fail me, before I do wrong.'

He was going to leave the room—she followed him, and
cried—'But my lord how shall I see again the unhappy object
of my treachery?'

'See her,' replied he, 'as one to whom you meant no injury,
and to whom you have done none.'

'But she would account it such, my lord.'

'We are not judges of what belongs to ourselves;'—he
replied,—'I am transported at the tidings you have revealed,
and yet, perhaps, I had better never have heard them.'

Miss Woodley was going to say something farther, but as
if incapable of attending to her, he hasted out of the room.

CHAPTER VI

MISS WOODLEY stood for some time to consider which way
she was to go.—The first person she met would enquire, why
she had been weeping to that excess her eyes were scarce dis-
cernible? and if Miss Milner was to ask the question, in what
words could she tell, or in what manner deny the truth?—To

avoid her, was her first caution, and she took the only method; she had a hackney-coach ordered, rode several miles out of town, and returned to dinner with so little remains of her swoln eyes, that complaining of the head-ache was a sufficient excuse for them.

Miss Milner was enough recovered to be present at dinner, though she scarce tasted a morsel. Lord Elmwood did not dine at home, at which Miss Woodley rejoiced, but at which Mr. Sandford appeared highly disappointed.—He asked the servants, several times, what his lordship said when he went out? they replied, 'nothing more than that he should not be at home to dinner.'—'I can't imagine where he dines?' said Sandford. —'Bless me, Mr. Sandford, can't you guess?' (cried Mrs. Horton, who by this time was made acquainted with his intended marriage), 'he dines with Miss Fenton to be sure.'— 'No,' replied Sandford, 'he is not there; I came from thence just now, and they had not seen him all day.'—Poor Miss Milner, on this, put a mouthful into her mouth; for where we hope for nothing, we receive small indulgences with joy.

Notwithstanding the anxiety and trouble under which Miss Woodley had laboured all the morning, her heart for many weeks had not felt so light as it did this day at dinner—The confidence she reposed in the promises of Lord Elmwood— the firm reliance she had upon his delicacy and his justice— the unabated kindness with which her friend received her, while no one suspicious thought, she knew, had taken harbour in her bosom—and the conscious integrity of her own intentions, however she might be misled by her judgment, all conspired to comfort her with the hope, she had done nothing she ought to wish recalled.—But although she felt thus tranquil, in respect to what she had divulged, yet she felt a great deal embarrassed with the dread of next seeing Lord Elmwood.

Miss Milner, not having spirits to go abroad, passed the

evening at home—she read part of a new opera, played upon her guitar, mused, sighed, occasionally talked with Miss Woodley, and so passed the tedious hours till near ten, when Mrs. Horton asked Mr. Sandford to play a game at piquet, and on his excusing himself, Miss Milner offered in his stead, and was gladly accepted.—They had just begun to play when Lord Elmwood came into the room—Miss Milner's countenance immediately brightened, and although she was in a negligent morning dress, and looked paler than usual, she did not look less beautiful—Miss Woodley was leaning on the back of her chair to observe the game, and Mr. Sandford sat reading one of the Greek Fathers at the other side of the fire place. Lord Elmwood as he advanced to the table bowed, not having seen the ladies since morning, or Miss Milner that day; they returned his salute, and he was going up to Miss Milner, (seemingly to enquire of her health,) when Mr. Sandford, laying down his book, said,

'My lord, where have you been all day?'

'I have been very busy,' replied his lordship, and walking from the card-table went up to him.

Miss Milner began to make mistakes, and play one card for another.

'You have been at Mr. Fenton's this evening, I suppose?' said Sandford.

'No, not at all to-day,' replied his lordship.

'How came that about, my lord?' cried Sandford.

Miss Milner played the ace of diamonds, instead of the king of hearts.

'I shall call to-morrow,' answered his lordship, and going with a very ceremonious air up to Miss Milner, said, 'He hoped she was perfectly recovered.'

Mrs. Horton begged her 'To mind what she was about.'

She replied, 'I am much better, sir.'

He then returned to Sandford again: but never, during all this time, did his eye once encounter Miss Woodley's, and she, with equal care, avoided his.

Some cold dishes were now brought up for supper—Miss Milner lost deal, and the game ended.

As they were arranging themselves at the supper-table, 'Do, Miss Milner,' said Mrs. Horton, 'have something warm for your supper? a chicken boiled? or something of that kind? you have eat nothing all day.'

With the feeling of humanity, and apparently no other sensation—but never did he feel philanthropy so forcibly—Lord Elmwood said, 'Let me beg of you, Miss Milner, to have something provided for you.'

The earnestness and emphasis with which these few words were pronounced, were more flattering than the finest turned compliment had been; her gratitude was expressed by blushes, and by assuring his lordship she was now 'so well as to be able to sup on what was before her.'—She spoke, however, and had not made the trial; for the moment she carried a piece to her lips, she laid it on her plate again, and turned paler, from the vain endeavour to force her appetite. Lord Elmwood had ever been attentive to her, but now he watched her as he would a child; and when he saw by her struggles she could not eat, he took her plate from her; gave her something else; and all with a care and watchfulness in his looks, as if he had been a tender-hearted boy, and she his darling bird, the loss of which, would embitter all the joy of his holidays.

This attention had something about it so tender, so officious,[1] and yet so sincere, that it brought the tears into Miss Woodley's eyes, attracted the notice of Mr. Sandford, and the observation of Mrs. Horton, while the heart of Miss Milner overflowed with a gratitude that gave place to no sentiment, except her love.

To relieve that anxiety her guardian expressed, she endeavoured to appear cheerful, and that anxiety, at length, really made her so.—He now pressed her to take one glass of wine with such solicitude, he seemed to say a thousand things beside—Sandford still made his observations, and being unused to conceal his thoughts before the present company, he said, bluntly,

'Miss Fenton was indisposed the other night, my lord, and yet you did not seem half so anxious about her health.'

Had Sandford laid all Lord Elmwood's estate at Miss Milner's feet, or presented her with that eternal bloom which adorns the face of a goddess, he would have done less to endear himself to her, than by that single sentence—she looked at him with the most benign countenance, and felt affliction that she had ever offended him.

'Miss Fenton,' (Lord Elmwood replied) 'has a brother with her; her health and happiness are in his care, Miss Milner's are in mine.'

'Mr. Sandford,' said Miss Milner, 'I am afraid I behaved very uncivilly to you last night; will you accept of an atonement?'

'No, madam,' returned he, 'I accept no expiation without amendment.'

'Well then,' said she, smiling, 'suppose I promise never to offend you again, what then?'

'Why then, you'll break your promise,' returned he, churlishly.

'Do not promise,' said Lord Elmwood, 'for he means to provoke you to it.'

In the like conversation the evening was passed, and Miss Milner retired to rest in far better spirits than the morning's prospect had given her to hope for. Miss Woodley too, had cause to be well pleased, but her pleasure was in a great measure eclipsed by the reflection, 'there was such a person as Miss Fenton;' she could not but fear, that in doing Miss Milner a right, she had, perhaps, done that lady a wrong—she wished she had been equally acquainted with her heart, as she was with Miss Milner's, and she would then have acted without injustice to either; but Miss Fenton had of late shunned their society, and even in their company she was of a temper too reserved to discover her mind; Miss Woodley was therefore obliged to act to the best of her judgment only, and leave all events to providence.

CHAPTER VII

WITHIN a few days, in the house of Lord Elmwood, every thing, and every person wore a new face.—His lordship was the profest lover of Miss Milner—she, the happiest of human beings—Miss Woodley partaking in her joy—while Mr. Sandford was lamenting with the deepest concern, that Miss Fenton had been supplanted; and what added most poignantly to his sorrow was, that she had been supplanted by Miss Milner.—Though a church man, he bore his disappointment with the impatience of one of the laity; he could hardly speak to Lord Elmwood; he would not look at Miss Milner, and was displeased with every body.—It was his intention when he first became acquainted with Lord Elmwood's resolution, to quit his house; and as his lordship had, with the utmost degree of inflexibility, resisted all his good counsel and advice upon this subject, he resolved, in quitting him, never to be his adviser or counsellor again.—But, in preparing to leave his friend, his pupil, his patron, and yet him, who, upon most occasions, implicitly obeyed his will, the spiritual got the better of the temporal man, and he determined to stay, lest in totally abandoning him to the pursuit of his own passions, he might make his punishment even greater than his offence.— 'My lord,' said he, 'on the stormy sea, upon which you are embarked, though you will not shun the rocks your faithful pilot would point out, he will, nevertheless, sail in your company, and lament over your watery grave. The more you slight my advice, the more you want it, and till you command me to leave your house, (as I suppose you will soon do, to oblige your lady) I will continue along with you.'

Lord Elmwood liked him sincerely, and was glad he took this resolution; yet as soon as his lordship's reason and affections had once told him, he ought to break with Miss Fenton, and marry his ward, he became so decidedly of that opinion, Sandford's never had the most trivial weight upon the subject, nor would he flatter the supposed authority he possessed over him, by urging him to remain in his house a single day, contrary to his inclinations. Sandford beheld, with grief, this firmness, but finding it vain to contend, submitted—not, however, with a good grace.

Amidst all the persons affected by this change in Lord Elmwood's marriage designs, Miss Fenton was, perhaps, the least—she would have been content to have married, she was contented to live single—Mr. Sandford was the first who made overtures to her on the part of Lord Elmwood, and the first sent to ask her to dispense with the obligation—She received both these proposals with the same insipid smile of approbation, and the same cold indifference at the heart.

It was a perfect knowledge of this disposition in his intended wife, which had given to Lord Elmwood's thoughts, on matrimony, the prospect of dreary winter; but the sensibility of Miss Milner had now reversed that prospect to perpetual spring; or the dearer variety of spring, summer, and autumn.

It was a knowledge also of this torpor in Miss Fenton's
nature, from which he formed the purpose of breaking with
her; for Lord Elmwood still retained enough of the priest's
sanctity, to have yielded up his own happiness, and even that
of his beloved ward, rather than have plunged one heart into
affliction by his perfidy. This, before he offered his hand to
Miss Milner, he was perfectly convinced would not be the
case—even Miss Fenton, herself, assured him, her thoughts
were more inclined towards the joys of Heaven than earth;
and as this circumstance would, she believed, induce her to
retire to a convent, she thought it a happy, rather than an
unhappy event.—Her brother, on whom her fortune devolved
if she took this resolution, was exactly of her opinion.

Lost in the maze of happiness which surrounded her, Miss
Milner oftentimes asked her heart, and her heart whispered
like a flatterer, 'Yes,' 'Are not my charms even more invincible
than I ever believed them to be? Dorriforth, the grave, the
sanctified, the anchorite[1] Dorriforth, by their force is animated
to all the ardour of the most impassioned lover—while the
proud priest, the austere guardian, is humbled, if I but frown,
into the veriest slave of love.'—She then asked, 'Why did I not
keep him longer in suspense? he could not have loved me
more, I believe; but my power over him might have been
greater still.—I am the happiest of women in that affection
he has proved to me, but I wonder whether it would exist
under ill treatment? if it would not, he still does not love me
as I wish to be loved—if it would, my triumph, my felicity,
would be enhanced.'—These thoughts were mere phantoms
of the brain, and never by system put into action; but repeatedly
indulged, they were practised by casual occurrences; and the
dear-bought experiment of being beloved in spite of her faults,
(a glory proud women ever aspire to) was, at present, the
ambition of Miss Milner.

Unthinking woman! she did not reflect, that to the searching eye of Lord Elmwood she had faults, with her every care to conceal or overcome them, sufficient to try all his love, and all his patience. But what female is not fond of experiments? to which, how few are there, that do not fall a sacrifice!

Perfectly secure of the affections of the man she loved, her declining health no longer threatened her; her declining spirits returned as before; and the suspicions of her guardian being now changed to the liberal confidence of a doating lover, she now again professed all her former follies, all her fashionable levities, and indulged them with less restraint than she had ever done.

For a while, blinded by his passion, Lord Elmwood encouraged and admired every new proof of her restored happiness; nor till sufferance had tempted her to proceed beyond her usual bounds, did he remonstrate.—But she, who as his ward, had been ever gentle, and (when he strenuously opposed) always obedient; he now found as a mistress, sometimes haughty; and to opposition, always insolent.—He was surprised, but the novelty pleased him.—And Miss Milner, whom he tenderly loved, could put on no change, or appear in any new character that did not, for the time she adopted it, seem to become her.

Among the many causes of complaint she gave him, want of œconomy in the disposal of her income was one.—Bills and drafts came upon him without number, while the account, on her part, of money expended, amounted but to articles of dress she sometimes never wore, toys that were out of fashion before they were paid for; and charities directed by the force of whim.—Another complaint was, as usual, extreme late hours, and often-times company he did not approve.

She was charmed to see his love struggling with his censure —his politeness with his anxiety—and by the light, frivolous, or resentful manner, in which she treated his admonitions, she triumphed in shewing to Miss Woodley, and, more especially to Mr. Sandford, how much she dared upon the strength of his affections.

Every thing in preparation for their marriage, which was to take place at Elmwood-House during the summer months, she resolved for the short time she had to remain in London, to let no occasion pass of tasting all those pleasures which were not likely ever to return; but which, eager as she was in their pursuit, she still placed in no kind of competition with those she hoped would succeed; those more sedate, and far greater joys she had in domestic contemplation—and often, merely to hasten on the tedious hours that intervened, she varied and diverted them with the many recreations her intended husband could not approve.

It so happened, and it was unfortunate it did, that a law-suit and some other intricate affairs that came with his title and estate, frequently kept Lord Elmwood from his house part of the day; sometimes the whole evening; and when at home, would often closet him for hours with his lawyers.— But while he was thus off his guard, Sandford never was— and had Miss Milner been the dearest thing on earth to him, he could not have watched her more narrowly; or had she been the frailest thing on earth, he could not have been more hard upon her, in all the accounts of her conduct he gave to Lord Elmwood.—His lordship knew Sandford's failing was to think ill of Miss Milner, he pitied him for it, and he pitied her for it—and in all the aggravation his representations gave to her real follies, affection for them both, in the heart of Dorriforth, stood between that and every other impression.

But facts are glaring; and he at length beheld those faults in their true colours, although previously pointed out by the prejudice of Mr. Sandford.

As soon as Sandford perceived his lordship's uneasiness, 'There, my lord!' cried he, exultingly, 'Did I not always say the marriage was an improper one?—but you would not be ruled—you would not see.'

'Can you blame me for not seeing,' replied his lordship, 'when you yourself were blind?—Had you been dispassionate, had you seen Miss Milner's virtues as well as her faults, I should have believed, and been guided by you—but you saw her failings only, and therein have been equally deceived with me, who have only beheld her perfections.'

'My observations, however, my lord, would have been of most use to you; for I have seen what to avoid.'

'But mine have been the most charitable,' replied his lordship, 'for I have seen—what I must always love.'

Sandford sighed, and lifted up his hands.

'Mr. Sandford,' resumed his lordship, with a voice and manner such as he puts on when not all the power of Sandford, or any other, can change his fixed determination, 'Mr. Sandford,' resumed he, 'my eyes are now open to every failing, as well as to every accomplishment; to every vice, as well as to every virtue of Miss Milner's; nor will I suffer myself to be again prepossessed in her favour by your prejudice against her—for I believe it was compassion at your unkind treatment of her, that first gained her my heart.'

'I, my lord?' cried Sandford, 'Do not load me with the burthen—with the mighty burthen of your love for her.'

'Do not interrupt me,' said his lordship; 'Whatever your meaning has been, the effect of your unkindness to her, is such as I say.—Now, I will no longer,' continued he, 'have an enemy such as you have been, to heighten her charms, which are too transcendent in their native state. I will hear no more complaints against her, but I will watch her closely myself— and if I find her mind and heart (such as my suspicions have of late whispered) too frivolous for that substantial happiness I look for with an object so beloved; depend upon my word— the marriage shall yet be broken off.'

'I depend upon your word; it *will* then,' replied Sandford, eagerly.

'You are unjust, sir, in saying so before the trial,' replied his lordship, 'and your injustice shall make me more cautious, lest I follow your example.'

'But, my lord——'

'My mind is made up, Mr. Sandford,' returned he, interrupting him, 'I am no longer engaged to Miss Milner than she shall deserve I should—but in my observations I will take care not to wrong her as you have done.'

'My lord, call my observations wrong, when you have reflected upon them as a man, and not as a lover—divest yourself of your passion, and meet me upon equal ground.'

'I will meet no one—I will consult no one—my own judgment shall be the judge, and in a few months, marry, or— *banish me from her for ever.*'

There was something in these last words, in the tone and firmness with which they were delivered, that the heart of Sandford rested upon with content—they bore the symptoms of a menace that would be executed; and he parted from his patron with congratulations upon his wisdom, and the warmest assurances of his firm reliance on his *word*.

Lord Elmwood having come to this resolution, was more composed than he had been for several days before; while the horror of domestic wrangles—a family without subordination—a house without œconomy—in a word, a wife without discretion, had been perpetually present to his mind.

Mr. Sandford, although he was a man of understanding, of learning, and a complete casuist; yet, all the faults he himself committed, were entirely—for want of knowing better.—He constantly reproved faults in others, and he was most assuredly too good a man not to have corrected and amended his own, had they been known to him—but they were not.—He had been for so long time the superior of all with whom he lived, had been so busied with instructing others, he had not recollected he himself wanted instructions—and in such awe did his severity keep all about him, that notwithstanding he had many friends, not one told him of his failings—(except just now Lord Elmwood, but who, in this instance, as a man in love, he would not credit)—Was there not then some reason for him to suppose he had no faults?—his enemies, indeed, hinted that he had, but enemies he never hearkened to; and thus, with all his good sense, wanted the sense to follow the rule, *Believe what your enemies say of you, rather than what is said by your friends*; this rule attended to, would make many a one amiable that is now the reverse, and had made him, a perfect upright character.—For could an enemy, to whom he would have listened, have whispered to Sandford as he left Lord Elmwood's study, 'Cruel, barbarous man! you go away with your heart satisfied, nay, even elated in the prospect, that Miss Milner's hopes, on which she alone exists; those hopes which keep her from the deepest affliction, and cherish her with joy and gladness, will all be disappointed—you flatter yourself it is for the sake of your friend Lord Elmwood you rejoice; because he has escaped a danger—you wish him well, but there is another cause for your exultation which you will not seek to know—it is, that in his safety shall dwell the punishment of his ward.—For shame! for shame! forgive her faults, as this of your's needs forgiveness.'

Had any one said this, to Sandford, whom he would have credited; or had his own heart suggested it, he was a man of that rectitude and conscientiousness, he would have returned immediately to Lord Elmwood, and have endeavoured to

strengthen all his favourable opinions of his intended wife—
but having no such monitor as this, he walked on, highly contented, and meeting Miss Woodley, said, with an air of
triumph,

'Where's your young lady?—where's Lady Elmwood?'

Miss Woodley smiled, and answered—she was gone with
such and such ladies to an auction.—'But why give her that
title already, Mr. Sandford?'

'Because,' answered he, 'I think she will never have it.'

'Bless me, Mr. Sandford!' said Miss Woodley, 'you shock
me!'

'I thought I should,' replied he, 'and that is why I tell it
you.'

'For Heaven's sake, what has happened?' cried she.

'Nothing new—her indiscretions only.'

'I know she is imprudent,' said Miss Woodley; 'I can see
she is often to blame—but then my lord surely loves her, and
love will overlook a great deal.'

'He does love her—but he has understanding and resolution.—He loved his sister too, tenderly loved her, and yet
when he had taken the resolution; passed his word he would
never see her again; even upon her death-bed he would not
retract it—no entreaties could prevail upon him.—And now,
though he maintains, and I dare say loves her child, yet you
remember when you brought him home he would not bear
him in his sight.'

'Poor Miss Milner!'—said Miss Woodley in the most pitying accents.

'Nay,' said Sandford, 'Lord Elmwood has not yet passed
his word, that he will never see her more—he has only
threatened to say so—but I know enough of him to know, his
threats are generally the same as the actions done.'

'You are very good,' said Miss Woodley, 'to acquaint me

of this in time: I may now warn Miss Milner of it, and she
may behave with more circumspection.'

'By no means,'—cried Sandford, hastily, 'What would you
warn her for?—it will do her no good—besides,' added he,
'I don't know whether his lordship does not expect secresy
from me on this subject, and if he does——'

'But, with all deference to your opinion,' said Miss Woodley, (and with all deference did she speak) 'don't you think,
Mr. Sandford, that secresy upon this occasion would be
wicked? for consider the anguish it may cause my friend, and
if by advising her we can save her from——' She was going on.

'You may call it wicked, madam, not to inform her of it,'
cried he, 'but I call a breach of promise (if I did give my
promise, which I don't say I did) much more sinful.'

'I suppose you are right; sir,' said Miss Woodley, with
humility; 'but if you have given *your* promise, I have not
given mine, and therefore may divulge——'

'There now!' cried Sandford, 'there is how you judge of
this matter.—You judge of things as they are in reality, not
what they are by construction; the only way to judge of any
thing.—If I did make a promise to Lord Elmwood—(which,
I again say, I don't know that I did)—the promise was, that I
would not communicate the secret; meaning, not tell it to
Miss Milner herself.—I have not; and therefore have kept my
word—and in revealing it to you, I did it with a full persuasion
you would conceal it; which confidence, on my part, binds you
as much as the most solemn promise you could have given.'

'The fault will be mine, then, not yours, if it comes to the
knowledge of Miss Milner?'

'Certainly.'

'Then, as it will be my fault, do not you, sir, be uneasy
about it.'—

He was going to explain again, but Miss Milner entered,

and put an end to the discourse.—She had been passing the whole morning at an auction, and had laid out near two hundred pounds in different things she had no one use for; but bought them because they were said to be cheap.— Among the rest was a lot of books on chemistry, and some Latin authors.

'Why, madam,' cried Sandford, looking over the cata- logue, where her purchases were marked by a pencil, 'do you know what you have done? you can't read a word of these books.'

'Can't I, Mr. Sandford? but I assure you, you will be vastly pleased with them when you see how elegantly they are bound.'

'My dear,' said Mrs. Horton, 'why have you bought china? you and Lord Elmwood have more now, than you have places to put them in.'

'Very true, Mrs. Horton—I forgot that—but then you know I can give these away.'

Lord Elmwood was in the room at the conclusion of this conversation———he shook his head and sighed.

'My lord,' said she, 'I have had a very pleasant morning, but I wished for you—if you had been with me I should have bought a great many other things; but I did not like to appear unreasonable in your absence.'

Sandford fixed his inquisitive eyes upon Lord Elmwood, to observe his countenance—his lordship smiled, but ap- peared thoughtful.

'And, oh! my lord, I have bought you a present,' said she.

'I do not wish for a present, Miss Milner.'

'What, not from me?—very well.'

'If you present me with yourself, madam, it is all I ask.'

Sandford moved upon his chair as if he sat uneasy.

'Why then, Miss Woodley,' said Miss Milner, '*you* shall

have the present.—But then it won't suit you—it is for a gentleman.—I'll keep it and give it to my lord Frederick the first time I meet with him.—I saw him this morning, and he looked divinely; I longed to speak to him.'

Miss Woodley cast, by stealth, an eye of apprehension upon Lord Elmwood's face, and trembled to behold it red as scarlet.

Sandford stared with both his eyes full upon him; then drew himself upright on his chair, and took a pinch of snuff upon the strength of his uneasiness.

A silence ensued.

After a short time—'You all appear very melancholy,' said Miss Milner; 'I wish I had not come home yet.'

Miss Woodley was in agony—she saw Lord Elmwood's extreme displeasure, and dreaded lest he should express it by some words he could not recall, or she could not forgive— therefore, whispering to her she had something particular to say to her, she took her out of the room.

The moment she was gone, Mr. Sandford rose nimbly from his seat, rubbed his hands, walked briskly across the room, then asked his lordship, in a cheerful tone, 'Whether he dined at home to-day?'

That which had given Sandford spirits to speak with cheerfulness, had depressed Lord Elmwood's so much, that he sat silent and dejected.—At length he answered, in a faint voice, 'No, I believe I shall *not* dine at home.'

'Where is your lordship going to dine?' asked Mrs. Horton; 'I thought we should have had your company to-day; Miss Milner dines at home, I believe.'

'I have not yet determined where I shall dine,' replied he, taking no notice of the conclusion of her speech.

'My lord, if you mean to go to the hotel, I'll go with you, if you please,' cried Sandford, officiously.

'With all my heart, Sandford,' replied his lordship; and they both went out together before Miss Milner returned to the apartment.

CHAPTER VIII

MISS WOODLEY, for the first time, disobeyed the will of Mr. Sandford; and as soon as Miss Milner and she were alone, informed her of all he had revealed to her; accompanying the recital with every testimony of sympathy and affection.—But had the genius of Sandford presided over this discovery, it could not have influenced the mind of Miss Milner to receive the intelligence, more exactly opposite to the intention of the informer. Instead of shuddering with fear at the menace Lord Elmwood had uttered, she boldly said, she 'Dared him to perform it.' 'He durst not,' repeated she.

'Why durst not?' said Miss Woodley.

'Because he loves me too well—because his own happiness is too dear to him.'

'I believe he loves you,' replied Miss Woodley, 'and yet there is a doubt if——'

'There shall be no longer a doubt,'—cried Miss Milner, 'I'll put him to the proof.'

'For shame, my dear! you talk inconsiderately—what do you mean by proof?'

'I mean, I will do something that any prudent man ought *not* to forgive; and yet, with that vast share of prudence he possesses, I will force him still to yield to his love.'

'But suppose you should be disappointed, and he should not yield?' said Miss Woodley.

'Then, I have only lost a man who had no regard for me.'

'He may have a great regard for you, notwithstanding.'

'But for the love I have, and do still bear my lord Elmwood, I will have something more than a *great regard* in return.'

'You have his love, I am sure.'

'But is it such as mine?—*I* could love *him* if he had a thousand faults.—And yet,' said she, recollecting herself, 'and yet, I believe, his being faultless, was the first cause of my passion.'

Thus she talked on—sometimes in anger, sometimes apparently jesting—till her servant came to tell her dinner was served.—Upon entering the dining-room, and seeing his lordship's place at table vacant, she started back. She was disappointed of the pleasure she expected in dining with him; and his sudden absence so immediately after the intelligence she had received from Miss Woodley, encreased her uneasiness.—She drew her chair, and sat down with an indifference, that said she should not eat; and as soon as she was seated, she put her fingers sullenly to her lips, nor touched her knife and fork, or spoke a word in reply to any thing that was said to her during the whole dinner.—Miss Woodley and Mrs. Horton were both too well acquainted with the good disposition of her heart, to take offence, or any notice of this behaviour.—They dined, and wisely said nothing either to provoke or sooth her. Just as the dinner was going to be removed, a loud rap came at the door—'Who is that?' said Mrs. Horton.—One of the servants went to the window, and answered, 'My lord and Mr. Sandford, madam.'—'Come back to dinner, as I live,' cried Mrs. Horton.—

Miss Milner still continued her position and said nothing—but at the corners of her mouth, which her fingers did not entirely cover, there were discoverable a thousand dimpled graces like small convulsive fibres, which a restrained smile on Lord Elmwood's return, had sent there.

His lordship and Sandford entered.

'I am glad you are returned, my lord,' said Mrs. Horton, 'for Miss Milner would not eat a morsel.'

'It was because I had no appetite,' returned she, blushing like crimson.

'We should not have come back,' said Sandford, 'but at the place where we went to dine, all the rooms were filled with smoke.'

'It has been a very windy day indeed,' said Mrs. Horton, 'and one part of this house, is now in a smother.'

Lord Elmwood put the wing of a fowl on Miss Milner's plate, but without previously asking if she chose any; yet she condescended to eat—they spoke to each other too in the course of conversation, yet it was with a reserve that appeared as if they had been quarrelling, and so felt to themselves, though no such circumstance had happened.

About two weeks passed away in this kind of distant behaviour on both sides; without either venturing a direct quarrel, and without either expressing (except inadvertently) their strong affection for each other.

During this time they were once, however, nearly becoming the dearest friends in expressions, as well as in sentiments.— This arose from a favour he granted in compliance to what he knew was her earnest desire; and, as a favour which he had refused to the repeated requests of many friends, she could not but esteem the high value of the obligation.

She and Miss Woodley had taken an airing to see the poor child, young Rushbrook; and on their return, his lordship inquiring of the ladies how they had passed their morning, Miss Milner frankly told him; and added, 'What pain it gave her to leave the child behind, as he still cried to come away with her.'

'Go for him then to-morrow,' said his lordship, 'and bring him home.'

'Home!' she repeated, with surprise.

'Yes,' replied he, 'if you desire it, this shall be his home—you shall be a mother, and I will, henceforward, be a father to him.'

Sandford, who was present, looked unusually sour at this high token of his lordship's regard to Miss Milner; yet, with resentment on his face, he wiped a tear of joy from his eye, for the boy's sake—his frown was the force of prejudice, his tear the force of nature.

Rushbrook was brought home; and whenever Lord Elmwood wished to shew a kindness to Miss Milner, without directing it immediately to her, he took his nephew upon his knee, talked to him, and told him, he 'Was glad they had become acquainted.'

In the various, though delicate, struggles for power between Miss Milner and her guardian, there was not one person witness to these incidents, who did not suppose, all would at last end in wedlock—for the most common observer perceived, ardent love was the foundation of every discontent, as well as of every joy they experienced.—One great incident, however, totally reversed the prospect of all future accommodation.

The fashionable Mrs. G—— gave a masked ball; tickets were presented to persons of the first quality, and among the rest, three were sent to Miss Milner.—She had never been at a masquerade,[1] and received them with ecstasy—more especially as the masque being at the house of a woman of fashion, she did not conceive there could be any objection to her going. —She was mistaken—the moment she mentioned it to Lord Elmwood, he desired her, somewhat sternly, 'Not to think of being there.'—She was vext at the prohibition, but more at the manner in which it was delivered, and flatly said, 'She should certainly go.'

She expected a severe rebuke for this, but what alarmed her much more, he never replied a word; but looked with a resignation which foreboded her more sorrow, than the severest reproaches would have done.—She sat for a minute reflecting how to rouse him from this composure—she first thought of attacking him with upbraidings; then she thought of soothing him; and at last of laughing at him.—This was the least supportable of all, and yet this she ventured upon.

'I am sure your lordship,' said she, 'with all your saintliness, can have no objection to my being present at the masquerade, provided I go as a Nun.'

He made no reply.

'That is a habit,' continued she, 'which covers a multitude of faults—and, for that evening, I may have the chance of making a conquest even of you, my lord—nay, I question not, if under that inviting attire, even the pious Mr. Sandford would not ogle me.'

'Hush,'—said Miss Woodley.

'Why hush?' cried Miss Milner, aloud, though Miss Woodley had spoken in a whisper, 'I am sure,' continued she, 'I am only repeating what I have read in books about nuns, and their confessors.'[1]

'Your conduct, Miss Milner,' replied Lord Elmwood, 'gives evident proofs what authors you have read; you may spare yourself the trouble of quoting them.'

Her pride was hurt at this, beyond bearing; and as she could not, like him, govern her anger, it flushed in her face, and almost forced the tears.

'My lord,' said Miss Woodley, (in a voice so soft and peaceful, it ought to have calmed the resentment of both,) 'my lord, suppose you were to accompany Miss Milner? there are tickets for three, and you can then have no objection.'

Miss Milner's brow was immediately smoothed; her eye

beamed hope; and she fetched a sigh in anxious expectation he would consent.

'I go, Miss Woodley?' he replied, with astonishment, 'Do you imagine I would play the buffoon at a masquerade?'

Miss Milner's face changed to its former state.

'I have seen many grave characters there, my lord,' said Miss Woodley.

'Dear Miss Woodley,' cried Miss Milner, 'why persuade Lord Elmwood to put on a mask, just at the time he has laid it aside?'

His patience seemed now to be tempted to its height, and he answered, 'If you suspect it, madam, you shall find me changed.'

Pleased, she had been able at last to irritate him, she smiled with a degree of triumph, and in that humour was going to reply; but before she could speak four words, and before she thought of it, he abruptly left the room.

She was highly offended at this insult, and declared, 'From that moment she banished him her heart for ever.' And to prove she set both his love and anger at defiance, she immediately ordered her chariot, and said, she 'was going to some of her acquaintance, whom she knew to have tickets, and with whom she would fix upon the dress she meant to appear in at the masquerade; for nothing, unless she was locked up, should alter the resolution she had taken, of being there.' To remonstrate at that moment, Miss Woodley knew would be in vain; the chariot came to the door, and she drove away.

She did not return to dinner, nor till late in the evening; Lord Elmwood was at home, but never once mentioned her name.

She came home, after he had retired to bed, and in great spirits; the first time she ever appeared careless what he might think of her behaviour:—but her whole thoughts were occupied upon the business she had been about, and her dress engrossed all her conversation as soon as Miss Woodley and she were alone.—She told Miss Woodley, she had been shewn the greatest variety of beautiful and becoming dresses she had ever beheld, and yet, said she, 'I have fixed upon a very plain one; but one I look so well in, you will hardly know me when I have it on.'

'You are seriously then resolved to go,' said Miss Woodley, 'provided you hear no more on the subject from your guardian?'

'Whether I do or not, Miss Woodley, I am equally resolved to go.'

'But you know, my dear, he has desired you not—and you used always to obey his commands.'

'As my guardian, I certainly did obey him; and I could obey him as a husband; but as a lover, I will not.'

'Yet that is the means, never to have him for a husband.'

'As he pleases—for if he will not submit to be my lover, I will not submit to be his wife—nor has he the affection I require in a husband.'

Thus, the old sentiments were repeated as heretofore, and prevented a separation till towards morning.

Miss Milner, for that night, dreamt less of her guardian than of the masquerade. On the evening of the next day it was to be; she was up early, breakfasted in her dressing-room, and remained there most of the day, busied in all the thousand preparations for the night; one of which, was to take every particle of powder out of her hair, and have it curled all over in falling ringlets.—Her next care was, that her dress should exactly fit, and display her fine person to the best advantage—it did so.—Miss Woodley entered as it was trying on, and was struck with astonishment at the elegance of the habit, and the beautiful effect it had upon her graceful person; but most of all,

she was astonished at her venturing on such a character—for
although it was the representative of the goddess of Chastity,
yet from the buskins,[1] and the petticoat made to festoon far
above the ankle, it had, on the first glance, the appearance of
a female much less virtuous.—Miss Woodley admired the
dress, yet objected to it; but as she admired first, her objections after had no weight.

'Where is Lord Elmwood?' said Miss Milner, 'he must not
see me.'

'No, for heaven's sake,' cried Miss Woodley, 'I would not
have him see you for the universe.'

'And yet,' returned the other, with a sigh, 'Why am I then
thus pleased with this dress? for I had rather he should admire
me than all the world beside, and yet he is not to see me in it.'

'But he would not admire you thus,' said Miss Woodley.

'How shall I contrive to avoid him,' said Miss Milner, 'if
he should offer to hand me into my carriage?—but I believe
he will not be in good humour enough for that.'

'You had better dress at the ladies' house with whom you
go,' said Miss Woodley; and this was agreed upon.

At dinner they learnt, his lordship was to go that evening
to Windsor, in order to be in readiness for the king's hunt,
early in the morning; and this intelligence having dispersed
Miss Milner's fears, she concluded to dress at home.

Lord Elmwood appeared at dinner in an even, but not in a
good-temper—the subject of the masquerade was never
brought up, or indeed was once in his thoughts; for though
he was offended at his ward's behaviour on the occasion, and
thought she committed a fault in telling him, 'She would go,'
yet he never suspected she meant to do so, not even at the time
she said it, much less that she would persist, coolly and
deliberately in so direct a contradiction to his will.—She, for
her part, flattered herself his going to Windsor, was intended

in order to give her an opportunity of passing the evening as she pleased, without his being obliged to know of it, and consequently to complain.—Miss Woodley, who was willing to hope as she wished, began to be of the same opinion; and, without reluctance, drest herself as a wood-nymph, to accompany her friend.

CHAPTER IX

AT half after eleven, Miss Milner's chair,[1] and another with Miss Woodley, took them from Lord Elmwood's house to call upon the party (a group of wood-nymphs and huntresses) which were to acompany them, and make up the suit of Diana.

They had not left the house two minutes, when a thundering rap came at the door—it was Lord Elmwood in a post chaise.—Upon some occasion the next day's hunt was put off: he had been made acquainted with it, and came from Windsor at that late hour.—After his lordship had told Mrs. Horton and Mr. Sandford, who were sitting together, the cause of his sudden return, and some supper was ordered for him, he inquired, 'What company had just left the house?'

'We have been alone the whole evening, my lord,' replied Mrs. Horton.

'Nay,' returned he, 'I saw two chairs, with several servants, come out of the door as I drove up; but what livery I could not discern.'

'We have had no creature here,' repeated Mrs. Horton.

'Nor has Miss Milner?' asked he.

This brought Mrs. Horton to her recollection, and she cried, 'Oh! now I know.'——And then checked herself, as if she knew too much.

'What do you know, madam?' said his lordship, sharply.

'Nothing'—said Mrs. Horton, 'I know nothing.' And she lifted up her hands and shook her head.

'So all people say, who know a great deal,' cried Sandford, 'and I suspect, that is at present your case.'

'Then I know more than I wish to know, I am sure, Mr. Sandford,' returned she, shrugging up her shoulders.

Lord Elmwood was all impatience. 'Explain, madam, explain,' cried he.

'Dear my lord,' said she, 'if your lordship will recollect, you may just have the same knowledge that I have.'

'Recollect what?' said he, sternly.

'The quarrel you and your ward had about the masquerade.'

'What of that? she is not gone there?' he cried.

'I am not sure she is,' returned Mrs. Horton, 'but if your lordship saw two sedan chairs going out of this house, I cannot but suspect it must be Miss Milner, and my niece going to the masquerade.'

His lordship made no answer, but rung the bell violently.— A servant entered.—'Send Miss Milner's woman hither,' said he, 'immediately.'—The man withdrew.

'Nay, my lord,' cried Mrs. Horton, 'any of the other servants could tell you just as well, whether Miss Milner is at home, or gone out.'

'Perhaps not,' replied he.

The maid entered.

'Where is your lady?' said he.

The woman had received no orders to conceal where her lady was gone, and yet some secret influence which governs the replies of all waiting women and chamber maids, whispered to her, she ought not to tell the truth.

'Where is your lady?' repeated Lord Elmwood, in a louder voice than before.

'Gone out, my lord,' she replied.

'Where?'

'My lady did not tell me.'

'And don't you know?'

'No, my lord,' she answered, and without blushing.

'Is this the night of the masquerade?' said he.

'I don't know, my lord, upon my word; but, I believe, my lord, it is not.'

Sandford, as soon as Lord Elmwood had asked the last question, run hastily to the table, at the other side of the room, snatched something from it, and returned to his place again—and as soon as the maid said, 'It was not the night of the masquerade,' he exclaimed, 'But it is, my lord, it is—yes, it is.' And showing a news-paper he held in his hand, pointed to the paragraph which contained the information.

'Leave the room,' said Lord Elmwood to the woman, 'I have done with you.'—She withdrew.

'Yes, yes, here it is,' repeated Sandford, with the paper in his hand.—He then read the paragraph: '*The masquerade at the honourable Mrs. G——'s this evening—*' 'This evening, my lord, you find:' '*it is expected will be the most brilliant, of any thing of the kind, for these many years past.*'

'They should not put such things in the papers,' said Mrs. Horton, 'to tempt young women to their ruin.' The word ruin, seemed to grate upon his lordship's ear, and he said to the servant who came to wait on him, while he supped, 'Take the supper away.'—He had not attempted to eat, or even to sit down; and he now walked backwards and forwards in the room, lost in thought and care.

A little time after, one of Miss Milner's footmen came in upon some occasion, and Mr. Sandford said to him, 'Pray did you attend your lady to the masquerade?'

'Yes, sir,' replied the man.

Lord Elmwood stopt himself short in his walk, and said to the servant, 'You did?'

'Yes, my lord,' replied he.

His lordship walked again.

'I should like to know what she was drest in,' said Mrs. Horton; and turning to the servant, 'Do you know what your lady had on?'

'Yes, madam,' replied the man, 'she was in men's cloaths.'

'How?' cried Lord Elmwood.

'You tell a story to be sure,' said Mrs. Horton to the servant.

'No,' cried Sandford, 'I am sure he does not; for he is an honest good young man, and would not tell a lie upon any account,—would you?'

Lord Elmwood ordered Miss Milner's woman to be again sent up.—She came.

'In what dress did your lady go to the masquerade?' asked his lordship, and with a look so extremely morose, it seemed to command her to answer in a word, and to answer truly.

A mind, with a spark of sensibility more than she possessed, could not have equivocated with such an interrogator, but her reply was, 'She went in her own dress, my lord.'

'Was it a man's, or a woman's dress?' asked his lordship with the same commanding look.

'Ha, ha, my lord,' (half laughing and half crying,) 'a woman's dress to be sure, my lord.'

On which Sandford cried,

'Call the footman up, and let him confront her.'

He was called; but Lord Elmwood, now disgusted with the scene, sat down at the farther end of the room, and left Sandford to question them.

With all the authority and consequence of a country magistrate, Sandford, with his back to the fire and the witnesses before him, began with the footman.

'In what dress do you say, you saw your lady, when you attended, and went along with her, to the masquerade?'

'In men's cloaths,' replied the man, boldly and firmly as before.

'Bless my soul, George, how can you say such a thing?' cried the woman.

'In what dress, do *you* say she went in?' cried Sandford to her.

'In women's cloaths, indeed, sir.'

'This is very odd!' said Mrs. Horton.

'Had she on, or had she not on, a coat?' asked Sandford.

'Yes, sir, a petticoat,' replied the woman.

'Do *you* say she had on a petticoat?' said Sandford to the man.

'I can't answer exactly for that,' replied he, 'but I know she had boots on.'

'They were not boots,' replied the maid, with vehemence, 'indeed, sir,' (turning to Sandford) 'they were only half boots.'

'My girl,' said Sandford, kindly to her, 'your own evidence convicts her.—What has a woman to do with *any* boots?'[1]

Impatient at this mummery, Lord Elmwood rose from his seat, and ordered the servants out of the room; and then looking at his watch, found it was near one. 'At what time am I to expect her at home?' said he.

'Perhaps not till three in the morning,' answered Mrs. Horton.

'Three! six, more likely,' cried Sandford.

'I can't wait with patience till that time,' answered his lordship with a most anxious sigh.

'You had better go to bed, my lord,' said Mrs. Horton, 'and by sleeping, the time will pass away unperceived.'

'If I *could* sleep, madam,' returned he.

'Will you play a game of cards, my lord?' said Sandford,

'for I will not leave you till she comes home; and though I am not used to sit up all night——'

'All night,' repeated his lordship, 'she durst not stay all night.'

'And yet, after going,' said Sandford, 'in defiance to your commands, I should suppose she dares?'

'She is in good company, at least, my lord,' said Mrs. Horton.

'She does not know herself, what company she is in,' replied his lordship.

'How should she?' cried Sandford, 'where every one hides his face.'

Till five o'clock in the morning, in such conversation as this, the hours passed away.—Mrs. Horton, indeed, retired to her chamber at two; and left the gentlemen to a graver discourse, but a discourse still less advantageous to poor Miss Milner.

She, during this time, was at the scene of pleasure she had pictured to herself, and all the pleasure it gave her was, that she was sure she should never desire to go to a masquerade again.—The crowd and bustle fatigued her—the freedom offended her delicacy—and though she perceived she was the first object of admiration in the place, yet there was one person still wanting to admire; and the remorse at having transgressed his injunctions for so trivial an entertainment, weighed upon her spirits, and added to its weariness.—She would have come away sooner than she did, but she could not, with any degree of good manners, leave the company with whom she went, and not till half after four were they prevailed on to return.

Day-light just peeped through the shutters of the room where his lordship and Sandford were sitting, when the sound of her carriage, and its sudden stop at the door, caused Lord Elmwood as suddenly to start from his seat.—He trembled extremely, and looked pale.—Sandford was ashamed to seem to notice it, yet he could not help asking him, 'To take a glass of wine.'—He took it—and for once evinced he was reduced so low, as to be *glad* of such a resource.

What passion thus agitated Lord Elmwood at this crisis, it is hard to define.—Perhaps it was indignation at Miss Milner's imprudence, and the satisfaction he felt at being on the point of revenge—perhaps his emotion arose from joy, to find she was safe—perhaps it was perturbation at the regret he felt that he must upbraid her—perhaps it was one alone of these sensations, but most probably, it was them all combined.

She, wearied out with the tedious night's dissipation, and less joyous than melancholy, had fallen asleep as she rode home, and when the carriage stopt, came half asleep out of it. —'Light me to my bed-chamber instantly,' said she to her woman, who waited in the hall to receive her.—But one of Lord Elmwood's valets went up to her, and answered, 'Madam, my lord desires to see you before you go to bed.'

'Your lord, man?' cried she, 'Is he not out of town?'

'No, madam, my lord has been at home ever since you went out, and has been sitting up with Mr. Sandford, waiting for your return.'

She was wide awake instantly.—The heaviness was removed from her eyes, but fear, grief, and shame, seized upon her heart.—She leaned against her woman, as if unable to support herself under those feelings, and said to Miss Woodley,

'Make my excuse—I can't see him to night—I am unfit— indeed I cannot.'

Miss Woodley was alarmed at the thought of going to him by herself, and thus perhaps aggravating him still more; she therefore said, 'He has sent for you; for heaven's sake, do not disobey him a second time.'

'No, dear madam,' cried her woman, 'for he is like a lion— he has been scolding me.'

'Good God!' exclaimed Miss Milner, (and in a tone that seemed prophetic) 'Then he is not to be my husband, after all.'

'Yes,' cried Miss Woodley, 'if you will only be humble, and appear sorry.—You know your power over him, and all may yet be well.'

She turned her speaking eyes upon her friend, the tears starting from them, her lips trembling; 'Do I not appear sorry?' she cried.

The bell at that moment rung furiously, and they mended their pace to the door of the apartment where his lordship was.

'No, this is only fright,'—replied Miss Woodley, 'Say to him you are sorry, and beg his pardon.'

'I cannot,' said she, 'if Mr. Sandford is with him.'

The servant opened the door, and she and Miss Woodley went in.—Lord Elmwood by this time was composed, and received her with a slight inclination of his head; she bowed to him in return, and said, with some marks of humility,

'I suppose, my lord, I have done wrong.'

'You have indeed, Miss Milner;' answered he, 'but do not suppose, I mean to upbraid you; I am, moreover, going to release you from any such apprehension *for the future.*'

Those last three words he spoke with a countenance so serious and so determined, with an accent so firm and so decided, they pierced through her heart.—She did not however weep, or even sigh; but her friend, Miss Woodley, knowing what she felt, exclaimed, 'Oh!' as if for her.

She herself strove with her anguish, and replied, (but with a faltering voice) 'I expected as much, my lord.'

'Then, madam, you may perhaps expect all that I intend?'

'In regard to myself,' she replied, 'I suppose I do.'

'Then,' said he, 'you may expect in a few days we shall part.'

'I am prepared for it, my lord,' she answered, and while she said so, sunk upon a chair.

'My lord, what you have to say farther,' said Miss Woodley, in tears, 'defer till the morning; Miss Milner, you see, is not able to bear it now.'

'I have nothing to say farther,' replied he, coolly, 'I have now only to act.'

'Lord Elmwood,' cried Miss Milner, divided between grief and anger, 'you think to frighten me by your menaces, but I can part with you; heaven knows I can—your late behaviour has reconciled me to a separation.'

On this he was going out of the room—but Miss Woodley, catching hold of him, cried, 'Oh! my lord, do not leave her in this sorrow—pity her weakness, and forgive it.'—She was proceeding, and he seemed inclined to listen to her, when Sandford called out in so sharp a tone,

'Miss Woodley, what do you mean?' she gave a start, and desisted.

His lordship turned to Sandford and said, 'Nay, Mr. Sandford, you need entertain no doubts of me; I have judged, and have deter——'

He was going to say determined; but Miss Milner, who dreaded to hear the word, interrupted the period, and exclaimed, 'Oh! could my poor father know the grief, the days of sorrow, I have experienced since his death, how would he repent his fatal choice in a protector!'

This sentence, wherein his friend's memory was recalled, with the additional allusion to her long, and secret affection for himself, affected Lord Elmwood much—he was moved, but ashamed of being so, and as soon as possible, conquered the propensity.—Yet, for a short interval, he did not know whether to go out of the room, or to remain in it; whether to speak, or to be silent.—At length he turned towards her and said,

'Appeal to your father in some other form, in that' (pointing to her dress) 'he will not know you.——Reflect upon him too in your moments of dissipation, and let his idea control your indiscretions—not merely in an hour of contradiction call peevishly upon his name, only to wound the dearest friend you have.'

There was a degree of truth, and a degree of feeling, in the conclusion of this speech, that alarmed Sandford, and he caught up one of the candles, and laying hold of his lordship's elbow, drew him out of the room, crying, 'Come, my lord, come to your bed-chamber, it is very late—it is morning—it is time to rise.' And by a continual repetition of these words, in a very loud voice, drowned whatever his lordship, or any other person, might have wished to have spoken, or heard.—In this manner, Lord Elmwood was taken out of the apartment, and the evening's entertainment concluded.

CHAPTER X

Two whole days passed in the bitterest suspense on the part of Miss Milner, while neither one word or look from Lord Elmwood, denoted the most trivial change of those sentiments he had declared on the night of the masquerade.—Still those sentiments, or intentions, were not explicitly delivered; they were more like intimations, than solemn declarations—for though he had said, 'He would never reproach her *for the future*,' and that 'she might expect they should part,' he had not positively said they should; and upon this doubtful meaning of his words, she hung with the strongest agitation of hope, and of fear.

Miss Woodley seeing the distress of her mind, (much as she endeavoured to conceal it) entreated, nay implored, of her, to permit her to be a mediator; to suffer her to ask for a private interview with Lord Elmwood, and provided she found him inflexible, behave with a proper degree of spirit in return; but if he appeared not absolutely averse to a reconciliation, to offer it to him in so cautious a manner, it might take place without farther uneasiness on either side. But Miss Milner peremptorily forbad this, and acknowledging to her friend every weakness she felt on the occasion, yet concluded with solemnly declaring, 'That after what had passed between her and Lord Elmwood, *he* must be the first to make a concession, before she herself would condescend to be reconciled.'

'I believe, I know Lord Elmwood's temper,' replied Miss Woodley, 'and I do not think he will be easily induced to beg pardon for a fault, which he thinks you have committed.'

'Then he does not love me.'

'Pshaw! Miss Milner, this is the old argument.—He may love you too well to spoil you—consider, he is your guardian as well as your lover, he means also to become your husband; and he is a man of such nice honour, he will not give you a specimen[1] of that power before marriage, which he does not intend to submit to hereafter.'

'But tenderness, affection, the politeness due from a lover to his mistress, demands this submission; and as I now despair of enticing, I will oblige him to it—at least I'll make the trial, and know my fate at once.'

'What do you mean to do?'

'Invite my lord Frederick to the house, and ask my guardian's consent for our immediate union; you will then see, what effect that has upon his pride.'

'But you will then make it too late for him to be humble.— If you resolve on this, my dear Miss Milner, you are undone at once—you may thus hurry yourself into a marriage with a

man you do not love, and the misery of your whole future life
may be the result.—Or, would you force Mr. Dorriforth
(I mean Lord Elmwood) to another duel with my lord
Frederick?'

'No, call him Dorriforth—' answered she, with the tears
stealing from her eyes, 'I thank you for calling him so; for by
that name alone, is he dear to me.'

'Nay, Miss Milner, with what rapture did you not receive
his love, as Lord Elmwood.'

'But under that title he has been barbarous; under the first,
he was all friendship and tenderness.'

Notwithstanding Miss Milner indulged herself in all those
soft bewailings to her friend—before Lord Elmwood she
maintained a degree of pride and steadiness which surprised
even him, who had perhaps ever thought less of her love for
him, than any other person.—She now began to fear she had
gone too far in discovering her affection, and resolved to make
trial of a contrary method.—She determined to retrieve that
haughty character which had inspired so many of her admirers
with passion, and take the chance of the effect upon this only
one, to whom she ever acknowledged a mutual love.—But,
although she acted this character well—so well, that every
one but Miss Woodley thought her in earnest—yet, with the
nicest and most attentive anxiety, did she watch even the
slightest circumstance, that might revive her hopes, or confirm her despair. Lord Elmwood's behaviour was calculated
to produce the latter—he was cold, polite, and perfectly indifferent.—Yet, whatever his manners now were, they did
not remove from her recollection what they had been—she
recalled, with delight, the ardour with which he had first
declared his passion to her, and the thousand proofs he had
since given of its reality.—From the constancy of his disposition, she depended a great deal, that those sentiments

were not totally eradicated; and from the extreme desire, which Mr. Sandford now, more than ever, discovered to depreciate her in his patron's esteem—from the now, more than common earnestness, with which he never failed to take Lord Elmwood from her company, whenever he had it in his power, she was led to believe, that while his friend entertained such strong fears of his lordship relapsing into love, she had reason to indulge the strongest hopes that he would.

But the reserve, and even indifference she had so well assumed for a few days, and which might perhaps have effected her designs, she had not the patience to persevere in, without calling levity to their aid.—She visited repeatedly without saying where, or with whom—kept later hours than usual—appeared in the highest spirits; sung, laugh'd, and never heaved a sigh, but when she was alone.

Still, Lord Elmwood protracted a resolution, he was determined not to break when once taken.

Miss Woodley was extremely uneasy, and with cause; she saw her friend was providing herself with a weight of cares, she would soon find too much for her strength to bear—she would have reasoned with her, but all her arguments had long since proved unavailing.—She strongly wished to speak to Lord Elmwood upon the subject, and (unknown to her) plead her excuse; but he apprehended Miss Woodley's intention and evidently shunned her.—Mr. Sandford was now the only person to whom she could speak of Miss Milner, and the delight he took to expatiate on her faults, was more sorrow to her friend, than not to speak of her at all. She, therefore, sat a silent spectator, waiting with dread for that time, when she, who now scorned her advice, would fly to her in vain for comfort.

Sandford had, however, said one thing to Miss Woodley, which gave her a ray of hope. During their conversation on this subject (not by way of consolation to her, but as a reproach to Lord Elmwood), he one day angrily exclaimed, 'And yet, notwithstanding all this provocation, he has not come to the determination to think no more of her—he lingers and hesitates—I never saw him so weak upon any occasion before.'

This was joyful hearing to Miss Woodley; still, she could not but reflect, the longer he was in coming to this determination, the more irrevocable it would be, when once taken; and every moment she passed, she trembled lest that should be the moment, in which Lord Elmwood resolved to banish Miss Milner from his heart.

Among the unpardonable indiscretions, she was guilty of during this trial upon the temper of her guardian, was the frequent mention of many gentlemen, who had been her profest admirers, and mentioning them with partiality.— Teased, if not tortured by this, Lord Elmwood still behaved with a manly evenness of temper, and neither appeared provoked on the subject, or insolently careless.—In a single instance, however, this calmness had nearly deserted him.

Entering the drawing-room, one evening, he suddenly started, on seeing Lord Frederick Lawnly there, in earnest conversation with Miss Milner.

Mrs. Horton and Miss Woodley were both indeed present, and Lord Frederick was talking in an audible voice, and upon some indifferent subjects; but with that impressive manner, in which a man never fails to speak to the woman he loves, be the subject what it will.—The moment Lord Elmwood started, which was the moment he entered, Lord Frederick arose.

'I beg your pardon, my lord,' said Lord Elmwood, 'I protest I did not know you.'

'I ought to entreat your lordship's pardon,' returned Lord Frederick, 'for this intrusion, which an accident alone has occasioned. Miss Milner has been nearly overturned, by the carelessness of a lady's coachman, in whose carriage she was, and therefore suffered me to bring her home in mine.'

'I hope you are not hurt,' said Lord Elmwood to Miss Milner, but his voice was so much affected, by what he felt, he could scarcely articulate the words.—Not with the apprehension she was hurt, was he thus agitated, for the gaiety of her manners convinced him that could not be the case, nor did he indeed suppose any accident, such as was mentioned, had occurred; but the circumstance of unexpectedly seeing Lord Frederick had taken him off his guard, and being totally unprepared, he could not conquer those signs of surprise, and the shock it had given him.

Lord Frederick who had heard nothing of his intended union with his ward, (for it was even kept a secret, at present, from every servant in the house) imputed this discomposure, to the personal resentment his lordship might bear him, in consequence of their duel; for, notwithstanding Lord Elmwood had assured the uncle of Lord Frederick, (who once waited upon him on the subject of Miss Milner) that all resentment was, on his part, entirely at an end; and that he was willing to consent to the lady's marriage with his nephew, if she herself would concur, yet Lord Frederick doubted the sincerity of this, and would still have had the delicacy not to have entered his house, but, encouraged by Miss Milner, and emboldened by his love. Personal resentment was then the construction he put upon Lord Elmwood's emotion on entering the room, but Miss Milner and Miss Woodley knew his agitation to arise from a far different cause.

After his entrance, Lord Frederick did not attempt to resume his seat, but bowing most respectfully to all present, took his leave; while Miss Milner followed him, as far as the door, repeating her thanks and gratitude for his protection.

Lord Elmwood was hurt beyond measure; but he had a second concern, and that was, he had not the power to conceal how much he was affected.—He trembled—when he attempted to speak, he stammered—he perceived his face burning with the blood that had flushed to it from confusion, and thus one confusion gave birth to another, till his state was pitiable.

Miss Milner, with all her assumed gaiety and real insolence, had not, however, the insolence to seem to observe his situation; she had only the confidence to observe it by stealth.— And Mrs. Horton and Miss Woodley, having opportunely begun a discourse upon some trivial occurrences, gave him time to recover himself by degrees—yet, still it was merely by degrees, for the impression this incident had made, was deep, and not easily to be erased.—The entrance of Mr. Sandford, who knew nothing of what had happened, was also some relief, and his lordship and he entered into a conversation, which they very soon retired into the library to terminate.—— Miss Milner, taking Miss Woodley with her, went directly to her own apartment, and there exclaimed to her friend, in rapture,

'He is mine—he loves me—and he is mine for ever.'

Miss Woodley congratulated her upon believing so, but confessed, she herself, 'had her fears.'

'What fears?' cried Miss Milner, 'don't you perceive he loves me?'

'I do,' said Miss Woodley, 'but that, I always supposed; and, I think, if he loves you now, he has still the good sense to know, he has cause to hate you.'

'What has good sense to do with love?' returned Miss Milner, 'If a lover of mine suffers his understanding to get the better of his affection——'

And the same arguments were again going to be repeated, but Miss Woodley interrupted her, by requiring an explanation

of her conduct, not in respect to her guardian, but to Lord
Frederick; whom, at least, she must allow, she was treating
with cruelty, if she only made use of his affection, to stimulate
that of Lord Elmwood.

'By no means, my dear Miss Woodley,'—returned she—
'I have, indeed, done with my lord Frederick from this day;
and he has certainly given me the proof I wanted of Lord
Elmwood's love; but then, I did not engage him to this, by
the smallest degree of hope.—No, do not suspect me of that,
while my heart was another's.—And I assure you, seriously,
it was from the circumstance we described, that he came with
me home—yet, I must own, that had I not had this design
upon Lord Elmwood's jealousy in idea, I would have walked
on foot through the streets, rather than have suffered his
rival's civilities.—But he pressed his services so violently,
and my lady Evans (in whose chariot I was, when the accident
happened) pressed me so violently to accept them, that he
cannot expect any farther meaning from my acquiescence,
than my own convenience.'

Miss Woodley was going to reply, when she resumed,

'Nay, if you intend to say I have done wrong, still I am not
sorry for it, while it has given me such convincing proofs of
Lord Elmwood's love.—Did you see him? I am afraid you did
not see how he trembled?—and that manly, firm voice
faltered, as mine does some times—his proud heart was
humbled too; as mine is some times.—Oh! Miss Woodley,
I have been counterfeiting indifference to *him*; I now find all
his indifference has been counterfeit too, and we not only love,
but we love equally.'

'Supposing this, all as you hope; I yet think it highly necessary, your guardian should be informed, seriously informed,
that it was mere accident, (for, at present, that plea seems but
as a subterfuge) which brought Lord Frederick hither.'

'No, that will be destroying the work so successfully began.
—I will not suffer any explanation to take place, but let my
lord Elmwood act just as his love shall dictate; and now I have
no longer a doubt of its excess, instead of stooping to him, I
wait in the certain expectation, of his submission to me.'

CHAPTER XI

IN vain, for three long days, did Miss Milner wait impatiently
for this submission; not a sign, not a symptom appeared—
nay, Lord Elmwood had, since the evening of Lord Frederick's
visit, (which, at the time it happened, seemed to affect him so
exceedingly) become just the same man, he was before the
circumstance occurred; except, indeed, something less
thoughtful, and now and then cheerful; but without the
smallest appearance, that his cheerfulness was affected.—
Miss Milner was vext; she was alarmed; but was ashamed to
confess those humiliating sensations, even to Miss Woodley—
she assumed, therefore, the vivacity she had so long assumed,
but gave way, when alone, to a still greater degree of melancholy than usual. She no longer applauded her scheme of
bringing Lord Frederick to the house, and trembled, lest, on
some pretence, he should dare to call again. But as these were
feelings her pride would not suffer her to disclose to her
friend, who would have condoled along with her, their effects
were doubly poignant.

Sitting in her dressing-room, one forenoon with Miss
Woodley, and burthened with a load of grief, she blushed to
acknowledge; while her companion was charged with apprehensions she was as loath to disclose; one of Lord Elmwood's
valets tapped gently at the door, and delivered a letter to Miss

Milner.—By the person who brought it, as well as by the address, she knew it came from Lord Elmwood, and laid it down upon her toilet, as if fearful to unfold it.

'What is that?' said Miss Woodley.

'A letter from my guardian,' replied Miss Milner.

'Good Heaven!' exclaimed Miss Woodley.

'Nay,' returned she, 'it is, I have no doubt, to beg my pardon.' But her reluctance to open it, plainly evinced she did not think so.

'Do not read it yet,' said Miss Woodley.

'I do not intend,' replied she, trembling extremely.

'Will you dine first?' said Miss Woodley.

'No—for not knowing its contents, I shall not know how to conduct myself towards him.'

Here a silence ensued—during this silence, Miss Milner took up the letter—looked earnestly at the hand-writing on the outside—at the seal—inspected into its folds—and seemed to wish, by some equivocal method, to guess at the contents, without daring to come at the certain knowledge of them.

Curiosity, at length, got the better of her fears; she opened the letter, and scarce able to hold it while she read, read the following words:

'Madam,

'While I considered you only as my ward, my friendship for you was unbounded—when I looked upon you as a woman formed to grace a fashionable circle, my admiration equalled my friendship—and when fate permitted me to behold you in the tender light of my betrothed wife, my soaring love left those humbler passions at a distance.

'That you have still my friendship, my admiration, and even my love, I will not attempt to deceive either myself or you, by disavowing; but still, with a firm assurance, I declare,

Prudence outweighs them all, and I have not, from henceforward, a wish to be regarded by you in any other respect,
than as one "who wishes you well."—That you ever beheld
me in the endearing quality of a destined, and an affectionate
husband, (such as I would have proved) my hopes, my vanity,
own the deception, and are humiliated—but I entreat you to
spare their farther trial, and for a single week, do not insult me
with the open preference of another.—In the space of that
time, I shall have taken my leave of you *for ever*.

'I shall visit Italy, and some other countries for a few years,
till I become once more reconciled to the change of state I am
enjoined; a change, I now most fervently wish could be entirely
dispensed with.

'The occasion of my remaining in England a week longer,
is to settle some necessary affairs, but chiefly that of delivering to a friend, a man of worth and tenderness, all those
writings, which have invested me with the power of my
guardianship—he will, the day after my departure (without
one upbraiding word), resign them to you in my name; and
even your father, could he behold the resignation, would concur in its propriety.

'And now, my dear Miss Milner, let not affected resentment, contempt, or levity, oppose that serenity, which, for the
week to come, I wish to enjoy.—By complying with this
request, give me to believe, that since you have been under my
care, you think I have, at least, faithfully discharged some part
of my duty.—And wherever I have been inadequate to your
wishes, attribute my demerits to some infirmity of mind,
rather than to a negligence of your happiness.—Yet, be the
cause what it will, since these faults have existed, I acknowledge them, and beg your pardon.

'However, time, and succession of objects, may eradicate
more tender sentiments; I am sure *never* to lose the liveliest

anxiety for your welfare—and with all that solicitude, which
I cannot describe, I entreat for your own sake, for mine—
when we shall be far asunder—and for the sake of your dead
father's memory, *call upon every important occasion, your
serious judgment to direct you.*

I am, Madam,
your sincerest friend,
ELMWOOD.'

After reading every syllable of this letter, it dropped from
Miss Milner's hands; but she uttered not a word.—There
was, however, a paleness in her face, a deadness in her eye,
and a kind of palsy over her frame, which Miss Woodley, who
had seen her in every stage of her uneasiness, never had seen
before.

'I do not want to read the letter,' said Miss Woodley, 'your
looks tell me its contents.'

'They will then discover to Lord Elmwood,' replied she,
'what I feel; but heaven forbid—that would sink me even
lower than I am.'

Scarce able to crawl, she rose, and looked in the glass, as if
to arrange her features, so as to impose upon him: alas! this
was of no avail; a serenity of mind, could, alone, effect what
she desired.

'You must endeavour,' said Miss Woodley, 'to feel that disposition, you wish to make appear.'

'I will,' replied she, 'I will feel a proper pride—and a proper
scorn of this treatment.'

And so desirous was she to attain the appearance of these
sentiments, she made the strongest efforts to calm her
thoughts, in order to acquire it.

'I have but a few days to remain with him,' she said to herself, 'and we part for ever—in those few days, it is not only

my duty to obey his commands, or rather comply with his request, but it is also my wish to leave upon his mind, an impression, which may not add to the ill opinion he has formed of me, but, perhaps, serve to diminish it.—If, in every other instance, my conduct has been blameable, he shall, at least in this, acknowledge its merit.—The fate I have drawn upon myself, he shall find I can be resigned to; and he shall be convinced, that the woman, of whose weakness he has had so many fatal proofs, is yet in possession of some forti-tude—fortitude to bid him farewell without discovering one affected, or one real pang, though her death should be the immediate consequence.'

Thus she resolved, and thus she acted.—The severest judge could not have arraigned her conduct from the day she received Lord Elmwood's letter, to the day of his departure.— She had, indeed, involuntary weaknesses, but none with which she did not struggle, and in general her struggles were victorious.

The first time she saw him after the receipt of his letter, was on the evening of the same day—she had a little concert of amateurs in music, and was, herself, singing and playing when he entered the room; the connoisseurs immediately per-ceived she lost the tune, but Lord Elmwood was no con-noisseur in the art, and did not observe it.

They occasionally spoke to each other during the evening, but the subjects were general—and though their manners every time they spoke were perfectly polite, they were not tinctured with the smallest degree of familiarity.—To describe his behaviour exactly, it was the same as his letter, polite, friendly, composed, and resolved.—Some of the company staid supper, which prevented the embarrassment that must unavoidably have arisen, had the family been by themselves.

The next morning each breakfasted in their separate

apartments—more company dined with them, and in the evening, and at supper, Lord Elmwood was from home.

Thus all passed on as peaceably as he had requested, and Miss Milner had not betrayed one particle of frailty; when, the third day at dinner, some gentlemen of his acquaintance being at table, one of them said,

'And so, my lord, you absolutely set off on Tuesday morning?'

This was Friday.

Sandford and he both replied at the same time, 'Yes.' And Sandford, but not Lord Elmwood, looked at Miss Milner when he spoke.—Her knife and fork gave a sudden spring in her hand, but no other emotion witnessed what she felt.

'Ay, Elmwood,' cried another gentleman at table, 'you'll bring home, I am afraid, a foreign wife, and that I shan't forgive.'

'It is his errand abroad, I make no doubt,' said another visitor.

Before his lordship could return an answer, Sandford cried, 'And what objection to a foreigner for a wife? do not crowned heads all marry foreigners? and who happier in the marriage state than some kings?'

Lord Elmwood directed his eyes to the side of the table, opposite to that where Miss Milner sat.

'Nay,' (answered one of the guests, who was a country gentleman) 'what do you say, ladies—do you think my lord ought to go out of his own nation for a wife?' And he looked at Miss Milner, for the reply.

Miss Woodley, uneasy at her friend's being thus forced to give an opinion upon so delicate a subject, endeavoured to satisfy the gentleman, by answering to the question herself: 'Whoever my Lord Elmwood marries, sir,' said Miss Woodley, 'he, no doubt, will be happy.'

'But what say you, young lady?' asked the gentleman, still keeping his eyes on Miss Milner.

'That whoever his lordship marries, he *deserves* to be happy,' returned she, with the utmost command of her voice and looks; for Miss Woodley, by replying first, had given her time to collect herself.

The colour flew to Lord Elmwood's face, as she delivered this short sentence; and Miss Woodley flattered herself, she saw a tear start in his eye.

Miss Milner did not look that way.

In an instant his lordship found means to change the subject, but that of his journey, still employed the conversation; and what horses, servants, and carriage he took with him, was minutely asked, and so accurately answered either by himself or by Mr. Sandford, that Miss Milner, although she had beheld her doom before, till now had received no circumstantial account of it—and as circumstances add to, or diminish all we feel, hearing these things told, encreased the bitterness of their truth.

Soon after dinner, the ladies retired, and from that time, though Miss Milner's behaviour still continued the same, yet her looks and her voice were totally altered—for the world, she could not have looked cheerfully; for the world, she could not have spoken with a sprightly accent; she frequently began in one, but not three words could she utter, before her tones sunk into the flattest dejection.—Not only her colour, but her features became changed; her eyes lost their brilliancy, her lips seemed to hang without the power of motion, her head drooped, and her dress was wholly neglected.—Conscious of this distrest appearance, and conscious of the weakness from whence it arose, it was her desire to hide herself from the only object she could have wished to have charmed.—Accordingly, she sat alone, or with Miss Woodley in her own apartment, as much as was consistent with that civility her guardian had requested, and which forbad her from totally absenting herself.

Miss Woodley felt so acutely the torments of her friend, that had not her reason told her the inflexible mind of Lord Elmwood was fixed beyond her power to shake, she had cast herself at his feet, and implored the return of his affection and tenderness as the only means to save his once beloved ward from an untimely grave. But her understanding—her knowledge of his lordship's firm and immoveable temper; and all his grievous provocations—her knowledge of his word, long since given to Sandford, 'That if one resolved, he would not recall his resolution.'—the certainty of the many plans that had been arranged for his travels, all agreed to convince her, that by any interference, she only exposed Miss Milner's tenderest love and delicacy to a contemptuous rejection.

If the conversation did not every day turn upon the subject of Lord Elmwood's departure—a conversation he evidently avoided himself—yet every day some new preparation for his journey, struck the ear or the eye of Miss Milner—and had she beheld a frightful spectre, she could not have shuddered with more horror, than when she unexpectedly passed his large trunks in the hall, nailed and corded, ready to be sent off to meet him at Venice.—At the sight, she flew from the company that happened to be along with her, and stole to the first lonely corner of the house to conceal her tears—she reclined her head upon her hands, and bedewed them with the sudden anguish that had overcome her.—She heard a footstep advancing towards the spot where she hoped to have been concealed; she lifted up her eyes, and beheld Lord Elmwood. —Pride was the first emotion his presence inspired—pride, which arose from the humility into which she was plunged.

She instantly stifled her tears, and looked at him earnestly, as if to imply, 'What now, my lord?'

He only answered with a bow, which expressed these words alone: 'I beg your pardon.' And immediately withdrew.

Thus each understood the other's language, without either uttering a word.

The just construction, which she put upon his looks and behaviour upon this occasion, kept up her spirits for some little time; and she blessed heaven, repeatedly, for the singular favour of shewing to her, clearly, by this accident, his negligence of her sorrows, his total indifference.

The next day was the eve of that, on which he was to depart —and the one on which she was to bid adieu to Dorriforth, to her guardian, to Lord Elmwood; to all her hopes at once.

The moment she awoke on Monday morning, the recollection, that this was, perhaps, the last day she was ever again to see him, softened all the resentment his yesterday's conduct had given birth to, and forgetting his austerity, and all she once termed, cruelties; she now only remembered his friendship, his anxious tenderness, and his love.—She was impatient to behold him, and promised to herself, for this last day, to neglect no one opportunity of being with him. For that purpose she did not breakfast in her own room, as she had done for several mornings before, but went into the breakfast-room, where all the family generally met.—She was rejoiced on hearing his voice as she opened the door, yet the sound made her tremble so much, she could scarcely totter to the table.

Miss Woodley looked at her as she entered, and was never so much shocked at seeing her; for never had she yet seen her look so ill.—As she approached, she made an inclination of her head to Mrs. Horton, and then to her guardian, as was her custom, when she first saw them in a morning—his lordship looked in her face as he bowed, then turned his eyes upon the fire place, rubbed his forehead, and began talking with Mr. Sandford.

Sandford, during breakfast, by accident, cast his eyes upon Miss Milner; his attention was caught by her deathly countenance, and he looked earnestly.—He then turned to Lord Elmwood to see if he was observing her appearance—he was not—and so much were her thoughts engaged on him alone, she did not once perceive Sandford gazing at her.

Mrs. Horton after a little while observed, 'It was a beautiful morning.'

Lord Elmwood said, 'He thought he heard it rain in the night.'

Sandford cried, 'For his part he slept too well to know.' And then (unasked) held a plate with biscuits to Miss Milner —it was the first civility he had ever in his life offered her; she smiled at the whimsicality of the circumstance, but took one in return for his attention.—He looked grave beyond his usual gravity, and yet not with his usual ill temper. She did not eat what she had so politely taken, but laid it down soon after.

Lord Elmwood was the first who rose from breakfast, and did not return to dinner.

At dinner, Mrs. Horton said, 'She hoped his lordship would, however, favour them with his company at supper.'

To which Sandford replied, 'No doubt, for you will hardly any of you see him in the morning; as we shall be off by six, or soon after.'

Sandford was not going abroad with Lord Elmwood, but was to go with him as far as Dover.

These words of his—'not see Lord Elmwood in the morning'— [never again to see him after this evening,] were like the knell of death to Miss Milner.—She felt the symptoms of fainting, and eagerly snatched a glass of wine,[1] which the servant was holding to Sandford, (who had called for wine) and drank a part of it.—As she returned the glass to the servant, she began to apologize to Mr. Sandford for her seeming rudeness, but before she could utter what she meant, he said, good-naturedly, 'Never mind—you are very welcome—I am glad you took it.'—She looked at him to observe, whether he had really spoken kindly, or ironically; but before his countenance could satisfy her, her thoughts were away from that trivial circumstance, and again fixed upon Lord Elmwood.

The moments seemed tedious till he came home to supper, and yet, when she reflected for how short a time the rest of the evening would continue, she wished to defer the hour of his return, for months.—At ten o'clock he arrived, and at half after ten the family, without any visitor, met at supper.

Miss Milner had considered, that the period for her to counterfeit appearances, was diminished now to a very short one; and she rigourously enjoined herself not to shrink from that little which remained.—The certain end, that would be so soon put to this painful deception, encouraged her to struggle through it with redoubled zeal; and this was but necessary, as her weakness encreased.—She therefore listened, she talked, and even smiled with the rest of the company, nor did their vivacity seem to arise from a much less compulsive source than her own.

It was past twelve, when Lord Elmwood looked at his watch, and rising from his seat, went up to Mrs. Horton, and taking her hand, said, 'Till I see you again, madam, I sincerely wish you every happiness.'

Miss Milner fixed her eyes upon the table before her.

'My lord,' replied Mrs. Horton, 'I sincerely wish you health and happiness likewise.'

He then went to Miss Woodley, and taking her hand, repeated much the same, as he had said to Mrs. Horton.

Miss Milner now trembled beyond all power of concealment.

'My lord,' replied Miss Woodley, a good deal affected, 'I sincerely hope my prayers for your happiness may be heard.'

She and Mrs. Horton were both standing as well as his lordship; but Miss Milner kept her seat, till his eye was turned upon her, and he moved slowly towards her; she then rose—and every one who was present attentive to what he would now say, and how she would receive what he said, cast their eyes upon them, and listened with impatience.—They were all disappointed—he did not utter a syllable.—Yet he took her hand, and held it closely between his.—He then bowed most respectfully, and left her.

No, 'I wish you well;—I wish you health and happiness.' No 'Prayers for blessings on her.'—Not even the word 'farewell,' escaped his lips—perhaps, to have attempted any of these, might have choked his utterance.

She had behaved with fortitude the whole evening, and she continued to do so, till the moment he turned away from her. —Her eyes then overflowed with tears, and in the agony of her mind, not knowing what she did, she laid her cold hand upon the person next to her—it happened to be Sandford; but not observing it was him, she grasped his hand with violence— yet he did not snatch it away, nor look at her with his wonted severity.—And thus she stood, silent and motionless, while his lordship lighted a candle, he took from the side-board, bowed once more to all the company, and retired.

Sandford had still Miss Milner's hand fixed upon his; and when the door was shut after Lord Elmwood, he turned his head to look in her face, and turned it with some marks of apprehension for the grief he might find there.—She strove to overcome that grief, and after a heavy sigh, sat down, as if resigned to the fate to which she was decreed.

Instead of following Lord Elmwood, as usual, Sandford poured out a glass of wine, and drank it.—A general silence ensued for near three minutes.—At last turning himself round on his seat, towards Miss Milner, who sat like a statue

of despair at his side, 'Will you breakfast with us to-morrow?'
said he.

She made no answer.

'We shan't breakfast before half after six,' continued he, 'I
dare say; and if you can rise so early—why do.'

'Miss Milner,' said Miss Woodley, (for she caught, eagerly,
at the hope of her passing this night in less unhappiness than
she had foreboded) 'pray rise at that hour to breakfast; Mr.
Sandford would not invite you, if he thought it would displease his lordship.'

'Not I,' replied Sandford, churlishly.

'Then desire her woman to call her,' said Mrs. Horton to
Miss Woodley.

'Nay, she will be awake, I have no doubt,' returned her
niece.

'No;' replied Miss Milner, 'since Lord Elmwood has
thought proper to take his leave of me, without even speaking
a word; by my own design, never will I see him again.' And
here a flood of tears burst forth, as if her heart burst at the
same time.

'Why did not *you* speak to *him?*' cried Sandford—'pray
did you bid *him* farewell?—and I don't see why one is not as
much to be blamed, in that respect, as the other.'

'I was too weak to say, I wished him happy;' cried Miss
Milner, 'but, heaven is my witness, I do wish him so from my
soul.'

'And do you imagine, he does not wish you so too?'
cried Sandford.—'You should judge him by your own
heart; and what you feel for him, imagine he feels for you, my
dear.'

Though '*my dear*' is a trivial phrase, yet from certain
people, and upon certain occasions, it is a phrase of infinite
comfort and assurance.—Mr. Sandford seldom said 'my dear'

to any one; to Miss Milner never; and upon this occasion, and from him, it was an expression most precious.

She turned to him with a look of gratitude; but as she only looked, and did not speak, he rose up, and soon after said, with a friendly tone he had seldom spoken with in her presence, 'I sincerely wish you a good night.'

As soon as he was gone, Miss Milner exclaimed, 'However my fate may have been precipitated by the unkindness of Mr. Sandford, yet, for that particle of concern he has shown for me this night, I will always be grateful to him.'

'Ay,' cried Mrs. Horton, 'good Mr. Sandford may show his kindness now, without any danger from its consequences. —Now his lordship is going away for ever, he is not afraid of your seeing him once again.' And she thought she praised him by this suggestion.

CHAPTER XII

WHEN Miss Milner retired to her bed-chamber, Miss Woodley went with her, nor would leave her the whole night —but in vain did she persuade her to go to rest, she absolutely refused; and declared she would never, from that hour, indulge the smallest repose.—'The part I undertook to perform,' cried she, 'is over; I will now, for my whole life, appear in my own character, and give a loose to the anguish I endure.'

As day light showed itself, 'And yet I might see him once again,' said she. 'I might see him within these two hours, if I pleased, for Mr. Sandford invited me.'

'If you think, my dear Miss Milner,' said Miss Woodley, 'that a second parting from Lord Elmwood, would but give you a second agony, in the name of heaven do not see him any more—but, if you think your mind would be easier, were you to bid each other adieu in a more direct manner than you did last night, let us go down and breakfast with him.—I'll go before, to prepare him for your reception—you shall not unexpectedly surprise him—and I will let him know, it is by Mr. Sandford's invitation you are coming.'

She listened with a smile to this proposal, yet objected to the indelicacy of her wishing to see him, after he had taken his leave—but as Miss Woodley, nevertheless, perceived she was inclined to infringe this delicacy, of which she had so proper a sense, she easily persuaded her, it was impossible for the most suspicious person (and Lord Elmwood was far from such a character) to suppose, that the paying him a visit at that period of time, could be with the most distant idea of regaining his heart, or of altering one resolution he had taken.

In this opinion, Miss Milner acquiesced, yet she had not the courage to come to the determination she would go.

Day light now no longer peeped, but stared broad upon them.—Miss Milner went to the looking-glass, breathed upon her hands and rubbed them on her eyes; put some powder into her hair;[1] yet said, after all, 'I dare not see him again.'

'You may do as you please,' said Miss Woodley, 'but I will. I that have lived for so many years under the same roof with him, and on the most friendly terms, and he going away, perhaps for these ten years, perhaps for ever; I should think it a disrespect not to see him to the last moment of his remaining in the house.'

'Then do you go,' said Miss Milner, eagerly, 'and if he should ask for me, I will gladly come, you know; but if he does not ask for me, I will not—and pray do not deceive me.'

Miss Woodley gave her her word not to deceive her; and soon after, as they heard the servants pass about the house, and the clock had struck six, Miss Woodley went to the breakfast-room.

She found Lord Elmwood there in his travelling dress, standing pensively by the fire place—and, as he did not dream of seeing her, he started when she entered, and with an appearance of alarm said, 'Dear Miss Woodley, what's the matter?'—She replied, 'Nothing, my lord; but I could not be satisfied without seeing your lordship once again, while I had it in my power.'

'I thank you,' he returned with a sigh, and the heaviest and most intelligent sigh, she ever heard him condescend to give. —She imagined, also, he looked as if he wished to ask how Miss Milner did, but would not allow himself the indulgence. —She was half inclined to mention her to him, and debating in her mind whether she should or not, when Mr. Sandford came into the room; saying, as he entered,

'For heaven's sake, my lord, where did you sleep last night?'

'Why do you ask?' said his lordship.

'Because,' replied Sandford, 'I went into your bed-chamber but now, and I found your bed made.—You have not slept there to-night.'

'I have slept no where;' answered his lordship, 'I could not sleep—and having some papers to look over, and to rise early, I thought I might as well not go to bed at all.'

Miss Woodley was pleased at the frank manner in which he made this confession, and could not resist the strong impulse to say, 'You have done just then, my lord, like Miss Milner, for she has not been in bed the whole night.'

Miss Woodley spoke this in a negligent manner, and yet, Lord Elmwood echoed back the words with solicitude and tenderness, 'Has not Miss Milner been in bed the whole night?'

'If she is up, why does not she come and take some coffee?' said Sandford, as he began to pour it out.

'If she thought it would be agreeable,' returned Miss Woodley, 'I dare say she would.' And she looked at Lord Elmwood while she spoke, though she did not absolutely address him; but he made no reply.

'Agreeable!' returned Sandford, angrily, 'Has she then a quarrel with any body here? or does she suppose any body here bears enmity to *her?*—Is she not in peace and charity?'

'Yes,' replied Miss Woodley, 'that I am sure she is.'

'Then bring her hither,' (said he) 'directly.—Would she have the wickedness to imagine we are not all friends with her?'

Miss Woodley left the room, and found Miss Milner almost in despair, lest she should hear Lord Elmwood's carriage drive off before her friend's return.

'Did he send for me?' were the words she uttered as soon as she saw her.

'Mr. Sandford did, in his presence,' returned Miss Woodley, 'and you may go with the utmost decorum, or I would not tell you so.'

She required no protestations of this, but readily followed her beloved adviser, whose kindness never appeared in half the amiable light as at that moment.

On entering the room, through all the dead white of her present complexion, she blushed to a crimson.—Lord Elmwood rose from his seat, and brought a chair for her to sit down.

Sandford looked at her inquisitively, then sipped his tea, and said, 'He never made tea to his own liking.'

Miss Milner took a cup, but had scarce strength to hold it.

It seemed but a very short time they were at breakfast, when the carriage, that was to take his lordship away, drove to the door.—Miss Milner started at the sound; so did he; but she had nearly dropped her cup and saucer: on which Sandford took them out of her hand, saying,

'Perhaps you had rather have coffee?'

Her lips moved, but he could not hear what she said.

A servant came in, and told Lord Elmwood, 'The carriage was at the door.'

He replied, 'Very well.' But though he had breakfasted, he did not attempt to move.

At last, rising briskly from his seat, as if it was necessary to go in haste, when he did go; he took up his hat, which he had brought with him into the room, and was turning to Miss Woodley to take his leave, when Sandford cried, 'My lord, you are in a great hurry.'—And then, as if he wished to give poor Miss Milner every moment he could, added, (looking about) 'I don't know where I have laid my gloves.'

His lordship, after repeating to Miss Woodley his last night's farewell, now went up to Miss Milner, and taking one of her hands, again held it between his, but still without speaking—while she, unable to suppress her tears as heretofore, suffered them to fall in torrents.

'What is all this?' cried Sandford, going up to them in anger.

They neither of them replied, or changed their situation.

'Separate this moment,'—cried Sandford—'Or resolve never to be separated but by death.'

The commanding, and awful manner in which he spoke this sentence, made them both turn to him in amazement! and almost petrified with the sensation his words had caused.

He left them for a moment, and going to a small book-case in one corner of the room, took out of it a book, and returning with it in his hand, said,

'Lord Elmwood, do you love this woman?'

'More than my life,' replied his lordship, with the most heartfelt accents.

He then turned to Miss Milner—'Can you say the same by him?'

She spread her hands over her eyes, and cried, 'Oh, heavens!'

'I believe you *can* say so;' returned Sandford, 'and in the name of God, and your own happiness, since this is the case, let me put it out of your power to part.'

Lord Elmwood gazed at him with wonder! and yet, as if enraptured by the sudden appearance of a change in his prospects.

She, sighed with a trembling kind of ecstasy; while Sandford, with all the pomp and dignity of a clergyman in his official character, delivered these words:

'My lord, while I thought my counsel might save you from the worst of misfortunes, conjugal strife, I importuned you hourly; and set forth your danger in the light it appeared to me.—But though old, and a priest, I can submit to think I have been in an error; and I now firmly believe, it is for the welfare of you both, to become man and wife.—My lord, take this woman's marriage vows; you can ask no fairer promises of her reform; she can give you none half so sacred, half so binding; and I see by her looks she will mean to keep them.— And my dear,' continued he, addressing himself to her, 'act but under the dominion of those vows, to a husband of sense and virtue, like him, and you will be all that I, himself, or even heaven can desire.—Now then, Lord Elmwood, this moment give her up for ever; or this moment constrain her by such ties from offending you, she shall not *dare* to violate.'

Lord Elmwood struck his forehead in doubt and agitation; but still holding her hand, he cried, 'I cannot part from her.'————Then feeling this reply as equivocal, he fell upon his knees, and cried, 'Will you pardon my hesitation?— and will you, in marriage, show me that tender love you have not shown me yet?—will you, in possessing all my affections, bear with all my infirmities?'

She raised him from her feet, and by the expression of her face, the tears with which she bathed his hands, gave him confidence.

He turned to Sandford—then placing her by his own side, as the form of matrimony requires, gave this as a sign for Sandford to begin the ceremony.—On which, he opened his book, and—married them.

While with a countenance—manner—and voice, so serious, and so fervent, did he perform these rites, that the idea of jest, or even of lightness, was far from the mind of every one present.

Miss Milner, covered with shame, sunk on the bosom of Miss Woodley.

When the ring was wanting, Lord Elmwood supplied it with one from his own hand, but throughout all the rest of the ceremony, appeared lost in zealous devotion to heaven.— Yet, no sooner was it finished; than his thoughts seemed to descend to this world.—He embraced his bride with all the transport of the fondest, happiest bridegroom, and in raptures called her by the endearing name of, 'wife.'

'But still, my lord,' cried Sandford, 'you are only married by your own church and conscience, not by your wife's; or by the law of the land;[1] and let me advise you not to defer that marriage long, lest in the time you disagree, and she yet refuse to become your legal spouse.'

'I think there is danger,' returned his lordship, 'and therefore our second marriage must take place to-morrow.'

To this the ladies objected, and it was left to Sandford to fix their second wedding-day, as he had done their first.—He, after consideration, gave four days interval.

Miss Woodley then recollected (for every one else had forgot it) that the carriage was still at the door to convey Lord Elmwood abroad.—It was of course dismissed—and one of those great incidents of delight Miss Milner that morning tasted, was to look out of the window, and see this very carriage drive from the door unoccupied.

Never was there a more rapid change from despair to happiness—to happiness most supreme—than was that, which Miss Milner, and Lord Elmwood experienced within one single hour.

The few days that intervened between this and their legal marriage, were passed in the delightful care of preparing for that happy day—yet, with all its delights inferior to the first; when every joy was doubled by the expected sorrow.

Nevertheless, on that first wedding-day, that joyful day, which restored her lost lover to her hopes again; even on that *very* day, after the sacred ceremony was over, Miss Milner— (with all the fears, the tremors, the superstition of her sex)— felt an excruciating shock; when, looking on the ring Lord Elmwood had put upon her finger, in haste, when he married her, she perceived it was a—MOURNING RING.[1]

VOLUME III

CHAPTER I

THROUGHOUT life, there cannot happen an event to arrest the reflection of a thoughtful mind more powerfully, or to leave so lasting an impression, as that of returning to a place after a few years absence, and observing an entire alteration in respect to all the persons who once formed the neighbourhood—To find some, who but a few years before were left in the bloom of youth and health, dead—to find children left at school, married, with children of their own—some persons who were in riches, reduced to poverty—others who were in poverty, become rich—those, once renowned for virtue, now detested for their vice—roving husbands, grown constant—constant ones, become rovers—the firmest friends, changed to the most implacable enemies—beauty faded.—In a word, every change to demonstrate 'All is transitory on this side the grave.'

Actuated by a wish, that the reflective reader may experience the sensation, which an attention to circumstances such as these, must cause; he is desired to imagine seventeen years elapsed, since he has seen or heard of any of those persons, who in the foregoing volumes have been introduced to his acquaintance—and now, supposing himself at the period of those seventeen years, follow the sequel of their history.

To begin with the first female object of this story.—The beautiful, the beloved Miss Milner—she is no longer beautiful—no longer beloved—no longer—tremble while you read it!—no longer—virtuous.

Dorriforth, the pious, the good, the tender Dorriforth, is

become a hard-hearted tyrant. The compassionate, the feeling, the just Lord Elmwood, an example of implacable rigour and injustice.

Miss Woodley is grown old, but less with years than grief.

The child Rushbrook is become a man, and the apparent heir of Lord Elmwood's fortune; while his own daughter, his only child by his once adored Miss Milner, he refuses ever to see again, in vengeance to her mother's crimes.

The least wonderful change, is the death of Mrs. Horton. Except

Sandford, who remains much the same as heretofore.

We left Lady Elmwood in the last volume at the summit of human happiness; a loving and beloved bride.—We begin this volume, and find her upon her death bed.

At thirty-five, her 'Course was run'—a course full of perils, of hopes, of fears, of joys, and at the end of sorrows; all exquisite of their kind, for exquisite were the feelings of her susceptible heart.

At the commencement of this story, her father is described in the last moments of his life, with all his cares fixed upon her, his only child—how vain these cares! how vain every precaution that was taken for her welfare! She knows, she reflects upon this; and yet, torn by that instinctive power which a parent feels, Lady Elmwood on her dying day has no worldly thought, but that of the future happiness of *her* only child.—To every other prospect before her, 'Thy will be done' is her continual exclamation; but where the misery of her daughter presents itself, the dying penitent would there, combat the will of heaven.

To state the progression by which vice gains a predominance in the heart, may be a useful lesson; but it is one so little to the satisfaction of most readers, that it is not meant to be related here, all the degrees of frailty by which Lady Elmwood fell;

but instead of picturing every occasion of her fall, come briefly to the events that followed.

There are, nevertheless, some articles under the former class, which ought not to be entirely omitted.

Lord Elmwood, after four years passed in the most perfect enjoyment of happiness, the marriage state could give; after seeing himself the father of a beautiful daughter, whom he loved with a tenderness nearly equal to his love for her mother, Lord Elmwood was then under the indispensable necessity of leaving them both for a time, in order to save from the depredation of his steward, a very large estate in the West Indies. His voyage was tedious; his residence there, from various accidents, prolonged from time to time till near three years had at length passed away.—Lady Elmwood, at first only unhappy, became at last provoked; and giving way to that impatient, irritable disposition she had so seldom governed, resolved, in spite of his injunctions, to divert the melancholy hours his absence caused, by mixing in the gayest circles of London. His lordship at this time, and for many months before, had been detained abroad by a severe and dangerous illness, which a too cautious fear of her uneasiness had prompted him to conceal; and she received his frequent apologies for not returning, with a suspicion and resentment they were calculated, but not intended, to inspire.

To violent anger, succeeded a degree of indifference still more fatal—Lady Elmwood's heart was never formed for such a state—there, where all the passions tumultuous strove by turns, one among them soon found the means to occupy all vacancies—that one was love.—The dear object of her fondest, truest, affections was away; and those affections painted the time so irksome that was past; so wearisome that, which was still to come; she flew from the present tedious solitude, to the dangerous society of one, whose every care to charm her, could not repay her for a moment's loss of him, whose absence he supplied.—Or if the delirium gave her a moment's recompense, what were her sufferings and remorse, when she was awakened from the fleeting joy by the unexpected arrival of her husband?—How happy, how transporting, had been that arrival a few months before!—As it had then been felicitous, it was now bitter—this word, however, weakly expresses—Language affords none, to describe Lady Elmwood's sensations on being told her lord was arrived, and that necessity only had so long delayed his return.

Guilty, but not hardened in her guilt, her pangs, her shame were the more excessive. She fled the place at his approach; fled his house, never again to return to a habitation where he was the master,—She did not, however, elope with her paramour, but escaped to shelter herself in the most dreary retreat; where she partook of no one comfort from society, or from life, but the still unremitting friendship of Miss Woodley.— Even her infant daughter she left behind, nor would allow herself the consolation of her innocent, but reproachful, smiles—she left her in her father's house that she might be under his protection; parted with her, as she thought for ever, with all the agonies that mothers part from their infant children: and yet even a mother scarcely can conceive how much more sharp those agonies were, on beholding the child sent after her, as the perpetual outcast of its father.

Lord Elmwood's love to his lady had been extravagant— the effect of his hate was extravagant likewise. Beholding himself separated from her by a barrier never to be removed, he vowed in the deep torments of his revenge, not to be reminded of her by one individual object; much less by one so nearly allied to her as her child. To bestow upon that his affections, would be, he imagined, still in some sort, to divide them with the mother.—Firm in his resolution, the beautiful Matilda was, at the age of six years, sent out of her father's house, and received by her mother with the tenderness, but with the anguish, of those parents, who behold their offspring visited with the punishment due only to their own offences.

During this transaction, which was performed by his lordship's agents at his command, he himself was engaged in an affair of still weightier importance—that of life or death:—he determined upon his own death, or the death of the man who had wounded his honour and his happiness. A duel with his old antagonist was the result of this determination; nor was the Duke of Avon (before the decease of his father and eldest brother, Lord Frederick Lawnly) backward to render all the satisfaction that was required.—For it was no other than he, whose love for Lady Elmwood had still subsisted, and whose art and industry left no means unessayed to perfect his designs;—No other than he, (who, next to Lord Elmwood, was ever of all her lovers most prevalent in her heart,) to whom Lady Elmwood yielded her own and her husband's future peace, and gave to his vanity a prouder triumph, than if she had never given her hand in preference to another. This triumph however was but short—a month only, after the return of Lord Elmwood, his Grace was called upon to answer for his conduct, and was left upon the spot where they met, so maimed, and defaced with scars, as never again to endanger the honour of a husband. As Lord Elmwood was inexorable to all accommodation; their engagement lasted for some space of time; nor any thing but the steadfast assurance his opponent was slain, could at last have torn his lordship from the field, though he himself was mortally wounded.

Yet even during that period of his danger, while for days he laid in the continual expectation of his own death, not all the entreaties of his dearest, most intimate, and most respected friends could prevail upon him to pronounce forgiveness to his wife, or suffer them to bring his daughter to him for his last blessing.

Lady Elmwood, who was made acquainted with the minutest circumstance as it passed, appeared to wait the news of her lord's decease with patience; but upon her brow, and in every lineament of her face it was marked, his death was an event she would not for a day survive—and she had left her child an orphan, to have followed Lord Elmwood to the grave.—She was prevented the trial; he recovered; and from the ample and distinguished vengeance he had obtained upon the irresistible person of the duke, in a short time seemed to regain his usual tranquillity.

He recovered, while Lady Elmwood fell sick and lingered—possessed of youth and a good constitution, she lingered till ten years decline, brought her to that period, with which the reader is now going to be presented.

CHAPTER II

IN a lonely country on the borders of Scotland, a single house by the side of a dreary heath, was the residence of the once gay, volatile Miss Milner—In a large gloomy apartment of this solitary habitation (the windows of which scarce rendered the light accessible)[1] was laid upon her death-bed, the once lovely Lady Elmwood—pale, half suffocated with the loss of breath; yet her senses perfectly clear and collected, which served but to sharpen the anguish of dying.

In one corner of the room, by the side of an old-fashioned stool, kneels Miss Woodley, praying most devoutly for her still beloved friend, but in vain endeavouring to pray composedly—floods of tears pour down her furrowed cheeks, and frequent sobs of sorrow break through each pious ejaculation.

Close by her mother's side, one hand supporting her head, the other wiping from her face the damp dew of death, behold Lady Elmwood's daughter—Lord Elmwood's daughter too—yet he far away, negligent of what either suffers.—Lady Elmwood turns to her often and attempts an embrace, but her feeble arms forbid, and they fall motionless.—The daughter perceiving those ineffectual efforts, has her whole face convulsed with sorrow; kisses her mother; holds her to her bosom; and hangs upon her neck, as if she wished to cling there, and the grave not to part them.

On the other side the bed sits Sandford—his hair grown white—his face wrinkled with age—his heart the same as ever ——The reprover, the enemy of the vain, idle, and wicked; but the friend, the comforter of the forlorn and miserable.

Upon those features where sarcasm, reproach, and anger dwelt to threaten and alarm the sinner; mildness, tenderness, and pity beamed, to support and console the penitent. Compassion changed his language, and softened all those harsh tones that used to denounce resentment.

'In the name of God,' said he to Lady Elmwood, 'that God who suffered for you, and, suffering, knew and pitied all our weaknesses—By him, who has given his word to *take compassion on the sinner's tears*, I bid you hope for mercy.—By that innocence in which you once lived, be comforted—By the sorrows you have known since your degradation, hope, in some degree, to have atoned—By that sincerity which shone upon your youthful face when I joined your hands; those thousand virtues you have at times given proof of, you were not born to die *the death of the wicked*.'

As he spoke these words of consolation, her trembling hand clasped his—her dying eyes darted a ray of brightness—but her failing voice endeavoured, in vain, to articulate.—At length, her eyes fixing upon her daughter as their last dear object, she was just understood to utter the word 'Father.'

'I understand you,' replied Sandford, 'and by all that influence I ever had over him, by my prayers, my tears,' (and they flowed at the word) 'I will implore him to own his child.'

She could now only smile, in thanks.

'And if I should fail,' continued he, 'yet while I live, she shall not want a friend or protector—all an old man like me can answer for'——here his tears interrupted him.

Lady Elmwood was sufficiently sensible of his words and their import, to make a sign as if she wished to embrace him; but finding her life leaving her fast, she reserved this last token of love for her daughter—With a struggle she lifted herself from her pillow, clung to her child—and died in her arms.

CHAPTER III

LORD ELMWOOD was by nature, and more from education, of a serious, thinking, and philosophic turn of mind. His religious studies had completely taught him to consider this world but as a passage to another; to enjoy with gratitude what Heaven in its bounty should bestow, and to bear with submission, all which in its' vengeance it might inflict—In a greater degree than most people he practised this doctrine; and as soon as the first shock he received from Lady Elmwood's conduct was abated, an entire calmness and resignation ensued; but still of that sensible and feeling kind, which could never force him to forget the happiness he had lost; and it was this sensibility, which urged him to fly from its more keen recollection as much as possible—this he alledged as the reason he would never suffer Lady Elmwood, or even her child, to be named in his hearing. But this injunction (which all his friends, and even the servants in the house who attended his person, had received) was, by many people, suspected rather to proceed from his resentment, than his tenderness; nor did he himself deny, that resentment mingled with his prudence; for prudence he called it not to remind himself of happiness he could never taste again, and of ingratitude that might impel him to hatred; and prudence he called it, not to form another attachment near to his heart; more especially so near as a parent's, which might a second time expose him to all the torments of ingratitude, from one whom he affectionately loved.

Upon these principles he formed the unshaken resolution, never to acknowledge Lady Matilda as his child—or acknowledging her as such—never to see, hear of, or take one concern whatever in her fate and fortune. The death of her mother appeared a favourable time, had he been so inclined, to have recalled this declaration which he had solemnly and repeatedly made—she was now destitute of the protection of her other parent, and it became his duty, at least to provide her a guardian, if he did not choose to take that tender title upon himself.—But to mention either the mother or child to Lord Elmwood was an equal offence, and prohibited in the strongest terms to all his friends and household: and as he was an excellent good master, a sincere friend, and a most generous patron; not one of his acquaintance or dependants, were hardy enough to draw upon themselves his certain displeasure, which was violent in the extreme, by even the official intelligence of Lady Elmwood's death.

Sandford himself, intimidated through age, or by the austere, and even morose, manners Lord Elmwood had of late years adopted; Sandford wished, if possible, some other

would undertake the dangerous task of recalling to his lordship's memory, there ever was such a person as his wife. He
advised Miss Woodley to indite a proper letter to him on the
subject; but she reminded him, such a step was still more
perilous in her, than any other person, as she was the most
destitute being on earth, without the benevolence of Lord
Elmwood. The death of her aunt, Mrs. Horton, had left her
sole reliance on Lady Elmwood; and now her death, had left
her totally dependant upon the earl—for her ladyship, long
before her decease, had declared it was not her intention, to
leave a single sentence behind her in the form of a will—She
had no will, she said, but what she would wholly submit to
Lord Elmwood's; and, if it were even his will, her child should
live in poverty, as well as banishment, it should be so.—But,
perhaps, in this implicit submission to his lordship, there was
a distant hope that the necessitous situation of his daughter
might plead more forcibly than his parental love; and that
knowing her abandoned of every support but through himself,
that idea might form some little tie between them; and be at
least a token of the relationship.

But as Lady Elmwood anxiously wished this principle upon
which she acted, should be concealed from his lordship's suspicion, she included her friend, Miss Woodley, in the same
fate; and thus, the only persons dear to her, she left, but at
Lord Elmwood's pleasure, to be preserved from perishing in
want.—Her child was too young to advise her on this subject,
her friend too disinterested; and at this moment they were
both without the smallest means of support, except through
the justice or compassion of his lordship.—Sandford had,
indeed, promised his protection to the daughter; but his
liberality had no other source than from his patron, with
whom he still lived as usual, except during the winter when
his lordship resided in town, he then mostly stole a visit to

Lady Elmwood—On this last visit, he staid to see her buried.

After some mature deliberations, Sandford was now preparing to go to Lord Elmwood at his house in town, and there to deliver himself the news that must sooner or later be told; and he meant also to venture, at the same time, to keep the promise he had made to his dying lady—but the news reached Lord Elmwood before Sandford arrived; it was announced in the public papers, and by that means came first to his knowledge.

He was breakfasting by himself, when the newspaper that first gave the intelligence of Lady Elmwood's death, was laid before him—the paragraph contained these words:

'On Wednesday last died, at Dring Park, a village in Northumberland, the right honourable Countess Elmwood— This lady, who has not been heard of for many years in the fashionable world, was a rich heiress, and of extreme beauty; but although she received overtures from many men of the first rank, she preferred her guardian, the present Lord Elmwood (then the humble Mr. Dorriforth) to them all— and it is said, they enjoyed an uncommon share of felicity, till his lordship going abroad, and remaining there some time, the consequences (to a most captivating young woman left without a protector) were such, as to cause a separation on his return.—Her ladyship has left one child, a daughter, about fifteen.'

Lord Elmwood had so much feeling upon reading this, as to lay down the paper, and not take it up again for several minutes—nor did he taste his chocolate during this interval, but leaned his elbow on the table and rested his head upon his hand.—He then rose up—walked two or three times across the room—sat down again—took up the paper—and read as usual.——Nor let the vociferous mourner, or the perpetual weeper, here complain of his want of sensibility—but let them remember Lord Elmwood was a man—a man of understanding—of courage—of fortitude—with all, a man of the nicest feelings—and who shall say, but that at the time he leaned his head upon his hand, and rose to walk away the sense of what he felt, he might not feel as much as Lady Elmwood did in her last moments.

Be this as it may, his lordship's susceptibility on the occasion was not suspected by any one—he passed that day the same as usual; the next day too, and the day after.—On the morning of the fourth day, he sent for his steward to his study, and after talking of other business, said to him,

'Is it true that Lady Elmwood is dead?'

'It is, my lord,' replied the man.

His lordship looked unusually grave, and at this reply, fetched an involuntary sigh.

'Mr. Sandford, my lord', continued the steward, 'sent me word of the news, but left it to my own discretion, whether I made your lordship acquainted with it or not.'

'Where is Sandford?' asked Lord Elmwood.

'He was with my lady,' replied the steward.

'When she died?' asked his lordship.

'Yes, my lord.'

'I am glad of it—he will see every thing she desired done.—Sandford is a good man, and would be a friend to every body.'

'He is a very good man indeed, my lord.'

There was now a silence.——Mr. Giffard then bowing, said, 'Has your lordship any farther commands?'

'Write to Sandford,' said Lord Elmwood, hesitating as he spoke, 'and tell him to have every thing performed as she desired.—And whoever she may have selected for the guardian of her child, has my consent to act as such.—Nor in one instance, where I myself am not concerned, will I contradict her will.'—The tears rushed to his eyes as he said this, and caused them to start in the steward's—observing which, he sternly resumed,

'Do not suppose from this conversation, that any of those resolutions I have long since taken are, or will be, changed— they are the same; and shall continue the same:—and your interdiction, sir, (as well as every other person's) remains just the same as formerly; never to mention this subject to me in future.'

'My lord, I always obeyed you,' replied Mr. Giffard, 'and hope I always shall.'

'I hope so too,' replied his lordship, in a threatening accent —'Write to Sandford,' continued he, 'to let him know my pleasure, and that is all you have to do.'

The steward bowed and withdrew.

But before his letter arrived to Sandford, Sandford arrived in town; and Mr. Giffard related to him word for word what had passed between him and his lord.—Upon every occasion, and upon every topic, except that of Lady Elmwood and her child, Sandford was just as free with Lord Elmwood as he had ever been; and as usual (after his interview with the steward) went into his lordship's apartment without any previous notice. His lordship shaked him by the hand as upon all other meetings; and yet, whether his fears suggested it or not, Sandford thought he appeared more cool and reserved with him than common.

During the whole day, the slightest mention of Lady Elmwood, or of her child, was cautiously avoided—and not till the evening, (after Sandford had rung for his candle to retire to rest, it was brought, and he had wished his lordship good night) did he dare to mention the subject.——He then, after taking leave, and going to the door—turned back and said, 'My lord,'——

It was easy to guess on what he was preparing to speak—
his voice failed, the tears began to trickle down his cheeks,
he took out his handkerchief, and could proceed no farther.

'I thought,' said Lord Elmwood, angrily, 'I thought I had
given my orders upon this subject—did not my steward write
them to you?'

'He did, my lord,' said Sandford, humbly, 'but I was set out
before they arrived.'

'Has he not *told* you my mind then?' cried his lordship,
more angrily still.

'He has;' replied Sandford,—'But'——

'But what, sir?'—cried Lord Elmwood.

'Your lordship,' continued Sandford, 'was mistaken in
supposing Lady Elmwood left a will; she left none.'

'No will? no will at all?'—said his lordship, surprised.

'No, my lord,' answered Sandford, 'she wished every thing
to be as you willed.'

'She left me all the trouble, then, you mean?'

'No great trouble, sir; for except two persons, her ladyship has not left any one else to hope for your protection.'

'And who are those two?' cried he hastily.

'One, my lord, I need not name—the other is Miss
Woodley.'

There was a delicacy and an humility, in the manner in
which Sandford delivered this reply, that Lord Elmwood
could *not* resent, and he only returned,

'Miss Woodley, is she yet living?'

'She is—I left her at the house I came from.'

'Well, then,' answered his lordship, 'you must see that my
steward provides for those two persons.—That care I leave to
you—and should there be any complaints, on you they fall.'

Sandford bowed and was going.

'And now,' resumed his lordship, in a stern and exalted

voice, 'let me *never* hear again on this subject.—You have full power to act in regard to the persons you have mentioned; and upon you their situation, their care, their whole management depend—but be sure, you never let them be named before me, from this moment.'

'Then,' said Sandford, 'as this must be the last time they are mentioned, I must now take the opportunity to disburthen my mind of a charge'——

'What charge?'—cried his lordship, morosely interrupting him.

'Though Lady Elmwood, my lord, left no will behind, she left a request.'

'Request'—said his lordship, starting—'If it is for me to see her daughter, I tell you now before you ask, I will not grant it—for by heaven' (and he spoke and looked most solemnly) 'though I have no resentment to the innocent child, and wish her happy, yet I will never see her.—Never, for her mother's sake, suffer my heart to be again softened by an object I might doat on.—Therefore, sir, if that is the request, it is already answered; my will is fixed.'

'The request, my lord,' replied Sandford, (taking out a pocket book from whence he drew several papers) 'is contained in this letter; nor do I rightly know what its contents are.'— And he held it out to him.

'Is it Lady Elmwood's writing?' cried his lordship, extremely discomposed.

'It is, my lord—She called for ink and paper and wrote it a few days before she died, and enjoined me to deliver it to you, with my own hands.'

'I refuse to read it,'—cried he, putting it from him—and trembling while he did so.

'She desired me,' said Sandford, (still presenting the letter) 'to conjure you to read it, *for her father's sake*.'

Lord Elmwood took it instantly.—But as soon as it was in his hand, he seemed distressed to know what he should do with it—in what place, to go to read it—or how fortify himself against its contents.—He appeared ashamed too, that he had been so far prevailed upon, and said, by way of excuse,

'For Mr. Milner's sake I would do much—nay, any thing, but that to which, I have just now sworn never to consent.—For his sake I have borne a great deal—for his sake alone, his daughter died my wife.—You know, no other motive than respect for him, prevented my divorcing[1] her.——Pray' (and he hesitated) 'was she buried with him?'

'No, my lord—she expressed no such desire; and as that was the case, I did not think it necessary to carry the corpse so far.'

At the word corpse, Lord Elmwood shrunk, and looked shocked beyond measure—but recovering himself, said, 'I am sorry for it;—for he loved *her* sincerely, if she did not love him—and I wish they had been buried together.'

'It is not then too late,' said Sandford, and was going on—but his lordship interrupted him.

'No, no—we will have no disturbing of the dead.'

'Read her letter then,' said Sandford, 'and bid her rest in peace.'

'If it is in my power,' returned his lordship, 'to grant what she asks I will—but if her demand is what I apprehend, I cannot, I will not, bid her rest by complying.—You know my resolution, and my disposition, and take care how you provoke me.—You may do an injury to the very person you are seeking to befriend—the very maintenance I mean to allow her daughter I can withdraw.'

Poor Sandford, all alarm at this menace, replied with energy, 'My lord, unless you begin the subject, I never will presume to mention it again.'

'I take you at your word,'—returned his lordship, 'and in consequence of that, and that alone, we are friends.—Good night, sir.'

Sandford bowed with all humility, and they went to their separate bedchambers.

CHAPTER IV

AFTER Lord Elmwood had retired into his chamber, it was some time before he read the letter Sandford had given him. He first walked backwards and forwards in the room—he then began to take off some part of his dress, but did it slowly. At length he dismissed his valet, and sitting down, took the letter from his pocket.—He looked at the seal, but not at the direction; for he seemed to dread to see Lady Elmwood's hand writing.—He then laid it on the table, and began again to undress. He did not proceed, but taking up the letter quickly, (with a kind of effort in making the resolution) broke it open. These were its contents:

'My lord,

'Who writes this letter I well know—I well know also to whom it is addressed—I feel with the most powerful force both our situations;—nor should I dare to offer you even this humble petition, but that at the time you receive it, there will be no such person as I am in existence.

'For myself, then, all concern will be over—but there is a care that pursues me to the grave, and threatens my want of repose even there.

'I leave a child—I will not call her mine, that has undone her—I will not call her yours, that will be of no avail.—I present her before you as the grand-daughter of Mr. Milner.—

Oh! do not refuse an asylum even in your own house, to the destitute offspring of your friend; the last, and only remaining branch of his family.

'Receive her into your household, be her condition there ever so abject.—I cannot write distinctly what I would—my senses are not impaired, but the powers of expression are.—The unfortunate child in the scripture (a lesson I have studied) his complaint,[1] has made this wish cling so fast to my heart, that without the distant hope of its being fulfilled, death would have more terrors than my weak mind could support.

'"*I will go to my father; how many servants live in my father's house, and are fed with plenty, while I starve in a foreign land?*"[2]

'I do not ask a parent's festive rejoicing at her approach—I do not even ask her father to behold her;—but let her live under his protection.—For her grandfather's sake do not refuse this—to the child of his child whom he trusted to your care, do not refuse it.

'Be her host; I remit the tie of being her parent.—Never see her—but let her sometimes live under the same roof with you.

'It is Miss Milner your ward, to whom you never refused a request, supplicates you—not now for your nephew Rushbrook, but for one so much more dear, that a denial——she dares not suffer her thoughts to glance that way—She will hope—and in that hope, bids you farewell, with all the love she ever bore you.

'Farewell Lord Elmwood—and before you throw this letter from you with contempt or anger, cast your imagination into the grave where I am lying.—Reflect upon all the days of my past life—the anxious moments I have known, and what has been their end.—Behold *me*, also—in my altered face there is no anxiety—no joy or sorrow—all is over.——My whole frame is motionless—my heart beats no more.—Look at my horrid habitation, too,—and ask yourself—whether I am an object of resentment?'

While Lord Elmwood read this letter, it trembled in his hand: he once or twice wiped the tears from his eyes as he read, and once laid the letter down for a few minutes. At its conclusion the tears flowed fast down his face; but he seemed both ashamed and angry they did, and was going to throw the paper upon the fire; he however suddenly checked his hand, and putting it hastily into his pocket, went to bed.

CHAPTER V

THE next morning, when Lord Elmwood and Sandford met at breakfast, Sandford was pale with fear for the success of Lady Elmwood's letter—his lordship was pale too, but there was beside upon his face something which evidently marked he was displeased—Sandford observed it, and was all humbleness, both in his words and looks, in order to soften him.

As soon as the breakfast was removed, his lordship drew Lady Elmwood's letter from his pocket, and holding it towards Sandford, said,

'That may be of more value to you, than it is to me, therefore I give it you.'

Sandford called up a look of surprise, as if he did not know the letter again.

''Tis Lady Elmwood's letter,' said his lordship, 'and I give it to you for two reasons.'

Sandford took it, and putting it up, asked fearfully 'What those two reasons were?'

'First,' said Lord Elmwood, 'because I think it is a relic

you may like to preserve—my second reason is, that you may show it to her daughter, and let her know why, and on what conditions I grant her mother's request.'

'You do then grant it?' cried Sandford joyfully; 'I thank you—you are kind—you are considerate.'

'Be not too hasty in your gratitude,' returned his lordship, 'you may have cause to recall it.'

'I know what you have said,' replied Sandford, 'You have said you grant Lady Elmwood's request—you cannot recall these words, nor I my gratitude.'

'Do you know what her request is?' said Lord Elmwood.

'Not exactly, my lord—I told you before, I did not; but it is no doubt something in favour of her child.'

'I think not,' replied his lordship, 'Such as it is, however, I grant it.—But in the strictest sense of the word—no farther; —and one neglect of my commands, releases my promise totally.'

'We will take care, sir, not to disobey them.'

'Then listen to what they are—and to you I give the charge of delivering them again.—Lady Elmwood has petitioned me in the name of her father, (a name I reverence) to give his grandchild the sanction of my protection.—In the literal sense, to suffer her to reside occasionally at one of my seats; dispensing at the same time with my ever seeing her.'

'And you will comply?'

'I will, till she encroaches on this concession, and dare to ask for a greater.—I will, while she avoids my sight, or the giving me any remembrance of her.—But, if, whether by design or by accident, I ever see or hear from her; that moment my compliance to her mother's supplication ceases, and I abandon her once more.'

Sandford sighed.—His lordship continued.

'I am glad her request stopped where it did.—I would rather

comply with her desires than not; and I rejoice they are such as I can grant with ease and honour to myself. I am seldom now at Elmwood House; let her daughter go there;—the few weeks or months I am down in the summer she may easily in that extensive house avoid me—while she does, she lives in security—when she does not, you know my resolution.'

Sandford bowed—his lordship resumed.

'Nor can it be a hardship to obey this command—she cannot lament the separation from a parent whom she never knew——' Sandford was going eagerly to prove the error of that assertion, but his lordship prevented him saying, 'In a word—without farther argument—if she obeys me in this, I certainly provide for her as my daughter during my life, and leave her a fortune at my death—but if she dares——'

Sandford interrupted the menace he saw prepared for utterance, saying, 'And you still mean, I suppose, to make Mr. Rushbrook your heir?'

'Have you not heard me say so? And do you imagine I have changed my determination? I am not given to alter my resolutions, Mr. Sandford; and I thought you knew I was not;—besides, will not my title be extinct, whoever I make my heir?—Could any thing but a son have preserved my title?'

'Then it is yet possible——'

'By marrying again, you mean?—No—no—I have had enough of marriage—and Henry Rushbrook I leave my heir. Therefore, sir——'

'My lord, I do not presume——'

'Do not, Sandford, and we may still be friends.—But I am not to be controlled as formerly; my temper is changed of late; changed to what it was originally; till your scholastic and religious rules reformed it. You may remember, how troublesome it was, to conquer my stubborn disposition in my youth;

then, indeed, you did; but in my manhood you will find the task more difficult.'

Sandford again repeated 'He should not presume——'

To which his lordship again made answer, 'Do not, Sandford;' and added, 'For I have a sincere regard for you, and should be loath at these years to quarrel with you seriously.'

Sandford turned away his head to hide his tears.

'Nay, if we do quarrel,' resumed his lordship, 'You know it must be your own fault;—and as this is a theme the most likely of any (indeed the only one on which we can have a difference such as we cannot forgive) take care never from this day to resume it;—indeed that of itself, is an offence I will not pardon.—I have been clear and explicit in all I have said; there can be no fear of mistaking my meaning, therefore all future explanation is unnecessary—nor will I permit a word, or a hint on the subject from any one, without showing my resentment to the hour of my death.' He was going out of the room.

'But before we bid adieu to the subject for ever, my lord—there was another person whom I named to you——'

'Do you mean Miss Woodley?—Oh, by all means let her live at Elmwood House too.—On consideration, I have no objection to see Miss Woodley at any time—I shall be glad to see her—do not let *her* be frightened at me—to her I shall be the same, I have always been.'

'She is a good woman, my lord,' cried Sandford, pleased.

'You need not tell me that, Mr. Sandford; I know her worth.'—And his lordship left the room.

Sandford, to relieve Miss Woodley and her lovely charge from the suspense in which he had left them, set off for their habitation the next day; in order himself to conduct them from thence to Elmwood House, and appoint some retired part of it for Lady Matilda, against the annual visit her father paid there. But before he left London, Giffard, the steward, took an opportunity to wait upon him, and let him know, that his lord had acquainted him, with the consent he had given for his daughter to be admitted at Elmwood Castle; and upon what restrictions; likewise that he had denounced the most severe threats, should these restrictions be broken. Sandford thanked Giffard for his friendly information, which served him as a second warning of the circumspection that was necessary; and having taken leave of his lordship under the pretence 'he could not live in the smoke of London,' he set out for the north.

It is unnecessary to say with what delight Sandford was received by Miss Woodley, and the hapless daughter of Lady Elmwood, even before he told his errand. They both loved him sincerely; more especially Lady Matilda; whose forlorn state, and innocent sufferings, had ever excited his compassion in the extremest degree, and had caused him ever to treat her with the utmost affection, tenderness, and respect. She knew, too, how much he had been her mother's friend; for that she also loved him; and being honoured with the friendship of her father, she looked up to him with reverence and awe. For Matilda (with an excellent understanding, a sedateness above her years, and early accustomed to the most private converse between Lady Elmwood and Miss Woodley) was perfectly acquainted with the whole fatal history of her mother; and was by her taught, that respect and admiration of her father's virtues which they justly merited.

Notwithstanding the joy of beholding Mr. Sandford, once more to cheer by his presence their solitary dwelling; no sooner were the first kind greetings over, than the dread of what he might have to inform them, possessed both poor Matilda and Miss Woodley so powerfully, their gladness was changed into affright.—Their apprehensions were far more forcible than their curiosity;—they durst not ask a question, and even began to wish he would continue silent upon the subject, on which they feared to listen.—For near two hours he was so.——At length, after a short interval from speaking, (during which they waited with anxiety for what he might next say) he turned to Lady Matilda, and said,

'You don't ask for your father, my dear.'

'I did not know it was proper,' she replied timidly.

'It is always proper,' answered Sandford, 'for *you* to think of him, though he should never think on you.'

She burst into tears, saying, she '*did* think of him, but she felt an apprehension at mentioning his name,'—and she wept bitterly while she spoke.

'Nay, do not think I reproved you,' said Sandford; 'I but told you what was right.'

'Nay,' said Miss Woodley, 'it is not for that she cries thus— she fears her father has not complied with her mother's request.—Perhaps not even read her letter?'

'Yes, he has read it,' returned Sandford.

'Oh Heavens!' exclaimed Matilda, clasping her hands together, and the tears falling faster still.

'Do not be so much alarmed, my dear,' said Miss Woodley; 'you know we are prepared for the worst; and you know you promised your mother, whatever your fate was, to submit with patience.'

'Yes,' replied Matilda, 'and I am prepared for every thing, but my father's refusal to my dear mother.'

'Your father has not refused your mother's request,' replied Sandford.

She was leaping from her seat in ecstasy.

'But,' continued he, 'do you know what her request was?'

'Not entirely,' replied Matilda, 'and since it is granted I am careless.—But she told me her letter concerned none but me.'

To explain perfectly to Matilda Lady Elmwood's letter,

and that she might perfectly understand upon what terms she was admitted into Elmwood House, Sandford now read the letter to her; and repeated, as nearly as he could remember, the whole of the conversation that passed between Lord Elmwood and himself; not even sparing, with an erroneous delicacy, any of those threats her father had denounced, should she dare to break through the limits he prescribed— nor did he try to soften, in one instance, a word his lordship uttered. She listened sometimes with tears, sometimes with hope, but always with awe, and terror, to every sentence wherein her father was concerned. Once she called him cruel —then exclaimed 'he was kind;' but at the end of Sandford's intelligence, concluded she was happy and grateful for the boon bestowed.—Even her mother had not a more exalted and transcendent idea of Lord Elmwood's worth, than his daughter had formed; and this little bounty just obtained, had not been greater in her mother's estimation, than it was now in her's.—Miss Woodley, too, smiled at the prospect before her— she esteemed Lord Elmwood beyond any mortal living—she was proud to hear what he had said in her praise, and over-joyed at the prospect she should be once again in his company; picturing, at the same time, a thousand of the brightest hopes, from watching every emotion of his soul, and catching every proper occasion to excite, or increase, his paternal senti-ments.—Yet she had the prudence to conceal those vague hopes from his child, lest a disappointment might prove fatal; and assuming a behaviour not too much elated or depressed, she advised they should hope for the best, but yet, as usual, expect and prepare for the worst.——After taking measures for quitting their melancholy abode; within the fortnight they all departed for Elmwood Castle.—Matilda, Miss Woodley, and even Sandford, first visiting Lady Elmwood's grave, and be-dewing it with their tears.

I T was on a dark evening in the month of March, that Lady Matilda, accompanied by Sandford and Miss Woodley, arrived at Elmwood Castle, the magnificent seat of her father. —Sandford chose the evening; rather to steal into the house privately, than by any appearance of parade, suffer Lord Elmwood to be reminded of it by the public prints, or by any other accident.—Nor would he give the neighbours or servants the slightest reason to suppose, the daughter of their lord was admitted into his house in any other situation than, that, which she really was.

As the porter opened the gates of the avenue to the carriage that brought them, Matilda felt an awful, and yet a gladsome sensation no terms can describe.—As she entered the door of the house this sensation increased—and as she passed along the spacious hall, the splendid staircase, and many stately apartments, wonder! with a crowd of the tenderest, yet most afflicting, sentiments rushed to her heart.—She gazed with astonishment!—she reflected with more.

'And is *my father* the master of this house?' she cried— 'And was my mother once the mistress of this house?'—Here a flood of tears relieved her from a part of that burthen, which was before insupportable.

'Yes,' replied Sandford, 'And you are the mistress of it now, till your father arrives.'

'Good God!' exclaimed she, 'and will he ever arrive? and shall I live to sleep under the same roof with my father?'

'My dear,' replied Miss Woodley, 'have not you been told so?'

'Yes,' said she, 'but though I heard it with extreme pleasure, yet the idea never so forcibly affected me as at this moment.—

I now feel, as the reality approaches, this has been kindness sufficient—I do not ask for more—I am now convinced, from what this trial makes me feel, that to see my father, would cause a sensation, a feeling, I could not survive.'

The next morning gave to Matilda more objects still of admiration and wonder, as she walked over the extensive gardens, groves, and other pleasure grounds belonging to the house. She, who had never been beyond the dreary, ruinate place where her deceased mother had chosen her residence, was naturally struck with amazement and delight at the grandeur of a seat, which travellers have come for miles to see, and not thought their time misspent.

There was one object, however, among all she saw, which attracted her attention above the rest, and she would stand for hours to look at it—This was a full length portrait of Lord Elmwood, esteemed a very capital picture, and a great likeness—to this picture she would sigh and weep; though when it was first pointed out to her, she shrunk back with fear, and it was some time before she dared venture to cast her eyes completely upon it. In the features of her father she was proud to discern the exact moulds in which her own appeared to have been modelled; yet Matilda's person, shape, and complection were so extremely like what her mother's once were, that at the first glance she appeared to have a still greater resemblance of her, than of her father—but her mind and manners were all Lord Elmwood's; softened by the delicacy of her sex, the extreme tenderness of her heart, and the melancholy of her situation.

She was now in her seventeenth year—of the same age, within a year and a few months, of her mother when she became the ward of Dorriforth.—She was just three years old when her father went abroad, and remembered something of bidding him farewell; but more of taking cherries from his hand as he pulled them from the tree to give to her.

Educated in the school of adversity, and inured to retirement from her infancy, she had acquired a taste for all those amusements which a recluse life affords—She was fond of walking and riding—was accomplished in the arts of music and drawing, by the most careful instructions of her mother—and as a scholar she excelled most of her sex, from the great pains Sandford had taken with that part of her education, and the great abilities he possessed for the task.

In devoting certain hours of the day to study with him, others to music, riding, and such recreations, Matilda's time never appeared tedious at Elmwood House, although she neither received nor paid one visit—for it was soon divulged in the neighbourhood upon what stipulation she resided at her father's, and intimated, that the most prudent and friendly behaviour of the friends both of her father and of herself, would be, to take no notice whatever that she lived among them: and as Lord Elmwood's will was a law all around, such was the consequence, of his will being known or supposed.

Neither did Miss Woodley regret the want of visitors, but found herself far more satisfied in her present situation, than her most sanguine hopes could have formed—She had a companion whom she loved with an equal fondness, with which she had loved her deceased mother; and frequently in this charming mansion, where she had so often beheld Lady Elmwood, her imagination pictured Matilda as her risen from the grave in her former youth, health, and exquisite beauty.

In peace, in content, though far from happiness, the days and weeks passed away till about the middle of August, when preparations began to be made for the arrival of Lord Elmwood.—The week in which he was to come was at length fixed, and some part of his retinue was arrived before him.—

When this was told to Matilda she started, and looked just as her mother at her age often times had done, when, in spite of her love, she was conscious she had offended him, and was terrified at his approach. Sandford observing this, put out his hand, and taking hers shook it kindly; and bade her (but it was not in a cheerful tone) 'not be afraid.' This gave her no confidence; and she began, before his lordship's arrival, to seclude herself in those apartments which were allotted for her during the time of his stay; and in the timorous expectation of his coming, her appetite declined and she lost all her colour.—Even Miss Woodley, whose spirits had been for some time elated with the hopes she had formed, on drawing near to the test, found those hopes vanished; and though she endeavoured to conceal it, she was replete with apprehensions.—Sandford, had certainly fewer fears than either; yet upon the eve of the day on which his patron was to arrive, he was evidently cast down.

Lady Matilda once asked him—'Are you certain, Mr. Sandford, you made no mistake in respect to what Lord Elmwood said, when he granted my mother's request? Are you sure he *did* grant it?—Was there nothing equivocal on which he may ground his displeasure should he hear I am here?—Oh! do not let me hazard the being once again turned out of his house! —Oh! save me from provoking him perhaps to curse me.'— And here she clasped her hands together with the most fervent petition, in the dread of what might happen.

'If you doubt my word or my senses,' said Sandford, 'call Giffard, and let him inform you;—my lord repeated the same words to him he did to me.'

Though from her reason Matilda could not doubt of any mistake from Mr. Sandford, yet her fears suggested a thousand scruples; and this reference to the steward she received with the utmost satisfaction, (though she did not think it necessary to apply to him) as it perfectly convinced her of the folly of those suspicions she had entertained.

'And yet, Mr. Sandford,' said she, 'if it is so, why are you less cheerful than you were? I cannot help thinking but it must be the expectation of Lord Elmwood here, which has caused in you this change.'

'I don't know;' replied Sandford, carelessly, 'but I believe I am grown afraid of your father.—His temper is a great deal altered from what it once was—he exalts his voice, and uses harsh expressions upon the least provocation—his eyes flash lightning, and his face is distorted with anger on the slightest motives—he turns away his old servants at a moment's warning, and no concession can make their peace.—In a word, I am more at my ease when I am away from him—and I really believe,' added he with a smile, but with a tear at the same time, 'I really believe I am more afraid of him in my age, than he was of me when he was a boy.'

Miss Woodley was present; she and Matilda looked at one another; and each saw the other turn pale, at this description.

The day at length came on which Lord Elmwood was expected to dinner.——It had been a high gratification to his daughter to have gone to the topmost window of the house, to have only beheld his chariot enter the avenue; but it was a gratification which her fears, her tremor, her extreme sensibility would not permit her to enjoy.

Miss Woodley and she sat down that day to dinner in their retired apartments; which were detached from the other part of the house by a gallery; and of the door leading to the gallery they had a key to impede any one from passing that way, without first ringing a bell; to answer which, was the sole employment of a servant who was placed there during his lordship's residence, lest by any accident he might chance to come near that unfrequented part of the house; on which occasion the man was to give immediate notice to his lady.

Miss Woodley and she sat down to dinner, but did not dine. —Sandford ate, as usual, with Lord Elmwood.—When the servant brought up tea, Miss Woodley asked him if he had seen his lord—The man answered, 'Yes, madam; and he looks vastly well.'—Matilda wept with joy to hear it.

About nine in the evening Sandford rung at the bell, and was admitted—and never was he so welcome—Matilda hung upon him, as if his recent society with her father had endeared him to her more than ever; and staring anxiously in his face, seemed to ask him to tell her something of Lord Elmwood, and something that should not alarm her.

'Well—how do you find yourself?' said he to her.

'How are you, Mr. Sandford?' she returned, with a sigh.

'Oh! very well,' replied he.

'Is my lord in a good temper?' asked Miss Woodley.

'Yes; very well,' replied Sandford, with indifference.

'Did he seem glad to see you?' asked Matilda.

'He shook me by the hand,' replied Sandford.

'That was a sign he was glad to see you, was it not?' said Matilda.

'Yes; but he could not do less.'

'Nor more,' replied she.

'He looks very well, our servant tells us,' said Miss Woodley.

'Extremely well indeed,' answered Sandford: 'and, to tell the truth, I never saw him in better spirits.'

'That is well:' said Matilda, and sighed a weight of fears from her heart.

'Where is he now, Mr. Sandford?'

'Gone to take a walk about his grounds, and so I stole here in the mean time.'

'What was your conversation during dinner?'

'Horses, hay, farming, and politics.'

'Won't you sup with him?'

'I shall see him again before I go to bed.'

'And again to-morrow!'—cried Matilda, 'what happiness!'

'He has visitors to-morrow,' said Sandford, 'coming for a week or two.'

'Thank heaven!' said Miss Woodley, 'he will then be diverted from thinking on us.'

'Do you know,' returned Sandford, 'it is my firm opinion, that his thinking of ye at present, is the cause of his good spirits.'

'Oh, heavens!' cried Matilda, lifting up her hands with rapture.

'Nay, do not mistake me;' said Sandford; 'I would not have you build a foundation for joy upon this; for if he is in spirits that you are in this house—so near him—positively under his protection—yet he will not allow himself to think that, is the cause of his content—and the sentiments he has adopted, and are now become natural to him, will remain the same as ever; nay, perhaps with greater force, while he suspects his weakness (as he calls it) acting in opposition.'

'If he does but think of me with tenderness,' cried Matilda, 'I am recompensed.'

'And what recompense would his kind thoughts be to you,' said Sandford, 'were he to turn you out to beggary?'

'A great deal—a great deal,' she replied.

'But how are you to know he has these kind thoughts, while he gives you no proof of them?'

'No, Mr. Sandford; but *supposing* we could know them without the proof.'

'But as that is impossible,' answered he, 'I shall suppose, till the proof appears, I am mistaken.'

Matilda looked deeply concerned that the argument should

conclude in her disappointment; for to have believed herself
thought of with tenderness by her father, would have alone
constituted her happiness.

When the servant came up with something by way of supper, he told Mr. Sandford his lordship was returned from his
walk and had enquired for him; Sandford immediately bade
his companions good night, and left them.

'How strange is this!' cried Matilda, when Miss Woodley
and she were alone, 'My father within a few rooms of me, and
yet I am debarred from seeing him!—Only by walking a few
paces I might be at his feet, and perhaps receive his blessing.'

'You make me shudder,' said Miss Woodley; 'but some
spirits less fearful than mine, might perhaps advise you to try
the experiment.'

'Not for worlds,' returned Matilda; 'no counsel could tempt
me to such temerity; and yet to entertain the thought, that it
is possible I could do this, is a source of great comfort.'

This conversation lasted till bed time, and later; for they sat
up beyond their usual hour to indulge it.

Miss Woodley slept little, but Matilda less—she awaked
repeatedly during the night, and every time sighed to herself,
'I sleep in the same house with my father! Blessed spirit of my
mother, look down and rejoice.'

CHAPTER VII

THE next day the whole Castle appeared to Lady Matilda
(though she was in some degree retired from it) all tumult and
bustle; as was usually the case while his lordship was there.
She saw from her windows servants running across the yards
and park, horses and carriages driving with fury, all the suit

of a nobleman; and it seemed sometimes to elate, at other times to depress her.

These impressions however, and others of fear and anxiety, which her father's first arrival had excited, by degrees wore away; and after some short time, she was in the same tranquil state she enjoyed before he came.

He had visitors, to stay a week or two; he paid some visits himself for several days; and thus the time passed, till it was about four weeks since he arrived; during which, Sandford, with all his penetration, could never clearly discover whether he had once called to mind his daughter was living in the same house. He had not named her (that was not extraordinary) consequently no one durst name her to him; but he had not even mentioned Miss Woodley, of whom he had so lately spoken in the kindest terms, and said, 'He should take pleasure in seeing her again.' From these contradictions in Lord Elmwood's behaviour in respect to her, it was Miss Woodley's plan neither to throw herself in his way, or avoid him. She therefore frequently walked about the house while he was in it, not indeed wholly without restraint, but at least with the show of liberty. This freedom, indulged for some time without peril, became at last less cautious; and no ill consequences arising from its practice, her scruples gradually ceased.

One morning, however, as she was crossing the large hall, thoughtless of danger, a footstep at a distance alarmed her almost without knowing why—She stopped for a moment, thinking to return; the steps approached quicker, and before she could retreat she beheld Lord Elmwood at the other end of the hall, and perceived that he saw her.—It was now too late to hesitate what was to be done; she could not go back, and had not courage to go on; she therefore stood still.—Disconcerted, and much affected at his sight, (their former intimacy coming to her mind, together with the many years, and many sad occurrences passed, since she last saw him) all her intentions, all her meditated plans how to conduct herself on such an occasion, gave way to a sudden shock—and to make the meeting yet more distressing, her very fright she knew must serve to recall more powerfully to his mind, the subject she most wished him to forget. The steward was with his lordship, and as they came up close by her side, Giffard observing him look at her earnestly, said softly, but so as she heard him, 'My lord, it is Miss Woodley.' Lord Elmwood's hat was off immediately, and coming to her with alacrity, he took her by the hand and said, 'Indeed, Miss Woodley, I did not know you—I am very glad to see you:' and while he spoke, shook her hand with a cordiality her tender heart could not bear—and never did she feel so hard a struggle as to restrain her tears. But the thought of Matilda's fate—the idea of awaking in his mind a sentiment that might irritate him against his child, wrought more forcibly than every other effort; and though she could not reply distinctly, she replied without weeping.—Whether he saw her embarrassment, and wished to release her from it, or was in haste to conceal his own; he left her almost instantly; but not till he had entreated she would dine that very day with him and Mr. Sandford, who were to dine without other company.—She courtesied assent, and flew to tell Matilda what had occurred.—After listening with anxiety and joy to all she told, Matilda laid hold of that hand she said Lord Elmwood had held, and pressed it to her lips with love and reverence.

When Miss Woodley made her appearance at dinner, Sandford, (who had not seen her since the invitation, and did not know of it) looked amazed!—on which his lordship said, 'Do you know, Sandford, I met Miss Woodley this morning, and had it not been for Giffard I should have passed her without

knowing her—but Miss Woodley, if I am not so much altered
but that you knew me, I take it unkind you did not speak first.'
——She was unable to speak even now—he saw it, and
changed the conversation; which Sandford was happy to join,
for in the present discourse he did not feel himself very comfortable.

As they advanced in their dinner, Miss Woodley's and
Sandford's embarrassment diminished; while Lord Elmwood
in his turn became, not embarrassed, but absent and melancholy.—He now and then sighed heavily—and called for wine
much oftener than he was accustomed.

When Miss Woodley took her leave, his lordship invited
her to dine with him and Sandford whenever it was convenient
to her;—he said many things, too, of the same kind, and all
with the utmost civility, yet not with that warmth with which
he had spoken in the morning—into that he had been surprised, while this coolness was the effect of reflection.

When she came to Lady Matilda, and Sandford had joined
them, they talked and deliberated on what had passed.—

'You acknowledge, Mr. Sandford,' said Miss Woodley, 'that
you think my presence affected Lord Elmwood so as to make
him much more thoughtful than usual; if you imagine these
thoughts were upon Lady Elmwood, I will never intrude
again; but if you suppose I caused him to think upon his
daughter, I cannot go too often.'

'I don't see how he can divide those two objects in his mind,'
replied Sandford, 'and therefore you must e'en visit him on,
and take your chance, what reflections you may inspire—but,
be they what they will, time, will take away from you that
power of affecting him.'

She concurred in the opinion, and occasionally walked into
his lordship's apartments, dined, or took coffee with him, as
the accident suited; and observed according to Sandford's

prescience, that time, wore off that impression her visits first made.—Lord Elmwood now became just the same before her, as before others.—She easily discerned, too, through all that politeness which he assumed—he was no longer the considerate, the forbearing character he formerly was; but haughty, impatient, imperious, and more than ever, implacable.

CHAPTER VIII

WHEN Lord Elmwood had been at his country seat about six weeks, Mr. Rushbrook, his nephew, and his adopted child, the friendless boy whom poor Lady Elmwood first introduced into his uncle's house, and by her kindness preserved there—arrived from his travels, and was received by his lordship with all that affectionate warmth due to the man he thought worthy to make his heir. Rushbrook had been a beautiful boy, and was now an extremely handsome young man; he had made an unusual progress in his studies, had completed the tour of Italy and Germany, and returned home with the air and address of a perfect man of fashion—there was, beside, an elegance and persuasion in his manner almost irresistible.—Yet with all those accomplishments, when he was introduced to Sandford, and put out his hand to take his, Sandford, with evident reluctance, gave it to him; and when Lord Elmwood asked him, in the young man's presence, 'if he did not think his nephew greatly improved?' he looked at him from head to foot, and muttered 'he could not say he observed it.' The colour heightened in Mr. Rushbrook's face upon this occasion, but he was too well bred not to be still in perfect good humour.

Sandford saw this young man treated in the house of Lord Elmwood with the same respect and attention as if he had been his lordship's son; and it was but probable the old priest should make a comparison between the situation of him, and of Lady Matilda Elmwood.—Before her, it was Sandford's meaning to have concealed his thoughts upon the subject, and never to have mentioned it but with composure, that was, however, impossible—unused to conceal his feelings, at the name of Rushbrook his countenance would always change, and a sarcastic sneer, and sometimes a frown of resentment, force their way in spite of his resolution.—Miss Woodley, too, with all her boundless charity and good will, was, upon this occasion, induced to limit their excess; and they did not extend so far as to reach poor Rushbrook—She even, and in *reality*, did not think him handsome or engaging in his manners—she thought his gaiety frivolousness, his complaisance affectation, and his good humour impertinence.—It was impossible to conceal those unfavourable sentiments entirely from Matilda; for when the subject arose, as it frequently did, Miss Woodley's undisguised heart, and Sandford's undisguised countenance, told them instantly.—Matilda had the understanding to imagine, she was, perhaps, the object who had thus deformed Mr. Rushbrook, and frequently (though he was a stranger to her, and one who had caused her many a jealous heartache) frequently she would speak in his vindication.

'You are very good,' said Sandford one day to her; 'you like him because you know your father loves him.'

This was a hard sentence to the daughter of Lord Elmwood, to whom her father's love would have been more precious than any other blessing—She, however, checked the assault of envy, and kindly replied,

'My mother loved him, too, Mr. Sandford.'

'Yes,' answered Sandford, 'he has been a grateful man to

your poor mother—She did not suppose when she took him into the house, when she intreated your father to take him, and through her caresses and officious praises of him to his uncle, first gave him that power he now possesses over him; she little foresaw, at that time, his ingratitude, and its effects.'

'Very true,' said Miss Woodley, with a heavy sigh.

'What ingratitude?' said Matilda; 'do you suppose Mr. Rushbrook is the cause my father will not see me? Oh do not pay Lord Elmwood's motives so ill a compliment.'

'I do not say he is the absolute cause,' returned Sandford; 'but if a parent's heart is void, I would have it remain so, till stored by its lawful owner—a usurper I detest.'

'No one can take Lord Elmwood's heart by force,' replied his daughter, 'it must, I believe, be a free gift to the possessor; and as such, whoever has it, has a right to it.'

In this manner she would plead the young man's excuse—perhaps but to hear what could be said in his disfavour, for secretly his name was bitter to her—and once she exclaimed in vexation, on Sandford's saying Lord Elmwood and Mr. Rushbrook were gone out shooting together,

'All that pleasure is now eclipsed which I used to take in listening to the report of my father's gun, for I cannot now distinguish his, from his parasite's.'

Sandford, much as he disliked Rushbrook—for this expression which comprised her father in the reflection, turned to Matilda in extreme anger; but as he saw the colour mount to her face, for what, in the strong feelings of her heart, had escaped her lips, he did not say a word—and by a flood of tears that followed after, he rejoiced to see how much she reproved herself.

Miss Woodley, vext to the heart, and provoked every time she saw Lord Elmwood and Rushbrook together, and saw the familiar terms on which this young man lived with his

benefactor, now made her visits to his lordship very seldom.—
If Lord Elmwood observed this, he did not appear to observe
it; and though he received her very politely when she did pay
him a visit, it was always very coldly; nor did she suppose if
she never went, he would ever ask for her. For his daughter's
sake, however, she thought it right sometimes to show herself before him; for she knew it must be impossible that, with
all his seeming indifference, Lord Elmwood could ever see her
without thinking for a moment on his child; and what one
fortunate thought might sometime bring about, was an object
too serious for her to slight.—She therefore, after remaining
confined to her apartments near three weeks, (excepting those
short and anxious walks she and Matilda stole, while Lord
Elmwood dined, or before he rose in a morning) went one forenoon into his lordship's apartments, where as usual, she
found him, Mr. Sandford, and Mr. Rushbrook.—After she
had sat about half an hour, conversing with them all, though
but very little with the latter, his lordship was called out of the
room upon some business; presently after Sandford; and now,
not much pleased with the companion with whom she was left,
she rose and was going likewise, when Rushbrook fixed his
speaking eyes upon her, and cried,

'Miss Woodley, will you pardon me what I am going to
say?'

'Certainly, sir—You can, I am sure, say nothing but what
I must forgive.'—But she made this reply with a distance and
a reserve, very unlike the usual manners of Miss Woodley.

He looked at her earnestly and cried,

'Ah! Miss Woodley, you don't behave so kindly to me as
you used to do!'

'I do not understand you, sir,'—she replied, very gravely;—
'Times are changed, Mr. Rushbrook, since you were last here
—you were then but a child.'

'Yet I love all those persons now, I loved then;' replied he; 'and so I shall for ever.'

'But you mistake, Mr. Rushbrook; I was not even then so very much the object of your affections—there were other ladies you loved better.—Perhaps you don't remember Lady Elmwood?'

'Don't I?'—cried he, 'Oh!' (clasping his hands and lifting up his eyes to heaven) 'shall I ever forget her?'

That moment Lord Elmwood opened the door; the conversation of course that moment ended; but confusion at the sudden surprise was on the face of both the parties—his lordship saw it, and looked at each by turns, with a sternness that made poor Miss Woodley ready to faint; while Rushbrook, with the most natural and happy laugh that ever was affected, cried, 'No, don't tell my lord, pray, Miss Woodley.'—She was more confused than before; and his lordship turning to him, asked what the subject was.—By this time he had invented one, and continuing his laugh, said, 'Miss Woodley, my lord, will to this day protest she saw my apparition when I was a boy; and she says it is a sign I shall die young, and is really much affected at it.'

Lord Elmwood turned away before this ridiculous speech was concluded; yet so well had it been acted, he did not for an instant doubt its truth.

Miss Woodley felt herself greatly relieved; and yet so little is it in the power of those we dislike to do any thing to please us, that from this very circumstance, she formed a still more unfavourable opinion of Mr. Rushbrook than she had done before.—She saw in this little incident the art of dissimulation, cunning, and duplicity in its most glaring shape; and detested the method by which they had each escaped Lord Elmwood's suspicion, and perhaps anger, the more, because it was so dexterously managed.

Lady Matilda and Sandford were both in their turns informed of this trait in Mr. Rushbrook's character; and although Miss Woodley had the best of dispositions, and upon every occasion spoke the strictest truth, yet in relating this occurrence, she did not speak all the truth; for every circumstance that would have told to the young man's advantage, *literally* slipped her memory.

The twenty ninth of October arrived; on which a dinner, a ball, and supper, was given by Lord Elmwood to all the neighbouring gentry—the peasants also dined in the park off a roasted bullock; several casks of ale were distributed, and the bells of the village rung.—Matilda, who heard and saw some part of this festivity from her windows, inquired the cause; but even the servant who waited upon her had too much sensibility to tell her, and answered, 'he did not know.' Miss Woodley however soon learnt the reason, and groaning with the painful secret, informed her, 'Mr. Rushbrook on that day was come of age.'

'My birth day was last week,' replied Matilda; but not a word beside.

In their retired apartments, the day passed away not only soberly, but almost silently; for to speak upon any subject that did not engage their thoughts had been difficult, and to speak upon the only one that did, had been afflictive.

Just as they were sitting down to dinner their bell gently rung, and in walked Sandford.

'Why are not you among the revellers, Mr. Sandford?' cried Miss Woodley, with an ironical sneer—(the first her features ever wore)—'Pray, were not you invited to dine with the company?'

'Yes,' replied Sandford; 'but my head ached; and so I had rather come and take a bit with you.'

Matilda, as if she had beheld his heart as he spoke, clung

round his neck and sobbed on his bosom: he put her peevishly away, crying, 'Nonsense, nonsense—eat your dinner.' But he did not eat himself.

CHAPTER IX

ABOUT a week after this, Lord Elmwood went out two days for a visit; consequently Rushbrook was for that time master of the house. The first morning he went a shooting, and returning about noon, enquired of Sandford, who was sitting in the room, if he had taken up a volume of plays left upon the table.—'I read no such things,' replied Sandford, and quitted the room abruptly. Rushbrook then rung for his servant, and desired him to look for the book, asking him angrily, 'Who had been in the apartment? for he was sure he had left it there when he went out.'—The servant withdrew to enquire, and presently returned with the volume in his hand, and 'Miss Woodley's compliments, she begs your pardon, sir, she did not know the book was yours, and hopes you will excuse the liberty she took.'

'Miss Woodley!' cried Rushbrook with surprise, 'she comes so seldom into these apartments, I did not suppose it was her who had it—take it back to her instantly, with my respects, and I beg she will keep it.'

The man went; but returned with the book again, and laying it on the table without speaking, was going away; when Rushbrook, hurt at receiving no second message, said, 'I am afraid, sir, you did very wrong in taking this book from Miss Woodley.'

'It was not from her I took it, sir,' replied the man, 'it was from Lady Matilda.'

Since he had entered the house, Rushbrook had never before heard her name—he was shocked—confounded more than ever—and to conceal what he felt, instantly ordered the man out of the room.

In the mean time, Miss Woodley and Matilda were talking over this trifling occurrence; and frivolous as it was, drew from it strong conclusions of Rushbrook's insolence and power.—In spite of her pride, the daughter of Lord Elmwood even wept at the insult she had received on this insignificant occasion; for the volume being merely taken from her at Mr. Rushbrook's command, she felt an insult; and the manner in which it was done by the servant, might contribute to the offence.

While Miss Woodley and she were upon this conversation, a note came from Rushbrook to Miss Woodley, wherein he entreated he might be permitted to see her.—She sent a verbal answer, 'She was engaged.' He sent again, begging she would name her own time. But certain of a second denial, he followed the servant who took the last message, and as Miss Woodley came out of her apartment into the gallery to speak to him, Rushbrook presented himself, and told the man to retire.

'Mr. Rushbrook,' said Miss Woodley, 'this intrusion is insupportable;—and destitute as you may think me of the friendship of Lord Elmwood'——

In the ardour with which Rushbrook was waiting to express himself, he interrupted her, and caught hold of her hand.

She immediately snatched it from him, and withdrew into her chamber.

He followed, saying in a low voice, 'Dear Miss Woodley hear me.'

At that juncture Lady Matilda, who was in an inner room, came out of it into Miss Woodley's.—Perceiving a gentleman, she stopped short at the door.

Rushbrook cast his eyes upon her, and stood motionless—his lips only moved. 'Do not depart, madam,' said he, 'without hearing my apology for being here.'

Though Matilda had never seen him since her infancy, there was no cause to tell her who it was that addressed her—his elegant and youthful person, joined to the incident which had just occurred, convinced her it was Rushbrook; and she looked at him with an air of surprise, but with still more, of dignity.

'Miss Woodley is severe upon me, madam,' continued he, 'she judges me unkindly; and I am afraid she will prepossess you with the same unfavourable sentiments.'

Still Matilda did not speak, but looked at him with the same air of dignity.

'If, Lady Matilda,' resumed he, 'I have offended you, and must quit you without pardon, I am more unhappy than I should be with the loss of your father's protection—more forlorn, than when an orphan boy, your mother first took pity on me.'

At this last sentence, Matilda turned her eyes on Miss Woodley, and seemed in doubt what reply she was to give.

Rushbrook immediately fell upon his knees—'Oh! Lady Matilda,' cried he, 'if you knew the sensations of my heart, you would not treat me with this disdain.'

'We can only judge of those sensations, Mr. Rushbrook,' said Miss Woodley, 'by the effect they have upon your conduct; and while you insult Lord and Lady Elmwood's daughter by an intrusion like this, and then ridicule her abject state by mockery, such as the present'——

He flew from his knees instantly, and interrupted her, crying 'What can I do?—What am I to say, to make you change your opinion of me?—While Lord Elmwood has been at home I have kept at an awful distance; and though every moment

I breathed was a wish to cast myself at his daughter's feet, yet as I feared, Miss Woodley, you were incensed against me, by what means was I to procure an interview but by stratagem or force?—This accident has given a third method, and I had not strength, I had not courage, to let it pass.—Lord Elmwood will soon return, and we may both be hurried to town immediately;—then how for a tedious winter could I sustain the thought that I was despised, nay perhaps considered as an object[1] of ingratitude, by the only child of my deceased benefactress.'

Matilda replied with all her father's haughtiness, 'Depend upon it, sir, if you should ever enter my thoughts, it will only be as an object of envy.'

'Suffer me then, madam,' said he, 'as an earnest you do not think worse of me than I merit, suffer me to be sometimes admitted into your presence.'

She scarcely permitted him to finish the period, before she replied, 'This is the last time, sir, we shall ever meet, depend upon it—unless, indeed, Lord Elmwood should delegate to you the control of me—his commands I never dispute.' And here she burst into a flood of tears.

Rushbrook walked to the window, and did not speak for a short time—then turning himself to make a reply, both Matilda and Miss Woodley were somewhat surprised to see, he had shed tears too.—Having conquered them, he said, 'I will not offend you, madam, by staying one moment longer; and I give my honour, that, upon no pretence whatever, will I presume to intrude here again.—Professions, I find, have no weight, and only by this obedience to your orders can I give a proof of that respect which you inspire;—and let the agitation I now feel, convince you, Lady Matilda, that, with all my seeming good fortune, I am not happier than yourself.'—And so much was he agitated while he delivered this, it was with difficulty he came to the conclusion.—When he did, he bowed with reverence, as if he had left the presence of a deity, and went away.

Matilda immediately entered the chamber she had come from, and without casting a single look at Miss Woodley, by which she might guess of the opinion she had formed of Mr. Rushbrook's conduct.—The next time they met they did not even mention his name; for they were ashamed to own any partiality in his favour, and were too just to bring any serious accusation against him.

But Miss Woodley the day following communicated the intelligence of this visit to Mr. Sandford, who not being present, and a witness of those marks of humility and respect which were conspicuous in the deportment of Mr. Rushbrook, was highly offended at his presumption; and threatened if he ever dared to force his company there again, he would acquaint Lord Elmwood with his arrogance, whatever might be the event.—Miss Woodley however, assured him, she believed he would have no cause for such a complaint, as the young man had made the most solemn promise never to commit the like offence; and she thought it her duty to enjoin Sandford, till he did repeat it, not to mention the circumstance, even to Rushbrook himself.

Matilda could not but feel a regard towards her father's heir in return for that which he had so fervently declared for her; yet the more favourable her opinion of his mind and manners, the more he became a proper object of her jealousy for the affections of Lord Elmwood, and was now consequently an object of greater sorrow to her, than when she believed him less worthy.—This was the reverse on his part towards her[1]— no jealousy intervened to bar his admiration and esteem, and the beauty of her person, and grandeur of her mien, not only confirmed, but improved, the exalted idea he had formed of her previous to their meeting, and which his affection to both her parents had inspired.——The next time he saw his bene-factor, he began to feel a new esteem and regard for him, for his daughter's sake; as he had at first an esteem for her on the foundation of his love for Lord and Lady Elmwood—He gazed with wonder at his uncle's insensibility to his own happiness, and longed to lead him to the jewel he cast away, though even his own expulsion should be the fatal conse-quence.—Such was the youthful, warm, generous, grateful, but unthinking mind of Rushbrook.

CHAPTER X

AFTER this incident, Miss Woodley left her own apartments less frequently than before—she was afraid, though till now mistrust had been a stranger to her heart, she was afraid duplicity might be concealed under the apparent friendship of Rushbrook; it did not indeed appear so from any part of his behaviour, but she was apprehensive for the fate of Matilda; she disliked him also, and therefore she suspected him.—For near three weeks she had not now paid a visit to Lord Elmwood, and though to herself every visit was a pain, yet as Matilda took a delight in hearing of her father, what he said, what he did, what his attention seemed most employed on, and a thousand other circumstantial informations, in the detail of which, Sandford would scorn to be half so particular, it was a deprivation to her, Miss Woodley did not go oftener.— Now too the middle of November had arrived, and it was expected his lordship would shortly quit the country.

Partly therefore to indulge her hapless companion, and partly because it was a necessary duty, Miss Woodley paid his lordship a morning visit, and staid dinner.—Rushbrook was officiously polite to her, (for that was the epithet she gave his attention in relating it to Lady Matilda) yet she owned he had not that forward impertinence she had formerly discovered in him, but appeared much more grave and sedate.

'But tell me of my father,' said Matilda.

'I was going, my dear—but don't be concerned—don't let it vex you.'

'What? what?' cried Matilda, frightened by the preface.

'Why, on my observing that I thought Mr. Rushbrook looked paler than usual, and appeared not to be in perfect health, (which was really the case) your father expressed the greatest anxiety imaginable; he said he could not bear to see him look so ill, begged him with all the tenderness of a parent to take the advice of a physician, and added a thousand other affectionate things.'

'I detest Mr. Rushbrook,'—said Matilda, with her eyes flashing indignation.

'Nay, for shame,' returned Miss Woodley: 'do you suppose I told you this, to make you hate him?'

'No, there was no occasion for that,' replied Matilda; 'my sentiments (though I have never before avowed them) were long ago formed; he was always an object which added to my unhappiness; but since his daring intrusion into my apartments, he has been an object of my hatred.'

'But now perhaps I may tell you something to please you,' cried Miss Woodley.

'And what is that?' said Matilda, with indifference; for the first intelligence had hurt her spirits too much to suffer her to listen with pleasure to any other.

'Mr. Rushbrook,' continued Miss Woodley, 'replied to your father, his indisposition was but a slight nervous fever, and he would defer a physician's advice till he went to

London—on which his lordship said, 'And when do you expect to be there?'—he replied, 'Within a week or two, I suppose, my lord.' But your father answered, 'I do not mean to go myself till after Christmas.'—'No indeed, my lord!' said Mr. Sandford, with surprise: 'you have not passed your Christmas here,' continued he, 'these many a year.'—'No,' returned his lordship; 'but I think I feel myself more attached to this house at present, than ever I did in my life.'

'You imagine then, my father thought of me, when he said that?' cried Matilda eagerly.

'But I may be mistaken,' replied Miss Woodley.—'I leave you to judge.—But I am sure Mr. Sandford imagined he thought of you, for I saw a smile over his whole face immediately.'

'Did you, Miss Woodley?'

'Yes; it appeared on every feature except his lips; those he closed fast together, for fear Lord Elmwood should perceive it.'

Miss Woodley, with all her minute intelligence, did not however acquaint Matilda that Rushbrook followed her to the window while his lordship was out of the room, and Sandford half asleep at the other end of it, and inquired respectfully and anxiously for her ladyship; adding, 'It is my concern for Lady Matilda which makes me thus indisposed: I suffer more than her; but I am not permitted to tell her so, nor can I hope, Miss Woodley, you will.'—She replied, 'You are right, sir.' Nor did she reveal this conversation, while not a sentence that passed except that, was omitted.

When Christmas arrived Lord Elmwood had many convivial days at Elmwood House, but the name of Matilda was never mentioned by one of his guests, and most probably never thought of.—During all those holidays she was unusually melancholy, but sunk into the deepest dejection when she was told the day was fixed on which her father was to depart for the season.—On the morning of that day she wept incessantly; and all her consolation was, 'She would go to the chamber window which was fronting the door he was to pass through to his carriage, and for the first time, and most likely for the last time of her life, behold him.'

This design was soon forgot in another:—'She would rush boldly into the apartment where he was, and at his feet take leave of him for ever.—She would lay hold of his hands, clasp his knees, provoke him to spurn her, which would be joy in comparison to this cruel indifference.'—In the bitterness of her grief, she once called upon her mother, and reproached her memory—but the moment she recollected the offence, (which was almost instantaneously) she became all mildness and resignation. 'What have I said?' cried she; 'Dear, dear saint, forgive me, and behold for your sake I will bear all with patience—I will not groan, I will not even sigh again—this task I set myself to atone for what I have dared to utter.'

While Lady Matilda laboured under these variety of sensations, Miss Woodley was occupied in bewailing and endeavouring to calm her sorrows—and Lord Elmwood, with Rushbrook, was prepared ready to set off.—His lordship, however, loitered, and did not once seem in haste to be gone.—When at last he got up to depart, Sandford thought he pressed his hand, and shook it with more warmth than ever he had done in his life.—Encouraged by this supposition, Sandford, with the tears starting in his eyes, said, 'My lord, won't you condescend to take your leave of Miss Woodley?'—'Certainly, Sandford,' replied his lordship, and seemed glad of an excuse to sit down again.

Impressed with the idea of the state in which she had left his only child, Miss Woodley, when she came before Lord Elmwood to bid him farewell, was pale, trembling, and in tears.—Sandford, notwithstanding his lordship's apparent kind humour, was shocked at the construction he must put upon her appearance, and cried, 'What, Miss Woodley, are you not recovered of your illness yet?' Lord Elmwood, however, took no notice of her looks, but after wishing her health and happiness, walked slowly out of the house; turning back frequently and speaking to Sandford or some other person who was behind him, as if part of his thoughts were left behind, and he went with reluctance.

When he had quitted the room where Miss Woodley was; Rushbrook, timid before her, as she had been before her benefactor, went up to her all humility, and said, 'Miss Woodley, we ought to be friends; our concern, our devotion is paid to the same objects, and one common interest should teach us to be friendly.'

She made no reply.—'Will you permit me to write to you when I am away?' said he; 'You may wish to hear of Lord Elmwood's health, and of what changes may take place in his resolutions—Will you permit me?'——At that moment a servant came and said, 'Sir, my lord is in his carriage and waiting for you.' He hasted away, and Miss Woodley was relieved from the pain of giving him a denial.

No sooner was the chariot, with all its attendants, out of sight, than Lady Matilda was conducted by Miss Woodley from her lonely retreat into that part of the house from whence her father had just departed—and she visited every spot where he had so long resided, with a pleasing curiosity that for a while diverted her grief.—In the breakfast and dining rooms she leaned over those seats with a kind of filial piety, on which she was told he had been accustomed to sit. And in the library she took up with filial delight, the pen with which he had been writing; and looked with the most curious attention into those books that were laid upon his reading desk.—But a hat, lying on one of the tables, gave her a sensation beyond any other she experienced on this occasion—in that trifling article of his dress, she thought she saw himself, and held it in her hand with pious reverence.

In the mean time, Lord Elmwood and Rushbrook were proceeding on their road with hearts not less heavy than those which they had left at Elmwood House, though neither of them could so well as Matilda tell the cause of the weight.

CHAPTER XI

YOUNG as Lady Matilda was during the life of her mother, neither her youth, nor the recluse state in which she lived, had precluded her from the notice and solicitations of a nobleman who had professed himself her lover. Viscount Margrave had an estate not far distant from the retreat Lady Elmwood had chosen, and being devoted to the sports of the country, he seldom quitted it for any of those joys which the town offered.—He was a young man, of a handsome person, and was what his neighbours styled 'a man of spirit.'—He was an excellent fox-hunter, and as excellent a companion over his bottle at the end of the chace—he was prodigal of his fortune in all cases where his pleasures were concerned, and as those pleasures were mostly social, his sporting companions and his mistresses (for these were also of the plural number) partook largely of his wealth.

Two months previous to Lady Elmwood's death, Miss Woodley and Lady Matilda were taking their usual walk in some fields and lanes near to their house, when chance threw Lord Margrave in their way, during a thunder storm in which they were suddenly caught; and he had the satisfaction to convey his new acquaintances to their home in his carriage, safe from the fury of the elements.—Grateful for the service his lordship had rendered them, Miss Woodley and her charge permitted him to enquire occasionally of their healths, and would sometimes see him.—The story of Lady Elmwood was known to Lord Margrave, and as he beheld her daughter with a passion such as he had been unused to overcome, he indulged it with the probable hope, that on the death of the mother Lord Elmwood would receive his child, and perhaps accept him as his son-in-law.—Wedlock was not the plan which Lord Margrave had ever proposed to himself for happiness; but the excess of his love on this new occasion, subdued every resolution he had taken 'against the marriage state, and not daring to hope for the consummation of his wishes by any other means, he suffered himself to look forward to that, as his only resource.—No sooner was the long-expected death of Lady Elmwood arrived, than his lordship waited with impatience to hear Lady Matilda was sent for and acknowledged by her father; for he meant to be the first to lay before Lord Elmwood his pretensions as a suitor.—But those pretensions were founded on the vague hopes of a lover only; and Miss Woodley, to whom he first declared them, said every thing possible to convince him of their fallaciousness.—As to the object of his passion, she was not only insensible, but totally inattentive to all that was said to her on the subject.—Lady Elmwood died without ever being disturbed with it; for her daughter did not even remember his proposals so as to repeat them again, and Miss Woodley thought it prudent to conceal from her friend, every new incident which might give her cause for fresh anxieties.

When Sandford and the ladies left the north and came to Elmwood House, so much were their thoughts employed with other ideas, Lord Margrave did not occupy a place; and during the whole time they had been at their new abode, they had never once heard of him.—He had, nevertheless, his whole mind fixed upon Lady Matilda, and placed spies in the neighbourhood to inform him of every circumstance in her situation.—Having imbibed an aversion to matrimony, he heard with but little regret, that there was no prospect of her ever becoming her father's heir; while such an information gave him the hope of obtaining her, upon the illegal terms of a mistress.

Lord Elmwood's departure to town forwarded this hope, and flattering himself that the humiliating situation in which Matilda must feel herself in the house of her father, might gladly induce her to take shelter under any other protection, he boldly advanced as soon as the Earl was gone, to make such overtures as his wishes and his vanity told him, could not be rejected.

Inquiring for Miss Woodley, he easily gained admittance; but at the sight of so much modesty and dignity in the person of Matilda, so much good will, and yet such circumspection in her companion; and the good sense and proper spirit which were always apparent in the manners of Sandford, his lordship fell once more into the despondency, of becoming to Lady Matilda nothing more important to his reputation, than a husband.

Even that humble hope was, however, sometimes denied him, while Sandford set forth the impropriety of troubling Lord Elmwood on such a subject at present; and while the Viscount's penetration, small as it was, discovered in his fair one much more to discourage than to favour his wishes.— Plunged, however, too deep in his passion to emerge from it in haste, he meant still to visit, and wait for a change to happier circumstances, when he was peremptorily desired by Mr. Sandford to desist from ever coming again.

'Wherefore, Mr. Sandford?' cried his lordship.

'For two reasons, my lord;—in the first place, your visits
might be displeasing to Lord Elmwood;—in the next place,
I know they are so to his daughter.'

Unaccustomed to be spoken to so plainly, particularly in
a case where his heart was interested, his lordship nevertheless submitted with patience; but in his own mind determined how long this patience should continue—no longer
than it served as the means to prove his obedience, and by that
artifice, secure his better reception at some future period.

On his return home, cheered with the huzzas of his jovial
companions, he began to consult those friends, what scheme
was best to be adopted for the accomplishment of his desires.
—Some, boldly advised application to the father, in defiance
to the old priest; but that was the very last method his lordship
himself approved, as marriage must inevitably have followed
Lòrd Elmwood's consent; besides, though a Peer, Lord Margrave was unused to rank with Peers; and even the necessary
formality of an interview with one of his equals, carried along
with it a terror, or at least a fatigue, to a rustic Baron.—Others,
of his companions advised seduction; but happily his lordship
possessed no arts of this kind to affect a heart appendant to
such a mind as Matilda's.—There were not wanting among
his most favourite counsellors some, who painted the triumph
and gratification of force; those assured him there was nothing
to apprehend under this head; as from the behaviour of Lord
Elmwood to his child, it was more than probable he would be
utterly indifferent to any violence that might be offered her.—
This last advice seemed inspired by the aid of wine; and no
sooner had the wine freely circulated, than this was always the
scheme which appeared by far the best.

While Lord Margrave alternately cherished his hopes and
his fears in the country, Rushbrook in town gave way to his

fears only—every day of his life made him more acquainted with the firm, unshaken temper of Lord Elmwood, and every day whispered more forcibly to his own heart, that pity, gratitude, and friendship, strong and affectionate as these passions are, are weak and cold to that, which had gained the possession of him—he doubted, but he did not long doubt, that which he felt was love.—'And yet,' said he to himself, 'it is love of that kind, which arising from causes independant of the object itself, can scarcely deserve this sacred title.— Did I not love Lady Matilda before I beheld her?—for her mother's sake I loved her—and even for her father's.—Should I have felt the same affection for her, had she been the child of other parents?—no. Or should I have felt that sympathetic tenderness which now preys upon my health, had not her misfortunes excited it?—no.'—Yet the love which is the result of gratitude and pity only, he thought had little claim to rank with his; and after the most deliberate and deep reflection, he concluded with this decisive opinion—He had loved Lady Matilda, in *whatever state*, in *whatever circumstances*; and that the tenderness he felt towards her, and the anxiety for her happiness before he knew her, extreme as they were, were yet cool and dispassionate sensations, compared to that which her person and demeanour had incited—and though he acknowledged, that by those preceding sentiments his heart was softened, prepared, and moulded, as it were, to receive this last impression, yet the violence of his passion told him genuine love, if not the basis on which it was founded, had been the certain consequence.—With a strict scrutiny into his heart he sought this knowledge, but arrived at it with a regret that amounted to despair.

To shield him from despondency, he formed in his mind a thousand projects, depicting the joys of his union with Lady Matilda; but her father's implacability stood foremost and confounded them all.—His lordship was a man who made but few resolutions—those were the effect of deliberation; and as he was not the least capricious or inconstant in his temper, they were resolutions which no probable event could shake.— Love, that produces wonders, that seduces and subdues the most determined and rigid spirits, had in two instances over- come the inflexibility of Lord Elmwood; he married Lady Elmwood contrary to his determination, because he loved; and for the sake of this beloved object, he had, contrary to his resolution, taken under his immediate care young Rushbrook; but the magic which once enchanted away this spirit of im- mutability was no more—Lady Elmwood was no more, and the charm was broken.

As Miss Woodley was deprived the opportunity of desiring Rushbrook not to write when he asked her the permission, he passed one whole morning in the gratification of forming and writing a letter to her, which he thought might possibly be shewn to Matilda.—As he durst not touch upon any of those circumstances in which he was the most interested, that, joined to the respect he wished to pay the lady to whom he wrote, limited his letter to about twenty lines; yet the studious manner with which these lines were dictated, the hope and fear they might, or might not, be seen and regarded by Lady Matilda, rendered the task an anxiety so pleasing, he could have wished it to have lasted for a year; and in all this magni- fying of trifles was discoverable, the never-failing symptom of ardent love.

A reply to this formal address was a reward he wished for with impatience, but he wished in vain; and in the midst of his chagrin at the disappointment, a sorrow, little thought of, occurred, and gave him a perturbation of mind he had never before experienced.—Lord Elmwood proposed a wife to him; and in a way so assured of his acquiescence, that if Rushbrook's life had depended upon his daring to dispute his benefactor's will, he would not have had the courage to have done so. There was, however, in his reply, and his embarrassment, something which his lordship discerned from a free concurrence; and looking steadfastly at him, he said, in that stern manner which he now almost constantly adopted,

'You have no engagements, I suppose? Have made no previous promises?'

'None on earth, my lord,' replied Rushbrook candidly.

'Nor have you disposed of your heart?'

'No, my lord,' replied he; but not candidly,—nor with the appearance of candour: for though he spoke hastily, it was rather like a man frightened than assured.—He hurried to tell the falsehood he thought himself obliged to tell, that the pain and shame might be over; but there Rushbrook was deceived; the lie once told was as troublesome as in the conception, and added to his first confusion, an encreasing one.

Lord Elmwood now fixed his eyes upon him with a sullen contempt, and rising from his seat, said, 'Rushbrook, if you have been so inconsiderate as to give away your heart, tell me so at once, and tell me the object.'

Rushbrook shuddered at the thought.

'I here,' continued his lordship, 'tolerate the first untruth you ever told me, as the false assertion of a lover; and give you an opportunity to recall it—but after this moment, it is a lie between man and man—a lie to your friend and father, and I will not forgive it.'

Rushbrook stood silent, confused, alarmed, and bewildered in his thoughts.—His lordship resumed,

'Name the person, if there is any such, on whom you have bestowed your heart; and though I do not give you the smallest hope I shall not censure your folly, I will at least not reproach you for having at first denied it.'

To repeat these words in writing, the reader must condemn the young man that he could hesitate to own he loved, if he was even afraid to name the object of his passion; but his lordship in his question had made the two answers inseparable, and all evasions of the second, Rushbrook knew would be fruitless, after having avowed the first—and how could he confess the latter? The absolute orders he received from the steward on his first return from his travels, were, 'Never to mention his daughter, any more than his late wife, before Lord Elmwood.'—The fault of having rudely intruded into Lady Matilda's presence, rushed too upon his mind; for he did not even dare to say, by what means he had beheld her.— But more than all, the threatening manner in which his lord-ship uttered this rational and seeming conciliating speech, the menaces, the severity which sat upon his countenance while he delivered those moderate words, might have intimidated a man wholly independent, and less used to fear him than his nephew had been.

'You make no answer, sir,' said his lordship, after waiting a few moments for his reply.

'I have only to say, my lord,' returned Rushbrook, 'that although my heart may be totally disengaged, I may yet be disinclined to the prospect of marriage.'

'May! May! Your heart *may* be disengaged,' repeated his lordship. 'Do you dare to reply to me equivocally, when I have asked a positive answer?'

'Perhaps I am not positive myself, my lord; but I will inquire the state of my mind, and make you acquainted with it very soon.'

As the angry demeanour of his uncle affected Rushbrook with fear, so that fear, powerfully (but with proper manli-ness) expressed, again softened the displeasure of Lord Elmwood; and seeing and pitying his nephew's sensibility, he now changed his austere voice, and said mildly, but firmly,

'I give you a week to consult with yourself; at the expiration of that time I shall talk with you again, and I command you to be then prepared to speak, not only without deceit, but without hesitation.' He left the room at these words, and left Rushbrook released from a fate, which his apprehensions had beheld impending that moment.

He had now a week to call his thoughts together, to weigh every circumstance, and to determine whether implicitly to submit to his lordship's recommendation for a wife, or revolt from it, and see some other more subservient to his will, appointed his heir.

Undetermined how to act upon this great trial which was to decide his future destiny, Rushbrook suffered so poignant an uncertainty, that he became at length ill, and before the end of the week which his uncle had allotted him for his reply, he was confined to his bed in a high fever.—His lordship was extremely affected at his indisposition; he gave him every care he could bestow, and even a great deal of his personal attendance.—This last favour had a claim upon the young man's gratitude, superior to every other obligation which since his infancy his benefactor had conferred; and he was at times so moved by those marks of kindness he received from Lord Elmwood, he would form the intention of tearing from his heart every trace Lady Matilda had left there, and as soon as his health permitted him, obey to the utmost of his views every wish his uncle had conceived.—Yet again, Matilda's pitiable situation presented itself to his compassion, and her beautious person to his love.—Divided between the claims of obligation to the father, and tender attachment to the daughter, his sickness was increased by the tortures of his mind, and he once sincerely wished for that death, of which he was in danger, to free him from the dilemma into which his affections had involved him.

At the time his illness was at its height, and he lay complaining of the violence of his fever, Lord Elmwood, taking his hand, asked him, 'If there was any thing he could do for him?'

'Yes, yes, my lord, a great deal,' he replied eagerly.

'What is it, Harry?' asked his lordship kindly.

'Oh! my lord,' replied he, 'that is what I must not tell you.'

'Defer it then till you are well,' said his lordship, fearful of being surprised, or affected by the state of his health, into any promises which he might hereafter find the impropriety of granting.

'And when I recover, my lord, you give me leave to reveal to you, that which I wish you to comply with, let it be what it will?'

His lordship hesitated——but seeing an anxiety for the answer, by his raising himself upon his elbow in the bed and staring wildly, Lord Elmwood at last said, 'Certainly—Yes, yes,' as a child is answered for its quiet.

That Lord Elmwood could have no idea what was the real petition which Rushbrook meant to present him is certain; but it is certain he expected he had some request to make, with which it might be wrong for him to comply, and therefore he avoided hearing what it was; for great as his compassion for him in his present state, it was not of force to urge him to give a promise he did not mean to perform.—Rushbrook on his part was pleased with the assurance he might speak when he was restored to health, but no sooner was his fever abated, and his senses perfectly recovered from the slight derangement his malady had caused, than the lively remembrance of what he had hinted alarmed him, and he was even afraid to look his kind, but awful relation in the face.—Lord Elmwood's cheerfulness, however, on his returning health, and his undiminished attention, soon convinced him he had nothing to fear—But, alas! he found too, he had nothing to hope.— As his health re-established his wishes re-established also, and with his wishes his despair.

Convinced now that his nephew had something on his mind which he feared to reveal, his lordship no longer doubted but some youthful attachment had armed his heart against any marriage he should propose; but he had so much pity for his present weak state, to delay that farther inquiry which he had threatened before his sickness, to a time when he should be wholly restored.

It was the end of May before Rushbrook was able to be present and partake in the usual routine of the day—the country was now prescribed him as the means of entire restoration; and as Lord Elmwood designed to leave London some time in June, he advised him to go to Elmwood House a week or two before him;—this advice was received with delight, and a letter was sent to Mr. Sandford to prepare for Mr. Rushbrook's arrival.

CHAPTER XII

DURING the illness of Rushbrook, news had been sent of his danger from the servants in town to those at Elmwood House, and Lady Matilda expressed compassion when she was told of it—she began to conceive the instant she thought he would soon die, that his visit to her had some merit rather than impertinence in its design, and that he might possibly be a more deserving man than she had supposed him to be. Even Sandford and Miss Woodley began to recollect qualifications he possessed, which they never had reflected on before, and Miss

Woodley in particular reproached herself that she had been so severe and inattentive to him.—Notwithstanding the prospects his death pointed out to her, it was with infinite joy she heard he was recovered; nor was Sandford less satisfied; for he had treated the young man too unkindly not to dread, lest any ill should befall him;—but although he was glad to hear of his restored health, when he was informed he was coming down to Elmwood House for a few weeks in the style of its master, Sandford, with all his religious and humane principles, could not help thinking, 'that provided the lad had been properly prepared, he had been as well out of the world as in it.'

He was still less his friend when he saw him arrive with his usual florid appearance: had he come pale and sickly, Sandford had been kind to him; but in apparent good health and spirits, he could not form his mouth to tell him he was 'glad to see him.'

On his arrival, Matilda, who for five months had been at large, secluded herself as she would have done upon the arrival of Lord Elmwood; but with far different sensations.—Notwithstanding her restriction on the latter occasion, the residence of her father in that house had been a source of pleasure, rather than of sorrow to her; but from the abode of Rushbrook she derived punishment alone.

When, from inquiries made to his own servant, who inquired again, Rushbrook found that on his approach Matilda had retired to her own confined apartments, the thought was torture to him; it was the hope of seeing and conversing with her, of being admitted at all times to her society as the mistress of the house, that had raised his spirits, and effected his perfect cure, beyond any other cause; and he was hurt to the greatest degree at this respect, or rather contempt, shown to him by her retreat.

It was, nevertheless, a subject too delicate to touch upon in any one sense—an invitation for her company on his part, might carry the appearance of superior authority, and an affected condescension, which he justly considered as the worst of all insults.—And yet, how could he support the idea that his visit had placed the daughter of his benefactor as a dependant stranger in that house, where in reality he was the dependant, and she the lawful heir.—For two or three days he suffered the torments of these reflections, hoping to come to an explanation of all he felt by a fortunate meeting with Miss Woodley; but when that meeting occurred, although he observed she talked to him with less reserve than she had formerly done, and even gave some proofs of the goodness of her disposition, yet she scrupulously avoided naming Lady Matilda; and when he diffidently enquired of her ladyship's health, a cold restraint spread over Miss Woodley's face, and she left him instantly.—To Sandford it was still more difficult to apply; for though they were frequently together, they were never sociable; and as Sandford seldom disguised his feelings, to Rushbrook he was always extremely severe, and sometimes unmannerly.

In this perplexed situation, the country air was rather of detriment than service to the invalid; and had he not, like a true lover, held fast to hope, while he could perceive nothing but despair; he had returned to town, rather than by his stay placed in a subordinate state the object of his adoration.—But still persisting in his hopes, he one morning met Miss Woodley in the garden, and engaging her a longer time than usual in conversation, at last obtained her promise 'She would that day dine with him and Mr. Sandford.'—But no sooner had she parted from him than she repented of her consent, and upon communicating it to Matilda, that young lady, for the first time in her life, darted upon her kind companion, a look of the most cutting reproach and haughty resentment.—Miss

Woodley's own sentiments had upbraided her before; but she was not prepared to receive so pointed a mark of disapprobation from her young friend, till now, duteous and humble to her as to a mother, and not less affectionate. Her heart was too susceptible to bear this disrespectful and contumelious frown from the object of her long-devoted care and concern; the tears instantly covered her face, and she laid her hands upon her heart, as if she thought it would break.—Matilda was moved, but she possessed too much of the manly resentment of her father, to discover what she felt for the first few minutes.—Miss Woodley, who had given so many tears to her sorrows, but never till now, one to her anger, had a still deeper sense of this indifference, than of the anger itself, and to conceal what she suffered, left the room.—Matilda, who had been till this time working at her needle, seemingly composed, now let her work drop from her hand, and sat for a little while in a deep reverie.—At length she rose up, and followed Miss Woodley to the other apartment.—She entered grave, majestic, and apparently serene, while her poor heart fluttered with a thousand distressing sensations.—She approached Miss Woodley (who was still in tears) with a sullen silence; and awed by her manners the faithful friend of her deceased mother exclaimed, 'Dear Lady Matilda, think no more on what I have done—do not resent it any longer, and on my knees I'll beg your pardon.' Miss Woodley rose as she uttered these last words; but Matilda laid fast hold of her to prevent the posture she offered to take, and instantly assumed it herself. 'Oh, let this be my atonement!' she cried with the most earnest supplication.

They interchanged forgiveness; and as this reconciliation was sincere, they each without reserve gave their opinion upon the subject which had caused the misunderstanding; and it was agreed that an apology should be sent to Mr. Rushbrook,

'That Miss Woodley had been suddenly indisposed,' nor could this be said to differ from the truth, for since what had passed she was unfit to pay a visit.

Rushbrook, who had been all the morning elated with the advance he supposed he had made in that lady's favour, was highly disappointed, vext, and angry when this apology was delivered to him; nor did he, nor perhaps could he, conceal what he felt, although his severe observer, Mr. Sandford, was present.

'I am a very unfortunate man,' said he, as soon as the servant was gone who brought the message.

Sandford cast his eyes upon him with a look of surprise and contempt.

'A very unfortunate man indeed, Mr. Sandford,' repeated he, 'although you treat my complaint contemptuously.'

Sandford made no reply, and seemed above making one.

They sat down to dinner;—Rushbrook eat scarce any thing, but drank frequently; Sandford took no notice of either, but had a book (which was his custom when he dined with persons whose conversation was not interesting to him) laid by the side of his plate, which he occasionally looked into, as the dishes were removing, or other opportunities served.

Rushbrook, just now more hopeless than ever of forming an acquaintance with Lady Matilda, began to give way to the symptoms of despair; and they made their first attack by urging him to treat on the same level of familiarity that he himself was treated, Mr. Sandford, to whom he had till now ever behaved with the most profound tokens of respect.

'Come,' said he to him as soon as the dinner was removed, 'Lay aside your book and be good company.'

Sandford lifted up his eyes upon him—stared in his face—and cast them on the book again.

'I say,' continued Rushbrook, 'I want a companion; and

as Miss Woodley has disappointed me, I must have your company.'

Sandford now laid down his book upon the table, but still holding his fingers in the pages he was reading, said, 'And why are you disappointed of Miss Woodley's company?—When people expect what they have no right to hope for, they have yet the assurance to complain they are disappointed.'

'I had a right to expect she would come,' answered Rushbrook, 'for she promised she would.'

'But what right had you to ask her?'

'The right every one has to make his time pass as agreeably as he can.'

'But not at the expence of another.'

'I believe, Mr. Sandford, it would be a heavy expence to you, to see me happy; I believe it would cost you even your own happiness.'

'That is a price I have not now to give,' replied Sandford, and he began reading again.

'What, you have already paid it away? No wonder that at your time of life it should be gone.—But what do you think of my having already squandered mine?'

'I don't think about you,' returned Sandford, without taking his eyes from the book.

'Can you look me in the face and say that, Mr. Sandford?— No, you cannot—for you know you *do* think of me, and you know you hate me.'——Here he drank two glasses of wine one after another; 'And I can tell you why you hate me,' continued he: 'It is from a cause for which I often hate myself.'

Sandford read on.

'It is on Lady Matilda's account you hate me, and use me thus.'

Sandford put down his book hastily, and put both his hands by his side.

'Yes,' resumed Rushbrook, 'you think I am wronging her.'

'I think you grossly insult her,' exclaimed Sandford, 'by this rude mention of her name; and I command you at your peril to desist.'

'At my peril! Mr. Sandford? Do you assume the authority of Lord Elmwood?'

'I do on this occasion; and if you dare to give your tongue a freedom'——

Rushbrook interrupted him—'Why then I boldly say, (and as her friend you ought rather to applaud than resent it) I boldly say, my heart suffers so much for her situation, I am regardless of my own.—I love her father—I loved her mother more—but she herself beyond either.'

'Hold your licentious tongue,' cried Sandford, 'or quit the room.'

'Licentious? Oh! the pure thoughts that dwell in her innocent mind, are not less sensual than mine towards her.—Do you upbraid me with my respect, my pity for her? These are the sensations which impel me to speak thus undisguised, even to you, my open—no, even worse—my secret enemy!'

'Insult *me* as you please, Mr. Rushbrook,—but beware how you mention Lord Elmwood's daughter.'

'Can it be to her dishonour that I pity her? that I would quit the house this moment never to return, so she supplied the place I withhold from her.'

'Go, then,' cried Sandford.

'It would be of no use to her, or I would.—But come, Mr. Sandford, I will dare do as much as you.—Only second me, and I will entreat Lord Elmwood to be reconciled—to see and own her.'

'Your vanity would be equal to your rashness.—You entreat?—She must greatly esteem those parental favours which your entreaties gained her!—Do you forget, young man, how short a time it is, since you were entreated for?'

'I prove I do not, while this anxiety for Lady Matilda, arises, from what I feel on that account.'

'Remove your anxiety, then, from her to yourself; for were I to let Lord Elmwood know what has passed now'—

'It is for your own sake, not for mine, if you don't.'

'You shall not dare me to it, Mr. Rushbrook,'—and he rose from his seat: 'You shall not dare me to do you an injury.— But to avoid the temptation, I will never again come into your company, unless my friend Lord Elmwood is present, to protect me and his child from your insults.'

Rushbrook rose in yet more warmth than Sandford. 'Have you the injustice to say I have insulted Lady Matilda?'

'To speak of her at all, is in you an insult.—But you have done more—You have dared to visit her—to force into her presence and shock her with your offers of services which she scorns; and of your compassion which she is far above.'

'Did she complain to you?'

'She, or her friend did.'

'I rather suppose, Mr. Sandford, you have bribed some of the servants to reveal this.'

'The suspicion becomes Lord Elmwood's heir.'

'It becomes the man, who lives in a house with you.'

'I thank you, Mr. Rushbrook, for what has passed this day— it has taken a weight off my mind.—I thought my disinclination to you, might perhaps arise from prejudice—this conversation has relieved me from those fears, and I thank you.' —Saying this he calmly walked out of the room, and left Rushbrook to reflect on what he had been doing.

Heated with the wine he had drank, (and which Sandford engaged on his book had not observed) no sooner was he alone, than he became at once cool and repentant.—'What had he done?' was the first question to himself—'He had offended Sandford'—The man whom reason as well as prudence had ever taught him to treat with respect and even reverence.—He had grossly offended the firm friend of Lady Matilda, and even by the unreserved, the wanton use of her name.—All the retorts he had uttered came now to his memory; with a total forgetfulness of all Sandford had said to provoke them.

He once thought to follow him and beg his pardon; but the contempt with which he had been treated, more than all the anger, withheld him.

As he sat forming plans how to retrieve the opinion, ill as it was, which Sandford formerly entertained of him, he received a letter from Lord Elmwood, kindly enquiring after his health, and saying he should be down early in the following week.—Never were the friendly expressions of his lordship half so welcome to him; for they served to sooth his imagination, racked with Sandford's wrath and his own displeasure.

CHAPTER XIII

WHEN Sandford acted deliberately he always acted up to his duty; it was his duty to forgive Rushbrook and he did so —but he had declared he would never 'be again in his company unless Lord Elmwood was present;'—and with all his forgiveness, he found an unforgiving gratification, in the duty, of being obliged to keep his word.

The next day Rushbrook dined alone, while Sandford gave his company to the ladies.—Rushbrook was too proud to seek to conciliate Sandford with abject concessions, but he endeavoured to meet him as by accident, and try what, in such a case, a submissive apology might effect.—For a day or two, all the schemes he formed on that head proved fruitless; he could never procure even a sight of him.—But on the evening of the third day, taking a lonely walk, he turned the corner of a grove, and saw in the very path he was going, Sandford accompanied by Miss Woodley; and, what agitated him much more, Lady Matilda was with them. He knew not whether to proceed, or to quit the path and palpably shun them—To one who seemed to put an unkind construction upon all he said and did, he knew to do either, would be to do wrong.— In spite of the propensity he felt to pass so near to Lady Matilda, could he have known what conduct would have been deemed the most respectful, whatever painful denial it had cost him, that, he would have adopted.—But undetermined whether to go forward, or to cross to another path, he still walked on till he came too nigh to recede; he then, with a diffidence not affected, but felt in the most powerful degree, pulled off his hat; and without bowing, stood silently while the company passed.—Sandford walked on some paces before, and took no farther notice as he went by him, than just touching the fore part of his hat with his finger.—Miss Woodley courtesied as she followed.—But Lady Matilda made a full stop, and said, in the gentlest accents, 'I hope, Mr. Rushbrook, you are perfectly recovered.'

It was the sweetest music he ever listened to; and he returned with the most respectful bow, 'I am better a great deal, ma'am,' and pursued his way as if he did not dare to utter another syllable.

Sandford seldom found fault with Lady Matilda; not because he loved her, but because she seldom did wrong— upon this occasion, however, he was half inclined to reprimand her; but yet he did not know what to say—the subsequent humility of Rushbrook had taken from the indiscretion of her speaking to him, and the event could by no means justify his censure.—On hearing her begin to speak Sandford had stopped; and as Rushbrook after replying, walked away, Sandford called to her crossly, 'Come, come along.' But at the same time he put out his elbow for her to take hold of his arm.

She hastened her steps, and did so—then turning to Miss Woodley, she said, 'I expected you would have spoken to Mr. Rushbrook; it might have prevented me.'

Miss Woodley replied, 'I was at a loss what to do;—when we met formerly, he always spoke first.'

'And ought now,' cried Sandford angrily—and then added, with a sarcastic smile, 'It is certainly the duty of the superior, to be the first who speaks.'

'He did not look as if he thought himself our superior,' replied Matilda.

'No,' returned Sandford, 'some can put on what looks they please.'

'Then while he looks so pale,' replied Matilda, 'and so dejected, I can never forbear speaking to him when we meet, whatever he may think of it.'

'And were he and I to meet a hundred, nay a thousand times,' replied Sandford, 'I don't think I shall ever speak to him again.'

'Bless me! what for, Mr. Sandford?' cried Matilda—for Sandford, who was not a man that repeated little incidents, had never mentioned the circumstance of their quarrel.

'I have taken such a resolution,'—answered he, 'yet I bear him no enmity.'

As this short reply indicated he meant to say no more, no more was asked; and the subject dropped.

In the mean time, Rushbrook, happier than he had been for months; intoxicated with joy at that voluntary mark of civility he had received from Lady Matilda, felt his heart so joyous, so free from every particle of malice, that he resolved in the humblest manner, to make atonement for the breach of decorum he had lately been guilty of to Mr. Sandford.

Too happy at this time to suffer a mortification from any treatment he might receive, he sent his servant to him into his study, as soon as he was returned home, to beg to know 'If he might be permitted to wait upon him, with a message he had to deliver from Lord Elmwood.'

The servant returned—'Mr. Sandford desired he would send the message by him, or the house steward.' This was highly affronting; but Rushbrook was not in a humour to be offended, and he sent again, begging he would admit him;— but the answer was, 'He was busy.'

Thus defeated in his hopes of reconciliation, his new transports felt an allay, and the few days that remained before Lord Elmwood came, he passed in solitary musing, and in-effectual walks and looks towards that path where he had met Matilda—she came that way no more—nor indeed scarce quitted her apartment, in the practice of that confinement she had to experience on the arrival of her father.

All her former agitations now returned.—On the day he arrived she wept—all the night she did not sleep—and the name of Rushbrook again became hateful to her.—His lord-ship came in extreme good health and spirits, but appeared concerned to find Rushbrook less well than when he went from town.—Sandford was now under the necessity of being in Rushbrook's company, yet he took care never to speak to him but when he was obliged; or to look at him but when he could not help it.—Lord Elmwood observed this conduct, yet he neither wondered, or was offended at it—he had always per-ceived what little esteem Sandford showed his nephew from his first return; but he forgave in Sandford's humour a thousand faults he would forgive in no other; nor did he deem this one of his greatest faults, knowing the claim to his partiality from another object.

Miss Woodley waited on Lord Elmwood as formerly; dined with him, and as heretofore related to the attentive Matilda all that passed.

About this time Lord Margrave, deprived by the season of all the sports of the field, felt his love for Matilda (which had been extreme while divided with the love of hunting) too violent to be subdued; and he resolved, though reluctantly, to apply to her father for his consent to their union;—but writing to Sandford this resolution, he was once more repulsed, and charged as a man of honour, to forbear to disturb the tranquillity of the family by any application of the kind.—To this Sandford received no answer; for his lordship, highly incensed at his mistress's repugnance to him, determined more firmly than ever, to consult his own happiness alone; and as that depended merely upon his obtaining her, he cared not by what method it was effected.

About a fortnight after Lord Elmwood came into the country, as he was riding one morning, his horse fell with him, and crushed his leg in so unfortunate a manner, as to be pronounced of dangerous consequence.—He was brought home in a post chaise, and Matilda heard of the accident with more grief than would, on such an occasion, appertain to the most fondled child.

In consequence of the pain he suffered his fever was one night very high; and Sandford, who seldom quitted his apartment, went frequently to his bed side; every time with the secret hope he should hear him ask to see his daughter—he was every time disappointed—yet he saw him shake with a cordial friendship the hand of Rushbrook, as if he delighted in seeing those he loved.

The danger in which Lord Elmwood was supposed to be,

was but of short duration, and his sudden recovery succeeded. —Matilda who had wept, moaned, and watched during the crisis of his illness, when she heard he was amending, exclaimed (with a kind of surprise at the novelty of the sensation) 'And this is joy that I feel!—Oh! I never till now knew, what those persons felt that experienced joy.'

Nor did she repine, like Mr. Sandford and Miss Woodley, at her father's inattention to her during his malady, for she did not hope like them—she did not hope he would behold her, even in dying.

But notwithstanding his lordship's seeming indifference while his indisposition continued, no sooner was he recovered so as to receive the congratulations of his friends, than there was no one person he evidently showed so much satisfaction at seeing, as Miss Woodley.—She waited upon him timorously and with more than ordinary distaste at his late conduct; when he put out his hand with the utmost warmth to receive her, drew her to him, saluted her, (an honour he had never in his life conferred before) and all with signs of the sincerest friendship and affection.—Sandford was present, and ever associating the idea of Matilda with Miss Woodley, felt his heart bound with a triumph it had not enjoyed for many a day.

Matilda listened with delight to the recital Miss Woodley gave on her return, and many times while it lasted exclaimed 'She was happy.' But poor Matilda's sudden transports of joy, which she termed happiness, were not made for long continuance; and if she ever found cause for gladness, she far oftener had motives for grief.

As Mr. Sandford was sitting with her and Miss Woodley one evening about a week after, a person rung at the bell and enquired for him; on being told of it by the servant, he went to the door of the apartment and cried 'Oh! is it you? Come in.'—An elderly man entered, who had been for many years the head gardener at Elmwood House; a man of honesty and sobriety, and with a large indigent family of aged parents, children, and other relatives, who subsisted wholly on the income arising from his place—The ladies, as well as Sandford, knew him well, and they all, almost at once, asked 'What was the matter?' for his looks told them something distressful had befallen him.

'Oh, sir!' said he to Sandford, 'I come to entreat your interest.'

'In what, Edwards?' said Sandford with a mild voice; for when his assistance was supplicated in distress, his rough tones always took a plaintive key.

'My lord has discharged me from his service,'—(returned Edwards trembling, and the tears starting in his eyes) 'I am undone, Mr. Sandford, unless you plead for me.'

'I will,' said Sandford, 'I will.'

'And yet I am almost afraid of your success,' replied the man, 'for my lord has ordered me out of his house this moment; and though I knelt down to him to be heard, he had no pity.'

Matilda sighed from the bottom of her heart, and yet she envied this poor man who had been kneeling to her father.

'What was your offence?' cried Sandford.

The man hesitated; then looking at Matilda, said, 'I'll tell you, sir, some other time.'

'Did you name me, before Lord Elmwood?' cried she eagerly, and terrified.

'No, madam,' replied he, 'but I unthinkingly spoke of my poor lady that is dead and gone.'

Matilda burst into tears.

'How came you to do so mad a thing?' cried Sandford, with the encouragement his looks had once given him, now fled from his face.

'It was unthinkingly,' repeated Edwards; 'I was showing my lord some plans for the new walks, and told him, among other things, that her ladyship had many years ago approved of them.—"Who?" cried he.—Still I did not call to mind, but repeated "Lady Elmwood, sir, while you were abroad"—As soon as these words were delivered, I saw my doom in his looks, and he commanded me to quit his house and service that instant.'

'I am afraid,' said Sandford, sitting down, 'I can do nothing for you.'

'Yes, sir, you know you have more power over my lord than any body—and perhaps you may be able to save me and all mine from misery.'

'I would if I could,' replied Sandford quickly.

'You can but try, sir.'

Matilda was all this while drowned in tears; nor was Miss Woodley much less affected—Lady Elmwood was before their eyes—Matilda beheld her in her dying moments; Miss Woodley saw her, as the gay ward of Dorriforth.

'Ask Mr. Rushbrook,' said Sandford, 'prevail on him to speak; he has more power than I have.'

'He has not enough, then,' replied Edwards, 'for he was in the room with my lord when what I have told you happened.'

'And did he say nothing?' asked Sandford.

'Yes, sir; he offered to speak in my behalf, but my lord interrupted him, and ordered him out of the room—he instantly went.'

Sandford now observing the effect which this narration had on the two ladies, led the man to his own apartments, and there assured him he durst not undertake his cause; but that if time or chance should happily make an alteration in his lordship's disposition, he would be the first to try to replace him.—Edwards was obliged to submit; and before the next day at noon, his pleasant house by the side of the park, his garden, and his orchard, which he had occupied above twenty years, were cleared of their old inhabitant, and all his wretched family.

CHAPTER XIV

THIS melancholy incident perhaps affected Matilda and all the friends of the deceased Lady Elmwood, beyond any other that had occurred since her death.—A few days after this circumstance, Miss Woodley, in order to divert the disconsolate mind of Lady Matilda, (and perhaps bring her some little anecdotes, to console her for that which had given her so much pain) waited upon Lord Elmwood in his library, and borrowed some books out of it.—He was now perfectly well from his fall, and received her with the same politeness as usual, but, of course, not with that particular warmth he had received her just after his illness.—Rushbrook was in the library at the same time; he shewed to her several beautiful prints which his lordship had just received from London, and appeared anxious to entertain, and give tokens of his esteem and respect for her.—But what gave her pleasure beyond any other attention was, that after she had taken (by the aid of Rushbrook) about a dozen volumes from different shelves, and had laid them together, saying she would send her servant to fetch them, Lord Elmwood went eagerly to the place where they were, and taking up each book, examined attentively what it was.—One author he complained was too light, another too depressing, and put them on the shelves again; another was erroneous and he changed it for a better; and thus he warned her against some, and selected other authors; as the most cautious preceptor culls for his pupil, or a fond father for his darling child.—She thanked him for his attention to her, but her heart thanked him for his attention to his daughter.—For as she herself had never received such a proof of his care since all their long acquaintance, she reasonably supposed Matilda's reading, and not hers, was the object of his solicitude.

Having in these books store of comfort for poor Matilda, she eagerly returned with them; and in reciting every particular circumstance, made her consider the volumes almost like presents from her father.

The month of September was now arrived, and Lord Elmwood, accompanied by Rushbrook, went to a small shooting seat, about twenty miles distant from Elmwood Castle, for a week's particular sport.—Matilda was once more at large; and one beautiful forenoon, about eleven o'clock, seeing Miss Woodley walking on the lawn before the house, she hastily took her hat to join her; and not waiting to put it on, went nimbly down the great staircase with it hanging on her arm.—When she had descended a few stairs, she heard a footstep walking slowly up; and, (from what emotion she could not tell,) she stopt short, half resolved to return back.—She hesitated a single instant which to do—then went a few steps farther till she came to the second landing place; when, by the sudden winding of the staircase,—Lord Elmwood was immediately before her!

She had felt something like affright before she saw him—but her reason told her she had nothing to fear, as he was far away.—But now the appearance of a stranger whom she had never before seen; an air of authority in his looks as well as in the sound of his steps; a resemblance to the portrait she had seen of him; a start of astonishment which he gave on beholding her; but above all—her *fears* confirmed her it was him.—She gave a scream of terror—put out her trembling hands to

catch the balustrades on the stairs for support—missed them
—and fell motionless into her father's arms.

He caught her, as by that impulse he would have caught
any other person falling for want of aid.—Yet when he found
her in his arms, he still held·her there—gazed on her attentively—and once pressed her to his bosom.

At length, trying to escape the snare into which he had been
led, he was going to leave her on the spot where she fell, when
her eyes opened and she uttered, 'Save me.'—Her voice un-
manned him.—His long-restrained tears now burst forth—
and seeing her relapsing into the swoon again, he cried out
eagerly to recall her.—Her name did not however come to
his recollection—nor any name but this—'Miss Milner—Dear
Miss Milner.'

That sound did not awake her; and now again he wished to
leave her in this senseless state, that not remembering what
had passed, she might escape the punishment.

But at this instant Giffard, with another servant, passed by
the foot of the stairs; on which, Lord Elmwood called to them
—and into Giffard's hands delivered his apparently dead
child; without one command respecting her, or one word of
any kind; while his face was agitated with shame, with pity,
with anger, with paternal tenderness.

As Giffard stood trembling, while he relieved his lord from
this hapless burthen; his lordship had to unloose her hand
from the side of his coat, which she had caught fast hold of
as she fell, and grasped so closely, it was with difficulty
released.—On taking the hand away his lordship trembled—
faltered—then bade Giffard do it.

'Who, I, my lord, I separate you?' cried he.—But recollecting himself, 'My lord, I will obey your commands whatever they are.' And seizing her hand, pulled it with violence
—it fell—and her father went away.

Matilda was carried to her own apartments, laid upon the bed, and Miss Woodley called to attend her, after listening to the recital of what had passed.

When Lady Elmwood's old and affectionate friend entered the room, and saw her youthful charge lying pale and speechless, yet no father by to comfort or sooth her, she lifted up her hands to heaven exclaiming, with a flood of tears, 'And is this the end of thee, my poor child?—Is this the end of all our hopes?—of thy own fearful hopes—and of thy mother's supplications?—Oh! Lord Elmwood! Lord Elmwood!'

At that name Matilda started, and cried, 'Where is he?—Is it a dream, or have I seen him?'

'It is all a dream, my dear,' said Miss Woodley.

'And yet I thought he held me in his arms,' she replied—'I thought I felt his hands press mine—Let me sleep and dream it again.'

Now thinking it best to undeceive her, 'It is no dream, my dear,' returned Miss Woodley.

'Is it not?' cried she, starting up and leaning on her elbow—'Then I suppose I must go away—go for ever away.'——

Sandford now entered.—Having been told the news he came to condole—But at the sight of him Matilda was terrified, and cried, 'Do not reproach me, do not upbraid me—I know I have done wrong—I know I had but one command from my father, and that I have disobeyed.'

Sandford could not reproach her, for he could not speak;—he therefore only walked to the window and concealed his tears.

That whole day and night was passed in sympathetic grief, in alarm at every sound, lest it should be a messenger to pronounce Matilda's destiny.

Lord Elmwood did not stay upon this visit above three hours at Elmwood House; he then set off again for the seat he had left; where Rushbrook still remained, and from whence his lordship had merely come by accident, to look over some writings he wanted dispatched to town.

During his short continuance here, Sandford cautiously avoided his presence; for he thought, in a case like this, what nature would not of herself do, no art, no arguments of his could effect—and to nature and to providence he left the whole.—What these two powerful principles brought about, the reader must judge, on perusing the following letter, received early the next morning by Miss Woodley.

VOLUME IV

CHAPTER I

*A letter from Giffard, Lord Elmwood's House Steward,
to Miss Woodley*

'Madam,

'My lord, above a twelvemonth ago, acquainted me he had permitted his daughter to reside in his house; but at the same time he informed me, the grant was under a certain restriction, which if ever broken, I was to see his then determination (of which he also acquainted me) put in execution. In consequence of Lady Matilda's indisposition, madam, I have ventured to delay this notice till morning—I need not say with what concern I now give it, or mention to you I believe, what is forfeited.—My lord staid but a few hours yesterday after the unhappy circumstance on which I write, took place; nor did I see him after, till he was in his carriage; he then sent for me to the carriage door, and told me he should be back in two days time, and added "Remember your duty." That duty, I hope, madam, you will not require I should mention in more direct terms.—As soon as my lord returns, I have no doubt but he will ask me if it is fulfilled, and I shall be under the greatest apprehension should his commands not be obeyed.

'If there is any thing wanting for the convenience of your and Lady Matilda's departure, you have but to order it, and it is at your service—I mean likewise any cash you may have occasion for. I should presume to add my opinion where you might best take up your abode; but with such advice as you will have from Mr. Sandford, mine would be but assuming.

'I would also have waited upon you, madam, and have delivered myself the substance of this letter; but I am an old man, and the changes I have been witness to in my lord's house since I first lived in it, has encreased my age many years; and I have not the strength to see you upon this occasion.— I loved my deceased lady—I love my lord—and I love their child—nay, so I am sure does my lord himself; but there is no accounting for his resolutions, or for the alteration his disposition has lately undergone.

'I beg pardon, madam, for this long intrusion, and am, and ever will be (while you and my lord's daughter are so) your afflicted humble servant,

ROBERT GIFFARD

Elmwood House,
 Sept. 12.'

When this letter was brought to Miss Woodley, she knew what it contained before she opened it, and therefore took it with an air of resignation—yet though she guessed the momentous part of its contents, she dreaded in what words it might be related; and having now no great good to hope for, hope, that will never totally expire, clung at this crisis to little circumstances, and she hoped most fervently the terms of the letter might not be harsh, but that Lord Elmwood had delivered his commands in gentle language.—The event proved he had; and lost to every important comfort, she felt grateful to him for this small one.

Matilda, too, was cheered by this letter, because she expected something worse; and the last line where Giffard said he knew 'his lordship loved her,' she thought repaid her for the purport of the other part.

Sandford was not so easily resigned or comforted—he walked about the room when the letter was shewn to him—called it cruel—stifled his tears, and wished to show his resentment only—but the former burst through all his endeavours, and he sunk into grief.

Nor was the fortitude of Matilda, which came to her assistance on the first onset of this trial, sufficient to arm her, when the moment came she was to quit the house—her father's house—never to see that, or him again.

When word was brought that the carriage was at the door, which was to convey her from all she held so dear, and she saw before her the prospect of a long youthful and healthful life, in which misery and despair were all she could discern; that despair seized her at once, and gaining courage from it, she cried,

'What have I to fear if I disobey my father's commands once more?—he cannot use me worse.—I'll stay here till he returns—again throw myself in his way, and then I will not faint, but plead for mercy.—Perhaps were I to kneel to him—kneel, like other children, and beg his blessing; he would not refuse it me.'

'You must not try,' said Sandford mildly.

'Who?' cried she, 'shall prevent my flying to my father?—have I another friend on earth to go to?—have I one relation in the world but him?—This is the second time I have been commanded out of the house.—In my infant state my cruel father turned me out; but then he sent me to a mother—now I have none; and I will stay with him.'

Again the steward sent to let them know the coach was waiting.

Sandford now, with a determined countenance, went coolly up to Lady Matilda, and taking her hand, seemed resolved to lead her to the carriage.

Accustomed to be awed by every serious look of his, she yet resisted this; and cried 'Would *you* be the minister of my father's cruelty?'

'Then,' said Sandford solemnly to her, 'farewell—from this moment you and I part.—I will take my leave, and do you remain where you are—at least till you are forced away.—But I'll not stay to be turned out—for it is impossible your father will suffer any friend of yours to continue here, after this disobedience.—Adieu.'

'I'll go this moment,' said she, and rose hastily.

Miss Woodley took her at her word, and hurried her immediately out of the room.

Sandford followed slow behind, with the same spirits as if he had followed at her funeral.

When she came to that spot on the stairs where she had met her father, she started back; and scarcely knew how to pass it. —When she had—'There he held me,' said she, 'and I thought I felt him press me to his heart, but I now find I was mistaken.'

As Sandford came forward to hand her into the coach, 'Now you behave well;' said he, 'by this behaviour, you do not entirely close all prospect of reconciliation with your father.'

'Do you think it is not yet impossible?' cried she, clasping his hand. 'Giffard says he loves me,' continued she, 'and do you think he might yet be brought to forgive me?'

'Forgive you?' cried Sandford.

'Suppose I was to write to him, and entreat his forgiveness.'

'Do not write yet,' said Sandford with no cheering accent.

The carriage drove off—and as it went, Matilda leaned her head from the window, to survey Elmwood House from the roof to the bottom.—She cast her eyes upon the gardens too—upon the fishponds—the coach houses even, and all the offices adjoining—which as objects she should never see again—she gazed at, as objects of importance.

CHAPTER II

RUSHBROOK, who at twenty miles distance, could have no conjecture what had passed at Elmwood House, (during the short visit Lord Elmwood made there) went that way with his dogs and gun in order to meet his lordship's chariot on its return and ride with him back—he did so—and getting into the carriage, told my lord eagerly the sport he had had during the day; laughed at an accident that had befallen one of his dogs, and for some time did not perceive but that his lordship was perfectly attentive.—At length, observing he answered more negligently than usual to what he said, Rushbrook turned his eyes quickly upon him and cried,

'My lord, are you not well?'

'Yes; perfectly well, I thank you, Rushbrook,' replied his lordship, and leaned back against the carriage.

'I thought, sir,' returned Rushbrook, 'you spoke languidly; I beg your pardon.'

'I have the head-ache a little,' answered he;—Then taking off his hat, brushed the powder from it, and as he put it on again, fetched a most heavy sigh; which no sooner had escaped him, than, to drown its sound, he said briskly,

'And so you tell me you have had good sport to-day?'

'No, my lord, I said but indifferent.'

'True, so you did.—Bid the man drive faster—it will be dark before we get home.'

'You will shoot to-morrow, my lord?'

'Certainly.'

'How does Mr. Sandford do, sir?'

'I did not see him.'

'Not see Mr. Sandford, my lord?—but he was out, I suppose—for they did not expect you at Elmwood House.'

'No, they did not.'

In such conversation Rushbrook and his uncle continued till the end of their journey.—Dinner was then immediately served, and his lordship now appeared much in his usual spirits; at least not suspecting any cause for their abatement, Rushbrook did not observe any alteration.

Lord Elmwood went however earlier to bed than ordinary, or rather to his bedchamber; for though he retired some time before his nephew, when Rushbrook passed his chamber door it was open; and he not in bed, but sitting in a musing posture as if he had forgot to shut it.

When Rushbrook's valet came to attend his master, he said to him,

'I suppose, sir, you do not know what has happened at Elmwood House.'

'For heaven's sake what?' cried Rushbrook.

'My lord has met Lady Matilda,' replied the man.

'How? Where? What's the consequence?'

'We don't know yet, sir; but all the servants suppose, her ladyship will not be suffered to remain there any longer.'

'They all suppose wrong,' returned Rushbrook hastily; 'my lord loves her I am certain, and this event may be the happy means, of his treating her as his child, from this day.'

The servant smiled and shook his head.

'Why, what more do you know?'

'Nothing more than I have told you, sir; except that his lordship took no kind of notice of her ladyship, that appeared like love.'

Rushbrook was all uneasiness and anxiety to know the particulars of what had passed; and now Lord Elmwood's inquietude, which he had but slightly noticed before, came full to his observation.—He was going to ask more questions, but he recollected Lady Matilda's misfortunes were too sacred, to be talked of thus familiarly by the servants of the family;—besides, it was evident this man thought, and but naturally, it might not be for his master's interest the father and the daughter should be united; and therefore would certainly give to all he said the opposite colouring.

In spite of his prudence, however, and his delicacy towards Matilda, Rushbrook could not let his valet leave him till he had inquired, and learnt all the circumstantial account of what had happened; except, indeed, the order received by Giffard; which being given after his lordship was in his carriage, and in concise terms, the domestics who attended him (and from whom this man had gained his intelligence) were of that unacquainted.

When the valet had left Rushbrook alone, the perturbation of his mind was so great, that he was at length undetermined whether to go to bed, or to rush into his uncle's apartment, and at his feet beg for that compassion upon his daughter, which he feared he had denied her.—But then again, to what dangers did he not expose himself by such a step? Nay, he might perhaps even injure her whom he wished to serve; for if his lordship was at present unresolved whether to forgive or to resent this disobedience to his commands, another's interference might enrage, and determine him on the latter.

This consideration was so weighty it resigned Rushbrook to the suspense he must endure till the morning; when he flattered himself, that by watching every look and motion of Lord Elmwood's, his penetration would be able to discover the state of his heart, and how he meant to act.

But the morning came, and he found all his prying curiosity was of no avail; his lordship did not use one word, one look, or action that was not customary.

On first seeing him, Rushbrook blushed at the secret with which he was entrusted; then contemplated the joy he ought to have known in clasping in his arms a child like Matilda—whose tenderness, reverence, and duty had deprived her of all sensation at his sight; which was in Rushbrook's mind an honour, that rendered him superior to what he was before.

They were in the fields all the day as usual; Lord Elmwood now cheerful, and complaining no more of the head-ache.—Yet once being separated from his nephew, Rushbrook crossed over a stile into another field, and found him sitting by the side of a bank, his gun laying by him, and he lost in thought. He rose on seeing him, and proceeded to the sport as before.

At dinner, he said he should not go to Elmwood House the next day, as he had appointed, but stay where he was, three or four days longer.—From these two small occurrences, Rushbrook would fain have extracted something by which to judge the state of his mind; but upon the test, that was impossible—he had caught him musing many a time before; and as to his prolonging his stay, that might arise from the sport—or, indeed, had any thing more material swayed him, who could penetrate whether it was the effect of the lenity, or the severity, he had dealt towards his child? whether his continuance there was to shun her, or to shun the house from whence he had turned her?

The three or four days for their abode where they were, being passed, they both returned together to Elmwood House.—Rushbrook thought he saw his uncle's countenance change as they entered the avenue, yet he did not appear less in spirits; and when Sandford joined them at dinner, his lordship went with his usual cheerfulness to him, and (as was his custom after any separation) put out his hand cheerfully to take his.—Sandford said, 'How do you do, my lord?' cheerfully in return; but put both his hands into his bosom, and walked to the other side of the room.—Lord Elmwood did not seem to observe this affront—nor was it done as an affront

—it was merely what poor Sandford felt; and he felt he could *not* shake hands with him.

Rushbrook soon learnt the news that Matilda was gone, and Elmwood House was to him a desert—he saw about it no real friend of hers, except poor Sandford, and to him Rushbrook knew himself now, more displeasing than ever; and all the overtures he made to him to be friends, he at this time, found more and more ineffectual.—Matilda was banished; and her supposed triumphant rival was, to Sandford, more odious than he ever had been.

In alleviation of their banishment, Miss Woodley with her charge had not returned to their old retreat; but were gone to a large farm house, no more than about thirty miles from Lord Elmwood's: here Sandford with little inconvenience visited them; nor did his lordship ever take any notice of his occasional absence; for as he had before given his daughter, in some measure, to his charge, so honour, delicacy, and the common ties of duty, made him approve rather than condemn his attention to her.

Though Sandford's frequent visits soothed Matilda, they could not comfort her; for he had no consolation to bestow suited to her mind—her father had given no one token of regret for what he had done. He had even inquired sternly of Giffard on his returning home,

'If Miss Woodley had left the house?'

The steward guessing the whole of his meaning, answered, 'Yes, my lord; and *all* your commands in that respect have been obeyed.'

He replied, 'I am satisfied,' and, to the grief of the old man, appeared really so.

To the farm house, the place of Matilda's residence, there came, besides Sandford, another visitor far less welcome; Viscount Margrave.—He had heard with surprise, and still greater joy, that Lord Elmwood had once more shut his doors against his daughter.—In this her discarded state, his lordship no longer burthened his lively imagination with the dull thoughts of marriage, but once more formed the brutal idea of making her his mistress.

Ignorant of a certain decorum which attended all Lord Elmwood's actions, he suspected his child might be in want; and an acquaintance with the worst part of her sex informed him, relief from poverty was the sure bargain for his success.—With these hopes, he again paid Miss Woodley and her a visit; but the coldness with which he was still received by the first, and the haughtiness with which the last, still kept him at a distance, again made him fear to give one allusion of his purpose: but he returned home resolved to write what he durst not speak—he did so—he offered his services, his purse, his house; they were rejected with contempt, and a still stronger prohibition given to his visits.

CHAPTER III

LORD ELMWOOD had now allowed Rushbrook a long vacation, in respect to his answer upon the subject of marriage; and the young man vainly imagined, his lordship's intentions upon that subject were entirely given up.—One morning however, as he was attending him in the library,

'Henry'——said his lordship, with a pause at the beginning of his speech, which indicated he was going to say something of importance, 'Henry——you have not forgot the discourse I had with you, a little time previous to your illness?'

Henry hesitated—for he wished to have forgotten it—but it was too strongly impressed upon his mind. His uncle resumed:

'What, equivocating again, sir?—Do you remember it, or do you not?'—

'Yes, my lord, I do.'

'And are you prepared to give me an answer?'

Rushbrook paused again.

'In our former conversation,' his lordship continued, 'I gave you but a week to determine—there is, I think, elapsed since that time, half a year.'

'About as much, sir.'

'Then surely you have now made up your mind?'

'I had done that, at first, my lord—provided it had met with your concurrence.'

'You wished to lead a bachelor's life, I think you said.'

Rushbrook bowed.

'Contrary to my will?'

'No, my lord, I wished to have your approbation.'

'And you wished for my approbation of the very opposite thing to that I proposed?—But I am not surprised—such is the gratitude of the world—and such is yours.'

'My lord, if you doubt my gratitude'——

'Give me a proof of it, Harry, and I will doubt of it no longer.'

'Upon every other subject but this, my lord, heaven is my witness your happiness'——

His lordship interrupted him. 'I understand you—upon every other subject, but the only one, my content requires, you are ready to obey me.—I thank you.'

'My lord, do not torture me with this suspicion; it is so contrary to my deserts, I cannot bear it.'

'Suspicion of your ingratitude!—you judge too favourably of my opinion;—it amounts to certainty.'

'Then to convince you, sir, I am not ungrateful,—tell me who the lady is you have chosen for me, and here I give you my word, I will sacrifice all my future prospects of happiness—all, for which I would wish to live—and become her husband, as soon as you shall appoint.'

This was spoken with a tone so expressive of despair, that Lord Elmwood replied,

'And while you obey me, you take care to let me know, it will cost you your future happiness.—This is, I suppose, to enhance the merit of the obligation—but I shall not accept your acquiescence on these terms.'

'Then in dispensing with it, I hope sir, for your pardon!'

'Do you suppose, Rushbrook, I can pardon an offence, the sole foundation of which, arises from a spirit of disobedience? —for you have declared to me your affections are disengaged. —In our last conversation did you not say so?'

'At first I did, my lord—but you permitted me to consult my heart more closely; and I have found I was mistaken.'

'You then own you at first told me a falsehood, and yet have all this time, kept me in suspense without confessing it.'

'I waited, sir, till you should enquire'——

'You have then sir, waited too long.' And the fire flashed from his eyes.

Rushbrook now found himself in that perilous state, that admitted of no medium of resentment,[1] but by such dastardly conduct on his part, as would wound both his truth and courage;—and thus animated by his danger, he was resolved to plunge boldly at once into the depth of his patron's anger.

'My lord,' said he, (but he did not undertake this task without sustaining the trembling and convulsion of his whole frame) 'My lord—waving for a moment the subject of my marriage—permit me to remind you, that when I was upon my sick bed, you promised, that on my recovery, you would listen to a petition I had to offer you.'

'Let me recollect,'—said his lordship. 'Yes—I remember

something of it.—But I said nothing to warrant any improper petition.'

'Its impropriety was not named, my lord.'

'No matter—that, you yourself must judge of, and answer for the consequences.'

'I would answer with my life, willingly--but I own I shrink from your anger.'

'Then do not provoke it.'

'I have already gone too far to recede—and you would of course demand an explanation, if I attempted to stop here.'

'I should.'

'Then, my lord, I am bound to speak—but do not interrupt me—hear me out, before you banish me from your sight for ever.'

'I will, sir,' replied his lordship, prepared to hear something that would displease him, and yet determined to hear with patience to the conclusion.

'Then, my lord'—(cried Rushbrook in the greatest agitation both of mind and body) 'Your daughter'——

The resolution his lordship had taken (and on which he had given his word to his nephew not to interrupt him) immediately gave way.—The colour rose in his face—his eyes darted lightning—and his hand was lifted up with the emotion, that word had created.

'You promised to hear me, my lord;' cried Rushbrook, 'and I claim your promise.'

His lordship now suddenly overcame his violence of passion, and stood silent and resigned to hear him; but with a determined look expressive of the vengeance that should ensue.

'Lady Matilda,' resumed Rushbrook, 'is an object that wrests from me the enjoyment of every blessing your kindness bestows.—I cannot but feel myself as her adversary—as one who has supplanted her in your affections—who supplies her place, while she is exiled, a wanderer, and an orphan.'

His lordship took off his eyes from Rushbrook, during this last sentence, and cast them on the floor.

'If I feel gratitude towards you, my lord,' continued he, 'gratitude is innate in my heart, and I must also feel it towards her, who first introduced me to your protection.'

Again the colour flew to Lord Elmwood's face; and again he could hardly restrain himself from uttering his indignation.

'It was the mother of Lady Matilda;' continued Rushbrook, 'who was this friend to me; nor will I ever think of marriage, or any other joyful prospect, while you abandon the only child of my beloved patroness, and load me with the rights, which belong to her.'

Here Rushbrook stopped—and Lord Elmwood was silent too, for near half a minute; but still his countenance continued fixed, with his unvaried resolves.

After this long pause, his lordship said composedly, but firmly, 'Have you finished, Mr. Rushbrook?'

'All that I dare to utter, my lord, and I fear, already too much.'

Rushbrook now trembled more than ever, and looked pale as death; for the ardour of speaking being over, he waited his sentence, with less constancy of mind than he expected he should.

'You disapprove my conduct, it seems;' said Lord Elmwood, 'and in that, you are but like the rest of the world—and yet, among all my acquaintance, you are the only one who has dared to insult me with your opinion.—And this you have not done inadvertently; moreover knowingly, willingly, and deliberately.—But as it has been my fate to be used ill, and severed from all those persons to whom my soul has been most attached; with less regret I can part from you, than was this my first trial.'

There was a truth and a pathetic sound in the utterance of these words that struck Rushbrook to the heart—and he beheld himself as a barbarian, who had treated his benevolent and only friend, with an insufferable liberty; void of respect for those gnawing sorrows which had imbittered so many years of his life, and in open violation of his most strict commands.— He felt he deserved all he was going to suffer, and he fell upon his knees, not so much to deprecate the doom he saw impending, as thus humbly to acknowledge it was his due.

Lord Elmwood, irritated by this posture, as a sign of the presumptuous hopes he might be forgiven, suffered now his anger to break through all bounds; and raising his voice, he cried in rage,

'Leave my house, sir,—Leave my house instantly, and seek some other home.'

Just as these words were begun, Sandford opened the library door; was witness to them, and to the imploring situation of Rushbrook.—He stood silent with amaze!

Rushbrook arose, and feeling in his mind a presage, that he might never from that hour, behold his benefactor more; as he bowed to him in token of obedience to his commands, a shower of tears covered his face;—but Lord Elmwood, unmoved, fixed his eyes upon him which pursued him with their enraged looks to the end of the room.—Here he had to pass Sandford; who, for the first time in his life, took hold of him by the hand, and said to Lord Elmwood, 'My lord, what's the matter?'

'That ungrateful villain,' cried his lordship, 'has dared to insult me.—Leave my house this moment, sir.'

Rushbrook made an effort to go, but Sandford still held his hand; and said to Lord Elmwood,

'He is but a boy, my lord, and do not give him the punishment of a man.'

Rushbrook now snatched his hand from Sandford's, and threw it with himself upon his neck; where he indeed sobbed like a boy.

'You are both in league,' exclaimed Lord Elmwood.

'Do you suspect me of partiality to Mr. Rushbrook?' said Sandford, advancing nearer to his lordship.

Rushbrook had now gained the point of remaining in the room; but the hope that privilege inspired (while he still harboured all the just apprehensions for his fate) gave birth, perhaps, to a more exquisite sensation of pain, than despair would have done.—He stood silent—confounded—hoping he was forgiven—fearing he was not.

As Sandford approached still nearer to Lord Elmwood, he continued, 'No, my lord, I know you do not suspect me, of partiality to Mr. Rushbrook—has any part of my behaviour ever discovered it?'

'You now then,' replied his lordship, 'only interfere to provoke me.'

'If that were the case,' returned Sandford, 'there have been occasions, when I might have done it more effectually—when my own heart-strings were breaking, because I would not provoke, or add to what you suffered.'

'I am obliged to you, Mr. Sandford,' said his lordship mildly.

'And if, my lord, I have proved any merit in a late forbearance, reward me for it now; and take this young man from the depth of despair in which I see he is sunk, and say you pardon him.'

Lord Elmwood made no answer—and Rushbrook drawing strong inferences of hope from his silence, lifted up his eyes from the ground, and ventured to look in his face; he found it composed to what it had been, but still strongly marked with agitation.—He cast his eyes away again, in confusion.

On which his lordship said to him—'I shall postpone your complying with my orders, till you think fit once more to provoke them—and then, not even Sandford, shall dare to plead your excuse.'

Rushbrook bowed.

'Go, leave the room, sir.'

He instantly obeyed.

While Sandford, turning to Lord Elmwood, shook him by the hand, and cried, 'My lord, I thank you—I thank you very kindly, my lord—I shall now begin to think I have some weight with you.'

'You might indeed think so, did you know how much I have pardoned.'

'What was his offence, my lord?'

'Such as I would not have forgiven you, or any earthly being besides himself—but while you were speaking in his behalf, I recollected there was a gratitude so extraordinary in the hazards he ran, that almost made him pardonable.'

'I guess the subject then,' cried Sandford; 'and yet I could not have supposed'——

'It is a subject we cannot speak on, Sandford, therefore let us drop it.'

At these words the discourse concluded.

CHAPTER IV

To the great relief of Rushbrook, Lord Elmwood that day dined from home, and he had not the confusion to see him again till the evening.—Previous to this, Sandford and he met at dinner; but as the attendants were present, nothing passed on either side respecting the incident in the morning.—

Rushbrook, from the peril which had so lately threatened him, was now in his perfect cool, and dispassionate, senses; and notwithstanding the real tenderness which he bore to the daughter of his benefactor, he was not insensible to the comfort of finding himself, once more in the possession of all those enjoyments he had forfeited, and for a moment lost.

As he reflected on this, to Sandford he felt the first tie of acknowledgement—but for his compassion, he knew he should have been at that very time of their meeting at dinner, away from Elmwood House for ever—and bearing on his mind a still more painful recollection; the burthen of his kind patron's continual displeasure. Filled with these thoughts, all the time of dinner he could scarce look at his companion without his eyes swimming in tears of gratitude, and whenever he attempted to speak to him, gratitude choaked his utterance.

Sandford on his part behaved just the same as ever; and to show he did not wish to remind Rushbrook of what he had done, he was just as uncivil as ever.

Among other things, he said 'He did not know Lord Elmwood dined from home, for if he had, he should have dined in his own apartment.'

Rushbrook was still more obliged to him for all this, and the weight of obligations with which he was oppressed, made him long for an opportunity to relieve himself by expressions.— As soon, therefore, as the servants were all withdrawn, he began:

'Mr. Sandford, whatever has been your opinion of *me*, I take pride to myself, that in my sentiments towards *you*, I have always distinguished you for that humane and disinterested character, you have this day proved.'

'Humane, and disinterested,' replied Sandford, 'are two flattering epithets for an old man going out of the world, and who can have no temptation to be otherwise.'

'Then suffer me to call your actions generous and compassionate, for they have saved me'——

'I know, young man,' cried Sandford interrupting him,
'you are glad at what I have done, and that you find a gratification in telling me you are; but it is a gratification I will not indulge you with—therefore say another sentence on the subject,
and' (he rose from his seat) I'll leave the room, and never come
into your company again, whatever your uncle may say to it.'

Rushbrook saw by the solemnity of his countenance he was
serious, and positively assured him he would never thank him
more; on which Sandford took his seat again, but he still
frowned, and it was many minutes before he conquered his
ill humour.—As his countenance became less sour, Rushbrook fell from some general topics he had eagerly started in
order to appease him, and said,

'How hard is it to restrain conversation from the subject of
our thoughts; and yet amidst our dearest friends, and among
persons who have the same dispositions and sentiments as our
own, their minds fixed upon the self-same objects, is this constraint practised—and thus society, which was meant for one
of our greatest blessings, becomes insipid, nay oftentimes more
wearisome than solitude.'

'I think, young man,' replied Sandford, 'you have made
pretty free with your speech to-day, and ought not to complain
of the want of toleration on that score.'

'I do complain,' replied Rushbrook; 'for if toleration was
more frequent, the favour of obtaining it would be less.'

'And your pride, I suppose, is above receiving a favour.'

'Never from those I esteem; and to convince you of it, I
wish this moment to request a favour of you.'

'I dare say I shall refuse it.—However—what is it?'

'Permit me to speak to you upon the subject of Lady
Matilda.'

Sandford made no answer, consequently did not forbid him—and he proceeded.

'For her sake—as I suppose Lord Elmwood may have told you—I this morning rashly threw myself into the predicament from whence you released me—for her sake, I have suffered much—for her sake, I have hazarded a great deal, and am still ready to hazard more.'

'But for your own sake, do not,' returned Sandford drily.

'You may laugh at these sentiments as romantic, Mr. Sandford, but if they are, to me they are nevertheless natural.'

'But what service are they to be, either to her, or to yourself?'

'They are painful to me, and to her would be but impertinent, were she to know them.'

'I shan't inform her of them, so do not trouble yourself to caution me against it.'

'I was not going—you know I was not—but I was going to say, that from no one so well as from you, could she be told my sentiments, without the danger of her resenting the liberty.'

'And what impression do you wish to give her, from her becoming acquainted with them?'

'The impression, that she has one sincere friend—that upon every occurrence in life, there is a heart so devoted to all she feels, she can never suffer without the sympathy of another—or ever can command him, and all his fortunes to unite for her welfare, without his ready and immediate compliance.'

'And do you imagine, that any of your professions, or any of her necessities, would ever prevail upon her to put you to the trial?'

'Perhaps not.'

'What, then, are the motives which induce you to wish her to be told of this?'

Rushbrook paused.

'Do you think,' continued Sandford, 'the intelligence will give her any satisfaction?'

'Perhaps not.'

'Will it be of any to yourself?'

'The highest in the world.'

'And so all you have been urging upon this occasion, is, at last, only to please yourself.'

'You wrong my meaning—it is she—her merit which inspires my desire of being known to her—it is her sufferings, her innocence, her beauty'——

Sandford stared—Rushbrook proceeded: 'It is her'——

'Nay stop where you are,' cried Sandford; 'you are arrived at the zenith of perfection in a woman, and to add one qualification more, would be an anti-climax.'

'Oh!' cried Rushbrook with warmth, 'I loved her, before I ever beheld her.'

'Loved her!' cried Sandford, with astonishment, 'You are talking of what you do not intend.'

'I am, indeed,' returned he in confusion, 'I fell by accident on the word love.'

'And by the same accident, stumbled on the word beauty; and thus by accident, am I come to the truth of all your professions.'

Rushbrook knew he loved; and though his affection had sprung from the most laudable motives, yet was he ashamed of it, as of a vice—he rose, walked about the room, and did not look Sandford in the face for a quarter of an hour.—Sandford satisfied he had judged rightly, and yet unwilling to be too hard upon a passion, which he readily believed must have had many noble virtues for its foundation, now got up and walked away, without saying any thing in censure, though not a word in its approbation.

It was in the month of October, and just dark, at the time

Rushbrook was left alone, yet from the agitation of his mind, arising from the subject on which he had been talking, he found it impossible to remain in the house, and therefore walked into the fields;—but there was another instigation, more powerful than the necessity of walking; it was the allurement of passing along that path where he had last seen Lady Matilda, and where, for the only time she had condescended to speak to him divested of haughtiness, and with a gentleness that dwelt upon his memory beyond all her other endowments.

Here he retraced his own steps repeatedly, his whole imagination engrossed with her idea, till the sound of her father's chariot returning home from his visit, roused him from the soft delusion of his trance, to dread the confusion and embarrassment he should endure, on the next meeting with his lordship. He hoped Sandford might be present, and yet he was now, almost as much ashamed to behold him as his uncle, whom he had so lately offended.

As loath to leave the spot where he was, as to enter the house, he remained there till he considered it would be ill manners in his present humiliated situation, not to show himself at the usual supper hour, which was immediately.

As he laid his hand upon the door of the apartment to open it, he was sorry to hear by Lord Elmwood's voice, he was in the room before him; for there was something much more conspicuous and distressing, in entering where he already was, than had his lordship come in after him.—He found himself, however, reassured by overhearing his uncle laugh and speak in a tone expressive of the utmost good humour to Sandford, who was with him.

Yet again, he felt all the awkwardness of his own situation; but making one courageous effort, opened the door and entered.—His lordship had been away half the day, had dined abroad, and it was necessary to take some notice of his return;

Rushbrook therefore bowed humbly, and what was more to his advantage, he looked humbly.—Lord Elmwood made a slight return to the salutation, but continued the recital he had begun to Sandford;—then sat down to the supper table—supped—and passed the whole evening without saying a syllable, or even casting a look in remembrance of what had passed in the morning.—Or if there was any token, that shewed he remembered the circumstance at all, it was the putting his glass to his nephew's when Rushbrook called for wine, and drinking at the time he did.

CHAPTER V

THE repulse Lord Margrave received, did not diminish the ardour of his pursuit; for as he was no longer fearful of resentment from the Earl, whatever treatment his daughter might receive, he was determined the anger of Lady Matilda or of her female friend, should not impede his pretensions.

Having taken this resolution, he laid the plan of an open violation of all right, all power, and to bear away that prize by force, which no art was likely to procure.—He concerted with two of his favourite companions, but their advice was, 'one struggle more of fair means.' This was totally against his lordship's will, for he had much rather have encountered the piercing cries of a female in the last agonies of distress, than the fatigue of her sentimental harangues, or elegant reproofs, such as he had the sense to understand, but not the capacity to answer.

Stimulated, however, by his friends to one more trial; in spite of the formal dismission he had twice received, he intruded another visit on Lady Matilda at the farm.—

Provoked beyond bearing at such unfeeling assurance, Matilda refused to come into the room where he was, and Miss Woodley alone received him, and expressed her surprise at the little attention he had paid to her explicit desire.

'Madam,' replied the nobleman, 'to be plain with you, I am in love.'

'I do not the least doubt it, my lord,' replied Miss Woodley, 'nor ought you to doubt the truth of what I advance, when I assure you, you have not the smallest reason to hope your love will be returned; for Lady Matilda is resolved *never* to listen to your passion.'

'That man,' he replied, 'is to blame, who can relinquish his hopes, upon the mere resolution of a lady.'

'And that lady would be wrong,' replied Miss Woodley, 'who should entrust her happiness in the care of a man, who can think thus meanly of her, and of her sex.'

'I think highly of them all,' returned his lordship; 'and to convince you in how high an estimation I hold her ladyship in particular, my whole fortune is at her command.'

'Your absenting yourself from this house, Lord Margrave, she would consider as a much greater mark of your respect.'

A long conversation, equally uninteresting as this, ensued; till the unexpected arrival of Mr. Sandford put an end to it.— He started at the sight of Lord Margrave; but his lordship was much more affected at the sight of him.

'My lord,' said Sandford boldly to him, 'have you received any encouragement from Lady Matilda, to authorise this visit?'

'None, upon my honour, Mr. Sandford; but I hope you know how to pardon a lover?'

'A rational one I do—but you, my lord, are not such, while you persecute the pretended object of your affection.'

'Do you call it persecution that I once offered her a share

of my title and fortune—and even now, declare my fortune is at her disposal?'

Sandford was uncertain whether he understood his meaning—but his lordship, provoked at his ill reception, felt a triumph in not detaining him long in doubt, and proceeded thus:

'For the discarded daughter of Lord Elmwood, cannot expect the same proposals which I made while she was acknowledged, and under the protection of her father.'

'What proposals then, my lord?' asked Sandford hastily.

'Such,' replied his lordship, 'as the Duke of Avon made to her mother.'

Miss Woodley quitted the room that instant.—But Sandford, who never felt resentment but to those in whom he saw some virtue, calmly replied,

'My lord, the Duke of Avon was a gentleman, a man of elegance and breeding; and what have you to offer in recompense for your defects in these?'

'My wealth,' replied he, 'opposed to her indigence.'

Sandford smiled, and answered,

'Do you suppose that wealth can be esteemed, which has not been able to make you respectable?—What is it which makes wealth valuable? Is it the pleasures of the table? the pleasures of living in a fine house? or riding in a fine coach? These are pleasures a lord enjoys, but in common with his valet.—It is the pleasure of being conspicuous, which makes riches desirable—but if we are conspicuous only for our vice and folly, had we not better remain in poverty?'

'You are beneath my notice.'

'I trust I shall continue so—and that your lordship will never again condescend to come where I am.'

'A man of rank condescends to mix with any society, when a pretty woman is his object.'

'My lord, I have a book here in my pocket, which I am eager to read; it is an author who speaks sense and reason—will you pardon the impatience I feel for such company; and permit me to call your carriage?'

Saying this he went hastily and called to his lordship's servants; the carriage drove up, the door was opened, and Lord Margrave, ashamed to be exposed before his attendants, or convinced of the uselessness of remaining any longer where he was, departed.

Sandford was soon joined by the ladies; and the conversation falling, of course, upon the nobleman who had just taken his leave, Sandford unwarily exclaimed, 'I wish Rushbrook had been here.'

'Who?' cried Lady Matilda.

'I do believe,' said Miss Woodley, 'that young man has some good qualities.'

'A great many,' returned Sandford, mutteringly.

'Happy young man!' cried Matilda: 'he is beloved by all those, whose affection it would be my choice to possess, beyond any other blessing this world could bestow.'

'And yet I question, if Rushbrook is a happy man,' said Sandford.

'He cannot be otherwise,' returned Matilda, 'if he is a man of understanding.'

'He does not want for that,' replied Sandford; 'although he has certainly many indiscretions.'

'But which Lord Elmwood, I suppose,' said Matilda, 'looks upon with tenderness.'

'Not upon all his faults,' answered Sandford; 'for I have seen him in very dangerous circumstances with your father.'

'Have you indeed?' cried Matilda: 'then I pity him.'

'And I believe,' said Miss Woodley, 'that from his heart, he compassionates you.—Now, Mr. Sandford,' continued she, 'though this is the first time I ever heard you speak in his favour, (and I once thought as indifferently of Mr. Rushbrook as you can do) yet now I will venture to ask you, whether you do not think he wishes Lady Matilda much happier than she is?'

'I have heard him say so,' answered Sandford.

'It is a subject,' returned Lady Matilda, 'which I did not imagine you, Mr. Sandford, would have permitted to have been lightly mentioned, in your presence.'

'Lightly!—Do you suppose, my dear, we turned your situation into ridicule?'

'No, sir,—but there is a sort of humiliation in the grief to which I am doomed, that ought surely to be treated with the highest degree of delicacy by my friends.'

'I don't know on what point you fix real delicacy; but if it consists in sorrow, the young man gives a proof he possesses it, for he shed tears when I last heard him mention your name.'

'I have more cause to weep at the mention of his.'

'Perhaps so—But let me tell you, Lady Matilda, your father might have preferred a more unworthy object.'

'Still had he been to me,' she cried, 'an object of envy.— And as I frankly confess my envy of Mr. Rushbrook, I hope you will pardon my malice, which is, you know, but a consequent crime.'

The subject now turned again upon Lord Margrave; and all of them being firmly persuaded, this last reception would put an end to every farther intrusion from his lordship, they treated his pretensions, and himself, with the contempt they inspired—but not with the caution they deserved.

CHAPTER VI

THE next morning early Mr. Sandford returned to Elmwood House, but with his spirits depressed, and his heart overcharged with sorrow.—He had seen Lady Matilda, the object of his visit, but he had beheld her considerably altered in her looks and in her health;—she was become very thin, and instead of the most beautiful bloom that used to spread her cheeks, her whole complexion was of a deadly pale—her countenance no longer expressed hope or fear, but a fixed melancholy—she shed no tears, but was all sadness.—He had beheld this, and he had heard her insulted by the licentious proposals of a nobleman, from whom there was no satisfaction to be demanded, because she had no friend to vindicate her honour.

Rushbrook, who suspected where Sandford was gone, and imagined he would return that day, took his forenoon's ride, so as to meet him on the road a few miles distance from the castle; for since his perilous situation with Lord Elmwood, he was so fully convinced of the general philanthropy of Sandford's character, that in spite of his churlish manners, he now addressed him, free from that reserve to which his rough behaviour had formerly given birth.—And Sandford on his part, believing he had formed an illiberal opinion of Lord Elmwood's heir (though he took no pains to let him know that opinion was changed) yet resolved to make him restitution upon every occasion that offered.

Their mutual greetings when they met, were unceremonious but cordial; and Rushbrook turned his horse and rode back with Sandford;—yet, intimidated by his respect and tenderness for Lady Matilda, rather than by fear of the rebuffs of his companion, he had not the courage to name her, till their ride was just finished, and they came within a few yards of the house—incited then by the apprehension he might not soon again enjoy so fit an opportunity, he said,

'Pardon me, Mr. Sandford, if I guess where you have been, and if my curiosity forces me to enquire for Miss Woodley's and Lady Matilda's health?'

He named Miss Woodley first, to prolong the time before he mentioned Matilda, for though to name her gave him extreme pleasure, yet it was a pleasure intermingled with confusion and pain.

'They are both very well,' replied Sandford, 'at least they did not complain they were sick.'

'They are not in spirits, I suppose?' said Rushbrook.

'No, indeed,' replied Sandford, shaking his head.

'No new misfortune has happened, I hope?' cried Rushbrook, for it was plain to see Sandford's spirits were unusually cast down.

'Nothing new,' returned he, 'except the insolence of a young nobleman.'

'What nobleman?' cried Rushbrook.

'A lover of Lady Matilda's,' replied Sandford.

Rushbrook was petrified.—'Who? What lover, Mr. Sandford?—explain!'

They were now arrived at the house; and Sandford, without making any reply to this question, said to the servant who took his horse, 'She has come a long way this morning; take care of her.'

This interruption was torture to Rushbrook, who kept close to his side, in order to obtain a farther explanation; but Sandford without attending to him, walked negligently into the hall, and before they advanced many steps they were met by Lord Elmwood.

All farther information was for the present, now wholly put an end to.

'How do you do, Sandford?' said his lordship with extreme kindness; as if he thanked him for the journey which he suspected he had been taking.

'I am indifferent well, my lord,' replied he, with a face of deep concern, and a tear in his eye, partly in gratitude for his lordship's civility, and partly in reproach for his cruelty.

It was not now till the evening, that Rushbrook had an opportunity of renewing the conversation, which had been so barbarously interrupted.

In the evening, no longer able to support the suspense in which he was; without fear or shame he followed Sandford to his chamber at the time of his retiring, and entreated of him, with all the anxiety he suffered, to reveal to him what he alluded to, when he made mention of a lover, and insolence to Lady Matilda.

Sandford seeing his emotion, was angry he had inadvertently mentioned the subject; and putting on an air of surly importance, desired if he had any business with him, to call in the morning.

Exasperated at so unexpected a reception, and at the pain of his disappointment, Rushbrook replied, 'He treated him cruelly, nor would he stir out of his room, till he had received a satisfactory answer to his question.'

'Then bring your bed,' replied Sandford, 'for you must pass your whole night here.'

He found it vain to think of obtaining any intelligence by threats, he therefore said in a timid persuasive manner,

'Did you, Mr. Sandford, hear Lady Matilda mention my name?'

'Yes,' replied Sandford, a little better reconciled to him.

'Did you tell her what I declared to you?' he asked with more diffidence still.

'No,' replied Sandford.

'It is very well, sir,' returned he vexed to the heart—yet again wishing to sooth him.

'You certainly, Mr. Sandford, know what is for the best— yet I entreat you will give me some farther account of the nobleman you named?'

'I know what is for the best,' replied Sandford, 'and I won't.'

Rushbrook bowed, and immediately left the room.—He went apparently submissive, but the moment he shewed this submission, he took the resolution of paying a visit himself to the farm where Lady Matilda resided; and of learning either from Miss Woodley, the people of the house, the neighbours, or perhaps from Lady Matilda's own lips, the secret which the obstinacy of Sandford had denied him.

He saw all the dangers of this undertaking, but none appeared so great as the danger of losing her he loved, by the influence of a rival—and though Sandford had named 'insolence,' he was in doubt whether what had appeared such to him, was such in reality, or would be considered as such by her.

To prevent his absence being suspected by Lord Elmwood, he immediately called his groom, ordered his horse, and giving those servants concerned, a strict charge of secresy, and some frivolous pretence to apologize for his not being present at breakfast (resolving to be back by dinner) he set off that night, and arrived at an inn about a mile from the farm at break of day.

The joy he felt when he found himself so near to the beloved object of his journey, made him thank Sandford in his heart, for the unkindness which had sent him thither.—

But new difficulties arose, how to accomplish the end for which he came;—he learnt from the people of the inn that a lord with a fine equipage had visited at the farm, but who he was, or for what purpose he went, no one could inform him.

Miserable to return with the same doubts unsatisfied with which he set out, and yet afraid to proceed to extremities that might be construed into presumption, he walked disconsolately (almost distractedly) about the fields, looking repeatedly at his watch, and wishing the time to stand still, till he was ready to go back with his errand compleated.

Every field he passed, brought him nearer to the house on which his imagination was fixed; but how, without forfeiting every appearance of that very respect he so powerfully felt, could he attempt to enter it?—he saw the indecorum, resolved not to be guilty of it, and yet walked on till he was within but a short orchard of the door. Could he then retreat?—he wished he could; but he now found he had proceeded too far, to be any longer master of himself.—The time was urgent; he must either be bold, and venture her displeasure; or by diffidence during one moment, give up all his hopes perhaps for ever.

With that same disregard to consequences, which actuated him when he dared to supplicate Lord Elmwood in his daughter's behalf, he at length went eagerly to the door and rapped.

A servant came—he asked to 'speak with Miss Woodley, if she was quite alone.'

He was shown into an apartment, and Miss Woodley entered to him.

She started when she beheld who it was; but as he did not see a frown upon her face, he caught hold of her hand, and said persuasively,

'Do not be offended with me.—If I mean to offend you, may I forfeit my life in atonement.'

Poor Miss Woodley, glad in her solitude to see any one from Elmwood House, forgot his visit was an offence till he put her in mind of it; she then said with some reserve,

'Tell me the purport of your coming, sir, and perhaps I may then have no cause to complain.'

'It was to see Lady Matilda,' he replied, 'or to hear of her health.—It was to offer her my services—it was Miss Woodley, to convince her, if possible, of my esteem.'

'Had you no other method, sir?' said Miss Woodley with the same reserve.

'None;' replied he, 'or with joy I should have embraced it; and if you can inform me of any other, tell me I beseech you instantly, and I will immediately be gone, and pursue your directions.'

Miss Woodley hesitated.

'You know of no other means, Miss Woodley,' he cried.

'And yet I cannot commend this,' said she.

'Nor do I.—Do not imagine because you see me here, I approve my conduct; but reduced to this necessity, pity the motives that have urged it.'

Miss Woodley did pity them; but as she would not own she did, she could think of nothing else to say.

At this instant a bell rung from the chamber above.

'That is Lady Matilda's bell,' said Miss Woodley; 'she is coming to take a short walk.—Do you wish to see her?'

Though it was the first wish Rushbrook had, he paused, and said, 'Will you plead my excuse?'

As the flight of stairs was but short, which Matilda had to come down, she was in the room with Miss Woodley and Mr. Rushbrook just as that sentence ended.

She had stept beyond the door of the apartment, when perceiving a visitor, she hastily withdrew.

Rushbrook, animated, though trembling at her presence,

cried, 'Lady Matilda, do not avoid me, till you know I deserve such a punishment.'

She immediately saw who it was, and returned back with a proper pride, and yet a proper politeness in her manner.

'I beg your pardon, sir,' said she, 'I did not know you, and I was afraid I intruded upon Miss Woodley and a stranger.'

'You do not then consider me as a stranger, Lady Matilda? and that you do not, requires my warmest acknowledgements.'

She sat down, as if overcome by ill spirits and ill health.

Miss Woodley now asked Rushbrook to sit—for till now she had not.

'No, madam,' replied he, with confusion, 'not unless her ladyship gives me permission.'

Lady Matilda smiled, and pointed to a chair—and all the kindness which Rushbrook during his whole life had received from Lord Elmwood, never inspired half the gratitude, which this single instance of civility from his daughter excited.

He sat down with the confession of the obligation, upon every feature of his face.

'I am not well, Mr. Rushbrook,' said Matilda, languidly; 'and you must excuse any want of etiquette, you meet with at this house.'

'While you excuse me, madam, what can I have to complain of?'

She appeared absent while he was speaking, and turning to Miss Woodley, said, 'Do you think I had better walk to-day?'

'No, my dear,' answered Miss Woodley; 'the ground is damp, and the air cold.'

'You are not well, indeed, Lady Matilda,' said Rushbrook, gazing upon her with the most tender respect.

She shook her head; and the tears, without any effort either to impel or restrain them, ran fast down her face.

Rushbrook rose from his seat, and with an accent and manner the most expressive, said, 'We are cousins, Lady Matilda —in our infancy we were brought up together—we were beloved by the same mother—fostered by the same father'——

'Oh!' cried she, interrupting him, and the tears now gushed in torrents.

'Nay, do not let me add to your uneasiness,' resumed he, 'while I am attempting to alleviate it.—Instruct me what I am to do to show my esteem and respect, rather than permit me thus unguided, to rush upon what you may misterm, cruelty or arrogance.'

Miss Woodley went to Matilda, took her hand, then wiped the tears from her eyes, while Matilda reclined against her, wholly regardless of Rushbrook's presence.

'If I have been the least instrumental to this sorrow,'—— said Rushbrook, with a face as much agitated as his mind.

'No,' said Miss Woodley in a low voice, 'you have not— she is often thus.'

'Yes,' said Matilda, raising her head, 'I am frequently so weak I cannot resist the smallest incitement to grief.—But do not make your visit long, Mr. Rushbrook,' she continued, 'for I was just then thinking, that should Lord Elmwood hear of this attention you have paid me, it might be fatal to you.'— Here she wept again, as bitterly as before.

'There is no probability of his hearing of it, madam,' Rushbrook replied; 'or if there was, I am persuaded he would not resent it; for yesterday, when I am confident he knew Mr. Sandford had been to see you, he received him on his return with unusual marks of kindness.'

'Did he?' said she—and again she lifted up her head; and her eyes for a moment beamed with hope and joy.

'There is something which we cannot yet define,' said Rushbrook, 'that Lord Elmwood struggles with; but when time shall have eradicated'——

Before he could proceed farther, Matilda was once more sunk into despondency, and scarce attended to what he was saying.

Miss Woodley observing this, said, 'Mr. Rushbrook, let it be a token we shall be glad to see you hereafter, that I now use the freedom to beg you will put an end to your visit.'

'You send me away, madam,' returned he, 'with the warmest thanks for the reception you have given me; and this last assurance of your kindness is beyond any other favour you could have bestowed.—Lady Matilda,' added he, 'suffer me to take your hand at parting, and let it be a testimony that you acknowledge me for a relation.'

She put out her hand—which he knelt to receive, but did not raise it to his lips—he held the boon too sacred—and only looking earnestly upon it, as it lay pale and wan in his, he breathed a sigh over it, and withdrew.

CHAPTER VII

SORROWFUL and affecting as this interview had been, Rushbrook as he rode home reflected upon it with the most inordinate delight; and had he not beheld decline of health, in all the looks and behaviour of Lady Matilda, his felicity had been unbounded.—Entranced in the happiness of her society, the thought of his rival never came once to his mind while he was with her; a want of recollection, however, he by no means regretted, as her whole appearance contradicted every suspicion he could possibly entertain, of her favouring the addresses of any man living—and had he remembered, he had not dared to have named the subject.

The time run so swiftly while he was away, that it was beyond the dinner hour at Elmwood House, when he returned. ——Heated, his dress, and his hair disordered, he entered the dining room just as the dessert was put upon the table.—He was confounded at his own appearance, and at the falsehoods he should be obliged to fabricate in his excuse; there was yet that which engaged his attention, beyond any circumstance relating to himself—the features of Lord Elmwood—of which his daughter's, whom he had just beheld, had the most striking resemblance; while hers were softened by sorrow, as his lordship's were rendered austere by the self-same cause.

'Where have you been?' said his lordship, with a frown.

'A chase, my lord—I beg your pardon—but a pack of dogs I unexpectedly met.'——For in the hacknied art of lying without injury to any one, Rushbrook, to his shame, was proficient.

His excuses were received, and the subject ceased.

During his absence that day, Lord Elmwood had called Sandford apart and said to him,—that as the malevolence which he once observed between him and Rushbrook had, he perceived, subsided; he advised him, if he was a well-wisher to the young man, to sound his heart, and counsel him not to act contrary to the will of his nearest relation and friend.—— 'I myself am too hasty,' continued Lord Elmwood, 'and, unhappily, too much determined upon what I have once (though, perhaps, rashly) said, to speak upon a topic where it is probable I shall meet with opposition.—You, Sandford, can reason with moderation.—For after all I have done for my nephew, it would be a pity to forsake him at last; and yet, that is but too likely, if he provokes me.'

'Sir,' replied Sandford, 'I will speak to him.'

'Yet,' cried his lordship sternly, 'do not urge what you say

for my sake, but for his—I can part from him with ease—
but he may then repent, and, you know, repentance always
comes too late with me.'

'My lord, I will use my endeavours for his welfare.—But
what is the subject on which he has refused to comply with
your desires?'

'Matrimony—have not I told you?'

'Not a word.'

'I wish him to marry, that I may then conclude the deeds
in respect to my estate—And the only child of Sir William
Winterton (a rich heiress) was the wife I meant to propose;
but from his indifference to all I have said on the subject, I
have not yet mentioned her name to him; you may.'

'I will, my lord, and use all my persuasion towards his
obedience; and you shall have, at least, a faithful account of
what he says.'

Sandford the next morning sought an opportunity of being
alone with Rushbrook—he then plainly repeated to him what
Lord Elmwood had said, and saw him listen to it all, and
answer with the most tranquil resolution, 'He would do any
thing to preserve the friendship and patronage of his uncle,
but marry.'

'What can be your reason?' asked Sandford—though he
guessed.

'A reason I cannot give to Lord Elmwood.'

'Then do not give it to me, for I have promised to tell him
every thing you say to me.'

'And every thing I *have* said?' asked Rushbrook hastily.

'As to what you have said, I don't know whether it has made
that impression on my memory, to repeat.'

'I am glad it has not.'

'And my answer to your uncle, is to be simply, that you will
not obey him?'

'I should hope, Mr. Sandford, you would put it in better terms.'

'Tell me the terms, and I will be exact.'

Rushbrook struck his forehead, and walked distractedly about the room.

'Am I to give him any reason for your disobeying him?'

'I tell you again, I dare not name the cause.'

'Then why do you submit to a power you are ashamed to own?'

'I am not ashamed—I glory in it—Are you ashamed of your esteem for Lady Matilda?'

'Oh! if she is the cause of your disobedience, be assured I shall not mention it, for I am forbid to name her.'

'And as that is the case, I need not fear to speak plainly to you.—I love Lady Matilda—or, unacquainted with love, perhaps it is only pity—and if so, pity is the most pleasing passion that ever possessed a human heart, and I would not change it for all her father's estates.'

'Pity, then, gives rise to very different sensations—for I pity you, and that sensation I would gladly exchange for approbation.'

'If you really feel compassion for me, and I believe you do, contrive some means by your answers to Lord Elmwood to pacify him, without involving me.—Hint at my affections being engaged, but not to whom; and add, that I have given my word, if he will allow me a short time, a year or two only, I will, during that period, try to regain them, and use all my power to render myself worthy the lady for whom he designs me.'

'And this is not only your solemn promise—but your fixed determination?'

'Nay, why will you search my heart to the bottom, when its surface ought to content you?'

'If you cannot resolve on what you have proposed, why do you ask this time of your uncle? for should he allow it you, at its expiration, your disobedience to his commands will be less pardonable than it is now.'

'Within a year, Mr. Sandford, who can tell what strange unthought-of events may not occur to change all our prospects? even my passion may decline.'

'In that expectation, then—the failure of which you yourself must answer for—I will repeat to his lordship, as much of this discourse as shall be proper.'

Here Rushbrook communicated his having been to see Lady Matilda, for which Sandford reproved him, but in less severe terms than his reproofs were in general delivered; and Rushbrook by his entreaties, now gained the intelligence who the nobleman was who had addrest Matilda, and on what views; but was restrained to patience by Sandford's arguments and threats.

Upon the subject of this marriage Sandford met his patron, without having determined exactly what to say, but rested on the temper in which he should find his lordship.

At the commencement of the conversation he said, 'Rushbrook begged for time.'

'I have given him time, have I not?' cried Lord Elmwood, 'What can be the reason of his thus trifling with me?'

Sandford replied, 'My lord, young men are frequently romantic in their notions of love, and think it impossible to have a sincere affection, where their own inclinations do not first point out the choice.'

'If he is in love,' answered his lordship, 'let him take the object, and leave my house and me for ever.—Nor under this destiny need he be pitied; for genuine love will make him happy in banishment, in poverty, or in sickness; it makes the poor man happy as the rich, the fool blest as the wise.'——

The sincerity with which Lord Elmwood had loved, was expressed more than in words, as he said this.

'Your lordship is talking,' replied Sandford, 'of the passion in its most refined and predominant sense; while I may possibly be speaking of a mere phantom, that has led this young man astray.'

'Whatever it be,' returned Lord Elmwood, 'let him and his friends weigh the case well, and act for the best—so shall I.'

'His friends, my lord?—What friends, or what friend has he on earth but you?'

'Then why will he not submit to my advice; or himself give me some substantial reason why he cannot?'

'Because there may be friendship without familiarity—and so it is between him and you.'

'That cannot be; for I have condescended to talk to him in the most familiar terms.'

'To condescend, my lord, is *not* to be familiar.'

'Then come, sir, let us be on an equal footing through you. —And now speak out *his* thoughts freely, and hear mine in return.'

'Why then, he begs for a respite for a year or two.'

'On what pretence?'

'To me, it was preference to a single life—but I suspect it is—what he imagines to be love—and for some object whom he thinks your lordship would disapprove for his wife.'

'He has not, then, actually confessed this to you?'

'If he has, it was drawn from him by such means, I am not warranted to say so in direct words.'

'I have entered into no contract, no agreement on his account with the friends of the lady I have pointed out,' said Lord Elmwood; 'nothing beyond implications have passed betwixt her family and myself at present; and if the person on whom he has fixed his affections should not be in a situation absolutely contrary to my wishes, I may, perhaps, confirm his choice.'

That moment Sandford's courage prompted him to name Lady Matilda, but his discretion opposed—however, in the various changes of his countenance from the conflict, it was plain to discern he wished to say more than he dared.

On which Lord Elmwood cried, 'Speak on Sandford—what are you afraid of?'

'Of you, my lord.'

His lordship started.

Sandford went on—'I know no tie—no bond—no innocence, a protection from your resentment.'

'You are right,' he replied, significantly.

'Then how, my lord, can you encourage me to speak on, when that which I perhaps would say, may offend you to hear?'

'To what, and whither are you *changing* our subject?' said his lordship.—'But, sir, if you know my resentful and relentless temper, you surely know how to shun it.'

'Not, and speak plainly.'

'Then dissemble.'

'No, I'll not do that—but I'll be silent.'

'A new parade of submission.—You are more tormenting to me than any one I have about me—Constantly on the verge of disobeying my commands, that you may recede, and gain my good will by your forbearance.—But know, Mr. Sandford, I will not suffer this much longer.—If you choose upon every occasion we converse together (though the most remote from the subject) to think upon my daughter, you must either banish your thoughts, or conceal them—nor by one sign, one item, remind me of her.'

'Your daughter did you call her?—Can you call yourself her father?'

'I do, sir—but I am likewise the husband of her mother.

————And, as such, I solemnly swear,'————He was proceeding with violence.

'Oh! my lord,' cried Sandford, interrupting him, with his hands clasped in the most fervent supplication—'Oh! do not let me draw upon her one oath more of your eternal displeasure—I'll kneel to beg you to drop the subject.'

The inclination he made with his knees bent to the ground, stopped Lord Elmwood instantly.——But though it broke in upon his words, it did not alter one angry look—his eyes darted and his lips trembled with indignation.

Sandford in order to appease him, bowed and offered to withdraw; hoping to be recalled.—He wished in vain—Lord Elmwood's eyes followed him to the door, expressive of the pleasure of his absence.

CHAPTER VIII

THE companions and counsellors of Lord Margrave, who had so prudently advised gentle methods in the pursuit of his passion, while there was left any hope of their success; now, convinced there was none, as strenuously commended open violence;—and sheltered under the consideration, that their depredations were to be practised upon a defenceless woman, who had not one protector, except an old priest, the subject of their ridicule;—assured likewise from the influence of Lord Margrave's wealth, all inferior consequences could be overborne, they saw no room for fears on any side, and what they wished to execute, with care and skill premeditated.

When their scheme was mature for performance, three of his lordship's chosen companions, with three servants, trained and tried in all the villainous exploits of their masters, set off for the habitation of poor Matilda, and arrived there about the twilight of the evening.

Near four hours after that time (just as the family were going to bed) they came up to the doors of the house, and rapping violently, gave the alarm of fire, conjuring all the inhabitants to 'make their way out immediately, as they would save their lives.'

The family consisted of but few persons, all of whom ran instantly to the doors and opened them; on which two men rushed in, and with the plea of saving Lady Matilda from the pretended flames, caught her in their arms, and carried her off; while all the deceived people of the house, running eagerly to save themselves, paid no regard to her being taken away, till looking for the cause for which they had been terrified, they perceived the stratagem, and the fatal consequences.

Amidst the complaints, sorrow, and affright of the people of the farm, Miss Woodley's sensations wanted a name—terror and anguish give but a faint description of what she suffered—something like the approach of death stole over her senses, and she sat like one petrified with horror.—She had no doubt who was the perpetrator of this wickedness; but how was she to follow? how effect a rescue?

The circumstances of this event, as soon as the people had time to call up their recollection, were sent to a neighbouring magistrate; but little could be hoped from that.—Who was to swear to the robber?—Who undertake to find him out?—Miss Woodley thought of Rushbrook, of Sandford, of Lord Elmwood, but what could she hope from the want of power in the two former?—what from the latter, for the want of will?—Now stupefied, and now distracted, she walked about the house incessantly, begging for instructions what she should do, or how to forget her misery.

A tenant of Lord Elmwood's, who occupied a small farm

near to that where Lady Matilda lived, and who was well
acquainted with the whole history of hers and her mother's
misfortunes, was returning from a neighbouring fair just as
this inhuman plan was put in execution.—He heard the cries
of a woman in distress, and followed the sound till he arrived
at a chaise in waiting, and saw Matilda placed in it by the side
of two men, who presented pistols to him as he offered to
approach and expostulate.

The farmer, uncertain who this female was, yet went to the
house she had been taken from (as the nearest) with the tale
of what he had seen; and there, being informed Lady Matilda
was her whom he had beheld, this intelligence, joined to the
powerful effect her screams had on him, made him resolve to
take horse immediately, and with some friends, follow the
carriage till they should trace the place to which she was conveyed.

The anxiety, the firmness discovered in determining on this
undertaking, something alleviated the agony Miss Woodley
endured, and she began to hope timely assistance might yet
be given to her beloved charge.

The man set out, meaning at all events to attempt her
release; but before he had proceeded far, the few friends that
accompanied him began to reflect on the improbability of their
success against a nobleman, surrounded by servants, with
other attendants likewise, and perhaps even countenanced by
the lady's father, whom they presumed to take from him;—
or if not, while Lord Elmwood beheld the offence with indifference, that was giving it a sanction, they might in vain
oppose.—These cool reflections, tending to their safety, had
their weight with the companions of the farmer; they all rode
back rejoicing at their second thoughts, and left him to pursue
his journey and prove his valour by himself.

CHAPTER IX

IT was not with Sandford, as it had lately been with Rushbrook under the displeasure of Lord Elmwood—to the latter
his lordship behaved, as soon as their dissention was over, as
if it had never happened—but to Sandford it was otherwise;
and that resentment which he had repressed at the time of the
offence, lurked in his heart and dwelt upon his mind for
several days; during which, he carefully avoided exchanging
a word with him, and gave every other demonstration of his
anger.

Sandford, who was experienced in the cruelty and ingratitude of the world, yet could not without difficulty brook this
severity, this contumely, from a man, for whose welfare, ever
since his infancy, he had laboured; and whose happiness was
still more dear to him, in spite of all his faults, than any other
person's.—Even Lady Matilda was not so dear to Sandford
as her father—and he loved her more that she was Lord
Elmwood's child, than for any other cause.

Sometimes the old man, incensed beyond bearing, was on
the point of saying to his patron, 'How, in my age, dare you
thus treat the man, whom in his youth you respected and
revered?'

Sometimes instead of anger, he felt the tear, he was ashamed
to own, steal to his eye, and even fall down his cheek.—Sometimes he left the room half determined to leave the house—
but these were all but half determinations; for he knew him
with whom he had to deal too well, not to know he might be
provoked to greater anger yet; and that should he once rashly
quit his house, the doors most probably would be shut to him
for ever.

In this humiliating and degraded state (for even many of the domestics could not but observe their lord's displeasure) Sandford passed three days, and was beginning the fourth, when sitting with his lordship and Rushbrook just after breakfast, a servant entered, saying as he opened the door to somebody who followed, 'You must wait till you have my lord's permission.'

This attracted their eyes to the door, and a man meanly dressed, walked in, following close to the servant.

The latter turned, and seemed again to desire the person to retire, but all in vain; he rushed forward regardless of his opposer, and in great agitation, cried,

'My lord, if you please, I have business with you, provided you will choose to be alone.'

Lord Elmwood, struck with the stranger's earnestness, bade the servant leave the room; and then said to him,

'You may speak before these gentlemen.'

The man instantly turned pale, and trembled—then, to prolong the time before he spoke, went to the door to see if it was shut—returned—yet still trembling, seemed unwilling to say his errand.

'What have you done,' cried Lord Elmwood, 'that you are in this terror? What have you done, man?'

'Nothing, my lord,' replied he, 'but I am afraid I am going to offend you.'

'Well, no matter;' (answered his lordship carelessly) 'only go on, and let me know your business.'

The man's distress increased—the water came to his eyes—and he cried in a voice of grief and of affright—'Your child, my lord!'——

Rushbrook and Sandford started; and looking at Lord Elmwood, saw him turn white as death.—In a tremulous voice he instantly cried,

'What of her?' and rose from his seat.

Encouraged by the question, the poor man gave way to his feelings, and answered with every sign of sorrow,

'I saw her, my lord, taken away by force—two ruffians seized and carried her away, while she screamed in vain to me for help, and tore her hair in distraction.'

'Man, what do you mean?' cried his lordship.

'Lord Margrave,' returned the stranger, 'we have no doubt has formed the plot—he has for some time past beset the house where she lived; and when his visits were refused, he threatened this.—Besides, one of his servants attended the carriage; I saw, and knew him.'

Lord Elmwood listened to the last part of this account with seeming composure—then turning hastily to Rushbrook, he said,

'Where are my pistols, Harry?'

Sandford rose from his seat, and forgetting all the anger between them, caught hold of his lordship's hand, and cried, 'Will you then prove yourself a father?'

Lord Elmwood only answered, 'Yes,' and left the room.

Rushbrook followed, and begged with all the earnestness he felt, to be permitted to accompany his uncle.

While Sandford shaked hands with the farmer a thousand times.

And he, in his turn, rejoiced as if he had already seen Lady Matilda restored to liberty.

Rushbrook in vain entreated Lord Elmwood; he laid his commands upon him not to stir from the castle; while the agitation of his own mind was too great to observe the rigour of this sentence upon his nephew.

During the hasty preparations for his lordship's departure, Sandford received from Miss Woodley the sad intelligence of what had happened;—but he returned an answer to recompense her for all she had undergone.

Within a few hours[1] Lord Elmwood set off, accompanied by his guide the farmer, and other attendants furnished with every requisite to ascertain the success of their enterprize— while poor Matilda little thought of a deliverer nigh, much less, that her deliverer should prove her father.

CHAPTER X

LORD MARGRAVE, black as this incident in his story must make him to the reader, still nursed in his conscience a reserve of virtue, to keep him in peace with himself.— It was his design to plead, to argue, to implore, nay even to threaten, long before he put his threats in force;—and with this and the following reflection he reconciled—as most bad men can— what he had done, not only to the laws of humanity, but to the laws of honour.

'I have stolen a woman certainly;' said he to himself, 'but I will make her happier than she was in that humble state from whence I have taken her.— I will even,' said he, 'now she is in my power, win her affections—and when, in fondness, she shall hereafter hang upon me, how will she thank me for this little trial, through which she will have passed to happiness!'

Thus did his lordship hush his remorse, while he waited impatiently at home, in expectation of his prize.

Half expiring with her sufferings, in body as well as in mind, about twelve o'clock the next night Matilda arrived; and felt her spirits revive by the still greater sufferings that awaited— for her encreasing terrors now rouzed her from that death-like weakness, brought on by fatigue.

Lord Margrave's house, to which he had gone previous to

this occasion, was situated in the lonely part of a well-known forest, not more than twenty miles distant from London:— this was an estate he rarely visited; and as he had but few of his servants here, it was a place which he supposed would be less the object of suspicion in the present case, than any other of his seats. To this, then, Lady Matilda was conveyed—a most superb apartment allotted her—and one of his lordship's confidential females placed to attend upon her, with all respect, and assurances of safety.

Matilda looked in this woman's face, and seeing she bore the features of her sex, while her knowledge reached none of those worthless characters of which this person was a specimen, she imagined none of those could look as she did, and therefore found consolation in her seeming tenderness.—She was even prevailed upon (by her promises to sit by her side and watch) to throw herself on the bed, and suffer a few minutes sleep— for sleep to her was suffering; her fears giving birth to dreams terrifying as her waking thoughts.

More wearied than refreshed with her sleep, she rose at break of day, and refusing to admit of the change of an article in her dress, she persisted to sit in the torn disordered habit in which she had been dragged away; nor would she taste a morsel of all the delicacies that were prepared for her.

Her attendant for some time observed the most submissive and reverential awe; but finding this had not the effect of gaining compliance to her advice, she varied her manners, and began by less servile means to attempt an influence.—She said her orders were to be obedient, while she herself was obeyed—at least in circumstances so material as the lady's health, of which she had the charge as a physician, and expected equal compliance from her patient—food and fresh apparel she prescribed as the only means to prevent death;

and even threatened her invalid with something worse, a visit from Lord Margrave, if she continued obstinate.

Now loathing her for the deception she had practised, more, than had she received her thus at first, Matilda hid her eyes from the sight of her; and when she was obliged to look, she shuddered.

This female at length thought it her duty to wait upon her worthy employer, and inform him the young lady in her trust would certainly die, unless there were means employed to oblige her to take some nourishment.

Lord Margrave, glad of an opportunity that might apologise for his intrusion upon Lady Matilda, went with eagerness to her apartment, and throwing himself at her feet, conjured her if she would save his life, as well as her own, to submit to be consoled.

The extreme disgust and horror his presence inspired, caused Matilda for a moment to forget all her weakness, her want of health, her want of power; and rising from the place where she sat, she cried, with her voice elevated,

'Leave me, my lord, or I'll die in spite of all your care; I'll instantly expire with grief, if you do not leave me.'

Accustomed to the tears and reproaches of the sex—though not of any like her—his lordship treated with contempt those menaces of anger, and seizing her hand, carried it to his lips.

Enraged, and overwhelmed with sorrow at the affront, she cried, (forgetting every other friend she had,) 'Oh! my dear Miss Woodley, why are you not here to take my part?'

'Nay,' returned his lordship, stifling a fit of laughter, 'I should think the old priest, would be as good a champion as the lady.'

The memory of Sandford with all his kindness, now rushed so forcibly on Matilda's mind, she shed a shower of tears, thinking how much he felt, and would continue to feel, for her situation.—Once she thought on Rushbrook too, and thought even *he* would be vext for her.—Of her father she did not think—she durst not—one single time the thought intruded, but she hurried it away—it was too bitter.

It was now quite night again; and near to that hour she came first to the house.—Lord Margrave, though at some distance from her, remained still in her apartment; while her female companion had stolen away.—His insensibility to her lamentations—the agitated looks he sometimes cast upon her—her weakly and defenceless state, all conspired to fill her mind with horror.

He saw her apprehensions pictured in her distracted face, disheveled hair, and the whole of her forlorn appearance,— yet, notwithstanding his former resolves, he could not resist the desire of fulfilling all her dreadful expectations.

He once again approached her, and was going again to take her hand; when the report of a pistol on the staircase, and a confusion of persons assembling towards the apartment deterred him.

He started—but looked more surprised than alarmed; while her alarm augmented; for she supposed this tumult was some experiment to intimidate her into submission.—She therefore wrung her hands, and lifted up her eyes to heaven in the last agony of despair, when one of Lord Margrave's servants entered hastily and cried,

'Lord Elmwood, sir.'

That moment her father entered—and with the unrestrained fondness of a parent, folded her in his arms.

Her extreme, her excess of joy on such a meeting; and from such anguish rescued, was still, in part, repressed by his awful presence.—The apprehensions to which she had been accustomed, kept her timid and doubtful—she feared to speak, or clasp him in return for his embrace, but falling on her knees

clung round his legs, and bathed his feet with her tears.——
These were the happiest moments she had ever known—
perhaps the happiest *he* had ever known.

Lord Margrave, on whom Lord Elmwood had not even
cast a look, now left the room; but as he quitted it, called out,
'My Lord Elmwood, if you have any demands on me'——
His lordship interrupted him,—'Would you make me an
executioner? The law shall be your only antagonist.'

Matilda, quite exhausted, yet upheld by the sudden transport she had felt, walked, as her father led her, out of this
wretched dwelling—more despicable than the cottage built
with clay.

CHAPTER XI

OVERCOME with the want of two night's rest from her cruel
fears, and all those fears now hushed; Matilda soon after she
was placed in the carriage with Lord Elmwood, dropped fast
asleep; and thus insensibly surprised, leaned her head against
her father in the sweetest slumber imagination can conceive.

When she awoke, instead of the usual melancholy prospect
before her view, she heard the voice of the late dreaded Lord
Elmwood, tenderly saying,

'We will go no farther to-night, the fatigue is too much for
her;—order beds here directly, and some proper persons to
sit up and attend her.'

She could only turn to him with a look of love and duty;
her tongue could not utter a sentence.

In the morning she found her father by the side of her bed.—
He inquired 'If she was in health sufficient to pursue her
journey, or if she would remain where she was?'

'I am able to go with you,' she answered instantly.

'Nay,' replied he, 'perhaps you ought to stay here till you are better?'

'I *am* better,' said she, 'and ready to go with you.'——Half afraid he meant to send her from him.

He perceived her fears, and replied, 'Nay, if you stay, so shall I—and when I go, I shall take you along with me to my house.'

'To Elmwood House?' she asked eagerly.

'No, to my house in town, where I intend to be all the winter, and where we shall live together.'

She turned her face on the pillow to conceal her tears of joy, but her sobs revealed them.

'Come,' said he, 'this kiss is a token you have nothing to fear.'—And he kissed her affectionately.—'I shall send too for Miss Woodley immediately,' continued he.

'Oh! I shall be overjoyed to see her, my lord—and to see Mr. Sandford—and even Mr. Rushbrook.'

'Do you know him?' said Lord Elmwood.

'Yes,' she replied, 'I have seen him twice.'

His lordship hoping the air might be a means of re-establishing her strength and spirits, now left the room and ordered his carriage; while she arose, attended by one of his female servants, for whom he had sent to town, to bring such changes of apparel as was requisite.

When Matilda was ready to join her father in the next room, she felt a tremor seize her, that made it almost impossible to appear before him.—No other circumstance now depending to agitate her heart, she felt more forcibly its embarrassment at meeting on terms of easy intercourse, him, whom she had been used to think of, but with that distant reverence and fear, which his severity had excited; and she knew not how to dare to speak, or look on him with that freedom her affection warranted.

After several efforts to conquer these nice and refined sensations, but to no purpose, she went at last to his apartment.—He was reading; but as she entered, put out his hand and drew her to him.—Her tears wholly overcame her.—He could have intermingled his—but assuming a grave countenance, he commanded her to desist from exhausting her spirits; and, after a few powerful struggles, she obeyed.

Before the morning was over she experienced the extreme joy of sitting by her father's side as they drove to town, and receiving during his conversation, a thousand proofs of his love, and tokens of her lasting happiness.

It was now the middle of November, and yet as Matilda passed along, the fields to her delighted eye appeared green; the trees in their bloom; and every bird seemed to sing the sweetest music—Never to her, did the sun rise upon a morning such as this—never did her imagination comprehend the human heart could feel happiness so true as hers.

On arriving at the house, there was no abatement of her felicity—all was respect and duty on the part of the domestics —all paternal care on the part of Lord Elmwood;—and she seemed to be at that summit of her wishes which annihilates hope, but that the prospect of seeing Miss Woodley and Mr. Sandford, still kept this pleasing passion in existence.

CHAPTER XII

RUSHBROOK was detained at Elmwood House during all this time, more from the friendly persuasions, nay even prayers, of Sandford, than by the commands of Lord Elmwood. He had, but for Sandford, followed his uncle and exposed himself to his severest anger, rather than have endured a state of the most piercing inquietude, such as he suffered till the news arrived of Lady Matilda's safety.—He indeed had little else to fear from the known, firm, and courageous character of her father, and the expedition with which he undertook his journey; but lover's fears are like those of women, and no argument could persuade either him or Miss Woodley (who had now ventured to come to Elmwood House) but that Matilda's peace of mind might be for ever destroyed before she was set at liberty.

The summons from Lord Elmwood for their coming to town, was received by each of this party with delight; but the impatience to obey it was in Rushbrook so violent, it was painful to himself, and extremely troublesome to Sandford; who wished, from his regard to Lady Matilda, rather to delay, than hurry their journey.

'You are to blame,' said he to him and to Miss Woodley, 'to wish by your arrival, to divide with Lord Elmwood that tender tie, with which obligations conferred ever binds the donor.—At present there is no one with him to share in the care and protection of his daughter, and he is under the necessity of discharging the duty himself; accustomed to this, it may become so powerful he cannot throw it off, even if his former resolutions should urge him to it.—While we remain here, therefore, Lady Matilda is safe with her father; but it would not surprise me, if on our arrival (especially if we are precipitate) he should place her again with Miss Woodley at a distance.'

To this forcible conjecture, they submitted for a few days, and then most gladly set out for town.

On their arrival, they were met, even at the door of the street, by Lady Matilda; and with an expression of joy, they did not suppose her features could have worn.—She embraced Miss Woodley! hung upon Sandford!—and to Mr. Rushbrook,

who from his conscious love only bowed at an humble distance, she held out her hand with every look and gesture of
the tenderest esteem.

When Lord Elmwood joined them, he welcomed them all
most sincerely; especially Sandford; with whom he had not
spoken for many days before he left the country, merely for his
alluding to the wretched situation of his daughter—And
Sandford (with his fellow travellers) now saw his lordship
treat that daughter with all the easy, natural fondness, as if
she had lived with him from her infancy.—He appeared, however, at times, under the apprehension, that the propensity of
man to jealousy, might give Rushbrook a pang at this dangerous
rival in his love and fortune—for though his lordship remembered well the hazard he had once ventured to befriend
Matilda, yet the present unlimited reconciliation was something so unlooked for, it might be a trial too much for his
generosity, to remain wholly disinterested on the event.—
Slight as was this suspicion, it did Rushbrook injustice.—He
loved Lady Matilda too sincerely; he loved her father's
happiness, and her mother's memory too faithfully, not to be
rejoiced at all he was witness of; nor did the secret hope that
whispered to him 'Their every blessing might one day be
mutual,' increase the pleasure he found, in beholding Matilda
happy.

Unexpected affairs in which Lord Elmwood had been for
some time engaged, diverted his attention for a while from
the marriage of his nephew; nor did he at this time find his
disposition sufficiently severe to exact from the young man a
compliance with his wishes, at the cruel alternative of being
for ever discarded.—He felt his mind, by the late incident,
too much softened for such harshness; he yet wished for the
alliance he had proposed; for he was more consistent in his
character than to suffer the sudden tenderness his daughter's

danger had awakened, to derange those plans so long pro-
jected; and never for a moment did he indulge—for perhaps
it had been an indulgence—the idea of replacing her exactly
in that situation to which she was born, to the disappointment
of all his nephew's expectations.

Milder now in his temper than he had been for years before,
and knowing he could be no longer irritated upon the subject
of his daughter, his lordship once more resolved to trust himself in a conference with Rushbrook on the subject of marriage,
meaning at the same time to mention Matilda as an opponent
from whom he had nothing to fear. But for some time before
Rushbrook was called to this private audience, he had by his
unwearied attention, endeavoured to impress upon Matilda's
mind, the softest sentiments in his favour.—He succeeded—
but not as he wished.—She loved him as her friend, her cousin,
her softer brother, but not as a lover.—The idea of love never
once came to her thoughts; and she would sport with Rushbrook like the most harmless child, while he, all impassioned,
could with difficulty resist telling her, what she made him
suffer.

At the meeting between him and Lord Elmwood, to which
he was sent for to give his final answer on that subject which
had once nearly proved so fatal to him; after a thousand fears,
much confusion and embarrassment, he at length frankly confessed his 'Heart was engaged, and had been so, long before
his lordship offered to direct his choice.'

Lord Elmwood desired to know 'On whom he had placed
his affections.'

'I dare not tell you, my lord,'—returned he, infinitely confused; 'but Mr. Sandford can witness their sincerity, and how
long they have been fixed.'

'Fixed!' cried his lordship.

'Immoveably fixed, my lord; and yet the object is as

unknowing of it to this moment as you yourself have been; and I swear ever shall be so, without your permission.'

'Name the object,' said Lord Elmwood, anxiously.

'My lord, I dare not—the last time I named her to you, you threatened to abandon me for my arrogance.'

Lord Elmwood started.——'My daughter!—Would you marry her?'

'But with your approbation, my lord; and that'——

Before he could proceed a word farther, his lordship left the room hastily—and left Rushbrook all terror for his approaching fate.

Lord Elmwood went immediately into the apartment where Sandford, Miss Woodley, and Matilda, were sitting, and cried with an angry voice and with his countenance disordered,

'Rushbrook has offended me beyond forgiveness.—Go, Sandford, to the library, where he is, and tell him this instant to quit my house, and never dare to return.'

Miss Woodley lifted up her hands and sighed.

Sandford rose slowly from his seat to execute his office.

While Lady Matilda, who was arranging her music books upon the instrument, stopped from her employment suddenly, with her face bathed in tears.

A general silence ensued, till Lord Elmwood, resuming his angry tone, cried, 'Did you hear me, Mr. Sandford?'

Sandford now, without a word in reply, made for the door—but there Matilda impeded him, and throwing her arms about his neck, cried,

'Dear Mr. Sandford, do not.'

'How!' exclaimed her father.

She saw the frown that was impending, and rushing towards him, took his hand fearfully, and knelt at his feet.—'Mr. Rushbrook is my relation,' she cried in a pathetic voice, 'my companion, my friend—before you loved me he was anxious for my happiness, and often visited me to propose some kindness.—I cannot see him turned out of your house without feeling for him, what he once felt for me.'

Lord Elmwood turned aside to conceal his sensations—then raising her from the floor, he said, 'Do you know what he has asked of me?'

'No'—answered she in the utmost ignorance, and with the utmost innocence painted on her face.—'But whatever it is, my lord, though you do not grant it, yet pardon him for asking.'

'Perhaps *you* would grant him what he has requested?' said his lordship.

'Most willingly—was it in my gift.'

'It is,' replied he. 'And go to him in the library, and hear what he has to say;—for on your will his fate shall depend.'

Like lightning she flew out of the room; while even the grave Sandford smiled at the idea of their meeting.

Rushbrook, with his fears all verified by the manner in which his uncle had left him, sat with his head reclined against a book case, and every limb extended with the despair that had seized him.

Matilda nimbly opened the door and cried, 'Mr. Rushbrook, I am come to comfort you.'

'That you have always done,' said he, rising in rapture to receive her, even in the midst of all his sadness.

'What is it you want?' said she. 'What have you asked of my father that he has denied you?'

'I have asked for that,' replied he, 'which is dearer to me than my life.'

'Be satisfied then,' returned she, 'for you shall have it.'

'Dear Matilda! it is not in your power to bestow.'

'But his lordship has told me it *shall* be in my power; and has desired me to give, or to refuse it you, at my own pleasure.'

'O Heavens!' cried Rushbrook in transport, 'Has he?'

'He has indeed—before both Mr. Sandford and Miss Woodley,——Now tell me what your petition is?'

'I asked him,' cried Rushbrook, trembling, 'for a wife.'

Her hand that had just then taken hold of his, in the warmth of her wish to serve him, now dropped down as with the stroke of death—her face lost its colour—and she leaned against the desk by which they were standing, without uttering a word.

'What means this change?' said he; 'Do you not wish me happy?'

'Yes,' she exclaimed: 'Heaven is my witness.—But it gives me concern to think we must part.'

'Then let us be joined,' cried he, falling at her feet, 'till death alone can part us.'

All the sensibility—the reserve—the pride, with which she was so amply possessed, returned to her that moment.—She started and cried, 'Could Lord Elmwood know for what he sent me?'

'He did,' replied Rushbrook—'I boldly told him of my presumptuous love, and he has yielded to you alone, the power over my happiness or misery.—Oh! do not doom me to the latter.'

Whether the heart of Matilda, such as it has been described, *could* sentence him to misery, the reader is left to surmise—and if he supposes that it did not, he has every reason to suppose their wedded life was a life of happiness.

He has beheld the pernicious effects of an improper education in the destiny which attended the unthinking Miss Milner—On the opposite side, then, what may not be hoped from that school of prudence—though of adversity—in which Matilda was bred?

And Mr. Milner, Matilda's grandfather, had better have given his fortune to a distant branch of his family—as Matilda's father once meant to do—so he had bestowed upon his daughter

A PROPER EDUCATION.[1]

FINIS

EXPLANATORY NOTES

Page 1. (1) The Preface was withdrawn after the 2nd edition.

(2) Cf. Pope: *An Essay on Criticism*, lines 233-4.

(3) Dating from *The Mogul Tale* (1784).

Page 2. (1) Possibly a theatrical manager, Thomas ('Jupiter') Harris at Covent Garden or George Colman at the Haymarket, though Boaden records no refusal of a play of hers at this date; or possibly a member of her rather unfortunate family, whom she often helped.

(2) Colley Cibber (1671-1757) actor and dramatist. Mrs. Inchbald probably refers to his *Apology for the Life of Mr Colley Cibber, comedian. With a historical view of the stage during his own time* (1740). I have not traced the anecdote.

VOLUME I

Page 3. (1) The English College at St. Omer in France. The sons of Catholic families were frequently educated at the English Colleges, conducted by the Jesuits, on the Continent. J. P. Kemble, who seems at one time to have been intended for the priesthood, was at Douai.

(2) The contrast is between reasonable belief (not exclusive of revealed knowledge) and practical wisdom, on the one hand, and irrational belief and practice, founded on fear and ignorance, on the other (cf. *OED* under *philosopher*, *philosophical*, and *superstitition*).

(3) The four cardinal virtues of Christian tradition.

Page 4. It was recognized usage among English Catholics until about the middle of the nineteenth century that daughters should follow their mother's religion. J. P. Kemble was the son of a mixed marriage; his sister, Sarah Siddons, was a Protestant. Sandford's objections to Miss Milner as Lord Elmwood's wife are not based on her Protestantism; a son of hers would be bred as a Catholic and the title would thus be preserved in a Catholic family. There is much less fuss about intermarriage in *A Simple Story* than in the converse case in *Sir Charles Grandison* of the hero's proposed union with Lady Clementina della Porretta.

Page 6. (1) The heroine has no Christian name; nor, with the exception of those whose titles necessitate its use (Lady Matilda, Lord Frederick Lawnly, Sir Edward Ashton, and Sir Harry Luneham) has anyone in the book, except Harry Rushbrook, whose uncle sometimes addresses him familiarly by it. The use of Christian names in the upper classes was virtually confined (except when addressing servants) to family intimacy, and not always found then (cf. Sir Peter and Lady Teazle in *The School for Scandal* and Mr. and Mrs. Bennet in *Pride and Prejudice*). Miss Milner is never seen in a relationship where the use of Christian names would be expected. Differences of age and social standing are reflected in a formal address, in private as well as in public. Cf. also Lord Elmwood's famous cry (vol. III, p. 274) only possible where the name of his ward, and later wife, was seldom spoken.

The name Milner may conceivably have been suggested by J. P. Kemble. John Milner, priest at Winchester (1779-1803) and later bishop and vicar apostolic in the Midland district, had been at school with him.

(2) A priest in England in the eighteenth century was described and addressed as 'Mr.'. 'Father' was introduced in the mid-nineteenth century.

(3) 2nd edition: thirty-five.

Page 16.   As a priest in England in the eighteenth century, Dorriforth's dress, behaviour, and lodgings were those of a private gentleman.

Page 20. = newspapers.

Page 21. = vows of celibacy. Dorriforth was not a monk.

Page 22. Cf. Pope: *Eloisa to Abelard*, lines 7-8. Eloisa (Héloïse) was a pupil of Peter Abelard, teacher of philosophy in the University of Paris in the first half of the twelfth century. She became his mistress. Lord Frederick misquotes. Pope wrote: 'And Eloisa yet must kiss the name.'

Page 34. (1) Sc. opposite to evil.

(2) A Protestant, therefore, since a Catholic could not hold the King's Commission.

(3) The maiden name of Mrs. Inchbald's mother was Rushbrook. Rushbrook Hall in the hundred of Thedwastre, south-east of Bury, an E-shaped, moated Elizabethan brick house, was the home of the Jermyns and one of the Catholic seats of the district.

Page 39. The Jesuits were expelled from the College of St. Omer in 1762 when the Order was suppressed in France. In 1763 the property was transferred by the French Government to the English secular clergy. Members of the Order were suffered to remain in France on the footing of secular priests, and those engaged in education were permitted to continue. They assumed such names as 'Fathers of the Faith'.

Page 40. Sc. by exposing Sandford's behaviour and forcing him to account for it.

Page 46. Mrs. Inchbald was acquainted with the life of the Catholic gentry in Suffolk on their estates. They provided for the religious needs of their co-religionists. As a girl she went to Mass at Coldham Hall in Standingfield parish, the seat of the Rookwoods, later Rookwood Gages, and Lady Gage of Hengrave Hall, north-east of Bury, visited her mother. Such descriptive detail as her narrative requires in vol. III is too general-ized to be traceable to these Elizabethan houses, and she may well have seen other mansions in Yorkshire and the north, where Catholic ladies be-friended her. One local touch, however, suggests that she had her home district in mind. The abduction of Lady Matilda leads to 'a well-known forest not more than twenty miles distant from London' (vol. IV, p. 326). This must be Epping Forest, near the route from Bury St. Edmunds.

Page 87. (1) Duelling was forbidden to all Catholics on penalty of ex-communication. This, however, cannot often have been enforced. A priest who shed blood would have been suspended, and Dorriforth acts cor-rectly in withholding his fire. Parson Woodforde mentions a Church of England clerical duellist in his *Diary*, 9 May 1801.

(2) = irrational apprehensions connected with religion.

VOLUME II

Page 94. = sceptic.

Page 100. Sc. Luneham. The name is supplied in later editions.

Page 101. Cf. the case of John Butler, Catholic Bishop of Cork, who suc-ceeded his nephew, Piers Edmund Creagh Butler, called Baron Dunboyne (the peerage was under forfeiture) in 1785, resigned his see in 1786 and applied to Rome for a dispensation to marry. When this was refused, he became a Protestant and married in 1787 at the age of nearly 70 (see *The Complete Peerage*, 1916). I owe this reference to the Revd. Gervase Mathew, O.P. If, however, the original draft of the novel ended in the marriage of Dorriforth and Miss Milner, Mrs. Inchbald was relying, ten years earlier, upon the assumption that such a dispensation would be granted.

Page 104. The biographical facts which may have provided incentive and suggestions for most of vol. II are as follows: Joseph Inchbald's sudden death in June 1779 removed a barrier between Mrs. Inchbald and J. P. Kemble. Both remained in the York company for 15 months and at one time he had lodgings in the same house as she did. He showed solicitude and affection, but did not propose. She received the attentions of another admirer, and had frequent differences with Kemble. In September 1780 she put an end to the situation by departing for Edinburgh and then London. In 1781–2 they acted together in Dublin. Kemble admired the actress Anna Maria Philips, later Mrs. Crouch, and London papers hinted at a marriage between them. In 1787 he married. 'He looked about him for quiet manners, steady principles, and gentle temper' (Boaden) and found them in Priscilla Brereton, widow of an actor (cf. Miss Milner's remarks on the placidity of Miss Fenton). Boaden frequently stresses Kemble's prudence; cf. vol. II, p. 175 where Lord Elmwood asserts that 'Prudence' outweighs his admiration and even his love for Miss Milner; also vol. III, p. 202, a waspish comment of the author's on the mixture of resentment and prudence in his motives.

See also under vol. II, p. 151, *masquerade*.

Page 117. The disguise of Lucifer, the evil angel, when he entered Eden as the Tempter.

Page 129. A nasalized modification of 'trickle'. Cf. *OED*. Mrs. Inchbald also uses the standard form; cf. vol. III, p. 207.

Page 130. 2nd edition: to know, this would have been not to love at all.

Page 134. Three distinct uses of this word were current in the eighteenth century, and Mrs. Inchbald has them all, viz., 'eager to serve or please'; 'zealous in duty'; 'unduly forward or meddlesome in proffering services' (see *OED*). Cf. vol. I, p. 28; vol. III, pp. 232, 242.

Page 138. = religious solitary, hence austere.

Page 151. Masquerades, to which the guests went in fancy dress and wearing masks, had an ambiguous reputation. Miss Harriet Byron in *Sir Charles Grandison* is abducted after a masquerade by a bad baronet, and blames herself for attending such a function. Captain Booth is unwilling to let his wife go to a masquerade in *Amelia*. Boaden tells us that Mrs. Inchbald went to a masquerade in winter, 1781, apparently in male habit (she had acted Bellario in Beaumont and Fletcher's *Philaster* at Covent Garden) and 'entertains no doubt' that she was accompanied

by the Marquess of Carmarthen,* who paid her visits at that time. He adds
that this incident is reflected in *A Simple Story*, and that she fashioned
Miss Milner out of her own indiscretions.

* Francis Godolphin Osborne, b. 1751, later Duke of Leeds. 'A light variable
young man', according to Horace Walpole (*Last Journal*, Jan. 1780), he was also
accomplished and elegant, Joseph Farington adds (*Diary*, 31 Mar. 1799): 'He was
too fond of low company, particularly that of Players.' At the time of his attentions to
Mrs. Inchbald, his first marriage had just been dissolved (see *The Complete Peerage*
under Leeds). He may have been the model for Lord Frederick Lawnly, later Duke
of Avon.

Page 152. The so-called 'nunnery books', sometimes taken from the
French, depicting monastic vice in sensational terms.

Page 155. = A covering for the foot and leg, reaching to the calf . . . a
half-boot (*OED*).

Page 156. A sedan chair, carried by two chairmen and accommodating
one person.

Page 160. Cf. Doreen Yarwood: *English Costume* (1952), p. 196. '[Women's
footwear] was of a slipper style, made of satin, silk or brocade, with an
ornate buckle on top. The heels were fairly high, and often made of red
leather. Less expensive types of slipper, commoner with the middle and
lower classes, were made of kid, fabric or leather.' Half-boots (i.e., reaching
to just below the calf of the leg) came in at the end of the eighteenth century.
Nankin half-boots are mentioned in Jane Austen's *The Watsons* (c. 1804).

Page 166. 4th edition: indulge you with any power before marriage.

Page 182. 4th edition: water.

Page 187. The use of powder in women's hair declined rapidly at the end
of the eighteenth century. Mrs. Inchbald, whose hair was a golden auburn,
was the first actress to appear without powder on the stage, at the Haymarket in 1783. Miss Milner, however, wore powder until the 4th edition
(1799) when the sentence is replaced by 'smoothed her hair and adjusted
her dress'. In 1795 Pitt placed his hair-powder tax on a personal basis at
a guinea a head. Miss Yarwood (op. cit.) says that powder was completely
out of fashion for women by 1795.

Page 192. All Catholics and Nonconformists were obliged to be married
in the Church of England, in addition to undergoing the ceremonies of
their own churches. Mrs. Inchbald was married in her sister's house on
9 June 1772 by a Catholic priest, and on 10 June by 'Protestant rites'
(Boaden).

Page 193. It is very unlikely that this omen of future unhappiness terminated the original version of *A Simple Story* if, as Boaden indicates, that covered no more than vols. I and II of the completed book. It must have been inserted when Mrs. Inchbald decided to fuse the two stories she had on hand. Modern readers (e.g. S. R. Littlewood, *Mrs. Inchbald and her Circle* [1921]) have failed to find a satisfactory reason for the continuation. Contemporaries fixed on the development of Dorriforth-Lord Elmwood as the principle of continuity. Mrs. Inchbald's strongest motive must have been to extend a tale that was slender and brief beside the growing bulk and complexity of the novel at the end of the century (cf. the works of Fanny Burney, Ann Radcliffe, and Robert Bage). As she was reluctant to enter into the collapse of the marriage she had imagined, she was thrown on the next generation. Boaden suggests *The Winter's Tale* as a model (vol. I, pp. 274 et seq.). It was not till 1802 that Kemble produced the play in London, with Mrs. Siddons as Hermione, but there need be no doubt that Mrs. Inchbald knew it. Boaden says that she had 'probably' acted both Hermione and Perdita. The likeness in plot and characters is very general, but Shakespeare did provide a precedent for extending a dramatic situation into the next generation and resolving it through the young people.

For further discussion of the reason for the continuation see the present Introduction, and Terry Castle, *Masquerade and Civilization: The Carnivalesque in Eighteenth-Century English Culture and Fiction* (1986). [JS]

VOLUME III

Page 199. The mildly Gothic (and doubtless symbolical) background to Lady Elmwood's penitence is the only point at which Mrs. Inchbald, though dealing with a cleric, an earl, and a castle, touches the fashionable mode.

Page 209. Lord Elmwood seems to think in the terms of English law rather than of Catholic marriage. The Catholic interest, however, disappears in vols. III and IV, except what remains to lend pathos to the changed relations of Sandford with that lofty aristocrat, his former pupil. Matilda and Rushbrook should, by English usage, be Protestants, but the point is never made. The lapse of Lord Elmwood's title is mentioned, but not that it is of importance to Catholics. Mrs. Inchbald probably aimed at variety and broadening the appeal of her book. The assumptions of vols. III and IV are those of general Christian belief and sentiment, as they are also in the near-contemporary *Nature and Art*. This is seen in Sandford's relations with Lady Elmwood and her daughter. Mrs. Inchbald, at this period, shows in her writings a 'philosophic' Christianity, broadly tolerant, with a minimum of dogma. She was certainly influenced by the liberal thinkers who were her friends (e.g. Godwin, Holcroft) but maintained an explicitly Christian allegiance. If J. P. Kemble is still relevant to Lord Elmwood at this point of the novel, it may be noted that he had virtually, though unostentatiously, withdrawn from his father's Church.

Page 211. (1) 2nd edition: The complaint of the unfortunate child in the scriptures (a lesson I have studied).

(2) Cf. Luke xv. 17-18. Lady Elmwood, though a Protestant, does not quote A.V. The lines seem to be a memorial conflation of the two verses in the English translation of the Vulgate, originally published by the English College at Rheims (1582).

Page 239. = a signal example of ingratitude.

Page 240. = the opposite was the case with Rushbrook.

VOLUME IV

Page 288. = (apparently) no moderation of Lord Elmwood's resentment.

Page 325. 2nd edition: a short hour.

Page 338. This moral is frequent in novels by women at the end of the eighteenth century. In *A Simple Story* it seems hardly to be integral to the development of the work, but need not therefore be dismissed as insincere. Boaden, thinking that Mrs. Inchbald is harking back to Mr. Milner's mixed marriage and advocating a Catholic education, exclaims: '*How* did it succeed with Dorriforth?' What she has in mind, however, is the indulgent, trifling upbringing of the society beauty, compared with her daughter's austere youth, in the comprehended presence of guilt and sorrow. Mr. Milner did not err in keeping his promise to his wife, but in not educating his daughter seriously.

The concern for 'a proper education' is seen as central in Gary Kelly's study, *The English Jacobin Novel 1780–1805* (1976). [JS]

The Oxford World's Classics Website

www.worldsclassics.co.uk

- Browse the full range of Oxford World's Classics online

- Sign up for our monthly e-alert to receive information on new titles

- Read extracts from the Introductions

- Listen to our editors and translators talk about the world's greatest literature with our Oxford World's Classics audio guides

- Join the conversation, follow us on Twitter at OWC_Oxford

- Teachers and lecturers can order inspection copies quickly and simply via our website

www.worldsclassics.co.uk

American Literature

British and Irish Literature

Children's Literature

Classics and Ancient Literature

Colonial Literature

Eastern Literature

European Literature

Gothic Literature

History

Medieval Literature

Oxford English Drama

Poetry

Philosophy

Politics

Religion

The Oxford Shakespeare

A complete list of Oxford World's Classics, including Authors in Context, Oxford English Drama, and the Oxford Shakespeare, is available in the UK from the Marketing Services Department, Oxford University Press, Great Clarendon Street, Oxford OX2 6DP, or visit the website at www.oup.com/uk/worldsclassics.

In the USA, visit www.oup.com/us/owc for a complete title list.

Oxford World's Classics are available from all good bookshops. In case of difficulty, customers in the UK should contact Oxford University Press Bookshop, 116 High Street, Oxford OX1 4BR.

	Women's Writing 1778–1838
WILLIAM BECKFORD	**Vathek**
JAMES BOSWELL	**Life of Johnson**
FRANCES BURNEY	**Camilla**
	Cecilia
	Evelina
	The Wanderer
LORD CHESTERFIELD	**Lord Chesterfield's Letters**
JOHN CLELAND	**Memoirs of a Woman of Pleasure**
DANIEL DEFOE	**A Journal of the Plague Year**
	Moll Flanders
	Robinson Crusoe
	Roxana
HENRY FIELDING	**Joseph Andrews and Shamela**
	A Journey from This World to the Next and The Journal of a Voyage to Lisbon
	Tom Jones
WILLIAM GODWIN	**Caleb Williams**
OLIVER GOLDSMITH	**The Vicar of Wakefield**
MARY HAYS	**Memoirs of Emma Courtney**
ELIZABETH HAYWOOD	**The History of Miss Betsy Thoughtless**
ELIZABETH INCHBALD	**A Simple Story**
SAMUEL JOHNSON	**The History of Rasselas**
	The Major Works
CHARLOTTE LENNOX	**The Female Quixote**
MATTHEW LEWIS	**Journal of a West India Proprietor**
	The Monk
HENRY MACKENZIE	**The Man of Feeling**
ALEXANDER POPE	**Selected Poetry**

An Anthology of Elizabethan Prose Fiction

An Anthology of Seventeenth-Century Fiction

Early Modern Women's Writing

Three Early Modern Utopias (Utopia; New Atlantis; The Isle of Pines)

FRANCIS BACON	Essays
APHRA BEHN	Oroonoko and Other Writings
	The Rover and Other Plays
JOHN BUNYAN	Grace Abounding
	The Pilgrim's Progress
JOHN DONNE	The Major Works
	Selected Poetry
BEN JONSON	The Alchemist and Other Plays
	The Devil is an Ass and Other Plays
	Five Plays
JOHN MILTON	Selected Poetry
SIR PHILIP SIDNEY	The Old Arcadia
IZAAK WALTON	The Compleat Angler